**B**

"Bursting with laughs and so much love, Sidney Karger's debut novel delivers a truly refreshing spin on the romantic comedy. It's full of funny, flawed, and poignant characters, set in the dreamy, sharply observed New York City that we love. *Best Men* is a bighearted, feel-good summer escape."

—Anderson Cooper, #1 *New York Times* bestselling author and journalist

"Sid's debut novel made me laugh out loud and feel alive."

—Amy Schumer, #1 *New York Times* bestselling author, comedian, and actor

"There's so much to love about Sid's brilliantly hilarious debut book. With sharp-witted dialogue; charming, smart characters; and tons of heart, *Best Men* is such a funny, clever, fresh take on modern romance. From start to finish, you won't stop laughing! I just loved it!!!!"

—Molly Shannon, *New York Times* bestselling author, comedian, and actor

"*Best Men* takes the reins of the rom-com and reinvents the genre in a thoroughly modern way. Karger's debut is inventive, hilarious, and satisfying; it's also a keenly observed portrayal of love and friendship. This is a hilarious, heartfelt charmer of a book."

—Grant Ginder, author of *Let's Not Do That Again* and *The People We Hate at the Wedding*

"With an unforgettable voice, *Best Men* is all at once funny, tender, and wise. A sexy, swoony, summer love story to get lost in!"
—Ashley Herring Blake, *USA Today* bestselling author
of *Iris Kelly Doesn't Date*

"This appealing debut . . . offers plenty to enjoy."
—*Publishers Weekly*

"Karger's debut is laugh-out-loud funny, and Max is the epitome of millennial dry humor. . . . Max and Paige's friendship is ultimately the star of the show, and readers will find their banter reminiscent of fan favorites like Amy Poehler and Tina Fey or Dan Levy and Annie Murphy."
—*Kirkus Reviews*

"With a spot-on gift for writing dryly witty banter and a deliciously acerbic sense of humor in the Nora Ephron mode, Karger . . . makes his fiction debut. A fun and flirty rom-com that is the perfect addition to beach bags and suitcases."
—*Booklist*

"The narrative voice is terrifically modern, punchy, and enjoyable."
—All About Romance

# The
# BUMP

## SIDNEY KARGER

BERKLEY ROMANCE
NEW YORK

BERKLEY ROMANCE
Published by Berkley
An imprint of Penguin Random House LLC
penguinrandomhouse.com

Copyright © 2024 by Sidney Karger

Penguin Random House supports copyright. Copyright fuels creativity, encourages diverse
voices, promotes free speech, and creates a vibrant culture. Thank you for buying an authorized
edition of this book and for complying with copyright laws by not reproducing, scanning,
or distributing any part of it in any form without permission. You are supporting writers
and allowing Penguin Random House to continue to publish books for every reader.

BERKLEY and the BERKLEY & B colophon are registered trademarks
of Penguin Random House LLC.

Library of Congress Cataloging-in-Publication Data

Names: Karger, Sidney, author.
Title: The bump / Sidney Karger.
Description: First edition. | New York : Berkley Romance, 2024. |
Identifiers: LCCN 2023052729 (print) | LCCN 2023052730 (ebook) |
ISBN 9780593439500 (trade paperback) | ISBN 9780593439517 (ebook)
Subjects: LCSH: Gay couples—Fiction. | Family planning—Fiction. |
Automobile travel—United States—Fiction. |
LCGFT: Romance fiction. | Road fiction. | Gay fiction. | Novels.
Classification: LCC PS3611.A7824 B86 2024 (print) |
LCC PS3611.A7824 (ebook) | DDC 813/.6—dc23/eng/20231120
LC record available at https://lccn.loc.gov/2023052729
LC ebook record available at https://lccn.loc.gov/2023052730

First Edition: May 2024

Printed in the United States of America
1st Printing

Book design by Daniel Brount

This is a work of fiction. Names, characters, places, and incidents either are the product
of the author's imagination or are used fictitiously, and any resemblance to actual persons,
living or dead, business establishments, events, or locales is entirely coincidental.

*This one's for J.M.*

"Don't you think it's kind of a waste for the two of us to . . ."

"Wander separately? Ah, but only one is a wanderer. Two, together, are always going somewhere."

—Scottie and Madeleine, *Vertigo*

# PROLOGUE

## DOLPHIN NOISES

**BIZ**

**M**Y BOYFRIEND AND I are trying to have a baby.

Let me clarify.

Wyatt and I are cozied up at opposite ends of the sofa with our feet—both in thick, fuzzy socks—meeting in the middle, occasionally playing a game of footsie as we scan through online databases of egg donors.

Our virtual baby-making is accompanied by the ample fire roaring next to us as an early December snowfall outside lightly dusts our Brooklyn street.

"Do we like Penelope?" Wyatt asks, his head excitedly popping up from his laptop to see what I think of another possible candidate who will share one-half of our future baby's DNA.

After eight months of scouring and debating every egg donor agency in the country—and several in Canada, Mexico and Europe—each woman's photo, bio, family history, SAT scores and all their other very personal information is starting to look the same.

"Is she the one whose dad is a commercial fisherman?" I ask.

"No, that was Anastasia," Wyatt says.

"Not to be confused with Evangeline."

"Or Dominque."

"Or Crystal H," I say. We both let out a laugh. "How are these names real?" I ask.

"Wait—are you kidding?"

"What do you mean?" I look up at Wyatt.

"Their real names are kept confidential unless the intended parents agree to meet."

"So we can know someone's grandmother had cataract surgery in early September twelve years ago, but they can't tell us their real name?" I ask.

"I thought you knew that," Wyatt says with a laugh. "You're cute."

"I'm kidding," I say, trying to save face. "Of course I knew that."

"You did not!" Wyatt teases. He stands, pulls me from the couch and squeezes me into him, only for the two of us to plunge back down into our sofa together in a love tangle.

"No wonder they all sound like soap opera characters from the eighties."

Our dog, Matilda, playfully runs over, tail wagging, curious about the commotion and wanting in on the fun.

"How's our baby girl?" We each pet Matilda, who yawns and stretches.

"I do like Penelope. Is she on the board?" I ask.

Wyatt stands to retrieve her printed headshot and tacks it on his highly organized corkboard full of profile photos and bios of possible egg donors. "She is now," he says.

If the words "Project Baby!" weren't written on a piece of

paper above the dozen photos of women, someone walking into our living room right now would think we're either casting a movie or solving a murder.

Wyatt sighs. "We've left no available egg donor unturned."

I stand next to him. "Every day feels like we're scrolling through a dating app," I say as we both survey our baby board.

Wyatt chuckles. "How would you know?"

"True," I say. Wyatt and I met fresh out of college on a ski trip in Colorado and fell in love immediately, so we never spent time online trying to find each other.

"I keep coming back to Mackenzie," I say, pointing to her smiling photo.

"Me too," Wyatt agrees. "She's my number one."

"She's my number one too. I thought you weren't sure."

"I'm going back and forth. I still think it's slightly weird she said her special skill is making dolphin noises."

"You really have to get over the dolphin noises," I say.

"If I'm putting my best foot forward in a bio to potential parents, I'd tell them I'm really good at hockey or a pretty decent chess player. Not imitating an aquatic mammal."

"She's quirky and unique," I point out. "And smart, funny, beautiful, creative, athletic, nurturing and heartfelt. And she loves animals."

"You're right," Wyatt says, rethinking his overthinking. "She is all of that. Her personal statement was the best one we read. And her video felt like she was talking directly to us. Okay, she's definitely my number one."

We both turn back and stare at Mackenzie's photo, full of hope.

"So should we do it? Should we finally pull the trigger on . . ." I make exaggerated air quotes. "Mackenzie?"

"I'll email the agency right now and make sure she's still available," Wyatt says as he turns to me with a giddy smile. "How about a little toast? I feel like finally deciding on an egg donor should be a mini-celebration."

"I'll break out some champagne," I say, walking into the kitchen and grabbing two glasses. Wyatt dances around with Matilda as our excitement builds.

I've always wanted to have a baby. Coming from a big, Italian family of five older sisters, I've wanted to recreate what I had growing up.

Starting a family is one of the first things Wyatt and I bonded over when we met. Both of us want to have a kid or three before we enter the wrong side of thirty.

We want family dinners and backyard barbecues and smiley face pancakes and pepperoni pizza parties. We want waterslide parks and camping and games and museums and bowling and trekking through canyons. We want graduations and birthday parties and sleepovers. We want laughter and music and dancing and funny impressions. We want watching a movie when it rains and falling into a pile of leaves and baking a chocolate cake for no reason.

Wyatt and I have endless conversations about all the things we want to do and how we can't wait to share our love with our future kids.

So why, all of a sudden, as Wyatt and I toast to this momentous occasion, as we slowly move another inch closer to actually having a baby, am I completely and totally freaking out?

# 1

## WYATT
### ONE AND A HALF YEARS LATER

'M STARTING TO WONDER if my boyfriend and I are going to make it. Not like, Will our crappy little car with our adorable but anxious mini-Airedale terrier in the back seat drive us from Brooklyn cross-country to California in time for the arrival of our baby? I mean I'm worried we aren't going to make it as a couple.

This morning as we suffer through early summer traffic just outside of New York, much later than the schedule I'd planned, I glance in the rearview mirror to see Matilda looking back at me with literal puppy dog eyes as she lets out a single piercing yelp.

"This is exactly what I did not want to happen," I say, flipping on my turn signal.

"Didn't want *what* to happen?" Biz asks, raising his bushy eyebrows and aiming his soulful green eyes at me.

"She looks like she's about to be sick," I say, gripping the wheel tightly.

"We just left Brooklyn. There's no way she's going to be sick," Biz says.

"We've been starting and stopping for an hour. Even I'm feeling a little barfy. If we'd left at the time I wanted, we would've avoided all this traffic."

"I'm sorry I made us five minutes late."

"Twenty minutes," I correct him.

"You're cute when you're stressed but . . ." Biz turns to look at Matilda moving in circles around her bed. "Don't freak out yet. She's just trying to get comfortable."

The cars in front of us finally start to crawl so I weave us toward an exit ramp.

"Where are we going?" Biz asks. The same question I've been asking myself lately.

"I just want to be safe," I say as I exit the highway, turning onto a gravel road.

We both climb out of the car. Biz grabs the leash. "I'll take her for a walk," he offers, leading Matilda out of the back seat toward a nearby forest. "She probably just has to pee."

"She can do whatever business she needs to do right here," I say, holding the other end of the leash. "She doesn't need to go in a forest. There are ticks in there."

"I'm not taking her in the forest. We'll go forest adjacent," Biz insists.

As we stand there, both competitively pulling the leash in opposite directions, Matilda throws up at our feet.

We look down and then back up at each other.

"Why do you do that?" I ask Biz, pulling doggie wipes from Matilda's bag and crouching down to gently wipe our dog's mouth. "You're okay, girl," I whisper in Matilda's ear.

"Do what?" Biz asks, massaging Matilda's chin. She shuts her eyes and lets out a sigh, comforted by her two dads.

"Always say the opposite of what I say."

"I do not say the opposite of what you say. *You* say the opposite of what *I* say." Biz sighs, getting frustrated.

"You just proved my point."

"Sometimes Matilda has to pee, other times she's carsick," Biz says, standing up. "How did I know which one she would choose this morning?"

"This isn't about our dog being sick, Biz. This is about me saying one thing and you saying another lately. I can't tell if you're being contrarian on purpose or not." I take control of the leash and Matilda once and for all.

"You were right. She was carsick, okay?" Biz says. "And don't say *contrarian*."

"Again, it's not about being carsick."

"Then what is it?" Biz asks.

I look at Biz and can't decide if I want to start our road trip by telling him what I think has been happening to us while standing in the middle of Westchester.

Biz has been trying to have as much fun as possible before the baby comes like it's his job. This road trip wasn't my idea. Biz wants a vacation, a chance to blow off some steam before our lives change forever. He keeps calling it a "babymoon."

Biz's determination to let loose is concerning me. It feels like he doesn't want the responsibility, or worse, like he's changing his mind entirely about being a father.

I would've preferred to fly to California for the birth like we had planned, but I compromised. I decided I could turn this trip into a chance for us to reconnect and see eye to eye.

"I'll take her for a quick walk for some fresh air," I say.

"Fine," Biz barks out. "See? We agree!" he says, as I turn to lead Matilda along the edge of the forest.

We weren't always this out of sync. Walking our dog through a patch of untamed grass while cars whiz by on the overpass, I think about the trips we've taken every summer along this same highway to our beloved Provincetown, the crown jewel of Cape Cod, when Biz and I were more relaxed with each other.

Usually, at this point in our drive, we'd start to feel the city melt away as we motored toward our special place, singing at the top of our lungs to Adele's "Rolling in the Deep" and whatever summer playlist that Biz made.

The first time we drove to Provincetown together as a couple, we stopped at our favorite coffee shop before leaving the city. They screwed up our order so the generous barista threw in two free slices of lemon-blueberry pound cake. Every trip after that, we made that pound cake our annual summer tradition, always laughing at how surprisingly delicious it tasted. This time though, we didn't stop at our coffee shop and our favorite pastry is a distant memory.

Ever since we officially chose our egg donor, the stress of building a family via surrogacy has taken ahold of us. To keep up with the finances, I've had to squirrel away as many directing gigs as possible.

In the past two months there was the Mucinex commercial I directed in LA, the Home Depot commercial in Atlanta and three commercials I shot back-to-back in Toronto for a bank. *Or maybe it was a credit union?* It's honestly all a blur.

I'm a storyteller. I tell stories. Sure, the stories I tell are dopey commercials no one pays attention to anymore, so you can continue watching the thing you want to watch in the first place, but they're still stories. They have a beginning, middle and end. There's always some kind of hero and a villain. Sometimes the stories are funny. Or clever. Or emotional, designed to pull at your heartstrings.

If I could tell longer stories, I would. I'd love to direct a James Bond–type movie with a gay twist, or maybe a prestige TV thriller about a detective investigating a murder while trying to pick up the pieces of her own messy life, but I'm not at that point in my career yet.

A couple days ago I directed another thirty-second story, this one about a dad who playfully steals his ten-year-old son's bagel and cream cheese. The son was our hero. The dad was kind of the villain, but in the end, he redeems himself.

To get the most out of the kid's performance, I channeled what little memories I have of my relationship with my own father when I was a kid, before he left us.

The best Christmas I ever had was when I was about six years old, and my parents woke up my brother and me, led us downstairs to the tree, and my father put his hands the size of dinner plates over my eyes. When I opened them, I saw a mountain of presents. I'd never been so excited in my life. It was the last Christmas I'd celebrated with my parents together.

So I told the kid actor to pretend the bagel was the best Christmas present his parents ever gave him. The kid nailed his performance. That probably seems like a lot of emotion just for a Philadelphia Cream Cheese commercial but I like to tell these mini stories with everything I have in my toolbox.

Truth be told, if I never hear "It's cheesy AND creamy!" ever again, I would be a happy man. That tagline the kid had to say over and over, until the client thought his energy was just right, reverberates in my brain like a bad one-hit wonder.

The story of Biz and I began when we met twelve years ago. We haven't been apart since.

But now I'm not sure which one of us is the hero and which one is the villain. I wish our relationship at this moment was something I could direct. Do another take. Have us go back to one. But this is real life and not a rehearsal. And despite having a baby on the way, right now I'm not totally confident our story is going to have a plot twist into a happy ending.

– – – – – – – ≻

MATILDA AND I RETURN FROM OUR WALK TO SEE BIZ STRETCHING HIS LEGS next to Virginia Woolf. We nicknamed our car, a tangerine-orange 1992 convertible Volkswagen Cabriolet, Virginia Woolf after buying it from Biz's coworker a few years ago still with its Virginia license plates. It also kind of looks like the famed author in profile if you squint really hard.

"Everything good?!" Biz asks, trying to smooth things over.

"She just sniffed everything in sight and peed like two drops. Nothing special," I say.

"Great," Biz says, staying neutral. Both of us are keeping an emotional distance.

As the three of us climb back into the car, the silent void between us is ripped open by my phone buzzing.

"It's Flora," I say, seeing her name pop up. "She's Face-Timing us."

"Now?" Biz asks.

Unlike our egg donor, we matched with Flora, our amazing surrogate, very quickly. We usually talk to Flora over video conference for a milestone that we'd like to share with her. Our first doctor's appointment. Hearing the baby's heartbeat. The baby kicking and fluttering. Lately, we've been talking to her once a week. We just spoke yesterday, so it's unusual for her to call again without messaging us first.

Biz and I shut our car doors in unison. This little act feels like the only thing that we've done together as a team lately. Besides that, Matilda and Flora feel like the only glue between us.

We turn to look at each other.

"Just pretend everything's normal," I say to Biz.

"No, I'm going to tell her we're arguing," Biz jokes.

"Put on your best perky face so we don't stress her out with any of our crap."

"Wyatt, just answer the phone."

I prop the phone on the dashboard, slide to answer and we wave hello.

"Hi, Flora," I say through a bright smile.

"Hey, Flora!" Biz shouts a little too loudly, leaning into the phone's frame, our shoulders clumsily bumping each other like everything is fine and dandy. The rare touch of our bodies is a reminder that we haven't been intimate in a couple months.

"Hi, guys! How's your *journey* going?" Flora asks with a smirk.

"It's been extremely journey-y," I reply.

"Yeah, we're totally journeying hard," Biz says.

Throughout this whole process, the three of us are always ready to joke about how many times people in the fertility industry use the word "journey." Where are you in the process of your *journey*? We're so happy to assist you on your *journey*. Has your *journey* been a *journey, Journey McJourney*?

Flora has the best sense of humor and she's been a dream surrogate. She and Gabrielle, her partner of nine years, live in

Baker, California, and have two beautiful, fun daughters we've met a couple times in person but mostly over various modes of technology.

A nurse who dabbles in self-portrait photography, Flora impressed us with her go-getter attitude, healthy lifestyle and love for her family. Over the months, I've shared some of the commercials I've directed, and Biz showed her clips of the old TV show he starred in, while Flora has shared her portfolio of Cindy Sherman–like photographs.

Also, Flora is a dog person like us. She has five rescue dogs, each named after a different Batman actor: Kilmer, Affleck, Keaton, Bale and Pattinson. We loved that we were signing up with an entire family who was on board with Flora's decision and were not only supportive, but also inspiring humans.

"Where are you guys?" Flora asks.

"We're still on our way to P-town," Biz explains. "Matilda had a pit stop."

"That's our little girl!" I say, trying to keep the mood light and definitely not thinking about any tension between me and Biz. Flora laughs at our familiar back and forth. So far it seems like she's buying our perfect couple act.

"So . . . I just wanted to tell you guys I'm seeing the doctor again this week."

"Didn't you just see her two days ago?" Biz asks, always quick to overreact.

"Yeah, but she wants to see me again in a few days just to make sure."

I swallow but adjust my voice to remain calm. "Just to make sure of what exactly?"

"You know, that everything is okay," Flora says. "I mean,

everything's okay! We're just nearing the finish line and she's keeping a close watch."

"So everything's okay," Biz repeats like it has to be true.

"Everything's great. Don't worry, guys. Just wanted you to be aware."

Trying to have a baby via surrogacy has given us so many unbelievable ups and downs during our very complicated *journey*. We're always prepared for any little surprise.

But this whole process has brought the differences between me and Biz more into focus. We're trying to achieve the same goal through two different approaches. I'm more of the organized one, planning every detail from the baby's name to the best schools.

Biz is more loosey-goosey, wanting to determine everything according to the baby's eventual personality. It's been challenging for us to find common ground.

"Sounds like it's just routine then?" Biz asks, looking for reassurance.

"Totally. Don't freak. Your baby is going to be amazing," Flora says.

I notice Biz biting his fingernail.

"We're not worried," I say, gently swatting Biz's hand from his mouth.

"Yeah, the baby'll be great. We'll all be great!" Biz tries to stay upbeat.

"You two go have fun and stay relaxed on your trip. I'll call you after the doctor's appointment, okay?" she says. Her soothing voice and maternal instincts are always a comfort.

"Thanks, Flora," Biz says.

Biz and I tilt our heads together and we wave goodbye with

big, happy smiles on our faces, which disappear the second Flora ends the call. Worry sets in.

"Oh my god," Biz says, shifting uncomfortably in his seat.

"Relax. Everything's fine," I say.

"Are you sure?" Biz asks.

"I'm sure," I say, trying to guide us through the unknown.

Even though our intimacy on the phone felt performative, it somehow brings us a little closer together. We let the conversation with Flora hang in the air, our imaginations getting the best of us.

Back on the road, we careen past New York state lines into Connecticut, and we're stuck in traffic again. Our conversation is at a standstill along with our car.

No music. No lemon-blueberry pound cake. Matilda is fast asleep in the back.

We need to try and make use of this drive, this road trip, to find our happy harmony again. I know it's possible. It's just going to take a little extra work for us to get there.

I think of something that will surely bring us together instead of focusing on all the things that are currently keeping us apart. I turn to Biz and ask, "Did you make a playlist for our trip?"

# 2

# WORLD'S TALLEST THERMOMETER

**BIZ**

THOUGHT YOU'D NEVER ASK," I say to Wyatt with a smile.

I search for the right song on my phone. It has to be up-beat to get us out of this funk.

We need to have fun! I mean, c'mon. We're about to have a baby. This is huge.

Life changing.

This is officially happening.

Oh my god. This is officially happening.

Ever since that day we decided on our egg donor, I've been having a ton of doubt if I'm going to be a good father. *Can I provide our kid with the same happy childhood I had?*

The idea for this trip came to me right after we found out Flora was pregnant. Basically, when shit got real.

*Vacation. Road trip. Babymoon!*

I have no idea how it happens, but these things just pop into my head, and I go with them. Look, I don't make the rules.

What if we took a road trip for some fun along the way to where the baby is born? The road trips I took with my family every year from Chicago to Door County, Wisconsin, are some of my greatest memories.

Plus, I'm not a fan of flying and I'll do anything to avoid being trapped forty thousand feet in the air.

I play "Rolling in the Deep." Its driving drum beat sends tingles up my neck. I turn to Wyatt and he bobs his head to the bass in approval.

"Good one," Wyatt says.

As Adele's raspy, smoky voice glides us along the highway, I wonder if this is the song we'll sing out loud to, like we usually do on our way to P-town.

Sure enough, the chorus comes and we belt out the lyrics at the top of our lungs together.

It feels good to finally connect and temporarily escape our worries.

If anyone wants to judge me for wanting to have some fun before having a baby, go ahead. I'm writing my own pregnancy *journey.*

Ugh, that word again.

The truth is, I'm hoping this road trip will clear my mind, and I can make sense of why I've been having major anxiety about becoming a father.

Ideally, Wyatt can let loose on this trip a little bit too before the baby comes. I also wanted to plan a vacation for him because he's been cranking out commercial after commercial, killing himself physically and emotionally with the pressure cooker of his work.

My job, on the other hand, could not be lower stakes compared to Wyatt's. I sit at a desk four days a week, writing copy for the Italian beat of a food magazine called *Chef's Kiss*. The toughest part about my job is finding a new synonym for the word *delicious*.

Glancing at Wyatt driving now, with his hands on the wheel precisely at ten and two, always in complete control, all I see are waves of stress emanating off him like a steaming bowl of minestrone.

I was right. He needs a break.

That's the thing about Wyatt though. It sounds corny but he inspires me to be better.

When it finally came time to researching the surrogacy process, Wyatt was the one who took charge. I came home one night from work and he'd made an impressive mood board of things that didn't even cross my mind. 1. Pros and Cons of Adoption vs. Surrogacy. 2. Legal Representation. 3. East Coast Fertility Clinics. 4. Nursery Necessities.

He's used to storyboarding commercials. Here he was mapping out our future family.

Sometimes I can't stand that he's so perfect. Let's just say I don't excel at spreadsheets.

But as much as I want kids, I wasn't prepared to feel this unprepared. Wyatt seems to have everything under control, asking all the right questions, knowing everything we need and always staying completely calm that we're about to co-father a human baby.

For me, the closer we head to our due date, the more intensely frightened I become.

It feels like at any minute, a shadowy figure is going to tap on my shoulder and tell me that Wyatt and our future baby are way out of my league.

The only way I was able to get Wyatt to say yes to a vacation before having a baby was by literally buttering him up.

A few months ago, one night I made his favorite dish, cacio e pepe. It wasn't until dessert, while savoring my homemade tiramisu (Mom's recipe), that Wyatt leaned back in his chair, scratched the back of his head and finally asked, "So what kind of road trip?"

The tiramisu was doing the trick.

"The kind where you take a trip. On a road," I said. We looked at each other as our brains surged with sugar-induced dopamine. The first taste of that cocoa powder dusting always does it.

I couldn't help but smile, thinking what an epic adventure we could have before we meet our little one.

My grin was matched with that wrinkle just above Wyatt's eyebrows, which forms when he overthinks something. It's so ruggedly cute but it telegraphs so much.

"We'd have to map something out," Wyatt said. *Of course he would say that.*

"Can't we just rent like an RV or something and play it by ear?" I asked.

"I knew you were going to say that. If we're serious, we should plan it," Wyatt said.

"I knew you were going to say *that*," I said. At least we find extreme comfort, never boredom, in how well we know each other. "I've always wanted to tour the South," I offered.

"The South?" Wyatt asked, making a face like he just ate a lemon. "That's the opposite direction of where we're going."

"Okay. I'm just spitballing here. No bad ideas," I said.

"Except I kinda think that going south is not a great idea."

"Oh! Here's a better idea: how about a food road trip where

we stop at the best restaurants and must-eats in different states?"
I suggested, thinking I could get a good article for the magazine out of it.

"Too Guy Fieri," Wyatt said. "What about a national park
road trip? We can see Yellowstone, Arches, Yosemite . . ."

"We've been to two of those already."

"Okay, what else ya got?" Wyatt asked.

"I don't need to workshop a road trip itinerary. I would literally get in our car and just drive."

"We have a baby on the way, Biz," Wyatt said. "We can't
just wander the country aimlessly like Beat poets on LSD, trying to find ourselves."

"That sounds amazing, actually," I said.

"What if we visit all the quirky landmarks? Go see the largest ball of ear wax or the world's tallest thermometer or whatever," Wyatt said.

I love it when he talks nerdy to me but I'd decided we needed
to have fun.

Like *real fun*.

"I personally need one last hurrah before we become tired
dads. If you really want a themed road trip, let's do a gay one,"
I said. "We can stop at all the gay resort destinations from New
York to California. We could even make it to Patrick and Nathan's wedding." Our old friends Patrick and Nathan recently
left New York for the mountains of Evergreen, Colorado, and
they're getting married a month before the baby is due. Wyatt
met Patrick in film school at Columbia and he especially didn't
want to miss the big day.

"That's not a bad idea," Wyatt said. "I'd love to make their
wedding, but a gay resort town trip feels like our 'Summer of
Hedonism.'"

Ah, our "Summer of Hedonism." It was when Wyatt wasn't working much and I was in between jobs. We spent one summer going back and forth from our Fire Island share house to a friend's house in P-town for various themed weeks. P-town is what the cool kids call Provincetown. We were there for the Fourth of July, Bear Week and, by mistake, Lesbian Week. The most fun we had that summer was Lesbian Week. "The pressure was off," Wyatt said.

"We can do Fire Island, P-town, Miami, then maybe Saugatuck. Remember our weekend there? It's the P-town of Michigan. Or neither of us have been to Rehoboth. Is there anything in the southwest? Austin is kinda queerish," I said.

"You're going all over the place again. We can't go up and down and zigzag across the country. That's too much driving and we'd never make the birth," Wyatt said.

"We don't wanna go straight either. Not if we're doing a gay trip." I was trying to be funny but it wasn't working.

Wyatt threw me a faux annoyed side-glance. I sighed in an overexaggerated way.

"What's wrong?" Wyatt asked.

"I'm just hoping we could be more spontaneous. Like a wanderlust Jack Kerouac *On the Road* situation, but this is totally fine," I said.

"Your idea is more of a *Thelma and Louise* situation," Wyatt said. "If we want gay resort towns, let's do this . . ." I love when he takes charge. "We'll start in Provincetown, then Saugatuck, then Patrick and Nathan's wedding in Colorado—"

"Oh! Maybe my cousins will let us stay at their place in Palm Springs after that," I said, getting excited.

"I like that idea," Wyatt said. "So Provincetown, Saugatuck,

Colorado, Palm Springs, then we can make our way to Baker for the baby."

I lit up. "All our favorite gay places."

It sounded perfect.

"Just no fast-food stops," I said. "Only quality food along the way."

"Deal," Wyatt agreed, making the gourmet food writer in me happy.

Wyatt, the organizer, the planner and always the director, spent the next week designing a whole itinerary. By the following week, he had every item we needed for our road trip *and* the birth, and we were still months away.

"Did you know the world's tallest thermometer is actually in Baker, California?" Wyatt asked me later one night. "I totally made that up!"

"Oh, wow," I said mildly amused.

"Diapers. Bottles. Blankets. The baby seat your parents gave us. Check. Check. Check. You're in charge of snacks and music . . ." Wyatt went on and on.

He can never wing it.

Winging it is my forte. I can't help it. I've always been in constant motion. My older sisters called me "Busy Body" as a little kid because I wouldn't stop running in circles around the house, bouncing off the walls, not able to sit still for more than ten minutes at a stretch. Everyone started calling me "Biz" and it stuck.

My nickname always felt right since my birth name, Massimo Giorgio Petterelli, made me stand out too much in my very all-American town of Arlington Heights, Illinois. I didn't know if the older boys in school stuffed me in gym lockers and made fun of me because I was second-generation Italian-American or because they knew I was gay or both.

My parents wanted me to live the American dream. When I was a kid they introduced me to a casting agent through a family friend, and I quickly booked a job walking the runway in a shopping mall fashion show, which snowballed into catalogue modeling jobs. That's when my sisters jokingly started calling me "Show Biz."

Before my junior year of high school, there was an open casting call in Chicago for a new Disney Channel sitcom called *Back in the Saddle* about a group of teenagers and their parents working on a dude ranch. I auditioned, and to everyone's surprise, I was hired as a lead, so I left Illinois for LA to shoot the show, which lasted for three seasons.

I started getting caught up with too many teen actors who just wanted to party all the time, and I needed to leave LA, so I enrolled in NYU. After graduation I was writing blogs about my teenage acting years, which turned into freelance journalism jobs. Somehow I stumbled into a staff writing job at the magazine. Now after all these years, I've gone full circle and I'm longing to get back into my days of performing.

After my playlist ends in the car, there's silence between us again. It feels like we're not agreeing on anything lately, and both of us are cautious not to say the wrong thing.

I decide to check in on my favorite nemesis Instagram account, @quaddaddiez. It's two handsome gay guys in their twenties who parade around their five-year-old quadruplets. The Quad Daddies's life seems impossibly perfect. Every post is taken in their ornate Salt Lake City McMansion, with their four kids always primped and poised.

"Funny" ugly Christmas sweaters during the holidays.

Sunday best pastels on Easter.

Matching swimsuits on a random Wednesday by the pool.

I'm fascinated by their need to post like twelve times a day. I can't look away.

For some reason, I've never shared @quaddaddiez with Wyatt.

Somewhere inside of me is envious, like I'll never live up to these perfect Instagays.

When I look over at Wyatt, he's studying the formation of traffic like he's about to make a chess move. He flips his turn signal on and expertly rolls us into the fast lane. His perfect posture and command of the steering wheel make me feel safe.

On top of being a calming force of nature, Wyatt Wallace is just a stud. His prematurely salt-and-pepper facial scruff. A head of dark blond wavy hair you can get lost in. His solid, brick-house build looks perfect in everything from a tux to sweaty gym clothes to a concert T-shirt and jeans. His affable demeanor is like a magnet in any social situation. Moms love him.

How can I measure up to this saintly creature who is so clearly going to be the greatest living dad on earth?

"*Take exit 36A to merge onto I-195 East,*" the GPS lady informs us. "*In six weeks, you're not going to be a good dad and you know it, Biz,*" I imagine her adding.

"How about another song?" I ask, trying to shake the voice inside my head that's making me question everything lately.

"Something kinda quiet. We're almost there," Wyatt suggests.

I immediately drown out my thoughts with "Ocean Eyes" by Billie Eilish as we race toward our favorite place on earth.

# 3

## PROVINCETOWN

**WYATT**

THE SMELL OF SALT air and that unmistakable early afternoon coastal sunlight wash over us like a gentle Evian spritz from heaven. A foghorn sounds in the distance as if announcing our arrival.

The dense summer traffic took us an hour and forty minutes longer than expected. I'm still in work mode because I can't help but think being this off schedule would sink the budget of one of my commercial productions. I hope it's not a sign of what's to come.

Leaving gray Connecticut, moving slowly through Rhode Island, and even slower through Massachusetts, Biz fell asleep to the soothing sounds of Billie Eilish. He's starting to open his eyes now, somehow sensing we're nearing the famously curved tip of Cape Cod.

"Nice nap?" I ask, glancing over at him, making an effort to connect. Those full lips and handsome face that I signed up for years ago always crush me. Even his pronounced nose has its own personality. If you were watching the cheesiest rom-com on basic cable, you wouldn't turn it off if Biz was the love interest. He wakes up from his car nap in a way that's so effortlessly rugged I think, *I'll never be that cool.*

"I wasn't even trying to sleep. It just happened." Biz yawns and rotates his head, coming alive. His superpower is sleeping. Cars, airplanes, movie theaters, coffee shops, barber chairs, his own birthday party as people are singing "Happy Birthday" to him. He finds sleep anywhere.

"My neck is killing me now." He turns to see Matilda, who's still sleeping like a baby and snoring like an old man.

"Are we already in Mass?" he asks.

"Don't call it Mass," I say, sort of joking but not really.

"Sorry. Massachusetts. Didn't mean to offend the native."

"It's like when people call San Francisco 'Frisco' or Chicago 'Chi-Town.'"

"You're right. That is annoying," Biz says with a laugh.

"That might be the first thing we've agreed on this whole trip."

"Not true. We agreed on the same music earlier," Biz disagrees.

"We're in Truro. Two-and-a-half minutes to Provincetown. Please acknowledge my smooth driving skills to accommodate your nap time."

"I forgot you need a handwritten thank-you card every time you drive," Biz says.

"A light ticker-tape parade will do," I say. "Also please acknowledge you're driving the next leg of the trip. I'll have some papers for you to sign, so you're legally obligated."

"Acknowledged. And I promise." Biz looks out the window at the surrounding forests. "I can't wait for margaritas on our balcony, then we can hit the Boatslip. Not in that order of course. But maybe in that order?"

The Boatslip hosts a nightly beachfront dance party that overspills with dozens of people, and it's not exactly the mood I'm in. Even though we're hitting resort destinations, I'm hoping this trip won't be a nonstop party and we can quietly luxuriate by bodies of water in the sun.

"I made a dinner reservation at the Red Inn at seven," I say. "I can already taste the first sweet oyster followed by a sip of crisp, dry rosé."

"Wait. Seven? That's prime cocktail hour," Biz says. "Why would you make a Red Inn rezzie so early in the trip? That's a last-night romantic-dinner kind of thing. Don't you want to just like see who's here? Dance? Blow off some steam?"

"It was the only reservation I could get all week. It's our favorite place. They have a happy hour raw bar."

I can tell Biz holds in whatever he was going to say next.

Neither one of us wants to argue, especially right now as we look up and see the passing sign welcoming us to Provincetown. That palpable silence between us reemerges as we hit the small-town traffic on Commercial Street, with its charming art galleries, souvenir stores, cafés and salt water taffy shops.

I'm quietly warmed to see the lovable, familiar swath of Americana tourists—strolling families, townies on their way to night shifts in restaurants and bars, and a smattering of gay guys in tank tops on their rented mountain bikes weaving through the pre-peak summer throngs.

"Is that Angel Mike?" I ask. A man in his seventies, who we see every summer always wearing large angel wings and a feathered halo, glides by on an electric scooter.

"Did his wings get bigger?" Biz asks.

More than a few guys turn to look at the fresh meat blowing into town. Biz glances around with a smile. Our vintage orange Virginia Woolf convertible with the top down fits perfectly in this colorful, quirky town, where standing out from the already unique crowd is a fun challenge.

Our feeling of bliss is interrupted when I spot Matilda in the rearview mirror pop her head up like the gopher in *Caddyshack*. She lets out her familiar yelp.

Without missing a beat, I drive past the Lobster Pot and pull over to the side of the road. Biz lifts Matilda out of the car, her body dry heaving, and sets her down on the sidewalk. Matilda's legs buckle and this time she marks her territory in her two dads' favorite vacation spot.

As I gaze up at the perfect deep blue sky and glimpse the Provincetown Monument, proudly standing above the entire town, I think, *We've arrived.*

"You're not in Kansas anymore, my pretties," someone says. We turn to see the disembodied voice belongs to a random drag queen dressed in a sepia-toned costume.

"Why, thank you, Wicked Witch of the West!" Biz says, immediately recognizing and entranced by her *Wizard of Oz* getup.

"That's Miss Gulch to you," she says, fully committed to her character with the evil voice and everything. "I'm Dorothy's neighbor."

She unlocks her bike that's tied to a fence and places her little dog, who vaguely resembles Toto, into a wicker basket. Biz and I stare in amused awe. That's when it hits me.

"Oh! You're the black-and-white version of the witch before Dorothy enters Oz!"

"You're quick. Don't look like such grumps. You're in P-town!"

She flashes a pearly smile and adds, "Cute car and your little dog too." She hops on her bike as the Wicked Witch theme music plays on a portable speaker attached to her handlebars, sending her off into the crowded street.

The Wicked Witch is not wrong. We probably don't look like the happiest campers.

I glance at Biz. Usually, we'd share a laugh, a knowing smile or a fun shrug at the locals. But he's cleaning Matilda's mouth with a doggy wipe. I can't help but wonder if he's purposely avoiding any connection because he's upset I just want a quiet dinner tonight.

We finally settle into our cute cottage, which is all gray cedar shingle surrounded by a white picket fence off Commercial Street. It's in a little nook in the West End, the quietest area that's removed from the buzzy, tourist part of town.

The tiny two-bedroom has a nautical theme throughout with lots of blues and whites, wooden anchor wall hangings and lamps made out of knotted rope.

The best part about the place is the balcony on the second floor that you enter through a spiral staircase, which looks either treacherous or fun, depending on your mood and how much you've had to drink. The balcony is just big enough for two blue Adirondack chairs and overlooks a small patch of backyard for Matilda to roam free. It's a slice of paradise.

After unpacking our bags and settling in, the close quarters feel almost too close compared to our somewhat spacious (for New York) Brooklyn apartment.

Biz returns from the specialty wine shop down the street holding up a small wheel of camembert and a bottle of pre-chilled rosé. "Welcome to P-town!" he says in the Wicked Witch voice, as we get comfortable in our balcony chairs with

Matilda already passed out from the long drive between our feet.

"Cheers, Richard Gere," he says.

"Cheers, Richard Gere," I return, smiling at our years-long inside joke that was born one weekend when we binged all the actor's movies.

We sip and stare at the horizon, taking in the spectacular, pink sky. Sometimes at night a mystical fog sets in on the town, and right now I can feel a version of it between us. I don't know how to see our way out of it.

"Your reservation is in an hour. Do you still want to go?" Pretty much everything is wrong with what Biz just said. *My* reservation and asking if I *still* want to go. As if we're not even together.

"Kinda. That was the plan," I say.

"That was *your* plan," he counters.

"I'm sorry you don't want to go to the best restaurant in town."

"It's not that. I just wanted something, you know, fun."

"More fun than the perfect setting, amazing food and hunky servers?"

"The first thing we always do in P-town is drop our bags and go to tea, check out the crowd, dance our asses off to Kylie Minogue or whoever then stumble into dinner afterward."

"Maybe it's time we do something different," I suggest.

"Just because we have a baby on the way?"

"Can't we have something civilized to kick off our trip? I'm not in the mood for messy drunken chaos."

"We'll have plenty of time to comment on the delicate taste of our oysters in a deathly quiet restaurant when we're eighty," Biz snaps.

Suddenly, I'd rather have dinner alone but I don't want to say this out loud. I make the thought disappear in a sip of wine. I haven't felt this far away from this person in, well, forever.

A memory of last summer pops into my head. We checked into our bed-and-breakfast just down the street and christened our room for the week by having a quick, sweaty romp in bed. My heart flutters thinking about it. This welcome party is the opposite of that.

I think of a plan that will hopefully suit both of us. "Why don't we just go to the restaurant tonight so they don't run us out of town for canceling and then do the Boatslip tomorrow. Deal?"

Biz's expression softens as he turns to me, knowing it's a peace offering.

The Red Inn is tucked away in a quiet spot near the end of town. Tonight, it's hardly deathly quiet. The popular restaurant is packed to the gills. We sit in a cramped two-top perched over the serene water, sharing Wellfleet oysters followed by creamy lobster corn chowder.

There's a famous lone red boat always anchored just in the near distance in the low-tide water, which I keep thinking I can always hop in if our dinner goes south.

As daylight disappears, we both seem too aware that the chattering people around us fill in our sporadic conversation.

"How do you like your oysters?" I ask, pretending I'm the cliché Biz said he's afraid of becoming. "Or should we wait until we're eighty years old to discuss?"

"Very fresh. Plump. Almost buttery," Biz jokes. "Dare I say . . . delicate?" We both laugh.

A mustached server in a tight T-shirt brings our entrees. Even our main dishes couldn't be more different as Biz cuts into his medium-rare fillet with Jack Daniel's sauce, and I take a bite of my fresh local scallops with hints of citrus.

"How did we get here?" Biz asks.

"We drove here in Virginia Woolf," I say. I'm being facetious. I know what Biz is really asking but I'm trying to make light of the situation.

"I mean us. As a couple," he says, motioning to our server. "How are we on such different pages right now? And by the way, if you deflect when I'm trying to have a serious conversation, it just makes me want to hop into that boat and paddle away."

I smile internally, at least we both had the same thought.

He's right though. Whenever Biz wants to talk things out, my natural default is humor. Somehow it's easier for me to go deeper with actors I work with, to find the emotional truth in their performance before I can find it within myself.

Biz puts on a huge smile, which seems random until I realize he's acknowledging our server, who's hovering over us.

"Did you need something else?" Mustache Guy asks.

"Can I do another spicy margarita?" Biz asks, to which the server nods as if understanding why he'd need a second cocktail. He looks at me.

"I'll have another rosé," I decide.

All the energy in the room shifts to a boisterous group of guys in their twenties near the bar. One bearded bearish guy kneels on one knee, presumably proposing to the bigger bearded bearish guy. Several people whip out their phones to capture the moment.

The guy standing shouts, "Yes, of course I'll marry you!" and the entire restaurant erupts into cheers. The two guys wildly make out as joyful tears stream down their friends' faces.

My stomach ties in knots that rival our nautical-themed lamps. I'm relieved that we ordered another round.

Marriage is a sore spot for us and the topic has been coming up a lot more now that we're about to become parents. Biz wants to get married and I remain a skeptic. Of course I love him and want to spend the rest of my life with him.

But I've seen what marriage did to my parents and I don't want to relive it. My mom never recovered after my dad left. Our love and our baby will tie Biz and me together forever. I just don't see the need to make it official.

We watch as the manager of the restaurant brings a platter of congratulatory shots to the grooms-to-be and their friends.

Biz slings back the final sip of his drink. After a beat, without looking at me, he announces, "Be right back." He pulls his chair out, abruptly scraping it against the wooden floor, and goes, avoiding eye contact.

# 4

## P-TOWN

**BIZ**

**H**APPY GAYS. PROPOSING TO each other. In our favorite place on
Earth.

This is so not what I need right now.

Not while Wyatt and I are this disconnected. It's stirring up
a lot of emotions for me.

I've floated the idea of getting married to Wyatt a few times
before, and I've never really gotten a straight answer why he
doesn't want to get hitched.

As our baby's due date draws closer, marriage is on my mind
a lot. Maybe this is why things between us seem forced. It's
funny how I'm the spontaneous one and yet here I am wanting
to plan our wedding.

Wyatt is amazing at so many things but sometimes communication isn't his strong suit. I'm an open book and I'll say what's
on my mind. He bottles it all up until he's ready to explode.

Staring at myself in the bathroom mirror, I resolve to let the
marriage thing go for this trip. I don't want to keep pushing

Wyatt on the idea and I just want to enjoy this time we have together before our lives change forever.

Maybe along the way we can rekindle our mojo.

That will make me a better dad anyway, right? *Right?!*

I check my phone and see a bunch of work emails. My boss knows I'm on a babymoon—I'm lucky enough to take advantage of my company's paternity leave.

If he needs new story ideas, there's a team of writers who can cover me. It's not that hard to come up with Italian food articles like:

"Top 24 Bomboloni to Eat Poolside."

"17 Veterans Day Pasta Recipes."

"The Perfect Anti–Valentine's Day Caprese Salad for One."

These articles are some of my finest contributions to society. You're welcome.

I do have work hanging over my head though. Right before I left, I pitched my boss a new feature that I could write so I wouldn't feel guilty taking so much time off.

"Where to Eat Italian on Your Next Road Trip."

It's during these pitch meetings that I remember this is not the job I'm destined to have. In high school, I told all of my friends I wanted the career trajectory of Ryan Gosling. I'd start on a kids' show, then grow up and move between meaty indie dramas and studio films. I have the kids' show under my belt but somehow my career has devolved into a writer for a food magazine on the Italian beat.

I'm admittedly pretty good at it.

Even my boss, Trent, can't hide his envy for the way I just rattle off fully formed clickbait headlines. Trent, with his graying beard like a divorced Gandalf, is a Harvard graduate and former artist and staff writer on the *Harvard Lampoon* humor magazine, facts that he loves to remind his underlings at least once a week.

In any case, I decide I'm not even going to look at work emails right now.

When I return to the table, the engagement party is seated next to me and Wyatt.

Of course.

They're going around the table, as everyone makes poignant toasts to the grooms-to-be.

I can choose to feel bad that it's not us celebrating our love with friends, but the truth is, these guys look SO HAPPY that it fills me with hope. My eyes cloud over watching them soak up each other's love.

Wyatt and I share a faint smile as I dig into my fillet and press on with our night.

－－－－－－－➤

THE NEXT MORNING, I WAKE UP TO THE SCENT OF FRESH COFFEE WITH A symphony of birds outside our bedroom window.

I stumble up the spiral staircase like a drunk baby.

Wyatt is sitting on the balcony, awake before me as usual. He turns as I enter, and I can see a million plans are already on his mind.

"We can pick up our bikes this morning before the beach, and I have lunch tentatively booked at the Lobster Pot but we can skip if we want to stay at the beach longer," he says, over-caffeinated.

"It's too early to use the word *tentatively*," I say, taking a sip of coffee, squinting, trying to wrap my head around all the sunlight pouring down on us.

Wyatt abruptly finishes his coffee, stands and walks back inside.

"What?" I can't tell if he's upset or refilling his mug. "You can use the word *tentatively*. I was just kidding," I call back into the cottage to no response.

A second later, Wyatt returns holding a beach umbrella. "Look what I found," he says like a little kid, opening it to display a giant white anchor on a blue background. "This house has everything."

I make a conflicted face.

"You don't like anchors?" Wyatt asks.

"You really want to go to the beach?"

"Of course. That's why we're here," he says, collapsing the umbrella.

The beach is *nice*. But the pool is *fun*.

The town pool is where everyone congregates when they arrive. Like a floating party.

"Cool," I say, stifling the urge to protest and trying to bridge the gap between us. "The beach it is then."

Later, walking through the streets of P-town feels like a self-guided tour of the Museum of Us. We pass by all our greatest work together.

Our favorite ice cream shop where we geeked out over talking with the filmmaker John Waters, the cute house we shared with our friends and their Australian friends, Café Heaven where Wyatt and I spent four hours one cozy lunch watching a torrential downpour outside.

Waiting for our bike rentals, we're stuck behind a group of guys taking their time to decide between mountain bikes or road bikes. It suddenly clicks that it's the engagement party from last night. I didn't immediately recognize them in their beach outfits and towels around their necks.

The grooms-to-be decide to rent a tandem bike. Then I notice they're wearing matching purple T-shirts that say, "I'm Engayged."

I turn to see Wyatt spot the guys, with a flash of recognition on his face, but he quickly averts his gaze. He pretends to admire the selection of bikes. He doesn't want to acknowledge it's the newly engaged guys. Maybe he doesn't care.

If I bring it up, he'll find an excuse not to talk about getting married like, "Why are you fixated on getting married when we have a baby to focus on," or "We're on vacation," or "It's a Tuesday."

It feels like complete freedom when we finally hop on our mountain bikes, wind in our sails, pushing us along the winding stretch of road toward Herring Cove Beach.

After locking our bikes to the old wooden fence, we begin the famous trek to the actual beach. We wade through an epic expanse of beautifully green marshes in water that's anywhere from a foot deep or up to your shoulders, depending on the tide.

"Leave it to the gays to find the furthest beach possible," I say every summer with our day packs slung over our shoulders and flip-flops in hand.

As we walk, I try to steer us into a fun memory. "Remember the Vikings?" I ask.

Wyatt takes my cue, happy to connect about something. "We melted!" he says with a laugh, remembering the first summer we went to P-town together for Fourth of July.

We didn't yet realize just how seriously people took their theme weeks in P-town.

"I think there must be a Viking-themed boat party?" Wyatt

said, walking onto Commercial Street that summer morning and seeing every other person dressed in a cheap plastic suit of armor, short shorts and sandals, waiting in line for their iced lattes.

Everyone, it seemed, received the memo except us.

After we scrambled all over town to put together makeshift sexy Thor costumes, laughing inside each quaint shop along the way, we finally fit in with the costumed throngs. We bought day passes to a boat party where we were held hostage for three hours in the middle of the water on the hottest day of the year.

We desperately tried to find shade and slathered on so much sunscreen that we looked like ghosts with helmets basically melting onto our heads.

We finally make it to the beach, with its long stretch of sand and smattering of pebbles, navigating past a few clumps of people to set up camp.

Wyatt throws down his towel. I throw down mine.

He pulls out the nautical-themed blue umbrella he found at the house and stakes it into the ground.

It's just big enough for two of us.

We're both sweating from the walk, ready for some shade.

Lying there next to Wyatt, all I hear are gentle waves rhythmically splashing hello.

Sometimes I wish Wyatt would use his directing skills and tell us what to say, when to say it and how to feel.

This strain between us is dampening the soul of our special place.

I stand to spray on some sunscreen. Anything for some action.

"Want some?" I ask Wyatt, hoping for a chance to make a physical connection.

"I put some on at the cottage," he says. So much for that move.

After covering my whole body, I turn to the left of us and see the husbears-to-be and their entourage again sitting right next to us. Colorful towels, umbrellas and a giant inflatable raft in the shape of a pizza slice.

We've run into them too many times not to say anything. "Looks like we're on the same schedule," I call out to their general direction.

The bigger one of the pre-marrieds wears a silver chain around his neck and a fluorescent green Speedo. He interrupts his sunbathing and turns to me. "Oh, hey! It's the Red Inn guys."

Wyatt and I both wave back. "Do we know them?" Wyatt asks quietly.

"They had their engagement party next to us last night," I whisper out of the corner of my mouth, reminding Wyatt. I'm surprised they remember us, the quiet ones in the corner.

"Are you two handsome boys having fun?" Speedo Bear asks. I'm paranoid that he detects we aren't exactly having the time of our lives.

"A blast so far," I shout back, overly enthusiastic. Wyatt turns to me, lifting an eyebrow, the sweat from the hot day making his face shiny. "Congrats on your engagement," I add.

"Thanks!" they both say with huge smiles, flashing their engagement rings at us. The smaller bear throws his arm around the bigger one and they fall back into the sand, a chaotic, hairy kissing machine.

I turn back to face the silence between me and Wyatt.

"*Are* we having fun?" Wyatt asks.

I nod but want to say not really. This gorgeous day doesn't deserve us. But I don't want to escalate whatever tension is circling us like a shark.

After the sun has had its way with us, we march back through the marsh to retrieve our bikes before having a late afternoon lunch.

The tide has risen to our hips so we carry our bags above our heads.

I feel my phone vibrate. Once. Twice. Three times.

Wyatt is way ahead of me, so I let him go and decide to check my email.

Fourteen messages from work. All from "Quipple."

Quipple is an all-knowing interoffice app that informs your managers of vacation time, updates your meeting calendar and monitors exactly how many bowel movements you've had that week, probably.

Trent is most likely trying to annoy me on vacation with his thoughts on my road trip piece.

I remind myself to tell Wyatt that I have a writing assignment. I'm sure he'll enjoy sampling all the Italian food in every town we hit.

Opening my email, I see the messages are, in fact, from Trent.

SUBJECT: Staffing Changes

As you're aware, we're in the process of restructuring.

I'm frozen. I slide my Ray-Bans onto my head for a closer look, plant my bare feet firmly in the watery, sandy muck and read on.

I've had the unfortunate task of choosing to let a few colleagues go and . . .

This can't be happening. I've been there for eight years.

The rest of Trent's email goes fuzzy and I just see words and letters lose all meaning.

Something about the parent company of the magazine becoming more fractured over the years. Migrating to digital this and the print version hanging on by a thread that.

I'm sure you understand . . .

This isn't easy . . .

I'm going to have to invite you to leave the company . . .

"Invite me to leave the company?" I ask out loud. There's no one around me as far as the eye can see. Wyatt is disappearing into the distance, not even turning around.

I can only imagine Trent typing his email as he eats a tuna sandwich, uncaring. His hairy gray mess of a beard catching god knows what food particles, trapped forever.

Surely there's something homophobic going on, I can't help but think, grasping for answers. I wonder if I have a case to bring to HR, especially because I'm on paternity leave. Or maybe it's just my time to leave.

I can't see who else is on the mass email, feeling bad for any of my coworkers finding out in such a cold way. I take another quick peek.

I'll be sure to give any referrals to your next employer . . .

This layoff stings, in a group email while I'm on vacation no less. A breeze brushes past me and I decide I can't let this sunlit slice of heaven where I'm standing now forever remind me of this news. I'm already moving on in my head. Because that's how I operate.

I slowly feel liberated that a food magazine won't define my identity anymore. Like a hundred pounds of rigatoni is lifted off my back.

I shut the email and close out of Quipple forever.

And then it sets in. Even before the baby is born I've already let my family down.

We're now a single-income couple about to have a baby in New York City.

How am I going to tell Wyatt?

# 5

## THE SALT MARSHES OF ZEN

**WYATT**

**H**OW AM I GOING to tell Biz I don't really want to go to the Boatslip tonight? It will be groups of sweaty men packed together like sardines in tank tops, flirting and drinking while everyone shouts over thumping dance music.

Debauchery is not the vibe I'm after on this trip.

I wasn't always a parent in training. Biz and I have had our share of messy fun together. We know our way around the famous underwear party in Fire Island. We can feel at home among the leather daddies at the grungy Eagle bar. We've spent New Year's on the beach in Rio. Countless Sunday Fundays on the glitzy rooftop of the Standard Hotel with the best of them? Check. Sing two hours of show tunes with musical theater nerds by the piano at Marie's Crisis? No problem. (Well, Biz can go two hours or more. I'm good for thirty minutes tops.) Been there, done all of that.

We were the first couple among our friends to move in

together in our twenties, so why can't we be the first responsible parents in our thirties?

Walking through this salt marsh is total Zen. I'm in a kind of trance with my thoughts, and when I reach our bikes, I look behind me to notice Biz has fallen way behind, a slow-moving silhouette making his way back.

I unlock my bike and take a swig from my water bottle. After several minutes of waiting, a sexy shirtless guy appears walking up the short path toward me, backlit by the brilliant sun. "Thanks for waiting," he says. I blink to realize it's Biz. I'm not sure which is more gorgeous, the scenery or my boyfriend.

"I was in the zone walking back. Sorry," I say. "It's so magical here. I thought maybe you wanted to float." When the tide in the marsh is this high, a fun thing to do is float on your back and let the water gently transport you.

"Why would I want to float?" Biz asks with a forced little laugh.

"That's your thing every summer. You float."

Biz says nothing. He unlocks his bike with a frustrated look on his face. Something feels off. He's quieter than normal and we feel even more disconnected than before we hit the beach.

He doesn't seem entirely happy to see me. I hope he doesn't regret spending the day at the beach instead of the pool. I have to meet him halfway if we're going to try and enjoy each other's company on this trip. I'll go where he wants to go.

"Boatslip tonight?" I ask.

"Nah," he says, hopping on his bike.

"What do you mean *nah*? I thought that's what you wanted to do." I hop on my bike and follow his lead.

"I'm just not in the mood anymore," Biz says as he pedals ahead, flying slightly downhill on the desolated street, back toward town. I'm not sure what's going on with Biz right now but one thing is always certain: his unpredictability keeps me on my toes.

Still in our bathing suits with our legs and feet sandy from the beach, we sit on the park bench outside of Relish and eat sandwiches. There's not much of a chance to connect because we're too busy making small talk with the crowd we see every summer, passing inside and out. We finish and take our banana puddings to go, deciding to have our dessert and some downtime at the cottage.

After a quick, glorious outdoor shower, I join Biz sitting on the balcony, where there's a warm breeze. I notice he hasn't eaten his pudding. He's just staring off into the middle distance. I smile uneasily as I sit.

"Trying to be healthy?" I ask, eyeing his cup of sweet banana deliciousness.

"You can have it if you want," he says, almost vacantly. It's obvious he didn't get a chance to talk things out last night and he wants to now. I'm dreading bringing up relationship stuff since this is the perfect time to just unwind and fall into a post-beach nap. "We should talk about some things," he says. I sigh, knowing he's right.

"Do you want to wait until dinner?" I ask, uncontrollably pushing it off. Why is this so hard for me? Why can't I show my vulnerable side like Biz?

"Not what I'm about to say, no," Biz says, looking at me with sober eyes. My whole body goes tense, wondering what he means.

Then my phone buzzes.

"It's Flora," I announce. Biz and I turn to each other. Another surprise call in two days.

"I wonder if she saw the doctor," Biz says. A swirl of emotions rises between us as we both sit up straight and pat down our sandy, salty beach hair.

I prop the phone up on a blue flower planter with an anchor on it and we all wave hello.

"Hi, Flora!"

"Hey, guys! Did you make it to P-town?" The sight of Flora on my phone temporarily glues us back together. "I'm so sorry— are you guys busy?" Flora asks.

"Not at all," I say, still unsure if we should be concerned about her call.

"Wyatt was busy stealing my banana pudding," Biz jokes.

"I was not. That's your banana pudding fair and square," I say.

"You were eyeing it," Biz says.

Flora laughs at our back and forth, thinking everything's fine between us.

"Are you still traveling to all the gay resort towns?" she asks.

"Yep. We're hitting all our favorite spots: P-town now, Saugatuck, then our friends' wedding in Colorado, then Palm Springs and then it's baby time," Biz says.

"Oh, that's so fun." Flora smiles.

"You guys look wrecked." Gabrielle, Flora's wife and always the blunt one, pops her head in to wave hi and pops right out.

"Beach fatigue," Biz says.

"We're just about to take a post-lunch nap," I say.

"I'm jealous," Flora adds, trying to get comfortable with her large stomach.

"Did you have news from the doctor?" Biz asks.

"Mommy, gimme that," Roxy interrupts. Flora's youngest appears on screen and wants her phone immediately.

"Someone's ready for their close-up," I say.

"Sweetie, this isn't your toy right now. Mommy's talking to Wyatt and Biz."

Roxy's giant mouth darkens the screen as if she's trying to eat the phone. "Hellooooooo!" she greets us then quickly disappears.

We both let out big laughs. "Such a cutie," I chime in.

"Sorry . . . I haven't seen the doctor yet. I'm scheduled to see her in a week. I just wanted to show you guys something," Flora says without giving anything away. Biz and I exchange curious looks. We never know if Flora's news is going to be good or bad. Everything is so out of our control, which is not my favorite way of operating.

The phone makes scratchy noises as the screen shakes and gets shoved around. *Is that a blanket covering the screen? Are they experiencing an earthquake? Did Roxy eat us?*

A ray of sunlight hits something round, like we're looking at a flesh-colored balloon. "Whoa," Biz says, in complete awe.

I'm staring intensely, trying to figure it out, like it's an optical illusion drawing.

"Can you see?" Flora asks.

"Beautiful," Biz says, smiling uncontrollably with tears in his eyes.

I tilt my head and my pulse quickens as I finally realize what we're looking at. "Awww, our baby," I say.

"Say hi!" Flora says, waving her hand in front of her stomach.

We coo to our glorious baby growing inside the belly of this woman we've met in person twice. For a split second I stare mournfully into all the moments we'll never have.

Because of our physical distance and nature of the surrogacy relationship, there will never be continuous bonding with Flora's belly. No feeling a spontaneous kick while watching movies on the couch. Or maybe a tiny karate chop. Our baby growing in someone else's stomach won't really know our voices until we meet in person.

Sure, all of this could, and some of it has happened over the phone. But there's an ache in my stomach that it just isn't the same. In all the surrogate materials we've read, none of it says: *first and foremost, you'll painfully miss the actual baby bump.*

"Your baby's feeling extra saucy today. All of their limbs are making themselves known. Elbows. Feet. Lots of jabbing happening," Flora informs us off-screen.

Biz watches with the same forlorn expression on his face. After a few minutes of letting us ogle over her belly, Flora quietly reappears on the phone.

"That's it. Just thought I'd share your fiery little one," Flora says.

Before we say our thank-you and goodbyes, Flora makes a point to tell us how excited she is to see us. We end the call saying something corny but true. That her generosity knows no bounds.

Biz and I stare at the phone with Flora and our baby no longer on screen.

"Do you ever regret that we'll never really get to experience the bump?" I ask Biz.

"All the time," Biz says, confirming something I've felt for a while too.

"We never did a professional photo shoot with Flora," I say.

"No playing Mozart in person," Biz says.

"No singing the same lullabies our moms sang to us."

"There's no bath time with her belly," Biz adds.

"No sitting behind her with our arms around her stomach in the style of Patrick Swayze and Demi Moore in *Ghost*," I say as we both laugh. "Maybe we're romanticizing the bump. Maybe it's just a small part of our *journey* that ultimately won't matter in the grand scheme of our kid's life."

"You know what *wasn't* romantic?" Biz reminds us. "Masturbating into a cup."

The first act of trying to conceive our baby. There was nothing sexy about the way the fertility nurse—the one with the cold, overly clinical disposition—asked if we wanted to share a room to deposit our *dual specimen*.

"She feels like she's imitating Sarah Paulson imitating Nurse Ratched," I said at the time.

The other option was to be in separate rooms. When we opted for one room, we couldn't believe this five-foot-by-five-foot cell that housed a single vinyl chair, where hundreds of would-be fathers sat, was the first step in making a baby.

"I am not sitting in that chair," Biz had said. We both wanted it to happen quickly. But first, our sexual appetite had to be stimulated by an outdated television connected to a weird motel-like cable box that offered a variety of adult films to choose from.

"Do people watch like full-length porn movies?" I asked.

Would we like twinks on twinks, twinks on daddies, daddies on daddies, cowboys on mechanics or mechanics on Army men? Or maybe we were interested in some hetero porn involving an "Adonis" with long flowing hair who looked like Fabio and his identical female partner.

We threw on some scene involving a shirtless, sweaty gardener working in the backyard with the beefy homeowner who was caught spying on him.

It became background white noise when we started kissing each other until we undid our pants, which slowly found their way down to our ankles.

A kaleidoscope of thoughts swirled through my mind: *the night we were intimate in Biz's first studio apartment . . . making out once during a hike at the top of Runyon Canyon . . . will the baby kind of look like both of us, hopefully?*

Our collective DNA released a second apart and we both almost missed our individual cups, making us laugh hysterically. "That was actually probably more romantic than what most people do," Biz said as we kissed on the lips one more time to mark the weight of the occasion.

"But," I reminded him, "most people don't have to hand Nurse Ratched a cup with stuff in it and send it off to be frozen after." We doubled over in giggles.

After our call with Flora, we nap, shower, change and walk Matilda. Later, as Biz and I saunter past the Boatslip, we see crowds of people pile in and hear some song of the summer I don't yet know spill out.

"Last chance," I say, letting Biz know we can still make the nightly ritual. I'm half hoping he won't want to go, half wanting him to stick to doing what he loves.

"I'm good," he says. He barely turns his head to look at the party. This seems especially off brand for Biz. He would go to the Boatslip every night if he had his way. The vacant expression on his face starts to worry me.

I'd made a reservation at our favorite Mediterranean spot on the east side of town called Strangers & Saints. "Loot, Plunder, Pillage & Play" reads the sign out front of the restored sea captain's house.

Cozied up on the candlelit front porch, we dig into our ricotta dumplings and Moroccan carrots as we sip our rosé-sake san-gria. I decide to let Biz take the wheel on the conversation.

"It's not so much that I want to tell you. It's something I have to tell you," Biz says, after I asked him what he wanted to tell me earlier.

"I'm all ears," I say. I can see whatever Biz *has* to tell me isn't coming easily. He sips his drink and tries to power through.

"Just promise me again you're not going to get upset," he says. Now he's scaring me but I guess we have to examine our relationship issues if we want to move forward.

"I won't get upset," I reassure him. I must look distracted because Biz tilts his head and squints at me. My phone has been buzzing in my shorts since we sat down, and I don't want to check it but it could be Flora with something urgent.

"Something wrong?" Biz asks, detecting I'm half listening.

"Sorry. My phone's been blowing up since we got here. Is yours?"

We both check our phones. It's my mom. I see she's called a bunch of times so I pick up.

"Hi, Mom. We're just at dinner. Can I call you back?" I ask. Biz leans back in his chair, slightly annoyed I'm taking the call.

"Something happened," she says on the other end of the phone, ignoring me.

"Can you be more specific?" I ask, putting down my fork. There's a drawn-out pause.

"It's your brother," she says cryptically.

"And . . . ?" I urge her to continue.

"He had an accident," Mom says, followed by another com-plicated pause. "I'm at the hospital now."

I feel a significant shift in my world, trying to process the news.

"What happened? Is he okay?" I ask, worried.

"Not exactly," my mom says, her voice quivering. "It might be a good idea if you come home, Wyatt."

I hold on to the phone, almost shaking. Biz stares at me, starting to freak out, waiting to hear his own fate.

# 6

## SNACKS, INTERRUPTED

**BIZ**

USUALLY, I'M THE ONE crying every summer when we leave P-town. I never want to leave.

Now it looks like Wyatt is about to cry and we just got here.

The expression on his face breaks my heart. Whatever his mom is saying on the phone has made him revert to being a helpless little kid. I want to take him into my arms and tell him everything will be alright.

"I think we have to leave," Wyatt says, hanging up with his mom. The tense lines on his face return. Even the corners of his mouth have gone rigid.

Dread fills my soul. "What?! Why?" I can't absorb all this bad news.

My first thought is, I hope nothing happened to his mom.

My second thought is a postcard image of P-town fading. Is our epic gay resort babymoon not going to happen?

"Alex is in the hospital" is all Wyatt can muster in a matter-of-fact way.

"What happened?" I ask.

"She just said he flipped on his bike."

"Is he okay?"

"I guess not if he's in the hospital," Wyatt says, worried.

I realize I've been holding my fork midair during this entire conversation, kept in suspense. I finally put it down.

Wyatt's younger brother, Alex, is the golden child of the two boys—the one his mom worshipped. He could do no wrong. But Wyatt is the one his mom has always gone to for emotional support.

"My mom needs me," Wyatt says, confirming my theory. "You can stay if you want. I know this isn't ideal timing."

"Are you kidding? I would never stay. We're in this together."

"I'm just giving you the option," he says, spreading his generosity thin. "I know how much you love it here."

"Your mom needs you and you need me," I decide. A thought pops into my mind. "Do you think we can come back though?"

"Biz, I have no idea. Plus, I don't think we'll want to drive back and forth if we're working our way out west."

"What about the cottage?"

"We'll have to eat the cost or try and get a refund."

P-town is going to have to wait for now. We both pause our night, gazing at the flickering candlelight between us. Our smiling server places our entrees in front of us as if nothing is happening.

- - - - - - - ➤

EARLY THE NEXT SUNNY MORNING, WE SECURE MATILDA IN HER DOG bed, climb into Virginia Woolf and motor out of town. I'm devastated to leave this cocoon of like-minded people on the edge of the earth. Our baby will be a teenager by the time we ever come back, I think.

I offer to drive so Wyatt doesn't have another thing to worry about. He pets Matilda, asleep in his lap, his emotional support animal for now.

No music on this leg of the trip. We're all too unsettled.

It's unfortunate that so much is happening when Wyatt and I can't even talk through any of the immediate road blocks between the two of us. We both know his brother's situation will have to take priority before we address our own issues.

We barely touched our dinner last night and skipped breakfast this morning.

Driving on an empty stomach is good for Matilda. But it's a nightmare for me.

"I wonder if we should grab a bite on the road before we get there," I gently suggest.

"Let's just drive and figure out food later," Wyatt says predictably as we head toward signs already pointing to Boston.

"Of course," I say, taking one hand off the wheel and squeezing Wyatt's shoulder for a second. Despite the unspoken issues between us, I just want Wyatt to know I'm here for him.

My stomach starts to growl, when I remember we have snacks. I reach behind my seat and fumble inside Matilda's tote bag, searching around the bag for way too long.

"What do you need in there? I'll get it," Wyatt offers, growing concerned about me multitasking while driving.

"I put a bag of chocolate covered almonds in there before we left."

"In Matilda's bag? That's dangerous. You shouldn't do that,"

Wyatt says, always reminding me of the possible fatal effects chocolate has on dogs.

"She's not going to eat a bag of chocolate almonds," I say, trying to defend my unwise decision.

"How do you know? She eats anything."

"The bag is sealed so . . . Would you mind?"

Wyatt sighs and twists around his seat to reach into the bag. What about *me needing food every two hours* doesn't he get?

"Tennis ball? No. Rubbery chew toy thing? No. Rawhide stick?" Wyatt flashes the stick near my face.

"Tempting. But no thank you," I say.

Matilda sits up, wagging her tail at the sight of the stick.

"Oops. Not for you," I tell our dog, who sighs in disappointment and wonders when these giants are going to let her out of this vomit machine.

Wyatt opens the bag of chocolate almonds and pours a few into my palm, giving me temporary relief. I catch him sneaking one or two himself and have to smile.

As much as I want to, I'm not sure how I'm going to tell Wyatt about losing my job. Not only is it crappy timing because of his family situation, but I don't want to let him down during this crucial point in our lives. Even under normal circumstances, telling him I was let go would be difficult. I'm hoping it will eventually become a blessing in disguise but right now the feeling of failure sets in.

None of this is helping my growing anxiety about becoming a good father. But I just can't tell Wyatt now. I don't want to toss a double whammy on him.

I decide I'll wait to break the news about my job until we find out what's happening with his brother.

# 7

## QUEEN B'S

**WYATT**

THE TWO-AND-A-HALF-HOUR DRIVE TO my mom's seems to happen in grueling slow motion. Even though I wasn't receptive to the Provincetown party that Biz seems to desperately want, trekking back to my hometown right now is not what I had in mind before the arrival of the baby.

Not that I don't want to be with my mom and brother—we're close enough—but surely the baby will bring my family together more often than our once-a-year Christmas visits. I just didn't think it would happen now.

The sea air scent of the Atlantic is replaced with the fresh smell of hospital as we arrive at Beth Israel, feeling bedraggled by the back-to-back long-distance driving.

With Matilda on her leash, walking slowly behind us, still waking up from her car sleep, we arrive at the front desk.

"May I help you?" the generically friendly receptionist asks us. Her plastic golden name tag tells the world she's "Phyllis." She looks like a former suburban soccer mom who raised three perfect children and is now creeping toward her seventies with a volunteer job that she dislikes but what else is she going to do with her time these days.

"We're looking for Alex Wallace?" I say.

While Phyllis types on her laptop, Biz curls up in a beige leather chair and looks like he wants to take a nap. He did most of the driving and it shows.

"Third floor," Phyllis says, eyeing Biz, disapproving of how comfortable he's becoming with his foot tucked under his leg.

"Thank you, Phyllis," I say, trying to get chummy with her. Her tight smile falls as she looks down and spots Matilda.

"Oh. No dogs allowed. Unless you have papers," Phyllis says.

"Papers?" I ask, my voice cracking on the second syllable.

"Papers declaring it's a service dog," she says.

"*She* isn't a service dog but thank you." Biz lets the lady have it from his lounge chair.

"We'll keep her outside," I say, trying to soften our approach.

The woman wants so badly to roll her eyes but she coldly ignores us and answers the phone. Biz stands, staring her down. I grab Matilda and shuffle us away from the front desk.

"Just relax. You can take M for a spin around the building," I say. "Not a big deal."

"I know but she's just so rude. Don't work in a friggin' hospital if you're going to treat people and animals like that."

I don't want to escalate Biz's frustration. I know he resents having to skip out on Provincetown early.

"Text me a status update," he says as he takes Matilda through the automatic doors outside where they'd both rather be anyway.

When the elevator transports me to the third floor, the

sounds of various machines beeping and hissing and pumping makes me miss the beach too.

I enter my brother's room, where my mom springs up from a chair and gives me a giant hug, as if she's been waiting for me. She won't let go.

Through our embrace, I see my sister-in-law, Megan, her eyes puffy and red from crying, her gigantic diamond ring always shockingly prominent. "Hi, Wyatt. Thanks for coming," Megan says upon seeing me. Even through her tears, her resting face always suggests she's disappointed in me. Like I'm not good enough to be her brother-in-law.

By the look my mom silently serves me, it's clear she's been here too long and needs to escape her daughter-in-law. "I am so happy to see you," my mom beams.

I step in farther but don't see my brother anywhere. I'm wary of all the cords and monitors around the room, worried they've taken him someplace even worse.

"Wyatt! Holy crap. You actually made it," Alex says, exiting the bathroom with a smile, looking slightly beaten up.

For a second, I don't recognize him. He has glossy eyes, a cut along the bridge of his nose, a few bruises on his arms and he's wearing a black wrist brace.

Even though he's two years younger than me, Alex is slightly taller. With his reddish hair and fair skin, he looks more like my mom than I do. It's hard to believe I used to give piggyback rides to this person who's now a grown adult man.

"We were in Provincetown so it wasn't too far," I say. Alex crushes me with his usual bear hug. Despite his appearance, I'm relieved he's stronger than ever.

"You should've seen him last night," my mom says, trying to

justify her reason for asking me here. "He could've taken a turn for the worse and I wanted you here just in case."

"Yeah, I kinda bounced back overnight," Alex admits.

"Leave it to Alex," Megan says, grabbing her husband's arm as if to suggest she owns him. Her ring looks like it could cut all of us at any second.

"They're giving him a CT scan today to check for any brain injuries," my mom says.

"What happened?" I ask.

"You know how Alex loves that dumb mountain biking," my mom offers.

"Seriously, Mom?" Alex protests.

"Please stop saying it's dumb, Beverly. It's his passion," Megan says. The condescending tone of her voice always sounds like the high school mean girl who tells you which day she and her sycophants wear pink and why you are not allowed to wear pink.

Alex's eyes helplessly pinball around, as if to say, *can't we all just get along?*

"It IS dumb," my mom continues, obviously stressed. "You just go in circles around a dirt path and you never get anywhere until you split your head open."

"Except I didn't split my head open," Alex says.

"Just tell me what happened," I say, trying to stay focused and defuse stress levels.

"It started raining. I was with my buddies. I took a wrong turn and smacked my head on a tree. Boom. Here we are," Alex says.

My mom bites her lower lip. She can't take it when her little prince is hurt. Me on the other hand, I'm supposed to swoop in and make everyone feel better.

"Alex is making it seem simpler than it was," Megan chimes in.

I'm sure there are three sides to this story.

"Were you wearing a helmet?" I ask.

"I forgot it," Alex admits.

"They were in Foxboro and didn't want to drive all the way back home." Megan is trying anything to make Alex not look bad.

"You didn't need to come. I'm honestly fine," Alex insists, not looking totally fine as he struggles to climb back into bed.

"They're saying he might have a concussion," my mom says to me. "I'm glad you're here."

"I don't have a concussion," Alex says. "Aren't you supposed to be on your babymoon thing?"

"We are but we wanted to make sure you were okay," I say.

Mom turns to me. "You look good, honey. Skinny. *Too* skinny. Are you eating? Any news with the baby? Oh, I'm so excited you're home! You can finally go through all your old boxes in the basement and get rid of some stuff. Where's Biz?"

"I'm fine. The baby's fine. Biz is outside with Matilda."

"You three can go visit with each other if you want. Alex probably needs a little rest right now anyway," Megan says.

In the hallway, my mom stabs the elevator down button and rolls her eyes, silently shaking her head at me. I can tell she's had enough of Megan.

"She's got a lotta balls, that one," my mom whispers about Megan. "She's making all the decisions without me. As if I'm not even there. I'm his *mother*, for chrissakes."

"Mom, you don't have to whisper. She can't hear us," I say, noticing a nurse walking by and looking at us suspiciously.

My mom looks at me and smiles. "Am I glad you're here."

Holding the elevator door open for my mom, I finally get a good look at what she's wearing: a yellow pleated pencil skirt with a matching belt, a crisp white button-down shirt with the collar popped and her ubiquitous high heels.

She waits until we walk out of the building to tie a floral silk scarf around her neck, draping it just so as it strikes me for the billionth time in my life just how stylish Ms. Beverly Wallace is for any occasion.

My mom was always a little higher profile and better dressed than other moms. It used to bother me as a kid, seeing Mom dressed to the nines, picking me up from hockey games with her freshly coiffed hair and makeup while the other moms wore basic yoga clothes they bought at Target.

The not-yet-out high school me never wanted to draw attention to myself, and the fact that the whole community gossiped about how increasingly fancy my mom dressed kept me mortified and resentful of her through my teen years. Young Wyatt Henry Wallace tried to hide the monogrammed clothing Mom insisted on buying me, often resorting to wearing my socks with the tiny "WHW" inside out.

When I was eight years old and my dad left us with basically nothing, my mom and her four best friends, Bonnie, Brenda, Barbra and Betty, started their own real estate business. "Queen B's Realty" became the community's top real estate agency and had dozens of billboards, bus shelters and local commercials to prove it. They were a tenacious group of women whose smiling faces on every corner turned them into Newton's honorary mayors. As an adult, I've learned to respect and embrace the amazing person my mom has become.

Looking around for Biz outside the hospital, I see a text from him telling me to walk across the street to the park. My mom can't get far enough away from Megan for a few minutes, even in her high heels, which she could run a marathon in.

"Bizzy! Matilda! How's my favorite son-in-law?" Mom throws out her arms and hugs Biz like he's her favorite kid.

"Beverly! How are you?! How's Alex?" Biz asks, as Mom kisses him hello.

"They're testing him for a possible concussion. I'm just worried. You hear all those stories of people hitting their head and they—" My mom can't even continue the thought.

"He'll be fine, Mom," I say, trying to console her.

I wave off my mom's genuine concern. It's a weird role I've always had to assume. The older brother savior. I just did it naturally until I grew up and realized I'd been playing substitute to my absent dad.

Once Alex married Megan, he didn't rely on me as much. As the third-generation heiress to a successful baby back rib chain, Megan has given Alex a whole new life. Alex became an executive within the company and now has everything he ever wanted.

"There you are," a determined voice says from afar as we all turn to see Megan approach, holding a box of Kleenex, wiping her runny nose.

"What's the matter? Is he okay?" Mom asks. "And how on earth did you find us?" she follows up, as if she really didn't want Megan to find us.

"The receptionist told me you guys were out here. Alex is okay. He's with the physical therapist," Megan says.

"Thank god. I thought something was wrong the way you're rushing out here." My mom's worried face softens.

"I was texting you but you weren't answering so I came out here," Megan says. "Evelyn and Melody's show is tonight. I don't want to leave but the nanny has to spend the night at her mother's house, which is like a forty-five-minute drive, because she's having a colonoscopy tomorrow and . . ."

As she continues, I notice my mom has full-on dissociated, her eyes almost disappearing into the back of her head. Mom can only take on so much stress and she certainly doesn't have the bandwidth to manage her son's nanny's colonoscopy.

"What's the show?" Biz chimes in. Clearly he's actually listening to her.

"They're performing *A Chorus Line*. It's so cute," says Megan. "I'm sad we'll miss it."

"*A Chorus Line*?" Biz perks up. Suddenly, we're firmly inside his wheelhouse. "Wait—isn't that a little adult? Your nieces are like ten." Biz aims this at me, not wanting to upset the easily upsettable Megan.

"They're nine but the school changed some of the lyrics so it's age appropriate," Megan says.

"Private school. They can do that kind of stuff," my mom says to us.

"Trust me, they cleared it with all the parents. It was a whole thing before the school year even started. Anyway, I don't want to leave Alex alone tonight," Megan says as she looks at my mom, who just stares back, conflicted.

"I can stay with Alex tonight," my mom offers.

Megan tilts her head in thought. She's intent on making the smarter move.

"I thought maybe you could take the kids to their play? I can't pull them," Megan says.

"I don't know if I want to leave my son for too long either though," Mom says.

"But they worked so hard on this show and their hearts will break," Megan insists.

"We can take them," Biz jumps in, which suddenly feels like the much-needed glue my family could use right now and always.

Biz and I glance at each other. I can't tell if he genuinely wants to start his parenting duties early or if he's trying to impress me. Either way, it's making me hopeful.

"Are you sure?" Megan asks, sizing both of us up. "I mean, it'd be such a big help, but only if you want to." Normally, she'd never let us babysit the kids—she's too controlling. But she has no choice in this unusual situation.

Come to think of it, we've never been with the kids on our own. Not living in the same city makes it harder to bond. But it doesn't help that Megan created codependent kids that used to cling to each of her legs and wouldn't let anyone except their nanny get near them. She even made their nanny sign her life away in blood with a lengthy legal contract and life-threatening nondisclosure agreement.

Megan is paranoid enough to think there's an organized army somewhere lurking around their cul-de-sac who wants to kidnap the fourth-generation heirs to a baby back rib chain.

"We'd love to do it," I say, happy to indulge my paternal instincts while simultaneously fulfilling my uncle duties.

"When and where is your next destination?" my mom asks with a subtext that screams *take me with you*.

"We should probably get back to P-town tomorrow," Biz says.

I raise an eyebrow. "We should?"

"We shouldn't?" Biz replies.

"I thought we agreed to just keep going west. Seems silly to go backward," I say, my whole body tensing up, knowing neither of us wants to have this conversation in front of my mom and Megan. "And we should wait to see how my brother is doing tomorrow."

I glance at my mom and Megan for support. They're both mesmerized by us airing our grievances like this in front of them. It's obvious Megan is fighting the urge to retract her ask.

"You're welcome to stay with me as long as you boys would like," my mom says, delighted for the distraction. "But promise me you'll go through all your old boxes when you get home? We can ship what you need back to Brooklyn."

"Yes, yes. I promise," I say.

Megan knows we're fully capable of babysitting, and yet in some cobwebbed, dusty nook of her mind, I'm sure she's letting herself imagine the worst. She pulls a tissue to silence the bad thoughts. "Thank you, guys." And blows her nose. "Just remember, they can be a handful. But they should be fine. They love their uncles."

"It could be like a trial run for being dads!" my mom adds.

# 8

## ONE SINGULAR SENSATION

### BIZ

**MISS P-TOWN.**

I miss morning coffee, sitting in a rocking chair overlooking Commercial Street. A bike ride through the dunes. Brunch and bloodies at Café Heaven. A sweaty dance party at Crown & Anchor. Post-barhopping slices of pizza at Spiritus.

I feel bad for Wyatt's brother but I just wasn't expecting to spend our babymoon in a hospital.

Okay, across the street from a hospital. But still.

It's especially disheartening to see how different Wyatt's relationship with his family is compared to mine. There's little chemistry between Wyatt and his brother. It's the complete opposite of how I interact with my sisters. Seeing Wyatt and his mom communicate always makes me long for the open and honest conversations I have with my parents.

It's nice though that we'll spend quality time with Wyatt's nieces. Even if babysitting them does, in fact, feel like some kind of cosmic test to see if we have what it takes to become fathers. And one I'm afraid I'll fail.

Later, with Wyatt's nieces, Evelyn and Melody, in the back seat of Virginia Woolf, we arrive at Awakenings. I'm shocked to discover it's just your average brick-and-mortar, two-story building.

Except, with an annual tuition of almost sixty thousand dollars and regularly voted as suburban Boston's number one private school, it's not average at all.

"What on earth are these people paying for?" I quietly ask Wyatt.

"The cafeteria food better be dipped in actual gold," he says.

We both stifle laughs.

"Wasn't *Awakenings* the name of a nineties movie?" Wyatt asks the girls, as I pull Virginia Woolf into the circular drive. Our cute little car is an orange sore thumb among the dozens of identical black SUVs filling up the school's parking lot. I love that we stand out. It's complete anarchy.

"Yes!" Melody, the gregarious, popular theater geek says. "Starring Robert De Niro and Robin Williams. It's a classic." Leave it to the nine-year-old to school the thirty-somethings. "Mom and Dad won't let us watch it because it has, quote, un-quote, adult themes. Tyler Shaewitz told me about it."

"Our school's called 'Awakenings' because they want to awaken your wallet so you pay them like the capitalist pigs they are," says Evelyn, the dark, brainiac, morose one, staring out the window.

"Why's this car so smelly?" Melody asks.

"It's old," Wyatt says. "Like us."

"Ew. Is it used?"

"Technically. Yes. We bought it from my coworker," I say.

"Why would you want someone else's stinky car?"

I realize that for a child of such privilege, this is not even in the realm of her imagination. "It's not stinky," I say.

"Biz . . ." Wyatt cautions me, not wanting to argue with the kids.

"But it is. Why didn't you just buy your own car?" Melody asks.

"Because we found this car at an affordable price," Wyatt explains.

"Plus, it's cool and vintage," I add.

"Oh, so you're like thrifters," Evelyn wisely says.

"Like thrift shoppers? Sure." Now I'm speaking her language.

"Okay, you two thespians!" Wyatt says to the girls. He's clearly trying to keep the mood light and upbeat. I get it. "It's showtime!"

After we park and enter, Wyatt tells me he's never been inside his nieces' school.

"With all the birthday cards and our once-a-year holiday visits here, it feels like we're a close family but we're really not," he tells me as we shuffle down the hallway.

I feel bad Wyatt's family isn't as tight-knit as mine. This is all just a blunt reminder for him that they've drifted apart even further over the years.

"When your baby comes, will they be our cousin?" Melody asks, wanting to get to the bottom of every passing thought in her head.

"Of course. Your dad and I are brothers," Wyatt says.

"But Dad told me the baby won't have a mom like us."

Oh god, here we go.

"That's true," Wyatt says with some hesitation on whether or not he should elaborate.

"We used an egg donor," I chime in.

"Eggs?" Now Evelyn perks up to this curious conversation.

"One lady is technically biologically linked to our child and another lady will give birth," I try to explain, used to this line of questioning. Almost everyone not familiar with how surrogacy works has asked us this.

Before Melody can ask a follow-up question, Wyatt interrupts. "I don't think we need to go into detail right before your show," he says.

"Parker Leventhal can fit a can of Pringles in his mouth," Evelyn informs us, happily derailing the conversation with random trivia about another boy they know, I guess.

We all stop and watch as the girls scream-squeal hello to some of their friends.

Seeing all these little ones interact makes my future-parent insecurity catch fire.

*Will our kid think we're dysfunctional?*

*What if our kid is bullied in school because they have gay dads?*

*Why are we bringing a child into this hellscape of a world?*

"Oh, hi. You're not Evelyn and Melody's dad." I turn to find a hard-core cute guy greeting me. "I'm Mr. Aronson, their theater director."

He fits the mold of everything you'd want in a drama teacher for your child.

The perfect beard. His best sport coat. The teardrop-shaped eighties-inspired glasses.

Not to mention, his wireless headset. Like he's Taylor Swift about to perform at Wembley Stadium.

Mr. Aronson swivels from me to Wyatt and says, "And *you're* not Evelyn and Melody's dad." His mock confusion charms us both.

Just now, I realize it's probably not a great idea to have two strange men show up inside a school in this day and age. But then I figure a domestic terrorist probably isn't going to pose as someone's guncle at a kids' production of *A Chorus Line*.

"Their dad, my brother, had an accident. So we're here instead. I'm Wyatt and this is my partner, Biz," Wyatt explains.

"Oh, right! It's coming back to me now. Opening-night stress!" Mr. Aronson says with a laugh as he glances at me. "Megan said she had to stay at the hospital and you'd be coming instead. I'm so sorry about Alex. I hope he has a speedy recovery. It's great to meet you both."

The three of us shake hands. Mr. Aronson and I smile and size each other up. Wyatt's eyes dart toward mine. I can tell he thinks we're inadvertently flirting.

Which we're not. At all. At least, I'm not.

Although, when Mr. Aronson shakes the hands of an impossibly young set of monied parents, anyone with a pulse can't help but catch his sizable bicep popping through his tweed blazer.

Immediately, I regret how inappropriate this thought is to have backstage at a school play. And it certainly won't help the strain in my relationship with Wyatt.

But now the guy is back and smiling at us.

"Where are you two from?" he asks, looking to bond with the (probably) only other gays in the building.

"We live in Brooklyn," I offer. "Prospect Heights, to be exact."

"Are you the one who chose *A Chorus Line*?" Wyatt asks, grinning and putting on the charm. It reminds me of when we first met, when Wyatt was genuinely interested in getting to know everything about me. I feel a pang of heartbreak this isn't directed at me.

"My teacher's assistant, Jocelyn, and I decided together. It was so ahead of its time," Mr. Aronson says.

"Biz is an actor," Wyatt says. He's always ready to shamelessly promote me to anyone and I love that about him.

"I was getting an actorly vibe," Mr. Aronson says, smiling.

"I am. Was," I say. "When I was a teenager mostly. I was on a show."

"What show?" he asks.

"*Back in the Saddle*," I say. "It was on the Disney Channel."

Mr. Aronson bursts with enthusiasm. "Oh my god, I used to love that show! You played Corey!" he beams.

"Good memory," I say.

"My favorite episode was when your identical twin shows up on the ranch."

"I had to shoot all those scenes twice. That was rough," I say.

"That is so funny. I watched your show every day after school. Wow," he says, squinting with curiosity. "What are you up to now?" The dreaded follow-up question.

"I write for a food magazine now so . . ."

*Oh, god. I'm not a magazine writer anymore*, I remind myself. The thought of both losing my actual job and disappointing this stranger that I'm no longer acting stings.

Thankfully the conversation veers away from my career and onto current Broadway musicals before Mr. Aronson wrangles the kids backstage.

Memories of my own school acting days flutter awake inside my soul as we enter the large auditorium in awe.

"These acoustics rival Radio City," I say.

"I'm glad their hefty annual tuition is being put to good use," Wyatt says quietly.

"There's no bar, right?" I ask Wyatt, half joking, as we take our seats close to the stage.

We stare at the red velvet curtain on stage as the rest of the audience shuffles in.

"Ogling Drama Teacher much?" Wyatt says, finally letting his dam break. I could tell he's stewing about some perceived sparks of chemistry between me and Mr. Aronson.

"Are you asking me or yourself that?" I wonder. Wyatt turns to me with a half smile, knowing I'm right. Even though Wyatt and I are monogamous, we both agree that admiring another handsome man here and there isn't the worst thing.

We aren't like our other friends Justin and Antonio, who have a well-documented open relationship with just about every eligible gay man in New York City. No judgments.

Nor are we like our married friends Grant and Noah, who are *supposed* to be monogamous with each other but secretly sleep with just about every eligible gay man in New York City. No judgments.

Hell, we aren't even like the Zachs, who are fully monogamous—except they're allowed hookups outside of the relationship with just a few rules: no kissing, no oral, no full-on sex and no repeat callers. Which basically means they're only allowed . . . *hand jobs?*

But I don't want to think about any of that. I want to stay present and just try to have a fun evening together.

"I'm excited for the show," I say.

"Thanks for enduring my family with me," Wyatt says.

"Of course. It's always nice to hang with Beverly and the gang."

"I feel bad we cut Provincetown short though."

"Don't be. It's kind of fun we're playing the role of Daddy Number One and Daddy Number Two to someone else's kids. For one night only. Before our own sparkling debut."

My secret stage fright is off the charts.

Seated in the plush seats, we catch the swirling activity around the theater. Moms and dads herd their little ones into their seats or onto their laps. Brothers and sisters hold bouquets of roses to give to their performing siblings after the show. The student ushers awkwardly hand out paper flyers cleverly made to look like Broadway Playbills.

Then I notice the confidence that these other, much younger parents have and it stuns me. I can only hope to reach that level of comfort when our kid is this age.

The theater's warm glow dims to total darkness. The show begins as Wyatt and I uncontrollably reach for each other's hand.

# 9

## DRAMA TEACHER DRAMA

### WYATT

**B**IZ HOLDING MY HAND feels so natural. His little extra squeezes give me a few quick pulses to let me know he's nothing but supportive. I squeeze back, feeling bad at how frustrated I can get sometimes but appreciating Biz for being here.

This is just like our usual theater date night where the lights dim and we instinctually hold each other's hand. In New York, we try to see a few shows throughout the year. I like seeing the most cutting-edge theater to give me visual ideas as a director, and Biz loves anything on Broadway to keep him connected to his acting roots. After each show we have our usual late-night dinner-and-drinks discussion, debating the performance for hours.

The only show we'd ever walked out early on was an experimental show on the Lower East Side that involved too many strobe and laser lights. The giant sign screaming, "THIS SHOW CONTAINS FLASHING LIGHTS!!!" at the entrance gave us both so much anxiety, we thought we'd have seizures before intermission. During an extended disco scene where the protagonist was murdered on the dance floor and the strobe lights continued for what seemed like half an hour, we bolted out as quickly as possible. We couldn't stop laughing at the fear-inducing sign and tried to calm our nerves afterward over tacos and margaritas.

The kids' show starts smoothly. Students of all ages and gender expressions play each role. One older girl belts out her number to the back of the house like a pro. Another very sporty boy mumbles his lines and looks like he'd perform better on a basketball court.

Then I remember they're kids. I shouldn't critique their performances, but it's hard to turn off my inner director. I make a mental note to take it easy on our own kid if they express interest in musical theater.

Out of the corner of my eye, I see Biz laughing, getting caught up in the emotion and mouthing along to the lyrics. Melody and Evelyn are the youngest in the cast and don't have major roles, but they're background players in the opening and closing numbers, performing their hearts out with gleeful energy.

Making some of the adult-themed lyrics more child-friendly proves both challenging and downright comical. "Tits and ass" becomes "grit and class."

Biz and I steal glances with each other throughout the performance. We've both scream-sung along with the original cast recording at home a million times.

When the entire cast comes together for the finale, my throat tightens. Seeing these kids perform with such confidence, I'm overcome with pride that my brother is raising two very awesome girls, and I can't wait until we do the same.

Biz and I hold back happy tears as the students bow to a wildly supportive standing ovation.

The school has a cast party inside the gym where all the families, faculty and students mingle and celebrate the fruits of their labor. There's a huge chocolate sheet cake made to look like a piano and cookies in the shape of the comedy and tragedy masks.

Biz and I stand there, holding plastic flutes of Prosecco as we watch Melody and Evelyn hug their fellow castmates and crew members, analyzing every last detail that no audience member would've ever caught.

"And when Hendrix swallowed their entire lyric in the second verse, I died."

"A room full of theater kids is born," I say.

"Hallelujah," Biz says. We smile at each other, feeling like proud fake dads.

A couple of the insular parents suspiciously pass their eyes over me and Biz, so we make a point to introduce ourselves to a few of them. A wave of relief settles as they finally realize we're not interlopers.

"I'm so glad Alex is okay," says one very concerned mom.

"Let us know what hospital so we can send flowers," offers another.

Everyone is flattered to learn that the school play is a stop on our way to the baby. More than a few of the progressive parents give me an overbearing vibe that suggests they still refer to their nine-year-olds as "four-hundred-sixty-nine-week-olds."

This whole night is like a flash forward into our future as dads. That's if we suddenly moved to the suburbs of Boston and became heiresses to a baby back rib fortune.

I've had enough of this *Big Little Lies: Midwest*, so I escape the inner sanctum of parents when I suddenly realize Biz is nowhere to be found.

I notice the twins are busy laughing and chatting with their friends. I toss back the rest of my Prosecco, pop a tragedy mask cookie in my mouth and exit the gym.

The sugar and bubbly collide inside my stomach, giving me a much-needed jolt of energy, so I speed-walk past the closed classrooms, the colorful library full of high-tech equipment and the cafeteria that looks like a Michelin-star restaurant. I feel both nostalgic for my crummy old public school and relieved I'm not still in school.

It occurs to me that Biz is probably getting fresh air somewhere outside. He doesn't like being pinned down too long, that one.

Opening the double doors, I step into the starry, cool night, which sends a refreshing shiver through my body. I can see for what feels like miles in front of me—no buildings and certainly none of the Manhattan supertalls obstructing the horizon.

Walking around the periphery of the school, I discover the athletic field and the air suddenly becomes fetid with what smells like a skunk. I don't want to come face-to-face with suburban wildlife, so I start to duck back inside when I hear faint laughter.

I walk the length of the dimly lit brick wall and turn the corner. From a distance, I spot the silhouette of Biz under a full moon. Turns out, it's not a skunk. It's weed.

Biz is standing under a weeping willow tree, the smoke billowing in the air like a thought bubble as he tilts his head back in laughter. *Is he laughing to himself?*

On the other side of the tree, my eyes go further into focus.

Biz laughs and shares a fat joint with Mr. Aronson, their bodies too close to each other for my taste.

Biz turns to see me. "Wyatt!" he calls, which sounds like something between jovial and getting caught.

My nieces' drama teacher and my boyfriend aren't just sharing a joint. They're sharing what could only be perceived as a romantic moment.

# 10

## ANGELS IN AMERICA

**BIZ**

**I** **DIDN'T DO ANYTHING WRONG.** Maybe Wyatt thought I did.

But I didn't.

Turns out the drama teacher is a father himself. Within seconds of talking with Mr. Aronson, I couldn't help but confess to him that I've been having fears of becoming a dad.

"Congrats! Your nieces were so great," Mr. Aronson said.

"Thanks so much. I'm having imposter syndrome because I'm about to become a dad myself but anyway . . ." I said.

I think he felt bad for me.

Okay, maybe I shouldn't have left the cast party and gone halfway around the building to a moonlit football field to smoke pot with a cute stranger.

Of course I think Mr. Drama is cute—who wouldn't? His resting *aw, shucks* face would grab anyone's attention. I also admittedly enjoy that he's a genuine fan of my old show.

But I'm innocent of any wrongdoing.

Plus, it's not like this guy is the type to break up a relationship. He's too . . . nice.

And it's not like I would ever cheat on Wyatt. It's one of the many things I love about us.

We're both monogamous to a fault.

But I can see by the pained expression on Wyatt's face as he approaches that he thinks I'm in the wrong. It's a mixture of jealousy, suspicion and hurt, which kills me.

"What are you guys up to?" Wyatt asks, trying to hide his emotion with a forced casual tone. I feel guilty for no reason.

"It's so great you guys are about to have a baby. I was just talking your husband's ear off about my two-year-old and our adoption journey," Mr. Aronson says brightly.

Wyatt and I share a look on his earnest use of the word *journey*.

"We're not married though," I clarify, glancing back at Wyatt, who looks away.

"Oh. Sorry. I just assumed. Boyfriends though, right?" Mr. Aronson needs to slap a label on us, which is understandable. Most people want to know if we're married, and it's always disappointing that I have to say we're just boyfriends. Somehow that never feels like it's enough.

"Yes. For now," Wyatt jokes. We all laugh but my smile fades quickly. The truth in his jest stings a little.

"You guys are going to be amazing dads. I can feel it," Mr. Aronson adds. He takes another quick puff then hands the joint to Wyatt, who politely declines. He offers it to me but I've had my share for the night.

"We should probably go," I say.

"Yeah, the girls have to get home," Wyatt adds.

"Of course!" Mr. Aronson says, holding out a pack of gum for all of us to take a stick.

The three of us walk back to the cast party where Wyatt and I collect the twins.

"Come back next year," Mr. Aronson says to us as we head for the exit. He smiles wide and announces, "We're doing *Angels in America*!"

We both smile. "You gotta love the guy," I say on our way out, immediately regretting my choice of words.

"Do you though?" Wyatt asks.

In the car, on the way back to Wyatt's mom's house, there are two very distinct conversations happening.

"Why would you do that?" Wyatt whispers at me so the girls won't hear.

"I want to play Roy Cohn in *Angels*," Evelyn tells Melody in the back seat.

"I didn't do anything. It was completely harmless. We just didn't want to," I mime smoking pot, "near the school," I explain, whispering back.

"Why? You're so not right for the role," a confused Melody says to Evelyn.

"Make out or smoke pot?" Wyatt asks, overreacting.

"So? It's called playing against type. Maybe I don't want to play ingenues my whole life," Evelyn says. "Roy Cohn is the villain I was born to play."

"I didn't make out with him. We were just having a good conversation about having kids and he offered me pot," I explain.

"I want to play the Angel," Melody says.

"I know but look at it from my perspective," Wyatt says.

"Do you even know what *Angels in America* is about?" Evelyn scoffs at her sister.

"I'm sorry that it *seemed* like something was going on but, trust me, it wasn't. So you have to let this go. It was all harmless," I say to Wyatt.

"It's about angels? In . . . America," Melody guesses.

Evelyn groans audibly. Wyatt groans audibly.

"It just feels like sometimes you're not interested in being equal partners with me," Wyatt continues. I can't believe he thinks that.

"What are you guys talking about up there?" Evelyn is done with her sister and wants in on the (other) adult conversation.

"We're just talking about how great you both were tonight," Wyatt says, smiling into the rearview mirror at our temporary little angels. "Your mom and dad would be so proud. Your uncles are very proud."

"That's not what you were talking about but okay," Evelyn says, nothing getting past her.

— — — — — — →

AFTER DROPPING THE TWINS OFF, WE DRIVE THE SHORT DISTANCE TO WYatt's childhood home in silence. I tell myself it's because we're both exhausted.

I know Wyatt is upset but I don't want to argue. I'm pretty sure Wyatt doesn't either.

Wyatt's mom returns from the hospital just as we arrive and tells us Alex is doing just fine. She and Wyatt decide to have a glass of wine after a long day. Wanting to give them some mother and son bonding time, I head upstairs.

Wyatt's childhood bedroom has become his mom's hybrid guest bedroom/real estate satellite office/home gym.

I collapse into an air mattress that Beverly made up, surrounded by a treadmill, a rack of pink dumbbells and her desk piled high with placards of her smiling real estate headshot.

I feel guilty for . . . I'm not sure exactly?

I'll admit, it was a moment of weakness on my part. When the drama teacher offered me pot, I saw it as a chance to let loose a little, take advantage of the babymoon we're supposed to be on. I needed to share how I'm worried about becoming a dad and that I won't measure up to Wyatt.

Sometimes it's easier to open up to a stranger than the ones we love.

I must've fallen asleep because Wyatt wakes me when he returns from downstairs. As he changes into his old gray Boston Bruins sleeping T-shirt, a fun thought pops into my head.

"Should we have make-up sex?" I ask, completely serious.

"Nope," Wyatt states emphatically, turning his back to me as he folds his clothes in a perfectly neat stack.

I'm scared we're never going to be intimate again. Especially after we have the baby. "Why not?" I ask.

"Because we haven't made up."

"Are we actually fighting? We could try and make up," I suggest.

"Why don't you go call your suburban Sondheim."

"Oh, come on. He was a fan and wanted to tell me all about his kid and his adoption *journey*. Plus, he had weed and that's it. Fine, I liked his glasses. But that's *really* it."

We hear footsteps approach and Wyatt slips onto the air mattress behind me, draping his arm over my body, as if nothing is wrong. His mom faintly knocks and pushes the door open. She appears almost in soft focus, wearing the nicest black nightgown thingy I've ever seen. It could easily double as a cocktail dress. She even dresses up to go to sleep.

"You two have everything you need?" she asks, placing two fancy bottles of sparkling water on a dresser.

"We're so good right now, Mom," Wyatt says.

I smile wide, feeling Wyatt give my thigh a tight squeeze under the covers. "We're great," I manage to let out.

"Stay hydrated and I'll see you in the morning. Love you both." She blows a kiss and leaves. The click of the door shutting coincides with Wyatt moving away from me.

It makes me feel like a toy he no longer wants.

"If she suspects anything, I'll never hear the end of it," Wyatt whispers. "Trying to figure out why we're fighting will become her new hobby."

"I'm not fighting. You're fighting."

"I'm not the one that snuck around to the football field, all hot for teacher," Wyatt says.

Seeing Wyatt in bed next to me now, I know my boyfriend always has the competition beat. From his tuft of dark chest hair poking out of his T-shirt to his meaty calves that peek out of the blanket. No one has made me sizzle quite the same way before or after I met Wyatt.

"Nothing happened and nothing would've happened for the eightieth time," I say. It's troubling that Wyatt refuses to see this. "Aren't we past petty jealousy at this point?"

"You've been so unpredictable lately that it's just setting off some alarm bells."

"Then let this be a lesson you can always trust me," I try to smooth things over. "Okay?"

He lets out a sigh and I can smell the minty fresh Crest

toothpaste on his breath as he tries to get comfortable on the cramped air mattress. He doesn't answer, mulling this over.

The truth is, I was also using Mr. Aronson as a sounding board for my worries going into parenthood. Are you able to get any sleep? How do you know what a crying baby needs? What if the kid doesn't even like you?

I sneak a glance at Wyatt, who's staring at the same contours in the cottage cheese ceiling he probably stared at when he was a closeted gay kid, unsure of how to come out.

I toss and turn in my stew of regret and humiliation for something I didn't even do.

"I can't sleep," Wyatt says.

We can hear his mom snoring now.

"Me neither," I say. But not because his mom is snoring. Because I don't know how to make any of this right.

"I overreacted," he admits. "I'm probably overthinking everything right now."

"You? Nah," I joke. "We need to talk about a lot of things," I continue, hopeful we can get past this.

"I know, but not in my childhood bedroom that's been converted into a multipurpose room with my mom snoring down the hall."

"Fair enough," I whisper with some disappointment.

The baggage between us has piled up like a broken airport carousel. I'm knee-deep in my insecurity about having a baby and losing my job isn't helping.

I can almost feel Wyatt thinking I won't be a good dad.

Before my thoughts get too heavy, my eye catches a section of the far wall cabinet filled with Wyatt's hockey medals and trophies. The last hint left that this was ever his bedroom.

"It's still so wild to me that you were a high school hockey star," I say.

"My brother was the real star," Wyatt says. "You should see his trophy case."

"Still can't believe what a jock you were," I say, genuinely impressed.

"You think my bubble butt was born in a gym?" Wyatt asks, eyes closed.

At least Wyatt can crack a joke. That means he's letting the teacher business go. We need to find a way to enjoy the next couple weeks.

But we also need to organize the messy drawers of our relationship. Our trust is broken if Wyatt thinks his partner of twelve years was about to hook up with his nieces' drama teacher.

Maybe I also need to understand why I felt the urge to escape my uncle duties to hang out with a stranger I'd just met. It was our one night of pretend fathering. Is the responsibility of parenting scaring me this much?

Maybe the larger issue isn't me and Wyatt.

Maybe it's just me.

Before I know it, Wyatt is asleep. I'm comforted by the sound of his deep breathing, which harmonizes with his mom, the crickets outside and the random creaks of the house.

There's a safety that surrounds me like a warm hug. A feeling that makes me miss my own childhood home and parents.

As I'm about to fall asleep, I make a decision.

We're going to make a detour to see my family in Chicago.

# 11

## THE MOTHERLOAD

**WYATT**

**WAKING UP THE NEXT** morning while Biz is still sound asleep, I've made a surprising decision. I want us to spend more time here with my mom.

Even with my childhood bedroom converted into my mom's weird office slash gym, it hits me that home is exactly where I want to be right now. Not only do I want to support Mom while Alex recovers, but it's nice to think some of her parenting skills can rub off on us in an unexpected crash course right before the baby's here.

I leave Biz asleep in bed, with his hairy bare right leg dangling off the air mattress, and walk to the kitchen where I'm greeted by the smells of French vanilla Coffee-Mate and Entenmann's mini powdered donuts. Two things we never buy in Brooklyn and sure signs that I'm home.

I'm slightly worried that my mom has gone off the deep end with her liquid coffee creamers though. In her always well-stocked pantry she has a half dozen flavors lined up including hazelnut, crème brûlée, pumpkin spice, peppermint mocha and . . . fat-free Rice Krispies Treats? Beverly needs a creamer-vention.

As I sit in my childhood kitchen, untouched since the eighties except for a brave iPhone charger hanging out of an outlet, Matilda scurries in and starts munching on her morning kibble.

I sink my fourth mini donut into my vanilla-flavored coffee and listen to the faint sounds of my mom talking on her landline in the living room. "It was all so sudden. *The accident.*" She whispers the word *accident* every time she says it. "The poor kids now have to deal with their dad's *accident.*" I'm also starting to wonder if my mom's Boston accent has gotten thicker or if I'm just not used to hearing it every day.

"That was Jackie. She says hi," Mom says, entering the kitchen after her call, wearing her perfect nightgown, large Crate and Barrel coffee cup in hand, referring to her childhood best friend, trusted confidant and doubles tennis partner. "You and Biz should have lunch with Chuck while you guys are here."

I go dead inside for a second as I sigh into my coffee and take a sip.

My mom and Jackie have spent a lifetime of trying to get me and Jackie's son Chuck to become friends. Chuck was different from most kids I knew growing up. He kept pet snakes, drove fast muscle cars that made loud noises and failed a grade. Maybe even two. Me and Chuck had nothing in common. Our mothers though, thick as thieves, still refuse to believe it.

It's impossible for me to imagine that a loose cannon like Chuck could ever be tamed for a civilized lunch in a booth eating a chopped salad. I try my best to ignore this evergreen request my mom suggests every trip home.

"How'd you two sleep? You can sleep in Alex's room, you know," Mom says.

*Don't tell her about Biz and the drama teacher.*

*Don't tell her you're having issues before the baby arrives.*

*Tell her everything is fine.*

I stand and rinse my cup in the sink. "My room is fine. Alex would kill me if we touched his old bedroom. I still don't know why you turned my bedroom into your office and not his."

"Your room was bigger. I needed more office space."

"Mm-hm." I know it's not true but sometimes I think she still favors Alex, her baby, over me.

"I talked to Megan this morning. She's so grateful you two were there for the girls. Bonding with the uncles."

"Anytime. The show was a hoot," I say. I wonder if I should break the headline news to my mom or Biz first that I want to stay a little longer. But I know how happy it would make Mom. "I think we could actually do it again because I want to stay a little longer."

She turns around, holding her giant bottle of fat-free cinnamon roll–flavored Coffee-Mate midair, completely giddy.

"That would be fabulous!" she says, tears of joy forming in her eyes, touched. "Oh, that makes me so happy."

"I just have to run it by Biz first."

"Where's Biz anyway? Still asleep?"

"You know him. He's a late sleeper."

We both turn to see Biz shuffling into the kitchen, right on cue, just having heard the news at the same time. A slightly confused look on his face.

"Run what by me?" Biz has an innocent quality to him in his fleece sweat shorts and faded *Spring Awakening* T-shirt, as the early morning light cascades through the kitchen windows onto his face. The incongruous image of a handsome, scruffy grown man standing in the kitchen where I grew up, next to a wall with pencil markings from measuring my height is not lost on me. I stand and shake the remains of my coffee around in my mug.

"You're up early," I say.

"It's almost eight thirty," he says.

"That's early for you," I say.

"Is it?"

I don't know if he sincerely doesn't understand how late he typically sleeps or if he's just in denial. I lean in and give him a peck on the lips because he's so damn cute.

"What if we stay here a few more days?" I ask. "We'll always have Provincetown," I say, somewhat jokingly. Biz tenses up.

My mom spots this exchange and quickly moves to the coffee machine, where she keeps an ear on us. A shudder runs through me. I just can't have my mom thinking there's a rift between us. It would upset her too much and conjure up bad memories of her relationship with my father.

"I thought we could help out Mom and my brother if he needs us."

Biz tries to wrap his head around the idea. "For how long?"

The whir of my mom's dated coffee machine cuts the tension.

"Sorry. Don't mind me," Mom says, glancing at us before placing her entire focus back on the machine as it spits out her favorite beverage.

"Just a couple days," I say. "Also, logistically, it doesn't make sense to go back east. We need to keep moving west toward California and our little one to-be." This could be more of a debate, but I can tell Biz is too self-conscious to engage with my mom in the room. She's now focused on loudly stirring her coffee creamer with a tiny spoon, pretending she's not listening.

"That makes sense," Biz concedes, quicker than I'd expected. He glances at my mom. "It'll be nice to spend a couple more days with your mom," Biz adds. He always knows the way to a mother's heart.

Mom finally turns around with a tight smile on her face, pretending everything is normal between us. And now I can see the wheels turning in her mind about all the fun things we can do. "Are you kidding? I fully insist you stay for a good week!" Mom says with joy washing over her. She hugs my waist and cradles her head into my ribs. It strikes me that maybe she's shrunk an inch? Or I'm just not used to seeing her out of high heels.

"A week? Let's not push it, Mom," I say. "I'll have to reconfigure our itinerary and see how much time we can fit in with the new driving schedule. Probably four days. It'll be good to spend time with you and with Alex too."

"Alex would love to see you both again," my mom says, overjoyed to bring her increasingly distant sons together whenever possible.

Biz shuffles toward a donut and coffee, making himself at home.

"Why don't we do this," Mom says. She's already referring to the three of us as *we*. "We'll all shower."

"Ew. Mom. We're not all showering together." Nothing feels safer or cozier to me than reverting to being an immature kid when I'm home. Maybe I need a temporary escape from impending adult responsibilities just as much as Biz.

"Wyatt Wallace. You know that's not what I mean," my

mom says, rolling her eyes toward Biz at my expense. "What are we gonna do with this one, huh?" she says, feigning exasperation. Back to the plan. "No, what I meant was we'll all shower. *Separately.*" She glares at me. "Weirdo . . . Then we'll check on Alex at the hospital. Megan is already there with the kids and said he's cleared for a concussion so he's going home today."

"That's great. We're here for you. Whatever you need us to do," I remind her.

"Once Alex is settled back home, then we'll have *a day*. The three of us! I can map out some fun things for us to do. Wyatt, you can touch all your bases at your childhood haunts. Biz, anything fun you'd like to do?"

A small bead of sweat forms on my forehead, thinking about the busy day ahead. I always forget that my mom is big on planning. Guess that's where I get the control gene. I've met my match.

"I wonder if we could build in some time to go to the gym?" Biz asks, probably seeing his future dad bod looming in the mirror. "All I'd need is a half hour."

"I just got a Peloton!" Mom shouts, scaring us both. "It's in the basement. I bought it as a gift to myself after I sold the Mandelbaum house. Skip the gym and you can be the first one to break it in." She lets out a little excited laugh, almost a chirp. With her boys home, this is her moment to shine as MOM in all caps.

- - - - - - - >

OUR FIRST STOP OF THE MORNING IS TO VISIT ALEX AT THE HOSPITAL. HE'S in his regular clothes and more than ready to leave. Megan collects the dozens of flowers and greeting cards from well-wishers while the kids watch *Angels in America* on their iPads.

"You're a machine," I tell Alex, always impressed by the star hockey player's strength.

"I still have to do physical therapy for the next few weeks but yeah. I kind of feel like new. This place is like a spa."

"Your kids were amazing last night," Biz says.

"They fuckin' loved spending time with you guys. You're going to crush it as dads," Alex says.

"We're staying another couple days with Mom," I say. I can feel Alex tensing up. "So we can all grab a bite to eat or something." I wish it wasn't always awkward between the two of us. It feels like we should be closer somehow, but it never comes naturally.

The overprotective Megan chimes in. "Oh, we'll be settling Alex in at home for at least a few weeks," she says. "He'll need to rest."

"Meg, I'm fine," Alex protests.

"I know but I'm not taking any chances. You guys are more than welcome to stop by. Maybe we can order in."

"Why don't we play it by ear," my mom says, always the diplomat. "Look what I brought." Mom gives Alex a giant bottle of Snickers-flavored coffee creamer. "Your fave!"

"You're the best," Alex says as he hugs Mom. She holds on to him tightly, afraid to let anything bad happen to her little one.

"Just text us. We'll figure it out," Alex says, both of us vaguely thinking this might not even happen.

After the hospital, our next stop is Huntington Court, a standard suburban shopping mall home to the local chain stores and restaurants of my youth. Mom insists on performing her favorite ritual with me whenever I come home: walk the entire mall. Biz steels himself for another guided tour.

*To your right is the Nordstrom bathing suit section where I had*

*my first kiss (with a girl) when I was in elementary school. We all
know how that turned out.*

*To your left, you'll see the former Abercrombie & Fitch store, now
a Sephora, where a group of teens from the wrong side of the tracks gave
me a wedgie and called me names for wearing a Madonna T-shirt.*

*And here's where I fell in love with directing, working as a highly
knowledgeable cashier at Blockbuster Video.*

For lunch, we sit in a large wooden booth at the Cloverleaf:
"Home of the Famous Motherload Baked Potato®." It's the
kind of booth that doesn't exist in New York. If it did, it would
be used as a communal table for fifteen strangers packed together. Many special occasions were held at the Cloverleaf including several of my childhood birthdays, graduation dinners
and even my ten-year high school reunion.

Our booth is next to "Boston's Longest Salad Bar." It's the
exact spot a teenage me came out to my mom and brother. I
remember a very Boston middle-aged woman dropped a spoonful of croutons when she heard me make my announcement.
She apologized profusely and tried to relate by saying her great-
uncle was gay. *Thanks, Crouton Lady.*

Finishing our potato skins, my mom wondered how she
could join a group for parents with LGBTQ kids. I still feel
lucky.

In the mall parking lot, walking to our car, Alex tried to
bank on our mom's generosity of spirit by asking, "If Wyatt can
be gay, can I get a tattoo?" to which Mom immediately stated a
nonnegotiable "That's not how it works" as the three of us
climbed into her station wagon.

Back at lunch, we eat loaded baked potatoes piled high with
cheddar cheese, thick cuts of bacon bits, green scallions and a
heaping spoonful of sour cream.

"Anyone want my bacon bits?" Mom asks, handing them out to us.

"Remember when Lindsay Millenbrook had her sweet sixteen here?" I ask my mom.

"She covered the ceiling in pink balloons," Mom says to Biz without missing a beat. We're trying to include him in yet another story about people from my childhood that he doesn't know. Biz raises a single eyebrow in acknowledgment. "You were the only boy," Mom adds before ordering us another round of Arnold Palmers.

After a while, Biz can only put up with so many of our memories. When I meet his gaze, it feels like we're losing him, so I need to redirect the conversation or else risk even further damage.

"Did you ever come here with your dad?" Biz asks before I can offer a new line of conversation to include him. He knows this is a tiny grenade to throw into a fun lunch with Mom. I rarely speak about my father and he has questions. Rightfully so.

If anyone has answers, Biz probably figures, my mom is the one who holds the key to the lockbox. It's been such a sore spot with Mom through the years that I stopped asking.

My mom and I both process Biz's question, working mentally through our collective Rube Goldberg–like labyrinth that grows more elaborate after each passing year.

"Oh, we don't need to bring that up, do we? Over baked potatoes?" Mom says, stabbing through her melted cheese, not wanting to go there. She shifts uncomfortably and turns visibly upset. Biz glances at me sheepishly, feeling bad he asked.

Usually, my mom papers over any father conversations with superficial memories and polite smiles. This time, though, it feels different. Maybe she's become more honest in her later years. Her body language is screaming *shut it down*.

For the first time in my life, I see my mom as a flawed adult. Also for the first time, I know with absolute certainty that there's something my mom isn't telling me about my father. I can tell Biz feels the same too.

Maybe it's some missing piece that would unlock my own potential as a dad. Whatever the mystery is, as long as we have some time while I'm here, I'm determined to uncover it.

# 12

## 'TIL BEV DO US PART

### BIZ

**I**T FEELS LIKE I'M in a throuple with Wyatt and Beverly.

The three of us are attached at the hip.

The next couple days, we browse all the quaint local shops, have dinner with Alex and his family and visit Beverly's sleek new office, where she introduces us to her fellow Queen B's, her best friends and chosen family. They all have larger-than-life personalities. "My sons, the famous director and actor!" Beverly beams. Neither of us have the heart to dispute that we're not actually famous. The women all gawk and probe us with questions on surrogacy.

One night, the three of us eat at an old-school Italian restaurant where Beverly and Wyatt know everybody. When I point out the tagline on the restaurant's menu, "You're Family When You're Here," is pretty much a rip-off of Olive Garden's "When You're Here, You're Family," Wyatt is not amused. He gets overly defensive of his beloved hometown.

Later, after the three of us share a pint of strawberry ice

cream at home in our pajamas while watching an ancient repeat of *The Golden Girls*, I feel like an actual Golden Girl.

"I think I'm gonna hit the hay," I announce in my best Blanche Devereaux.

"In the middle of the episode?" Beverly asks, as if I'm missing an important plot point.

"I'll have Wyatt catch me up later," I joke.

It's our third night in the guest room/office/gym, and I'm longing for the warmth of my own childhood home filled with lots of people. This is perfectly fine but there's something cold and disjointed about Wyatt's family, whereas mine feels more like superglue.

A few minutes after I settle into the air mattress, Wyatt enters. He undresses, staring into space, and I can tell more thoughts are weighing on his mind.

"Did Rose find her father?" I ask.

"You'll have to find out in the chilling conclusion of . . . *The Golden Girls*."

Poor choice of words on my part. The talk of Wyatt's dad at lunch the other day disappeared faster than our bacon bits, never mentioned again.

Wyatt slips into the air mattress and our knees knock briefly. I swallow as it sends a charge through my entire body. Wyatt's energy does that to me. Even with the two of us mired in tension, his left knee can make me long for him.

I'll ignore my needs for now as I hear Wyatt let out a loaded sigh.

I need to bring up my job but Wyatt is so clearly preoccupied with everything else that it's been difficult to find the right moment. Whatever's going on with this family, they need an outside mediator to step in and unpack their history.

"Are you thinking about the stuff with your dad?" I ask, trying to connect.

"Of course. It's hard to let it go," he says with a release as if he's been waiting to talk this out. "She's not telling me something about my father."

"When was the last time you spoke to him?" I ask.

"When I was little."

"Maybe it's time you investigate," I suggest.

"How?" Wyatt wonders, genuinely flummoxed.

"Ask your mom."

"Whenever Alex and I brought him up over the years, she'd always change the subject or tell us how awful he was. It was burned into our brains that he was basically a monster, and when I hit my twenties, I suspected there had to be more to her story. But she won't even go there."

"What about Alex? Doesn't he want to know more?" I ask.

"He got enough attention from my mom so maybe he didn't need any answers."

We both pause as we hear padded footsteps down the hallway. Then a door quietly shuts.

Wyatt lowers his voice, not wanting his mom to hear. "He's also way more focused on Megan and her whole family at this point."

"Maybe you should look your dad up online," I say.

"Trust me. I have."

"Any other family members you can talk to?"

"There's my one weird aunt. My dad's sister. She lives in Albuquerque. We've never had any kind of relationship. I met her once the summer before college," Wyatt says.

"Might be worth contacting her again."

"I never did find out if she was lying or not."

"What do you mean?"

"She came over for lunch and my mom made this huge spread. At one point, Mom excused herself to find some photo of my father, Richard. Aunt Katherine leaned in and said, 'Your mom will never tell you but . . . you should know the truth about your dad.'"

I sit up, mouth agape. The look on my face says, *I need you to continue immediately.*

"She wanted to tell me more but stopped herself when my mom came back," Wyatt says.

"Why the hell didn't you probe?!" I ask.

"Because it was all so cryptic and my mom always said my aunt made up stories. Plus, I was too busy dealing with being gay and about to go to college."

"That is some messy soap opera shit," I say, taking this all in.

When we're in Wyatt's hometown, this never really happens. Wyatt never spends this much time thinking and talking about his family the way I do when we go to my hometown.

It's a refreshing change.

Suddenly, in my mind, Wyatt's family situation has taken priority over our own unresolved problems. It's a lot juicier, and hey, who doesn't want a distraction from their own life?

I'm committed to helping him get to the bottom of this.

# 13

## HOLLYWOOD FUN TIME

**WYATT**

IT'S BEEN IMPOSSIBLE TO splinter off from Mom. Monopolizing my time is her favorite hobby when I'm home. I don't mind it. She's a ball of energy and we all enjoy each other's company.

And now with pending fatherhood just a few weeks away, it feels poetic to get to the bottom of my own paternal situation.

The problem is, I'm not exactly sure where to begin.

I've been texting with Alex the past couple days, trying to probe him for any answers about our father, but he's either not that interested or busy with physical therapy.

Puffy white clouds dot vivid blue skies so Mom decides it's a perfect day to visit her healing spot, Berkshire Botanical Garden. We can take Mom on long walks there for some nature therapy that will hopefully induce her to spill some beans about my father. With all the questions Biz was asking me last night, I can tell he's on board.

Strolling over a small red bridge toward Mom's favorite bonsai tree in the Japanese gardens, we see a cute family standing in front of the wildly shaped plant. The dad has a buzz cut with a football player build, and he's wearing Oakley sunglasses, standing in awe with his two kids and beautiful wife. He looks like if someone drew Mark Wahlberg from memory.

We maneuver around them to soak up a good look at the tree but they're not budging. I feel the dad glance at me a few times.

The gardens are populated with more people than expected, which makes it hard to have any meaningful conversation with my mom. When we've all had enough flowers and trees and plants, we head toward the parking lot, looking for Mom's car.

That's where Biz and I spot Mark Wahlberg-y loading up his tank-sized SUV with his family as he steals another glance at me.

"Hot zaddy checking you out again, two o'clock," Biz quietly says so Mom doesn't hear.

"He did that in the Japanese garden," I say.

"I saw. I bet he's closeted."

"Can you not?" I say. "We're with my mom." If it's true, I actually can't believe a guy with his wife and kids could so blatantly cruise me like this.

"There she is!" my mom yells, finally finding her car.

I do a double take. Yep, the daddy is unashamedly checking me out. He looks me up and down. Have some decency in front of your family, Mr. Fake Wahlberg.

We head to the car, forgetting all about him. I'm lost in thought on how to get my mom back on track of uncovering my father's story.

"Wyatt Wallace?!?" someone yells behind us, just before we climb into the car. I turn to see the daddy squinting at me, barreling toward us.

"Wait—you know him?" Biz asks.

"I don't think so," I say, trying to place the guy. His wife doesn't look familiar either.

The guy stands in front of me now with a huge smile on his face and a brawny hand extended. I'm trying to discern who this person is masked behind the sunglasses and the muscles. Somewhere on his face I catch a glimpse of a high school acquaintance I once knew. That mischievous smirk with the thin lips is the giveaway before it clicks into place.

"Jeremy Lowinger?" I ask. I'm still not convinced this *older man* is my former high school classmate. In my mind, everyone my age is still seventeen. I adjust my age radar.

"I thought that was you before. How've you been, man?" Jeremy's grip is strong and friendly. "How ya doin', Mrs. Wallace?"

We were good friends in grade school but drifted apart in high school. Jeremy and I played peewee hockey together. I have to admit that it's good to see him. The sheer number of years we've known each other cuts deep.

"Hi, honey!" my mom says, not having a clue who this person is, as she bloops off her car alarm. She calls anyone she doesn't know *honey*.

"This is my partner, Biz," I say.

"Right. I heard you were gay," Jeremy says. A grand piano of awkwardness comically falls on our heads. "I didn't mean . . . that wasn't negative meaning in any way."

I smile and let him squirm.

"This is my wife, Kim." Kim has an immediate fun, upbeat charm and looks like she teaches a spin class. She's not someone I recognize from school. At least that I can remember.

"So nice to meet you." Kim looks at Jeremy, as if signifying *this* is what he should've said to Biz.

"Aren't you a big-time movie director or something?" Jeremy asks, revealing the misinformed gossip of old classmates. I've sworn off all social media, but in the past, I had posted one or two pics of my director's chair on different jobs. I see how someone could quickly glimpse that and immediately think *Important Movie Director*.

Not *director of adult diaper commercials*.

"Commercial director. Mostly." I don't elaborate and probably should've just said yes.

"He's being modest. He's extremely talented," Biz says. Always so supportive.

"That is so effin' cool, man." Jeremy is extremely earnest and excited. Doesn't he know I'm just a wannabe movie director who has fallen into directing dumb commercials and has no idea how to get out of it? "I always knew you'd be a Hollywood director." He doubles down on the Hollywood thing. I'm so far removed from Hollywood, I'm in Uzbekistan. "You knew all those movies and stuff growing up."

"Right. I mean, I live in New York, not Hollywood, but yeah." This, I realize, is way too nuanced for Jeremy. *Just let him think you're Steven Spielberg*, I tell myself.

"Remember Pat Wisniewski?" Jeremy asks.

"Of course."

"His band's playing at the Toadstool next Saturday night. They're like Creed meets Puddle of Mudd. You should totally come."

I have no clue how to react to this early 2000s band mash-up. It's so bad, it's good? Biz scrunches his face, just as confused as I am about the whole encounter.

"Darn," I try to sound genuinely disappointed. "We're only here a few nights."

"Then come to Archie's party tonight. You'll know a bunch of us. Sam, Katie, Alice, Mikey P. . . . We'll all be there. Bring your dude."

Before I can answer, Biz immediately chimes in. "We'd love to!" I get it. He needs to escape my mom for five minutes and make our trip feel more like the babymoon he's been wanting this whole time. As much as I want to spend more quality time with my mom, even I think a party sounds like a good idea.

"What's your number? I'll text you the address." Jeremy takes out his phone, which looks like a matchbook inside his giant hands.

- - - - - - - →

LATER IN THE AFTERNOON, WE TAKE MOM'S CAR AND AFTER A FORTY-FIVE-minute drive into a suburb I'm not totally familiar with, Biz and I pull into a crowded parking lot of the address that Jeremy gave us.

It's a monstrosity of a building called Hollywood Fun Time Pizzeria Palace.

"It's just a bunch of words smooshed together," I say, as we eye the garish sign out front, complete with "Hollywood" stage lights flashing on and off.

Kids and their parents swarm the parking lot, entering and exiting the building.

"Oh my god, is this a kid's party?" Biz asks.

"Maybe it's an ironic adult party," I say, giving my old friend the benefit of the doubt.

"He said it's Archie's birthday. Isn't that someone you went to high school with?"

"I don't remember an Archie now that I think about it."

Inside is a throwback pizza place with arcade games, pinball machines, a ball pit and three different stages populated with various animatronic animal characters singing jamborees. Like an off-off-off-*way-off*-brand Chuck E. Cheese.

Excited kids line up to hand in the paper tickets each game spits out when they win, in exchange for a cheap plastic toy. Despite the chaos, it's refreshing to see kids interacting with one another and real live arcade games, as opposed to their phones and iPads.

After getting used to the idea that this is probably a kid's birthday party, I can't help but smile at the fun everyone is having.

We spot a small group of adults holding bottles of Miller Lite, huddled around a few Skee-Ball games, cheering each other on. I have to adjust my eyes when I see them. These are no longer my classmates from high school. They're fully fledged adult humans, some with children older than the age when I first met a couple of them.

"My dudes! You want beers?" Jeremy is the first to greet us, with giant hugs. Before we can ask if they have a craft cocktail menu, two Miller Lites are shoved at us.

"When in Hollywood Fun Time Pizzeria Palace . . ." I say as we clink bottles. Biz gulps his down with a shrug, both of us committed to having some fun.

I immediately recognize Tim, my Spanish class friend during all four years of high school, who only ever called me by my Spanish class name. "Mateo! Que pasa?!" He looks good; thicker though. Like he eats beer kegs for breakfast.

Then there's Alice, my very good friend from elementary school. "Remember we used to poke holes in bologna and put them on our faces?!" she asks. Her perfect social media persona doesn't lie. Pearl earrings, a gold watch, expensive blonde haircut with a severe chop. I knew that Alice and Tim were married, but it's still a mild shock to see them together in real life. They cocreated a baby furniture company and recently sold it to Ikea for a lot of dough.

Mikey P., not to be confused with Mikey G., as they were known growing up, is still calling himself Mikey even though he's no longer twelve and is now a dentist whose patients call him Dr. Mikey. He has the whitest teeth on the planet.

And of course, Katie. She's an entrepreneur, starting many successful eco-friendly businesses. The latest one is a bottled water company that services people in Mozambique. She was always a saint. Which is why it's hard to believe she's now married to her stay-at-home husband, Neil. Growing up, Neil's mediocrity was legendary. Judging by the way he badly plays Skee-Ball while letting Katie deal with their kids, nothing has changed.

After Skee-Ball, we eat bland pizza and have birthday cake for Jeremy's youngest, Archie, while watching a stage full of animatronic bears, coyotes and some sort of large rodent/duck creature sing a medley of Beatles songs.

Several beers and cardboard circles of cheese and pepperoni later, the old gang starts to appear exactly that: old. Up close, I notice none of them are as well-kept as they had first appeared to be. And the drunker they get, the messier, more revealing they become.

Jeremy's silver daddy, salt-and-pepper hair isn't a distinction of age. The more I examine it, I realize it's a shock of gray, wiry hair that seems to be a direct result of extreme stress. This man is prematurely gray because of extenuating life circumstances. Of course I have no scientific data to back this up but every gray hair on his head seems to tell a story. The increasingly heavy-duty bags under his eyes only support my theory.

The cracks in the very put-together Alice start to show too. Sure, on the outside she's perfect, but as Biz quietly points out, "Did you notice she's downed more beers than anyone?"

"You guys don't have any drugs by any chance?" Alice asks us.

"Sorry, no," I say as she openly texts her drug dealer.

As the night turns darker, figuratively and literally, Mikey P. drunkenly explains to us that we should "never get married and *never* have kids." He slurs through his cautionary tale.

"We have four kidsh. *Four!* Now we can't afford *shit*! And I'm a dentisht! I'm currently being shued by three different people. Two I can't talk about. Fine, I'll talk about 'em—I mishdiagnosed oral canshur on them. Sheriously, don't have kidsh."

Biz looks shell-shocked.

We turn to see all their kids either chasing each other at full speed around the room, screaming, or having meltdowns.

Jeremy's nine-year-old defiantly rips off the Whac-A-Mole mallet and starts bopping innocent kids on the head with it. "WHACK! WHACK! WHACK!" he shouts with each victim.

Alice's kids drain her purse for more money to play games like tiny vampires.

Mikey P. has to carry his wailing daughter over his head like a surfboard out of the place.

Tim's son unzips his pants, stands proudly over the ball pit and starts peeing, waving his stream back and forth like a weak sprinkler.

Biz and I glance at each other, holding in laughter.

Before we know it, we're in another suburb, walking with the gang down a pristine sidewalk in Jeremy and Kim's subdivision called "Briar Manors," which sounds like someone lazily slapped together the two fanciest names they could think of.

In a last-ditch effort to cling to their childhood, the adults put their kids to bed and we're cajoled into doing something I used to do as a teenager: pool hopping. We walk down a darkened, quiet street, aimlessly searching for the biggest swimming pool to jump into.

"Remember all those pools you took us to?" Jeremy asks me.

Biz turns to me. "Is that true?" His eyes fill with excitement. This is the first time I've seen him this present all night and possibly the entire trip.

"I did it once or twice," I admit, trying to downplay my guilt.

"Oh, please. You were the OG pool hopper," Alice says.

"Mr. Hollywood *invented* pool hopping!" Jeremy says, to which everyone bursts into a giggle fit.

"Oh my god. The Linderman house. It's perfect," Mikey P. says as we stand in front of a plain-looking house that's not exactly a manor, as per the name of the subdivision.

"Are you sure no one's home?" Tim asks, cautiously.

"Let's just go!" I yell-whisper. As Biz and I lead everyone through the side yard, a jolt of unhinged energy bursts through me that I haven't felt since maybe high school.

"We're finally going to have some fun on this trip!" Biz says with such giddiness, I realize in this moment that he's truly convinced once we have a baby, we'll absolutely no longer have fun. He has to realize we'll need to strike a balance.

We enter the backyard through a flimsy gate, and I run in, leading the group.

I'm the first one in the pool, doing a messy cannonball like

I did in high school. The thrill is intoxicating. Everyone jumps in after me with their own unique signature move. The pool is chilly at first, but the more we swim, the warmer and more exhilarating it becomes.

The women congregate by the diving board, giggling about the illicit nature of it all. The guys splash each other, roughhousing like they're back in gym class.

I swim up to Biz and fling my arms around him as we stare up into the nighttime sky sparkling with a million stars. It's worth it just to see the pure joy on Biz's face.

We all turn as a light goes on in the upstairs bedroom. Someone is home.

None of us move.

I'm freaking out, suddenly wondering what the hell we're doing. Biz is loving it.

My chest tightens when we hear a police siren "Bloop!" a single time as it speeds into the driveway. The red and blue swirling lights fill the backyard, creating iridescent shapes in the swimming pool that would be beautiful if they weren't so terrifying.

A wiry police officer walks bowlegged through, highlighting us with his flashlight as most of us scurry out of the pool.

"What seems to be the problem, officer?" Jeremy is the first to speak, casually doing a breast stroke down the length of the pool. *What a weird thing to say*, I think. It's not like we're being pulled over on the highway for speeding.

"The problem? The problem is that you're in a swimming pool that's not your own. This is considered trespassing, sir." The cop moves closer, pointing his flashlight at Jeremy's face. "Wait—*Lowinger*?! Is that *you*?"

"Officer Brewer!" Jeremy and the cop know each other.

I catch a solid glimpse of his face. Actually, we all know the cop. We graduated high school with him. It's Mark Brewer.

"You guys need to get out of here." He swings his flashlight onto the faces of everyone else and says hi as we slip our clothes back onto our wet bodies.

"Remember Wyatt Wallace?" Jeremy asks him.

"Mateo! I used to cheat off you in Spanish," Officer Brewer says.

"Hola," I say and wave, embarrassed for all of us.

An older woman with long gray hair watches with a scowl through her kitchen window as we're escorted off her premises and told to go home.

In the street, Officer Brewer pretends to read us our rights, and we all have a big laugh. We walk back to Jeremy and Kim's house, leaving wet footprints on the pavement.

In our final moments together, Biz and I decline having more beers in the backyard by the fire pit with the gang and instead say our farewells.

On the way back to Mom's, I turn to look at Biz as he drives, noticing how fresh and handsome he looks with his hair still wet in the dark of night.

"Well, that was sufficiently weird but fun," I say.

"I have to say, I'm impressed." Biz grins.

"With what?" I ask.

"I honestly didn't think you had it in you."

"Had what in me? Fun? You seriously don't think I know how to have fun?" I ask, genuinely surprised this is something that crossed his mind. "I know I've been . . . focused lately but I'm not that bad," I say.

"You've told me once or twice about your old pool hopping, but I didn't realize you were *the king* of pool hopping."

"We didn't even jump off the roof tonight," I say with a grin. "We used to do that all the time."

"You did not jump off the roof. Jesus, I would never. That would freak me out," Biz says as he turns to smile at me. "It's nice seeing you let loose."

"If you ever doubt that I can't have fun, just remember tonight and my legendary status as the number one pool hopper."

"Noted," Biz says.

Then my face falls, remembering something.

"What is it, Mr. Hollywood?" Biz asks, seeing this.

"All those kids," I say. "They were demons from hell."

"Oh, I know. What did their parents do to them? Your friends all seem a little broken. And they all look ten years older than us," Biz says. He's not wrong. "Are you sure you graduated high school with them?"

"Sure did," I say.

Biz narrows his eyes and turns to me. "Are we sure we want to have a kid?" he jokes.

"Yes," I say to Biz. "We just don't want *their* kids."

# 14

## FIVE WEEKS AND FIVE SISTERS

**BIZ**

IN BED THE NEXT morning, I slowly wake up, thinking about those kids from last night.

The screaming and the hitting and the jittery, high energy I couldn't begin to match no matter what designer club drug I tried.

I pray those kids are not an indication of our future. But maybe their behavior says more about their parents. I hope?

Wyatt is of course wide-awake next to me, holding a mug of coffee with his mom's smiling real estate face on the side. His brow is furrowed in concentration as he reads something on his phone. Matilda yawns at our feet.

He's shirtless and sexy and it's turning me on. I want to jump him right now.

But I still feel blocked by a distance between us. A wall stands in the way of our intimacy.

This feels like the night we first met and I was immediately shy around him. Like this smart, hot, athletic, successful guy would never give me the time of day.

My phone vibrates and I reach for it. A message in the epic group text I've had with my five older sisters for years.

Today it's from Zia.

ZIA

**FIVE MORE WEEKS!!!**

Their weekly countdown freaks me out and always reminds me of how unprepared I feel, but I smile at the patchwork of emojis each sister sends. I start typing back, when Wyatt notices I'm up.

"Good morning to you too," Wyatt says. His scratchy morning voice always gets me going.

"Good morning. I didn't want to disturb you. You seem so focused," I say, sitting up, the air mattress making noises like we're on a raft. Our shoulders are in line now, almost touching. "What time is it? What are you doing?" I ask.

"Almost eight. I'm working on getting us a refund with the rental company for the Provincetown house. It may be twenty-five percent of the total but it's something. Oh, and I redid our itinerary. We can leave first thing tomorrow for Saugatuck. We can make up some lost Provincetown time there, spend a few extra days, which is perfect."

"Can we talk about that and some other things for a sec?"

Wyatt puts his phone down and climbs out of bed, getting dressed.

"Maybe we can later? My mom is already texting me to help fix the back screen door. I'm like her handyman when I come home. Makes me realize how much Alex is never around."

Wyatt really knows how to slip out of any meaningful conversation when he wants to.

"Okay, but we need to talk," I remind him.

"We'll have plenty of time to talk on the road," Wyatt says. "I'll meet you downstairs?" He goes without giving me a chance to protest.

I need to tell Wyatt about my job. But we're on his home turf and I don't want us getting into it in front of his mom. I sigh and stretch, realizing our conversation will have to wait.

But the news about my job is eating me up and I have to spill to someone. I splinter off my family group text and message Zia. She's the closest sister to me in age and we tell each other everything.

BIZ
**i got fired.**

I don't find a need to sugarcoat it.

ZIA
**WHAT?!?!?!?!?**

Zia reacts immediately. She's always on her phone and I love her for that.

BIZ
**yup. in a fucking group email.**

It feels good to let this information out.

ZIA
**What assholes. I've read how companies are doing that now. That sucks!!!!**

BIZ

i know. especially with
the baby coming.

ZIA

I didn't want to say anything
about that. What are you gonna
do for work? This is kind of
huge news.

BIZ

maybe i'll go back into acting?
i dunno. this is the worst
possible timing. please don't
tell anyone.

ZIA

I won't. I'm so sorry Biz.

BIZ

yeah. thanks.

ZIA

Wyatt better make that $$$$ now.

BIZ

ugh. so depressing. we'll
make it work.

ZIA

You always do.

BIZ

oh—i think i want to
come home.

ZIA

WHEN???????

BIZ

like this week. tomorrow
maybe? i have to convince
wyatt first.

ZIA

On your babymoon? Where
are you now??

BIZ

why not? we're at wyatt's
mom's house right now.
long story.

ZIA

Oh, if you're visiting his family, you
HAVE to come home. We can
finally throw you a baby shower!

BIZ

do we have to? haha

ZIA

Yes!!! Text me later. Driving now.

BIZ
i will. love u

ZIA
Love you too.

– – – – – – –>

**LATER, THE THREE OF US SPEND THE MORNING GRABBING COFFEE AND** popping into more shops.

"Alex texted and said they can't come to dinner tonight," Wyatt informs me and Beverly in between bites of clam chowder at their favorite lunch spot.

"Why? Is he okay?" Beverly asks, growing concerned.

"He said he's headachy and wants to take it easy."

"Oh, god. I better go over there."

"Mom, he's fine. Megan is there. You know Alex. He likes his downtime."

"But we should all be together on your last night," Beverly says.

"We had dinner the other night, and we'll come back with the baby," Wyatt says.

"I'll have to change our reservation to three then," Beverly says, giving in.

"I can cook tonight," I offer.

Beverly perks up. It's probably not often someone makes dinner for her, and I can tell she loves the idea. To be honest, I'm getting tired of Wyatt's generic childhood restaurants and need something delicious. "This one's a keeper," she says about me.

Wyatt and I share a look of mutual appreciation.

The rest of the afternoon, I hit the grocery store, then hop on Beverly's Peloton in the basement for a good thirty minutes while Wyatt fixes a towel rack in the powder room. He's a good handyman to have around.

I make a feast of a dinner. Bruschetta with sheep's milk ricotta, sea salt and herbs, pappardelle al limone and homemade tiramisu. We even polish off a bottle of red wine with Beverly drinking more than both of us.

"I think it's time for bed," Beverly says, unexpectedly early.

"What about our nightcap and *Golden Girls*?" Wyatt asks. This is now our nightly routine.

"I just need to collapse," Beverly says.

"I was hoping we'd at least get to finish our conversation about my father," Wyatt says to everyone's surprise.

Beverly suddenly goes quiet and tries to redirect.

"Honey, with one son just out of the hospital and the other driving across the country about to have a baby, all this worrying has gotten to me," Beverly says, standing up from the dining table. "I can't have too many things on my plate," she says while surveying the mess of pots and pans.

"Don't worry," I say, swigging my wine. "Wyatt and I will clean up."

Wyatt stays silent, disappointed.

"That was an incredible meal, Biz. I've decided I'm going to make you guys a nice send-off breakfast in the morning," she says, not wanting to be outdone by my culinary skills.

"Mom, no," Wyatt says, knowing his mom isn't exactly the best cook on the planet. "We'll grab something on the way out of town."

"I have it all planned. But do me one favor. I've been asking you this since day one. Clean out some of your boxes downstairs before you leave? Biz can help you."

"We will," Wyatt says as we watch Beverly wave and wobble out of the room. That's when I notice something. Wyatt's mom is getting older. She's not limping or anything dramatic, just a slight stiffness and a vague look of someone climbing through her sixties. This was also the first trip we didn't hear talk of her doubles tennis games or her speed-walks for charities, I suddenly realize.

And Beverly making a meal at home is unheard of. She's self-described "better at making reservations," always on top of the latest restaurants and local nightlife. She really must be slowing down.

When Wyatt's eyes meet mine, I sense he's thinking what I'm thinking. Neither of us has paid much attention to our parents' health or state of being—a luxury for a child to think of their parents as immortal, godlike creatures.

"She's looking older," Wyatt whispers. "And of course she won't talk about anything."

I shrug, not wanting him to focus on it. "We should do what she wants and clean out your boxes."

Wyatt sighs deeply, knowing I'm right.

Who knows. Maybe this unexpected activity can bring us closer and give us a chance to chat about everything. I grab another bottle of wine, two glasses and we head downstairs.

# 15

## BOXES AND BOXES AND BOXES

**WYATT**

**M**OM'S WOOD-PANELED BASEMENT IS always freezing and smells like pine potpourri that she keeps in little glass bowls in every corner. In full Wallace form, my mom's neatly organized shelves of bulk foods and paper products are as impressive as ever. I make a mental note to create a coffee-table book out of her stack of real estate lawn signs, showing off years of outdated outfits and hairstyles.

"We had so many tournaments here," I say, sliding my finger across the dusty old Ping-Pong table my brother and I used to bond over.

The boxes Mom wants me to sort through are dozens of blue Rubbermaid containers.

"Oh. *My*. God," I say upon seeing the containers piled high to the ceiling. My boxes to the right. Alex's boxes to the left.

"You're going to have to come back to sort through all these," Biz says, handing me a glass of wine. We spend the next hour poring through containers to find my baby clothes, yearbooks, school report cards, more hockey medals and, if anyone had questioned whether I was actually gay, one box containing dozens of *People* magazines that I made my mom subscribe to. "I read it for the articles about movies," I joke to Biz.

"Just admit you got it for the annual Sexiest Man Alive," Biz teases. We both crack up at the truth.

I throw lots of stuff away that I don't want and memory lane starts to become memory long stretch of highway.

"This is such a treasure trove," I say. "I want to keep all of this kind of stuff for our own kid one day." I look up to see Biz down the last of his wine.

"I can't look at any more of your childhood macaroni sculptures," Biz says.

"Why don't you ever want to talk about the future of our kid?" I ask as I pack up a box.

"What do you mean? Why don't you ever want to talk about our present? And that's not true. I do want to talk about the future of our kid."

"You don't though. There's no planning ahead. Thinking about schools and activities and college," I say.

"Wyatt, we've been planning this for years," Biz says, slightly in shock.

"The baby isn't going to be a baby forever. We have to think about what's after that."

"I'm trying. I'm not the biggest planner like you," Biz admits, which is fair.

The furnace interrupts us with a *knock, knock*. It startles us both. My heart pounds. It sounds like a ghost trapped inside the walls, begging to escape.

Before letting our imagination get the best of us, we mentally regroup. One by one, we stack the containers back to their original formation. Biz seems annoyed. Then something catches my eye.

"What's that?" I ask.

Biz turns, trying to make out what I see.

In the corner of the basement is another stack of blue containers.

"Probably all of your mom's holiday stuff," Biz says.

I step closer for a better look. A couple boxes read, "Alex and Wyatt's Father." I blink, wondering what it could be.

"What's in them?" Biz asks.

"I don't know. I've never seen any of my father's stuff before. I didn't even know she had anything."

"You think she doesn't want you to see it?"

"No. The opposite," I say. "I think she *does* want me to see these."

"What is with you people and not communicating?!" Biz says, dumbfounded. He has a good point.

Like a giant game of reverse Jenga, I dismantle the boxes. Biz watches as we both sit cross-legged on the rust-colored carpet with one box.

I carefully pop off the container's lid and pull out a large photo album. I look at Biz, suggesting the album looks unfamiliar to me.

"Looks like a wedding album," he says.

"I wonder if Alex knows about this," I say.

The brown leather-bound cover with gold trim creaks open to laminated pages of my parents' wedding. My mom looks luminous and impossibly young as ever, perfect in her white wedding dress, eyes that telegraph happiness, youth and hope.

Nothing could prepare me for what I see next.

"Is that . . ."

"My father," I say as I focus in on the groom in the photo.

He's ruggedly handsome with a taller frame than my memory of him. I've seen five, maybe six photos of him in my entire life but never this album. Flipping through the delicate photographs, a crinkly sound with every turn, I'm in awe. My mom had always downplayed their wedding through the years. I certainly never knew there was an ornate photo album.

*Oh, it was a small affair*, she'd always said. My mind's image of my father has faded over time. Now here are actual photos of him. Never-seen-before footage.

I want to pinch and zoom in on every feature of his face. To study the lines and memorize each contour. Chills creep up my spine, seeing a photo of my father laughing, so alive, caught in a rare candid moment where he isn't posing.

"He looks exactly like you," Biz says before I can even think it.

"You think?" I ask even though I can see it now. It's uncanny.

We both study the last photo of my mother and father standing in an embrace. Their expressions seem indifferent. Almost disconnected from each other.

A flood of life experiences comes to mind that I wish I could've shared with him. Everything about my life. Biz. The baby on the way. Moving to New York, my dream city. Getting into the Directors Guild. That one time I worked with Lady Gaga. All of it. "Of course my mom wanted me to find this bin. Why else would she keep asking me to organize my boxes? They were organized to perfection."

"Maybe that's why she wanted you to come home so badly. I don't even think it was about Alex," Biz says. I look up at him, knowing he's probably right.

"I've always wondered why there were no photos," I say. "We never saw trips they took. Birthdays. Photos of my father haphazardly holding me as a baby. None of it."

"That's so sad," Biz says. "We have more photos and home movies than we know what to do with."

As I place the wedding album back in its home, in the box I promise myself to visit in the future, I open the next container. Brown packing paper fills the top of the container.

I lift the endless amount of brown paper, like tearing off never-ending wrapping paper on a Christmas present.

I stare at what I find for a few seconds.

"What is it?" Biz asks, fully invested in this treasure hunt of family secrets.

It's a letter still sealed in its envelope. I pick it up and see it's addressed to me in care of Mom. Curious shock flickers onto Biz's face when we both look inside the container at the same time.

We see dozens and dozens of letters neatly stacked on top of one another.

All from my father, Richard Wallace, addressed to me.

# 16

## RETURN TO SENDER

**BIZ**

THE NEXT MORNING, WYATT and I wake up at the same time.

He's perplexed. In a daze.

"Don't tell my mom we found the letters yet," he says to me as I stretch awake.

"I won't but she probably knows," I say.

Wyatt isn't ready to reveal to his mom what he learned about his dad.

Makes sense. I still haven't told Wyatt about my job. How can I now?

The smell of bacon pulls us both out of our cloud of confusion.

"Let's just get through this breakfast," Wyatt says as we both manage to get out of bed.

Lemon poppy seed ricotta pancakes, crispy bacon, a spinach and goat cheese quiche, freshly squeezed orange juice. Beverly has prepared an impressive breakfast for us, officially outdoing my dinner last night.

I secretly want mimosas but then I remember we have to take turns driving.

Beverly is even wearing a send-off outfit: a smart plum-colored pantsuit with matching eyeglasses. She looks like the commander of a futuristic army.

I imagine she's keeping herself busy all morning to avoid the bittersweet feeling she experiences every time her son leaves home.

She even showers us with a half dozen new onesies for the baby. Stylish outfits from the chic grandma-to-be.

"Any word from Alex or Megan?" Wyatt asks. He has intense eye contact with his mom, like he wants to say more. I could tell something like resentment is probably sizzling inside him, like the nearby bacon. I just wish he would say something to his mom.

"Oh, his headache is gone. Megan texted this morning and said he wanted to go for a run. I'm gonna visit them after you guys leave." Her voice cracks with vulnerability on the word "leave." "You'll come back with the baby and see them?"

"Of course. We want the cousins to be friends," Wyatt says.

Beverly doesn't want us to go. We're fun and up for doing just about anything—more than Alex and Megan, who usually keep to themselves. We make Bev feel like a peer. Our fun friend.

"Thanks for clearing out your boxes," Beverly says. "I saw you emptied a few."

"I threw some things away but I'll have to do more next time we're back. Lots of stuff I don't remember," Wyatt says.

A loaded pause hangs in the air. I've known him long enough that I can tell when he's holding back.

"Oh my god. It smells like heaven," I say. Someone needs to keep the conversation moving if they're not going to actually talk about anything real.

"We can eat if you guys are ready. I know you like your bacon extra crispy." Beverly places a hefty pitcher of orange juice in the middle of the picture-perfect kitchen table. I snap an overhead photo of the Instagram-ready spread.

"I'm not sure we can eat all this. I don't want to feel full while driving," Wyatt says. Now everything is starting to emerge with a slightly angry, bitter tone.

"Eat what you can," Beverly says, gesturing for us to sit. Matilda waddles in and Beverly seamlessly pulls a treat out for her to munch on.

"No!" Wyatt shouts, scaring everyone including Matilda.

"What?" Beverly asks.

"Matilda can't eat right before we get in the car. She throws up. You know that. Jesus," Wyatt overreacts.

He tries pulling the tiny morsel out of Matilda's mouth but she won't budge. She swallows it whole, almost smiling at getting away with it. And of course now she wants a full meal.

"Oh, one little treat isn't going to do anything." Beverly attempts to smooth it over.

"You don't know our dog. She gets sick every five seconds. You're not helping."

"It's okay, Wyatt. Relax," I say, for the sake of Beverly.

I hand Wyatt a piece of bacon, hoping to diffuse his sideways emotion.

As we fuel up with Beverly's power breakfast, I see Wyatt torturing himself, waiting for the right moment to bring up the letters. It's all so troubling to me.

Beverly realizes she hasn't asked enough about my family. While Wyatt broods over his black coffee, I go into depth about each of my sisters and parents. Later, Beverly and I fake argue over who will do the dishes with Beverly winning. Before I know it, we're loading up Virginia Woolf, ready to leave.

We stand in Beverly's driveway saying our goodbyes under the morning sun. I give Beverly a giant hug and her warm embrace makes me feel like her third son.

"Don't let him backseat drive you," she jokes at Wyatt's expense. We both laugh too hard, knowing how true this is, but Wyatt doesn't find it funny or he's ignoring us. His focus is on opening the convertible top. We could all use some fresh air.

The mechanics of the car keep Wyatt busy. He manually rolls down the windows, lifts the roof up and over the car, pushes it down hard to make sure it's snugly open. It's his way of delaying his turn to say goodbye to his mom.

Finally . . . "Bye, Mom," he says flatly and hugs Beverly like a wet noodle. As Wyatt pulls apart before Beverly is ready, she blinks, knowing something is off.

"You seem like you're in a hurry," she says.

I swear, the passive aggression between these two people is off the charts. My family would never let this wound sit unattended, festering.

"We've got almost three thousand miles to cover. Just want to get going," Wyatt says.

Wyatt lifts Matilda into her little bed in the back seat and we both run around the car a few times, making sure our luggage is all there and everything is tucked away.

"Drive safely, you two. And text me when you get to Saugatuck," Beverly calls out to me because it seems like Wyatt isn't even paying attention.

When we close the doors, Beverly starts waving a hand in front of her eyes.

"*Here come the waterworks*," Wyatt says under his breath.

"Darn it, I told myself not to do this!" she says as tears well in her eyes and an ugly cry ripples through, giving her short, sharp spasms, like she's about to give birth to an alien.

"Don't worry, Beverly. We'll call you every five minutes," I joke.

"Please do, Biz," she sniffs, pulling out a rumpled tissue from her pocket, which looks like she's already used it for a pre-cry cry. She blows her nose and waves as Wyatt snaps his seat-belt shut tight, getting out one last microaggression.

"Don't forget my turkey sandwiches. I threw in some Ruffles too." She's never once packed us a farewell lunch when we've visited. She must feel extra bad. "Next time I see you, you'll be dads!" Beverly realizes out loud. "Love you both!" she yells.

"Love you!" I call out. But Wyatt stays silent. He just tightly smiles and waves. He can't summon those words right now. Wyatt has quick eye contact with his mom before he backs out of the driveway.

Knowing Wyatt, he'll have to process what he discovered on the road first. He needs to form a solid take on those letters. And then he'll have to reassess his relationship with his mom. And now his dad.

I look back and see Wyatt's mom dabbing her eyes with the tissue and waving at the end of the driveway. It's the exact same tableau every time we visit. Only this time, Wyatt doesn't share her tears.

I can sense his blood start to boil.

Virginia Woolf travels as far as the house next to Beverly's and stops.

That's when we hear the sound.

Matilda throws up.

- - - - - - →

AFTER I CLEAN UP MATILDA'S BED, WE EVENTUALLY MAKE IT ONTO A LONG stretch of highway as the bossy GPS lady on Wyatt's phone continues to tell us where to go. With Matilda finally napping, we settle into an uneasy silence.

"I feel like you let your mom off too easy," I begin.

"What do you mean?"

"It just seems like you're in denial about your dad's letters the same way she's been."

Wyatt glances at me, maybe thinking I'm right. "I'm not like you. I need a minute to process all of this. Of course I won't let her off easy. It's hurtful what she did."

We turn to look at each other. I'm proud that Wyatt can admit he's hurt. A step in the right direction.

"I know there are two sides to every story," Wyatt says. "But I just need to figure out the next move with my mom. It's always been that way with us."

"Maybe it's time to face the truth," I suggest.

"You're a hundred percent right," Wyatt admits.

Scrolling through my phone, I see a new work email.

It's a form letter from my job listing my severance package (eight months—one month for every year I was there) and continuing insurance benefits (one year).

*I'm going to be such an awesome dad*, I immediately joke to myself.

Seriously, though. How am I going to be a father if I can't hold down a job?

*As discussed, your employment will terminate . . .*

Reality sets in.

Stressed-out gray hairs sprout and worried forehead lines form on my face by the second.

I know I'll have to tell Wyatt eventually. But not yet. I should tell him while we're in the car though. He can't push me out of a moving vehicle.

How ironic that I'm telling Wyatt to face the truth when I'm not ready to face my own.

"Everything okay?" Wyatt asks, sensing the weight of my silence. Does he know what I was reading?

Or maybe he's projecting and wants me to ask *him* if everything is okay.

"Yeah. Why? Just ignoring a work email," I say, staring straight out of the windshield. It's the truth, after all. "Everything okay with you?"

Wyatt nods.

So much is left unsaid between us. But first, I have to tell him about my plan to go home.

# 17

## SAGE

**WYATT**

'M UNSETTLED. THE LETTERS from my father have created an extra pain in my heart. It's not like I can magically make everything better with Biz and expect him to comfort me. In the past, we've been able to bounce back from our differences immediately. It just sucks that this time feels different. At a time when I need him the most.

I'll eventually need answers from my mom but there are so many obstacles standing in my way. The situation with me and Biz, our trip, the baby. Right now, I just have to get my mind off this building trauma.

"Find some music?" I ask Biz as I drive. He's already on it, scrolling through his phone for road trip songs. "No show tunes, please."

"How about something moody like Rufus Wainwright?" Biz suggests.

He hits play as a noisy semitruck plows next to us. It's the exact same orange color as Virginia Woolf. From a bird's-eye view, it probably looks like we're the newborn puppy detaching ourselves from our mom.

Biz lifts his arm and pulls down on an imaginary horn, signaling to the frowning truck driver to honk. My adrenaline races slightly.

"What is that? Why're you doing that?" I ask.

"I don't know. Didn't you ever do that as a kid? Try and get truck drivers to honk?"

"Of course, but that was in the before times. When people were friendly and not everyone was a potential homophobe with road rage and an AR-15."

"Oh my god. Is that how you see the world?" Biz asks.

"I'm just saying. You don't know how someone's going to react to that gesture. Maybe we're appropriating truck driver culture and he could be offended."

"You're right. I'm sure he wouldn't want us imitating his people," Biz says sarcastically.

My thoughts veer back to my mom. When it comes to analyzing and discussing this stuff, I'm not as good as Biz. Somehow, I just don't have the same tools. I need to occupy my mind with something else.

"Let's play a game," I suggest, realizing I don't know a single car trip game.

"I'm good," Biz says, taking a selfie with the sleeping Matilda and turning his face upward to soak up some sun.

"How about we come up with a baby name then," I try.

"Okay, I vote for Oprah Winfrey the second," Biz jokes.

"C'mon. I'm serious. We have four weeks and six days to decide."

"You already know my thoughts on this," Biz pushes back.

"We can't just wait until the baby comes to choose a name," I say.

"Why not?" Biz asks, genuinely not understanding why this isn't a good idea.

"No one wants to be born into this world without a name."

"Naming our baby isn't something to pre-plan," Biz says.

"Oh, god. Here we go."

"What? It's a feeling. A vibe," Biz explains. "We have to see the baby in order to name the baby."

"We could do city names. Find the new Brooklyn or Rio. How about . . ." I wait for the first passing sign on the road. "I-90 East?" I joke.

"I know you want to plan everything but you have to give me this one. I'm telling you, the name will come to us when we meet the baby."

This is so difficult for me to wait but I'm doing it for Biz. He knows I already have two unisex names picked out: Harper, because of my favorite author, and Cassidy, my mom's maiden name.

We've had endless conversations about baby names. At first, it was a friendly disagreement, something funny to quibble over. Like how Biz jokes I'm going to be the disciplinarian dad and he'll be the easygoing one. But eventually the baby name discussion became a point of contention during the course of our *journey*. The more I wanted a name set in stone, the more Biz wanted to wing it after the baby was born.

Sage was a baby name that Biz had briefly considered before holding steady on his rule to name the baby later. We met a cute Border Collie named Sage on a walk one September morning in Prospect Park. There's an off-leash section before nine a.m.

where we bring Matilda to freely frolic with her doggie friends. This particular Sunday was the first day of fall and, as it often happens in New York, the temperature strictly adhered to the exact changing of the seasons. It snapped into autumnal weather with temperatures in the low fifties. So the off-leash area wasn't too crowded that morning, with people avoiding the frosty, crisp air.

The second we'd popped off Matilda's leash and presented her with a tennis ball to fetch, a medium-sized dog ran up to her. The dogs did their usual dance and sniff while the owners only addressed the dogs as a way of projecting their true feelings at a distance.

This owner was a woman in her forties, with smart features, bouncy dirty blond hair, a loud, booming voice, and she was dressed in expensive designer athleisurewear.

"He's cold this morning," the woman said about her dog but really about herself.

"I know, she almost didn't want to go out," Biz said about Matilda but really himself.

"Aw, they like each other," the woman said about our dogs and as a way to signal she likes us. "What's her name?"

"Matilda," I said.

"Hi, Matilda. This is Sage, your new friend," the woman said.

Biz looked up from the dogs. The woman did too and for the first time we all had eye contact. "Oh, cool name. I love that. What kind is he?"

"Border Collie."

"You have such a great voice. So distinct," Biz said, somehow sensing she was a fellow performer. It took the woman by surprise that Biz had transitioned the conversation from the dogs to the people. It rarely gets personal in New York City dog parks.

"Thank you." The woman watched the dogs smell each other's butts before reluctantly adding, "I do voice-over work."

"No way. I'm an actor. Was . . ." Biz said.

"'When you live with moderate to severe plaque psoriasis . . .'"

"That's you?!" Biz asked, genuinely impressed as she nodded with a laugh.

"You're perfect. We've totally heard you before," I said.

The dogs chased each other in circles, getting along like gangbusters, as we all talked about acting, dog breeds, dog parks and acting again. When a lull in the conversation finally presented itself, we all looked down to find our dogs had disappeared behind a tree. Sage was wildly humping Matilda. A frightened look on Matilda's face told us she wanted to run away but was cornered.

"Sage, no!" the voice-over artist demanded before physically removing Sage from Matilda. Embarrassed, she said her goodbyes and left immediately, cradling her horny, panting dog in her arms.

"I don't think that was Sage's first offense," I said, kneeling down to make sure Matilda was okay. Right away, she bounced back to playing fetch.

"Probably not," Biz said, keeping an eye on Matilda and the surrounding area for any more horndogs. "But I love that name for a baby," he added.

It was a nice change of pace for me to hear Biz thinking about baby names but I wasn't sure this was the one. "Are you seriously considering naming our baby after a dog who just violated our dog?" With a name like that, I would only ever think of this aggressive dog. "And do we really want our child named after an aromatic herb?"

"Oh my god, you're right," Biz said. I felt bad I shot down his name idea but at least he agreed with me on this one.

‐ ‐ ‐ ‐ ‐ ‐ ‐ ➤

THIRTY MINUTES LATER ON THE HIGHWAY, BIZ NEGLECTS HIS DJING DUTIES and he's fast asleep. Luckily, Rufus Wainwright keeps me going for a couple hours until my stomach starts to growl.

I remember spotting a "Taco Bell—Exit 42" sign a few exits ago. I look over at the still sleeping Biz and decide to pull off the highway. If the foodie is not awake, you don't get to object to fast food. "Dems da rules," I quietly say out loud to myself.

"Rerouting . . . Rerouting . . . Rerouting . . ." says our GPS lady.

"Where are we going?" Biz stirs awake, sitting up.

"Just getting lunch," I say. Biz looks at the passing fast-food places: Subway, KFC, McDonald's, Chevys.

"I don't approve," he says.

"Come on. You know Taco Bell is my fast food of choice on the road."

"Isn't there anything else?" he asks, still waking up from his nap but coherent enough to demand Michelin-star-quality food.

"I'm not listening to you. We're doing the Bell," I say as we pull into a parking space.

"Then at least do the drive-through?"

"I thought we'd have lunch inside. Make it fancy," I say.

"What about the sandwiches your mom made?"

"Not really in the mood for those," I say, not wanting a reminder of my mom right now.

Something must be on Biz's mind because he immediately stops objecting and goes along with my plan. Even though I promised him no fast food on this trip. I throw the car in park and glance at him twice to make sure he's okay.

He turns to me and in true Biz fashion, he has a smirk on his face that says he's about to throw a wrench into our plans.

# 18

## PATRIOTIC DONUTS

**BIZ**

DON'T WANT TO GO to Saugatuck anymore," I summon up the courage to tell Wyatt.

"Okaaay," Wyatt says, taking a bite of his chipotle cheddar chalupa combo, processing my change of plans in a booth at Taco Bell. "Why not?"

"I think going to your hometown and seeing you with your mom and brother has inspired me. I'd really love if we spent a few days in Chicago with my family."

The broken dynamic between Wyatt and his family has actually made me long for the warm cohesiveness of my own.

"I get it. Quid pro quo. You do realize going to Boston wasn't on the itinerary. It was a family emergency," Wyatt says.

"Oh, it's not a competition. Like, at all." I hold up my pathetic bean burrito, inspecting it all over, like it's toxic sludge.

"You always get the wrong things at fast-food places," Wyatt says.

"Probably because you shouldn't eat fast food to begin with."

I take a microbite, discovering the taste and texture inside my mouth.

The professional food writer in me is judging.

After a few bites, though, I can admit that this tastes . . . pretty good?

"You can have my mom's sandwiches in the car if you don't like it," Wyatt says.

"It's fine, actually." I look down at Matilda, leashed to the leg of the table. She's looking up at us expectantly, wagging her tail. "No, sweetie. You can't have this. Stick with dog food."

Wyatt takes a huge bite of his chalupa with satisfaction and lets out an exaggerated "Mmmmmm," pretending he's a character in one of his commercials.

"So, are you okay with going to Chicago to see my family instead of Saugatuck?" I ask.

"Of course. We can cancel our hotel. You know I'd rather spend quality time with just family than mingle with a bunch of overly friendly gay bears with excessive back hair."

"Actually, that sounds amazing right now," I joke. "But no, I feel like seeing my family might be cozier. It feels right to touch both of our home bases before the baby's here. Maybe my sisters have some wise advice."

"Totally agree. Your sisters can finally have the baby shower they've been wanting to throw us," Wyatt adds.

"Zia said the same thing. We'll see if they follow through on that."

"You know your family loves a good party."

Going to Chicago for the holidays is always a fascinating experience for Wyatt. Unlike his tiny family, I have seven hundred thousand close relatives: besides my five older sisters, there are dozens of aunts, uncles, and cousins, with nieces and nephews that multiply every year and my incredible parents at the center of us all.

Wyatt once said my family is like the funny, good-looking, thoughtful sitcom family you grew up watching and wished you had.

Leaving Taco Bell, I text my sisters and call my parents to confirm we're coming. My mom and dad—never not on speakerphone together—literally scream. They're always ready to welcome their son and his boyfriend at the drop of a hat.

Back on the highway, I'm in the driver's seat.

Wyatt needs to adjust his internal Excel spreadsheet to exclude the Saugatuck leg of our trip, reimagining a few days with the Petterellis.

We'll spend time at home with an endless parade of fun, games and long, dynamic conversations over excellent Italian food and red wine.

"So what do you think happened? With my mom and stuff?" Wyatt asks, handing me half of Beverly's turkey sandwich. I guess *and stuff* means his dad. It's probably wise to use the drive between Massachusetts and Illinois to dissect his own family. With my family, there won't be any alone time between us. "You haven't said much about it."

"I didn't think you were ready to share. And I didn't want to pry," I say.

"Yeah, but aren't you curious?" he asks.

"Of course I am. Don't turn a thing into another thing."

"I'm not turning anything into anything."

"Then just tell me what you're thinking about it all."

If I don't bring up things first, Wyatt assumes I'm not interested. His penchant for bottling everything up is cute until he's about to burst.

"I stayed up last night reading some of the letters I took," Wyatt says, testing my curiosity level.

I finish half of my sandwich and notice he's barely touched his. "Can I eat your sandwich if you don't want it?"

"Oh my god. I'm telling you something deeply troubling and you're talking about sandwiches."

"We can multitask. Okay, letters. Go. What did they say?" I ask.

He says nothing.

"I'm waiting for the second episode of this limited series to drop," I say.

He's keeping me in suspense and I need answers.

"He started writing to Alex and me when we were in college."

I swallow and start to choke a little. The noise wakes up Matilda, who tilts her head and looks at me with concern. I'm coughing from a particularly dry part of the sandwich—Beverly was light on the mayo—but also in disbelief from what I'm hearing. "Are you serious?" I ask.

"There was one letter where he talked about me growing up without him and that he was sorry."

"Sorry for leaving?" I ask.

"I guess . . ." Wyatt says, holding back tears. He suddenly can't continue. Saying this all out loud is too much for him.

"That's pretty unbelievable," I say. We both stare out into the vast stretch of highway before us. I want him to share more but Wyatt stays quiet for now and I follow his lead.

- - - - - - - ->

BOSTON TO THE SUBURBS OF CHICAGO IS A SIXTEEN-HOUR TRIP BUT Wyatt wants us to drive straight through without stopping anywhere for the night. It's a couple hours more than Saugatuck and he hadn't built in a stopover for that trip.

As a driver, I tend to be distracted. Even when I'm behind the wheel, I need to read almost every sign we pass and I'll usually have to comment on it.

"Cracker Barrel—next exit. Aren't they racist or something?"

"Ain't Paul's Church. Someone scratched off the S!"

"Shinni*cock*? That can't be a real town."

Hey, it makes for great conversation starters.

I'll often use my knees to steer while playing DJ, which I'm doing right now. Of course, this never sits well with Wyatt, who wants both hands at ten and two at all times.

"Can you just pick a song?" Wyatt asks as a maniac in a matte-black, souped-up Mustang with tinted windows cuts in front of us, causing me to lose control of the wheel for a second and swerve onto the shoulder.

Wyatt is more shaken than I am. I remain calm.

"I'll do the music. You focus on the road," Wyatt says, frazzled, reaching for my phone and scanning for songs.

"That was not my fault. Look at that guy!" I say as we watch the Mustang gun ahead, in and out of cars, doing the same thing to every other car on the road.

"What an asshole!" Wyatt says.

"I need snacks to calm my nerves," I decide, seeing a billboard for a convenience store.

"Didn't you just eat two sandwiches and chips?" Wyatt asks, eternally amazed at how much food I can consume.

"That was over two hours ago."

Before Wyatt can object, I exit the highway in search of a store in the middle of nowhere. We've already crossed through

Pennsylvania and into Ohio. It makes me hungry just thinking about how much driving we're doing.

"What are you looking for?" Wyatt asks.

"There was a sign for a food store type thing."

There's nothing but empty road in front of us.

"Is this the right way?" Wyatt wonders, as we both see the sky darken ahead of us.

"I'm not sure now. We'll find something."

"I thought you saw a sign. You can't just wing this right now," Wyatt says.

"Every gas station on the planet has solid snacks. I just need like a protein bar or cashews or something. Don't worry," I say evenly.

Wyatt shakes his head and looks out the window as wind picks up.

A few minutes prior on the highway, the horizon had been an endless golden sunset. Now, spiking in the distance are a few lightning bolts. The skies turn almost blurry.

A storm is coming.

To top off the apocalyptic-aliens-landing feeling, this exit shows little sign of civilization.

"We need to put the top up," Wyatt says, his eyes laser focused on the approaching storm.

We spot a sign far down the road and pull into the parking lot of an oily-looking independent mechanic shop that may or may not still be in business.

Beaten-up old cars and pickup trucks seem forever parked in the burnt-out grass in front. Matilda jolts up on all fours to see where we're taking her now.

"This is every beginning to every horror movie," Wyatt says.

We park and jump out of the car to pull the roof back up. We make a pretty good team when it's needed.

Just as we slam our doors shut, the threshold of the storm reaches us, depositing a few raindrops onto our windshield, which quickly turns into a heavy downpour.

We laugh and rejoice, just having missed getting soaking wet. Matilda wags her tail and barks, wanting to join in on the random excitement.

"Snack time!"

"Are you kidding?" Wyatt says. "We need to get back on the highway if we want to make it to Chicago."

"Just give me five minutes to find food," I say.

Wyatt tenses up.

Our car races through the rain, onto some back road. I'm determined to scratch the itch of my sweet and salty cravings. Except for the ominous pounding of rain, we drive in silence.

Wyatt quietly fumes that things might not go according to plan.

Luckily, before Wyatt blows a gasket, I find the convenience store I was looking for called "Bucks Creek Deli and Groceries."

"I'll just run right in. You want anything?" I ask. Wyatt shakes his head, wanting to move on. Matilda lets out a sharp little bark, perhaps warning me not to go?

I fling myself out of the car, into the rain. Hurrying from the car to the store, now drenched, I think, *Well, at least I'm getting in my steps.*

Road trips can really screw with your exercise routine.

I have to remind myself we're as far away from New York City as it gets when I enter and see the oddest assortment of items for sale: a clothing rack full of camouflage hunting vests, bow and arrows hanging on a wall and display cases devoted entirely to knives.

I quickly scan every rack but can't find any snacks.

I approach the front counter where I find the world's entire supply of cigarettes.

"Hello?" I call out, looking around. I peer back by the knives. Not a soul.

When I turn back around, I'm startled to find a grim-looking older couple (the owners maybe?) exiting the back room.

They eye me, suspicious.

The woman has fried, bleached-blonde hair and a generous amount of eyeliner. The man wears a Bass Pro Shops flannel button-down from fifty years ago and has a protruding Adam's apple that's strangely off-center.

Wyatt was right. This is the older couple in a horror movie who warns the naive tourist not to go in *them there* mountains.

I'm a little scared.

As I approach the counter, I arrange my face into an open, friendly way, looking around to see if there are any potential witnesses just in case this couple wants to lock the door and hunt me down.

"Lovely weather we're having," I joke as the rain slaps the store windows like a car wash. I instantly realize they're not going to appreciate my humor.

They look at me like I'm an exotic zoo animal.

I glance down to make sure I'm not wearing my "I'm With Her" T-shirt. Luckily, I'm wearing a faded green hoodie. It's from J. Crew but it could pass for Walmart.

"You wanna buy a knife?" the man asks.

"Me? Oh, no. Thank you. I'm all set for knives at the moment."

"You were looking at 'em," the woman says, almost in an accusatory way.

"Ah, I see." I clock a video camera clipped to the cash register, staring directly at me. I suddenly feel guilty for no reason. Desperate to get out of there, I almost give up my need for something to munch on. But I can't leave after dragging Wyatt here. "I'm looking for the snacks?"

"Snacks?" the man claps back.

"Like chips, pretzels, peanut M&M's. I'd settle for a Twizzler." *I do not want a Twizzler.*

They stare at me blankly. "All we have are Millie's donuts." The man points to a dirty plastic container with three homemade donuts, each with red, white and blue frosting that look like they were made three Fourth of Julys ago. "They're on sale."

I let out a little confused laugh that I feel could maybe charm them.

It doesn't.

Before I know it, I'm race-walking back to the car in the rain, carrying a small paper bag of the donuts. I glance over my shoulder just because.

Wyatt is now in the driver's seat, ready to take over, so I climb into the passenger seat, shut the door and pound down the lock with my fist.

"Let's get the hell outta here," I say.

"Why? What was in there?" Wyatt asks, his gaze pointed at me.

"Knives. Go."

Wyatt sees me stuff the bag in the glove compartment. "What'd you get?"

"Three stale patriotic donuts. Please just drive."

Wyatt is amused and confused. We drive toward the highway as I explain the "deli and groceries" may have been an illegal front for weapons. I don't know how Ohio laws work.

Unfortunately, my cravings will have to wait because there's no way in hell I'm eating these donuts.

"I can't find the highway heading east." Wyatt panics, white-knuckling the steering wheel now that the heavy rain is pummeling us. The wind goes berserk, making Virginia Woolf sway back and forth on the road. It feels like we could tip over at any second.

The three of us freak out.

"I'm not getting a signal for GPS," I say, refreshing my maps app.

"I think it's the other way." Wyatt slows down.

It's a torrential downpour now and we can't see one foot in front of us.

The windshield wipers are on high.

We brace as Wyatt flips on his turn signal and turns into a nearby parking lot. Without warning, when Wyatt accelerates on the turn, the car hydroplanes.

For a quick moment, it feels like a roller-coaster drop.

Wyatt's eyes flash at me in terror.

Matilda stands up in her bed, her skinny legs wobbling to stay balanced.

Wyatt slams on the brakes and it feels like our minds disconnect from our bodies as the car spins around in circles twice, donuting in the middle of the road before careening into a nearby ditch.

# 19

## MILLIE AND DENNIS
## AND A CAT NAMED STEVE

**WYATT**

**T**HE THREE OF US sit in shock, without a scratch or a bruise on us, that we can tell for now. The car is thankfully upright. It's like we'd reached a higher plane of consciousness for a few seconds, aware that we just survived a potentially fatal accident.

We flew into heaven, fist-bumped God, who told us everything is going to be alright, and descended back down to Earth in slow motion.

"Are you okay?" I ask Biz, winded, my whole body still a bundle of nerves.

"Yeah, are you?" Biz asks.

We turn in unison to see Matilda. She gets comfortable on her bed like nothing happened.

We inhale and exhale, watching the rain, collecting ourselves. A pickup truck zooms by and we know how lucky we are that no other cars were around when we spun out of control.

"That was intense." I exhale, trying to process.

"That scared the shit out of me," Biz says. "I'm so glad it was you behind the wheel and not me."

"For a split second during the spin, I imagined our baby being born into the world without parents," I say. "Sorry if that sounds morose but it's the truth."

"The newborn's dads met their destiny in a small town in Ohio after buying expired donuts," Biz says, imitating an imaginary news reporter.

Relief setting in, we check our phones to find zero reception.

"I don't remember how to get back on the highway and there's no visibility."

"You know I have no sense of direction," Biz admits.

I can't help but let my next thought slip out. "I'm not saying we shouldn't have stopped for snacks but . . ."

"Here it comes. I knew you were going to somehow blame me for this," Biz says, throwing his hands in the air.

"I'm just saying you could've waited," I say.

"I'm sorry that I need food to survive."

"Survive?! You had like three lunches. You ate both of our sandwiches *and* Taco Bell. It's like you constantly—"

"I'm sorry, are you counting my calories too? I was hangry. And I was just going through the motions of eating Taco Bell, remember? I didn't even enjoy it. Fine, I loved it," Biz admits.

"So you won't eat Taco Bell but you're perfectly fine with roadside junk food?!"

"Actual meals shouldn't be fast food. Snacks are different."

"Says the supposed food expert. Your logic makes no sense."

"Don't question my logic," Biz says, which we both know is impossible. "And I am a food expert."

"Just be happy we're alive right now," I say, trying to redirect the course of our conversation. "Let's figure out how to get out of here."

In the distance, two blob-like figures come into focus through the rain. They look like the aliens from *Arrival*: faceless and shapeless but somehow able to mobilize.

"What the fuck is that?" Biz asks.

"Are we being abducted right now?"

The blobs quickly approach the car.

"Oh my god, it's the creepy couple from the knife and donut shop," Biz says.

I roll down my window just enough to talk, trying to avoid the rain.

"Don't roll down your window!" Biz screams. "We just cheated death and now we're possibly inviting it into our car. We have no idea what this couple is capable of."

Before I can join Biz's panic party, the blobs are right in front of me.

"You boys okay?" the man asks. The couple is wearing matching army green ponchos with hoods. I'm just happy they aren't white ponchos with hoods.

"We're fine. Just a little shaken up," I say. They both look inside our car and nod at Biz. He throws them a tiny thumbs-up through the window. They glance in the back seat at Matilda with smiles that suggest they want to make her their chew toy.

"We saw the whole thing. You're lucky there's no traffic in this area," the man says.

"Where you headed?" the woman asks.

"Illinois." I decide it sounds better to say the rural sounding Illinois rather than reference the big city of Chicago.

"You can't drive out tonight," the man says. "Not in this vehicle."

I look at Biz. We both know it's true. With the steady rain and the time, it's nearing pitch-black outside.

"Rain's supposed to go all night. Won't let up till morning," the woman says.

"Well, thank you. For that . . . kind info." I have no idea what else to say. And by the worried look on Biz's face, he's still not sure they come in peace.

"There's a bed-and-breakfast about a mile down the road. I hear there's vacancy."

"Cute little homey place. They take doggies, too. 'Bout five stop signs down. You can't miss it . . . Unless you're on drugs." She raises an eyebrow, suspicious. That came out of nowhere.

"We don't do drugs. But thank you for the tip," Biz says.

"We'll discuss and figure out our options. So nice of you to come out here in the rain like this," I say.

"Take care now," the man says. They slowly step away and casually walk back to their store like there aren't gusts of wind pummeling them at a hundred miles per hour.

I quickly roll up the window. "Do not eat those donuts. They could be laced with something then we wake up locked in their sex dungeon, hanging by our genitals."

"Trust me. I won't."

"What should we do? This rain is awful and I can't see anything," I say, thinking a bed-and-breakfast sounds pretty good at the moment.

After ten minutes of weighing the pros and cons, we pull into the B&B down the street with a wooden sign out front that's creatively named "Bed & Breakfast—Since 1972." Sure enough, as promised by the couple, the sign says there's vacancy.

It's an old, three-story home, every room lit up, with a grand, wraparound porch, set back in the woods. I half expect a crack of thunder and lightning to appear as we enter.

Inside, Matilda shakes out her wet fur, spraying rainwater all over the reception area. It's deadly quiet. We look around the ornate foyer, complete with wooden armoires containing dozens of ceramic animals of all shapes and sizes.

The room smells like Clorox wipes and eggs.

An older woman with bleached-blonde hair and excessive eyeliner appears behind the reception desk. "May I help you?"

Biz looks like he's in shock. He's holding an *are you kidding me right now* face. It slowly dawns on me that she's the knife and donut woman.

"Hi. It's us," I say to zero face recognition. "Yeah, so, we'd love a room?"

"Let me check what we have available."

Biz glances at me, losing all patience. "Um. Hello. We just met you on the road and I was in your store?"

"Oh, right. How are you two boys doin'?" She licks her forefinger and flips through her reservation book.

"You guys own this place too?" Biz asks. It's the question on both of our minds.

"Yup," she says, not acknowledging the weirdness of omitting this factoid before. She flicks through the reservation book again. "I'm afraid we only have one room tonight."

"Sold!" I say, wanting nothing more than to take a hot shower, have dinner and go to sleep.

The lady looks up at us with one raised eyebrow. "One room for both you fellows?"

*Oh no*, I think. Here comes the conversation where somehow it's our job to make her feel comfortable that we sleep together.

"Yep. We're partners," Biz says without even thinking. He's so much better than me when it comes to not caring what people think.

She gives us a quick little smile that suggests she has our number now, which I'm not sure is good or bad. I'm betting two guys sharing a bed is the furthest thing from her mind.

She writes something in the hotel guest book with perfect penmanship. We wait one full minute until she's done. Matilda whimpers, hungry, tired and cold. *Same, Matilda*, I think, *same*.

"Where you boys from?" her husband asks, appearing from the back room, also not acknowledging we just met them. Biz and I share a quick look.

"New York," Biz says, almost defiantly. "Brooklyn, actually."

"Bless your hearts," she says. Again, this could be good or bad. I'm still not sure. "I'm Millie. This is Dennis."

After several minutes of explaining we live nowhere near Times Square, we get our room key and walk up to our third-floor room.

It's a voluminous space with a working fireplace, wood trim and more ceramic lambs, frogs and ducks. It somehow feels less like a guest room and more like someone has been living here as recently as thirty minutes ago.

"Feels like we're in their actual bedroom," I say. I'm admittedly not as easygoing with hotel rooms as Biz. I like things a certain, sterile way. Not lived-in. In fact, I'd prefer a sign in every hotel room that reads, "No human being has ever stepped foot in this room."

"It's totally clean and fine. And it's just one night," Biz reminds me. We stare at the antique lamps, flowery window treatments and wooden rolltop desk. "At least there are no creepy ceramic baby dolls staring at us."

I silently point to the corner of the room where there is, in fact, a glass cabinet full of creepy ceramic baby dolls staring at us.

"Should we have dinner?" Biz says.

We can't get out of there fast enough.

The living room has been reconfigured into a restaurant with a few tables comfortably dotted throughout. So basically, it's a living room with a few tables.

"Any apostrophe?" Biz asks.

"No apostrophe," I say, as we share a laugh at our inside joke.

In the beginning of our relationship, Biz and I had discovered that neither of us had been to Maine so we took a romantic road trip one Valentine's Day weekend where we stayed at our first ever B&B with the cutesy name "Sweethearts Inn." We were still celebrating all our milestone firsts. "Should we introduce our friends to each other?" "Is it okay if I leave my toothbrush here?" "Let's go on a trip somewhere." We couldn't wait for our love nest in a log cabin.

Once inside, we quickly realized that the "Sweethearts" in the name of the bed-and-breakfast wasn't referring to "sweethearts" plural having a lovey-dovey getaway.

Sweetheart was the nickname of the owner, a gregarious woman with a loud, piercing voice and jackhammer laugh who was on top of every guest at every second of the day. Let's just say, you had to be in the mood for Sweetheart.

She wanted to have breakfast, lunch and afternoon wine and cheese on the porch with everyone every day, and if you weren't on time, she'd knock on your door, expecting you to join the group. She demanded we play board games, try her latest homemade cherry pie and listen to her long-winded stories. She even persuaded Biz to arm-wrestle.

We laughed that Sweetheart, the smothering host, neglected

to put an apostrophe in the name of her fine establishment. "Sweetheart's Inn" would've been more accurate than "Sweethearts Inn."

In contrast to Sweethearts Inn, the dining room at "Bed & Breakfast" is completely empty. The only noise is the rain splattering the windows outside. We wonder if there are actually other people staying here like Millie told us.

We look around, taking in the eclectic décor with the mismatched chairs, red and white checked tablecloths and framed needlepoint of various farm animals on the walls.

I reach under the table and squeeze Biz's knee as Biz squeezes my hand. We smile at each other, both finally feeling warm and safe after today's scare.

Movement suddenly catches our peripheral vision and we both turn to see an incredibly skinny brown cat with an elongated tail walking slowly across the room. The cat turns to see the human strangers and yawns, revealing serrated teeth. It looks like a mini velociraptor unhinging its jaw, ready to make us its supper.

We hear a throat clear. "That's Steve," Millie says, standing directly behind us, startling both of us.

I'm sure Biz is thinking what I'm thinking: the name "Steve" sounds like a first draft.

"His full name is Stephen King. Named after our favorite writer," Millie says in a gleeful, macabre way.

To recap, the owners of a completely empty, possibly haunted bed-and-breakfast have named their cat after a legendary horror writer. Not sure if we need to hear this right now.

"Is it possible to have dinner?" Biz asks, chopping his way past the weirdness with a virtual machete.

"Of course. Daddy's putting on the finishing touches as we speak."

Biz and I discreetly share a look. *Daddy*. There's no way that guy is her dad. They look the same age and, if anything, she seems slightly older than him.

"Oh. Daddy's what I call my husband," she explains, detecting our confusion. "After six kids all calling him Daddy, I sometimes forget his first name." She laughs, which makes the two of us force polite laughs. I guess we're relieved?

"Six kids. Wow," I say.

"Tell me about it. Got the stretch marks to prove it. Lasagna okay?" Millie asks.

To me, this sounds like the perfect rainy night dinner. To Biz, the Italian food connoisseur, they are setting him up for potential disappointment.

Sitting at a table by the large bay windows, still alone in the dining room with a nearby fire flickering hello every so often, it does feel strangely romantic.

My heart races with warmth that I can share an intimate moment with Biz, until Millie and Dennis return with salads. Dennis serves me and Millie serves Biz. They time it perfectly in unison the same way a team of servers would perform at Le Bernardin in Manhattan. Crisp lettuce with fresh tomatoes and tasty goat cheese.

Before we know it, the couple serves our lasagna entrees and Biz is delightfully surprised by the complex flavors and high-end presentation. Millie and Dennis linger during our first bite, watching raptly. We shower them with praise for a home-cooked meal.

Out of nowhere, Millie dramatically changes the course of our small talk.

"We know you're gay," she says.

I almost do a spit take. Biz freezes mid-bite. I swallow, wondering how to navigate this.

"Congrats?" Biz says. He can't help but administer a sarcastic tone as his defense mechanism. We stare at the couple, unsure of where this is going.

Did they poison our lasagna after all?

"We'd just like to say . . ." Millie pauses, maintaining a poker face for five seconds too long. The air of suspense makes us both unsettled. "Our son is gay too."

"And so is our daughter," Dennis adds.

"And our other child is nonbinary. They're bisexual."

We smile. This could've been game over but instead we've hit jackpot and our slot machine just keeps spitting out gold coins. The couple stands by our table expectantly.

"Would you like to join us for dinner?" I'm guessing they don't have many people in these parts to talk to about their kids.

They bring out the pan of lasagna and a bottle of red wine and we share the meal. We ask them questions about parenting three queer kids and three straight ones. Millie tells us how their son wrote them a letter to come out, their daughter revealed it to them (and her entire high school) in her graduation speech as the valedictorian and how they walked in on their other kid having sex with their boyfriend.

There's talk of our upcoming baby and the couple asks us every question under the sun. *Did you meet the egg donor? You mean the egg donor and the surrogate are not the same? How did you find the surrogate? What if she wants to keep the baby? Did you try adoption?*

Millie and Dennis tell us they feel less alone hearing our stories.

After at least three bottles of wine, a delicious chocolate cake and lively conversation, the night comes to an end. There's nothing I want more than to go to sleep in our cozy, weird room.

I carry in our luggage, deciding to bring the bundle of letters from my father to our room. Spending the night with these two awesome parents has made me forlorn for my own.

I wonder if my own father would've loved me the way Millie and Dennis love their kids.

Biz and I collapse in bed next to each other; I read through a couple of my father's letters while Biz texts with his sisters.

Two sentences into reading one letter and I'm filled with an emptiness I wasn't expecting. At the exact same time I put away the letters, Biz puts away his phone. There will be more time to read what my father wanted me to hear but for now, it's time to sleep.

We turn off our lamps and hear a scratch at the door. We look at each other with mild fright. Are there ghosts here after all? Another scratch. And another.

"What is that?" Biz asks.

Deciding to be the butch one, I throw off the covers and cautiously open the door.

I look down. "It's Steve the cat," I say. Stephen King confidently strides in and glides into Matilda's bed. Matilda doesn't mind as the two furry creatures exhale and fall asleep next to each other.

Biz and I fall into each other's arms, like it's the most natural thing to do. I have a smile on my face, realizing that we're cuddling for the first time on this trip.

Maybe our unexpected hosts brought Biz and I a little closer together tonight.

I listen to the pitter-patter of the tempest outside, feeling safe and not wanting to let go of Biz, but wondering when the storm between us will finally clear.

# 20

## THE PETTERELLIS

**BIZ**

**B**ED. CHECK.

Breakfast. Check.

After promising the kind Millie and Dennis to send them a picture of the baby, we're back on I-90, heading for my family's house.

The downpour, which seemed like it was never going to end last night, is finally gone.

Top down, dry highway, blue skies.

Rounding Lake Michigan past Gary, Indiana, I've firmly forgotten about our Saugatuck plans. At this point, it's easier to spend time with my family than hope Wyatt will want to let loose in another resort town.

"What do we have planned with the Petterellis?" Wyatt asks, smelling like a faint whiff of the citrus, eucalyptus soap Millie and Dennis had provided back at the B&B.

Not only were they a lovely couple but they had quality bath products.

"Um. Nothing? You know my family. They're not planners like your mom and you," I remind him. "We'll hang, see all the kids, eat good food and drink great wine. I've been texting with my mom and sisters. They're all so excited."

Unlike Wyatt's mom, who couldn't reimagine his bedroom fast enough after he left for college, my parents kept each kid's bedroom a shrine to our childhood. They even added onto the house, creating bedrooms for the grandkids. When I go home, the whole family sleeps over, forever holding on to the past while making room for the new generations.

When we finally cross the border into Illinois, heading toward Arlington Heights, my hometown about forty minutes northwest of Chicago, I send a message to my sisters and they all immediately reply with enthusiasm.

Heart emojis!

An old photo of all of us as kids wearing goofy pajamas!

A funny GIF of Chris Farley wildly dancing!

Slight anxiety fills me as we near my house. My sisters, all old pros when it comes to parenting, are bound to make me feel inferior and unprepared for fatherhood.

It's nothing that they'll do intentionally, of course. Just my own insecurity creeping in again. They're all just so good at being moms. How will I ever measure up?

"*At the next light, turn right,*" the GPS lady informs us.

I forgot to tell Wyatt to turn it off.

"*In one mile, good luck being a dad, Biz,*" she continues.

"Please kill GPS lady," I say to Wyatt. I reach for his phone and shut her down.

"Are those . . . welcome home balloons?" Wyatt asks as we arrive at my nice but modest two-story Tudor-style childhood home. My family hung a beautiful sculpture of balloons in various sizes and shades of gold cascading around the frame of the front doors.

"They sure are," I say, not surprised my family has already gone to great lengths to make us feel at home. "My sisters have probably already made six hundred trips to Party City."

When we pull into the driveway, packed with cars, we see more than a dozen people waving at us, bursting with anticipation.

"Looks like the gang's all here," Wyatt says with an overwhelmed face.

"That's actually not everyone," I realize, studying the crowd and noticing a couple teenage nieces and nephews are not present.

"Wait—how is that not everyone?" Wyatt asks.

"Are you forgetting not all families are small like yours?"

"I'm not used to this many people congregating in one spot, let alone a single family," Wyatt says.

I slurp the last of my caramel macchiato Frappuccino we'd picked up along the way, knowing I need to be *on* for my large family.

Wyatt finishes his Americano and grabs my drink for an extra hit of caffeine.

My parents, sisters, their husbands and kids, aunts, uncles and a few cousins all stand there, waving, greeting us. Some of them jump up and down like game show contestants. Two sisters hold boxes filled with cupcakes and cookies that read, "Baby-to-Be!"

We peel ourselves out of Virginia Woolf and step into the party. Matilda jumps free from the back seat and immediately joins the fold of several dogs like she's reuniting with old friends.

"Welcome *hooooooome!*" sings one sister.

"You made it!" calls another.

"I can't believe you weren't going to include us on your ba-bymoon trip!" Zia shouts.

"We're here, aren't we?" I say, falling into a sea of hugs.

None of my sisters strayed outside of their birthplace of sub-urban Chicago so it's easy enough for them to plan a welcoming committee for their little brother.

When he directs a commercial, Wyatt has a handy cheat sheet of every actor's name. I suggested he do the same with my cast of characters when we first started dating.

My parents, Giovanni (Gio) and Sylvia, and my sisters, An-tonia, Marisa, Daniella, Nicole and Zia.

My nieces and nephews playfully tumble around us, shout-ing out all the games they want to play with us while we're home: UNO! Clue! Pictionary! Several video games we've never heard of!

All of the chaos from outside eventually moves inside where we're hit by an inviting whiff of simmering pasta sauce with plenty of garlic.

"Mom's been prepping since she heard you were coming," Daniella says.

Sprawled out on the kitchen table are dozens of freshly made ricotta-filled ravioli that my mom made, recruiting some of the husbands to help roll them, per usual.

Quickly, everywhere we look—literally everywhere—each room fills up, buzzing with family. Each group is louder than the next: teenagers on the sofa watch a movie, kids on the living room floor play with toys, my dad and brothers-in-law in the kitchen drink red wine, dipping garlic bread into my mom's gravy, my sisters surround us, wanting to know every last detail of our trip and, especially, the current baby status.

Almost immediately, my sisters fall into the older sibling role, mildly bullying me for answers.

"Tell us where you've been."

"Tell us where you're going next."

"Tell us the baby's name."

*Tell us, tell us, tell us!*

As the voices project and the laughter escalates, I remember when I was a kid, I sometimes longed for a quieter life. These people are LOUD.

Wyatt, having grown up with one brother and one mom, always remarked that this is the kind of large, boisterous family he used to want.

Maybe we'll meet somewhere in the middle with our own.

Later, after having to repeat herself a few times so the whole gang can hear her, my mom emphatically declares, "Dinner! Is! Ready!"

More balloons that read "Hello, Baby!" float above one long dining table filled with candles and vases of baby's breath on the deck outside, which overlooks Mom and Dad's sizable backyard. The newly renovated swimming pool, firepit, and gazebo with a huge TV to watch movies outside look incredible as always.

My mom instructs everyone to sit anywhere they want with my nieces and nephews off to the side at their own kiddie section.

"I can never get over how long this table is," Wyatt says quietly to me, always comparing my family's large dinner table to his three-person dinners he grew up with in Boston. "Feels more like a town hall meeting than a dinner."

"Accurate," I say.

"We've got homemade ravioli, there's fried calamari, prosciutto, salami, four kinds of bruschetta and rigatoni with meat sauce in case the ravioli isn't enough," my mom informs us.

"And copious vino!" my dad adds.

"We! Love! Caaaaaarbs!" I say in my best Oprah voice. Everyone laughs.

As we eat and drink, with each sister clamoring to get the scoop on us, some family members start speaking Italian and I know they've lost Wyatt, making him feel monolingual.

I always see slight shock register on Wyatt's face that there's this whole other language that I speak fluently.

After the first time Wyatt met my family, he told me he felt *othered* in a way he'd never felt before and wondered if we kept slipping into Italian in order to talk about him.

Of course we did.

Wyatt always reminds me that my facial expressions and body language change when I speak Italian and that I start to eerily resemble my sisters with their wildly animated hand gestures, raised passionate voices, physical touching and ferocious laughter.

Tonight's dinner conversation is as lively as ever. But it's been a minute since I've been home and half the time I don't even know who the hell my family is talking about.

"Have you talked to Loretta?"

"Not since Benji's christening."

"She and Sonny asked me if they should invite Leo and Marissa to Carter and Dom's wedding, but I told Mallory she better clear it with Jay before Laurie finds out from Teddy."

"Do you know all these people?" Wyatt leans over to ask me.

"No clue," I say out of the side of my mouth.

Another rare moment during this trip when we feel like we're on each other's team.

Wyatt and I both crunch down on grilled bruschetta dripping with creamy gorgonzola, figs and honey. "Oh my god," Wyatt says with his mouth full of deliciousness. "I live here now."

My mom laughs and kisses Wyatt on the cheek. She senses my sisters fusing at the hip and feels the need to intervene. "Okay, girls. Biz and Wyatt didn't drive sixteen hours with a puking dog to listen to stories about Sharon and Tom and Dick and Harry and whoever the hell else you're talking about," Mom says.

The girls blink, not realizing—never realizing—they're prioritizing their own bubble.

"Can we not say 'puke' at the dinner table?" my dad asks.

"You just did," my mom says as we all laugh.

"Chicagoland's greatest comic duo," my brother-in-law says.

"What's up with the baby?" Zia asks.

"Four and a half more weeks and we're dads," Wyatt slips in before I can.

In between sips of wine, my sisters eye me, wondering how this makes me feel.

*Happy?*

*Excited?*

*Freaking the fuck out?*

They can mind-read me like no one else.

"If you need baby clothes, I can give you all of Jake's," Antonia offers.

"I'm happy to unload all of Gigi's old clothes," Marisa says.

"Mom, you are NOT giving away my baby clothes," Gigi, now ten and equipped with a reactive personality, chimes in from the kids' table before abandoning half of her food to go sit under a tree in the backyard, presumably to sulk. The rest of the kids take this as their cue that dinner is over as they all flee the kids' table to play cornhole or jump on the trampoline.

"That reminds me . . ." My mom disappears into the house and reappears, showering us with shopping bags full of presents. "Let the baby shower begin!"

Wyatt and I unwrap gifts to find swaddle blankets, teether toys, building blocks, booties and a calming cloud mobile that emits ambient noise.

"Thank you all so much!" Wyatt says, beaming with excitement.

"How are we going to fit all this into our car?" I ask, staring at all the foreign baby items.

"It's okay. We'll ship them to you in Brooklyn," my oldest sister says, trying to calm me.

My mom gives us a half dozen onesies. Each one is a different food theme with little images of hamburgers, pizza and . . . sushi?

"Thanks, Sylvia! I love the sushi one," Wyatt says, completely in his element.

"Is that sushi?" my mom asks, putting on her reading glasses for closer inspection. "Huh. I thought they were cupcakes."

My brain does a flash forward. I'm desperately trying to pull a onesie on our screaming baby while Wyatt looks on with disappointment. I snap back into the present and I've started to sweat a little. I remind myself that the wine I'm gulping is not water.

Everyone is on board this fast-moving train and I'm still buying my ticket.

"You can spend all your time dressing up your little one and sending us photos now that you were laid off, Biz," Zia says.

I freeze. The wind is knocked out of me.

I can feel my cheeks turn tomato red. I fill with guilt.

Wyatt, in the middle of freshening up his glass of red wine, forgets to stop pouring as it cascades over the rim of the glass, onto his hand and all over the table.

My family, knowing me all too well, immediately understands by the look on my contorted face that I haven't yet told Wyatt about work.

I'd made the mistake of texting the news about my job to only one person, Zia, who also happens to be President and CEO of Family Gossip.

*What was I thinking?!*

Of course Zia told everyone. Maybe I subconsciously knew the news would spread so I didn't have to humiliate myself over and over again with each family member.

And now Wyatt.

Silence falls over the table. Wyatt glances at me, trying to be nonchalant. Then he looks around the table, wondering who else knew.

"Wait, I thought you would've told everyone by now," Zia says, feeling caught.

"Looks like you got some 'splaining to do!" Paul, Zia's very animated husband, says in a Ricky Ricardo impression. Paul's entire personality is imitating TV and movie characters from a bygone era.

No one thinks this is funny; the weight of me withholding information from Wyatt hangs in the air. Zia shoots her husband a *shut up* look and mouths a genuine *sorry* to me.

For five full minutes, the entire table erupts into chaotic Italian. Everyone yell-talks at each other, pointed words flying like bullets across the table in every direction.

Wyatt watches me alternate from defending myself to yelling at my sisters to feeling bad about the entire situation.

While the family continues talking, I mouth *I'll explain later* to Wyatt.

I feel awful. I'm an idiot for not telling him sooner.

My mom tries to save dinner. "Who's ready for some tiramisu?!"

Wyatt mops up his spilled red wine with paper napkins. My dad watches both of us sympathetically.

I can tell that underneath the neutral face that Wyatt is politely trying to maintain, he's silently hurt and betrayed.

# 21

## WE ARE FAMILY

**WYATT**

'M TRYING TO UNDERSTAND why Biz didn't tell me he was laid off from his job.

After dinner, while everyone splits up to play board games—the kids figure out if Mrs. Peacock did it with a wrench in the billiards room, the sisters draw pictures while their husbands guess what they are—I head to the kitchen for more wine.

"I'm so sorry," Biz says, finding me midpour. The sound of people laughing, yelling and exclamations in Italian during game playing can be heard down the hall.

I turn around to face him, trying not to get heated. "Yeah, it would've been nice not to be the last person to know you got fired."

"I was laid off. But I'm sorry. I texted Z about it and . . . you know how she is. She says she can keep a secret and of course she never does."

"So you're blaming your sister?" I ask, genuinely hurt that

we're apparently keeping secrets from each other at this point in our relationship.

"What? No. It just slipped out with her in text," Biz says, trying to cover.

"Then are you going to tell me what happened?" I ask, my eyes trained on the wine I'm about to down.

"Biz and Wyatt! Are you playing or what?!" Marisa shouts from the other room. We all know she's disturbingly competitive when it comes to board games. She *needs* to win.

"They told me in a fucking *mass email*," Biz says, releasing a pained sigh like he's been holding this in for a while.

"When?" I probe.

"When we were in P-town," Biz says, feeling bad. "I wanted to tell you."

"Why didn't you?" I ask, not understanding.

"There was never a good moment," Biz says as he swallows, feeling caught.

"Hours of driving in silence and there wasn't one good moment?" I'm genuinely confused.

"You were preoccupied with your mom and brother. And then all the stuff with your dad. I didn't want to dump more on you. Plus, you're not very good at . . . opening up about things."

"Don't turn this back on me. This is *your job*. Our livelihood. I've been busting my ass with work lately and we're about to have . . ." I stop myself, suddenly self-conscious if anyone's listening. I lower my voice. "We're about to have a baby, Biz. This isn't something to take lightly."

"Obviously I know that," Biz says.

"How are we going to be good partners and especially

co-parents if there isn't complete honesty and transparency between us?" I ask.

Biz squints. "I honestly can't believe you're the one telling me this. And wouldn't your first thought be, *By the way, I'm sorry you got laid off*?"

"Guys?!?" Marisa calls out again. "GUYS!!!"

We're both conflicted. We want to continue hashing this out but we don't want to ruin the night. I suppress my frustration. "Just go. We can talk later," I let him off the hook for now.

"Sorry I didn't tell you, okay?" Biz holds my gaze. "Do you want to play with us?"

I'm terrible at Pictionary. Last Christmas when I played with the Petterellis, I had to draw a butternut squash and his sisters kept laughing at me, saying it looked like a dildo.

"I'll meet you in there," I say, wanting to escape but fearful of being talked about in hushed tones if I don't show.

After gathering myself (and more wine), I walk into the living room where the sisters and their husbands sit. Daniella is the only one not playing, lounging in a comfy chair with her glass of wine, legs thrown to the side, contently flipping through the ads of the Sunday editions of the *Chicago Tribune* and *Sun-Times*. The oldest sister, Daniella is an extreme couponer and lover of horoscopes. Riffling through the inky pages at family events, she'll often interject, "You see this?! Two bucks off Dove hand soap!" or "Hey, Antonia, aren't you a Virgo? Someone older and wiser than you might rain on your parade this autumn."

Even though this is the Petterellis' after-dinner ritual every time we visit, I'll never get used to seeing a group of adults squeezed together on couches, laughing and having fun. They look like actors in a board game commercial.

This is the opposite of what my family did growing up. After dinner, we became islands. My mom would sit in the kitchen, sealing envelopes for her real estate mass mailings. Alex was in his room watching a hockey game. And I was in my bedroom watching a classic movie. The three of us wouldn't speak to each other until the next morning.

The Petterellis all turn to see me enter. I'm trying not to think about Biz's news.

"Have a seat, Wyatt," Nicole says, taking me out of my misery as I hover in the doorway. Nicole's husband, Gabe, is sitting next to her at the end of the sofa. He's gym-hunky with over-pronounced deltoids and looks like he auditioned but didn't cast on *Jersey Shore*. Gabe scooches closer to his wife and slaps the empty spot on the sofa, inviting me to sit.

"You guys know I'm bad at Pictionary," I say, taking a seat.

Biz sits across the coffee table from me on the opposing team. We share a guarded look. He smiles with red wine-stained teeth, appreciative I'm trying to be a team player while attempting to get on my good side.

I'm pushing down any mixed emotions for the sake of keeping up family appearances.

"We're not playing Pictionary," Nicole informs us. She folds up the game as the sisters clear the giant coffee table and bring out various baby accessories.

A worried look appears on Biz's face. "What are we playing instead?" he asks.

"Tonight . . ." Marisa dramatically announces. "We play baby shower games!"

"Toldja we were doing this," Zia says to Biz with an apologetic smile.

I feel warmed that Biz's nurturing sisters want to celebrate us almost-dads. But I look up and see Biz go rigid, filling with dread.

It pains me to see Biz not sharing the same level of enthusiasm for the baby at this stage as he had a few months ago.

First, everyone competes to see who can drink an entire baby bottle filled with red wine. I chug mine and look over at Biz, who's barely trying. The competitive Marisa wins.

Then we play "feed the baby," where we partner off and feed our spouses tiramisu while we're both blindfolded. I clumsily feed Biz, feeling even less connected with a blindfold on. Marisa and her husband win. They double high-five with a fierceness that frightens me.

Next, we "deliver the baby" where we each put a balloon under our shirts and deliver it in the most creative way possible; an act that feels especially weird for two guys having a baby via surrogacy. Biz excuses himself to go to the bathroom. Marisa does some overdramatic acting that she's seen in every movie of a woman giving birth and declares herself the winner.

"And now," Marisa continues, as Biz returns. "This one's just for Biz and Wyatt. A diaper relay race!"

Two sisters bring out their old Cabbage Patch Dolls and hand one to each of us.

"Put these blindfolds on and whoever can change their doll's diaper first wins!" Marisa states.

Biz tosses the doll on the coffee table.

"This is so stupid," Biz says, averting his eyes as everyone looks at him.

I cradle mine like an actual baby. "Why? It's good practice," I say.

"See! Wyatt's a good sport. *C'mon*, Biz!" Marisa shouts.

"I'm not putting a diaper on your old dumb doll," Biz insists.

"And who takes care of a baby while blindfolded?" Biz asks. I'm not sure why he's trying to get out of playing.

"It's called fun," I say as I ready my blindfold. "Isn't that what this babymoon is about?" I glimpse Biz scowl at me after I say this.

"Put the diaper on the damn doll, Biz," Gabe demands.

"You have thirty seconds," Marisa says. "Ready?"

"No," Biz says emphatically. He slumps down in the corner of the couch where I imagine Biz would pout as a kid.

"It'll be fun, just do it," says another husband, egging Biz on.

I tie on my blindfold and I can't see if Biz is even participating.

"Ready. Set. C'mon, Biz," Marisa cajoles him one more time. "Go!"

I lift the legs of the doll and seal the tabs of the diaper securely, somehow knowing instinctively what to do. Maybe babysitting my little brother all those years while our mom worked late turned me into a parent before I knew it.

Everyone cheers as I slip off my blindfold. The diaper fits on the doll perfectly.

"That wasn't even fifteen seconds!" Marisa says as she fist-bumps me. "You rule!"

I see Biz's baby is diaper-less. Biz is still glued to the corner of the couch, hiding his misery in a sip of wine. He didn't even play the game.

"Guess we know who's changing the diapers," Gabe says as everyone cracks up at the expense of their baby brother.

– – – – – – – – ⟶

LATER, INSIDE BIZ'S CHILDHOOD BEDROOM, BIZ SNAPS THE DOOR SHUT.

"You okay?" I ask, seeing he hasn't shaken the night off yet.

Biz nods.

"Why didn't you want to play any of those games?" I ask.

"I'm just tired and want to sleep," he grumbles. Biz strips to his boxer briefs and crawls into his double bed, like he's willing this night to be over. I undress and join him.

"It's always strange being naked in your childhood bed," I can't help but say. I pull the blue and tan striped comforter, Bed Bath & Beyond circa 2002, up to my chest.

"I know. Tell my mom," Biz says. "She refuses to touch anything in here. It's like she thinks I went missing as a teenager and never came back. It's exactly how I left it."

Biz takes off his underwear and throws them onto his chair shaped like a baseball glove.

The weight of the evening settles over us.

"I'm honestly sorry for not telling you I was laid off."

"Why didn't you?"

"I needed to process it and there hasn't exactly been an ideal time to tell you," Biz rationalizes.

"But you told your sisters," I say, the hurt and anger rising in me again. "I just can't believe this. It's the worst timing ever," I accidentally say this a little loud for both of our tastes. The entire family is staying in all the rooms surrounding us and can probably hear everything. I look down at Matilda, who flops onto her back in her bed. Not a care in the world.

Biz speaks in a loud whisper. "Can we keep it down, please? But I mean, Jesus, Wyatt. Don't you think I know this isn't good timing? I'm hurt too. This sucks. But it doesn't matter now. It wasn't meant to be. If I really think about it, I was slowly dying at that job anyway."

My cheeks go hot. Panic overwhelms me. "Don't you under-stand how all those ridiculous directing jobs have been killing me?" I unleash again. "And now I'll have to take even more gigs to cover the baby expenses."

"I know. I'm not suggesting you have it easy," Biz says.

I release a frustrated sigh. Then I calmly inhale, revising my tone. "Okay," I say, trying to meet Biz halfway. "So what are you gonna do?"

"I don't know. I'll write for other places," Biz says.

We both stare at the opposite wall where there's a giant poster of Biz and his cast from *Back in the Saddle*, five smiling teenagers wearing western shirts, cowboy hats and cowboy boots, standing in the entrance of a horse stable.

"Maybe I'll get back into acting. Start auditioning again," Biz continues. "I miss it."

"I'm sure you do. You were good," I say, staring at the teenage Biz I never knew. "But freelance writing and auditions aren't going to pay for raising a kid in New York City."

"Then maybe we move out of Brooklyn. We can go somewhere cheaper. I don't know."

"Now you want to move out of New York?" I ask. This is something new.

"It's not out of the question. I wouldn't mind . . . *this*." Biz waves his hands around the room. "My parents have it made in a house like this. It's nice. Roomy. I mean, do we really want to raise our baby without a backyard and a barbecue?"

I let a long pause sit between us. In a robotically calm way, with my nerves shot, I peel off the covers, climb out of bed and walk across the room. I carefully step over Matilda's squeaky toys so I won't wake her, the floor covered in plushy roadkill.

I start pulling clothes out of my bag.

"What are you doing?" Biz asks, alarmed.

"I'm trying to have a logistical conversation with you about our finances and you're talking about a frickin' barbecue," I say.

"Fine, forget the barbecue, okay? It was a dumb metaph— Seriously, where are you going?" Biz asks. "Can you please talk to me?"

I'm trying to remain calm. "Biz. I'm just frustrated that somehow you got fired weeks before our baby is due. I know you're close with your sisters but I can't believe I wasn't the first person you told. And I'm sad that you're not showing any enthusiasm for raising our baby. Not participating in any of those baby shower games is very telling. I don't know, it's like you just want to escape what's about to happen to us."

After putting on a pair of sweatpants and a hoodie, I look up at a silenced Biz. He has tears in his eyes. "I'm not going out. I just need to be alone for a minute," I say.

Biz sits there, watching me quietly leave and shut the door.

Walking through Biz's house, I have so many memories. That first Christmas we spent here when we had sex on Biz's double bed. That one Thanksgiving where we karaoked in our underwear in the basement while everyone was asleep. That time we flew here to meet Biz's latest baby niece and cuddled with her all night.

One thing we've never done in Biz's childhood home is have an argument.

I sit at the darkened kitchen counter, spotlit only by a single overhead light, pouring myself one last glass of red wine. The house has so many little noises. The ice maker. The wind rattling the patio screen door. The last flicker of the fireplace in the living room.

I sip my wine and cringe at the spearmint taste mixed with

cabernet, remembering I just brushed my teeth. *I'll power through it*, I think and sip again.

I hear the floorboards creak and see Daniella walking into the kitchen, startling me.

"Oh, I'm so sorry," Daniella says. "I had no idea you were here. You scared me too." She's wearing a cozy, tie-dyed University of Illinois sweatshirt.

"Sorry," I whisper.

She collects her piles of coupons off the kitchen table. "No, *I'm* sorry. I wanted to grab these before someone stole them," she says with a little laugh. Even I know that no one in this family except Daniella wants anything to do with that pile of coupons.

"Good idea," I reassure her.

She smiles and spots my wine. "That looks so good right now for some reason." She thinks before deciding. "Want company?"

"Please," I say. I rarely get one-on-one time with anyone in the family, let alone the coveted oldest sister.

Daniella pours herself a sizable glass of wine, making me suspect she didn't really come into the kitchen for her coupons. "You must think our family is so wacky."

"All families that aren't yours are wacky," I say.

Daniella thinks. "You know, when we speak Italian, we're not talking about you. Just so you know."

"Oh, yeah. No. I know that." I try to sound like I don't care, swallowing my white lie in another sip.

"Well, maybe a little bit," she says, breaking into a smile. We laugh together as a trail of four silhouettes wearing various sweatshirts walk in. Antonia in a Chicago Bears sweatshirt. Zia in her Ohio State matching sweats. Nicole in a Grateful Dead hoodie. A fleece Patagonia for Marissa.

"Midnight snackage?" Zia asks.

"Where's lil Bizzy boy?" Nicole wonders.

"You know, we call him Biz because of all the biscotti he ate as a kid," Marisa tells me.

"I thought it was because he was an annoying little busy-body," Daniella says.

"Wrong. It's because he was in show biz," Nicole argues.

Their debate is interrupted by Daniella taking out the large tinfoil tray of leftover tiramisu. Zia takes out six forks and hands them out to her sisters and me.

"Here ya go. You're an official sistah now," Zia says to me.

"To the sistahs!" they all say in unison as we clink forks. One by one, we dig into the chocolaty, velvety dessert, *mmm*ing and *yum*ing. We analyze the conversation at dinner, steer clear of the job stuff and discuss all things babies.

"I thought I heard chocolate," Biz says, appearing out from the shadows.

Zia hands him a fresh fork and he goes to town along with us. "I missed my handsome boyfriend," Biz says, trying to smooth us over in front of his family.

"When are you two going to get married already?" Zia asks.

"Exactly. You're having a baby but no wedding?" Antonia, the traditional one, adds.

I take another bite of tiramisu, stress-chewing with my mouth shut, eyes tilted down at the fast-disappearing dessert, avoiding yet another conversation grenade.

"We'll see what happens," Biz speaks for both of us. The girls all steal glances at one another. *Another point of contention*, they probably think.

Which it is. Biz, coming from such a large family, with his stable parents, and me with my single mom and estranged dad. We see the world differently. I don't need the traditional family setup. I just want to focus on the baby. We're together. Who needs marriage? It certainly didn't work for my parents.

But this is nice for me, the sisters I've never had. I'm realizing that having this big of a family gives you so many different perspectives. A large family also lets you share a midnight snack while you get a serious case of the giggles.

But I know that the outstanding issues Biz and I have won't resolve while we're in Chicago. Not in front of Biz's entire family.

Biz caps off their wedding questions with, "Whatever happens, all I know is I love this man with all my heart."

I pause for a good ten seconds before letting out, "Me too." Each sister swoons.

And while I appreciate Biz's cute gesture, I smile through my red wine, tiramisu and toothpaste mouth, thinking to myself, he's not getting off the hook this easily.

# 22

## DAD

**BIZ**

FOLD IT IN HALF, diagonally. Take the two ends and make a double knot.

Place it around your neck.

Put the ends through the loop and adjust accordingly.

The European loop, aka the Parisian knot, aka the Italian twist.

Whatever it's called, my dad, Gio, an effortless dandy, always rocks his scarf like a classically handsome Italian GQ model. Go, Dad!

Growing up, I never really took notice of my extremely stylish dad. I figured every father wore Italian loafers and head-to-toe Brunello Cucinelli.

I was always—embarrassed isn't exactly right, more like self-conscious—by a few things.

First, my dad was way older than the rest of my friends' dads. By ten to fifteen years. Having an older dad never bothered me, but I noticed at school plays and science fairs that other people were aware that my dad was different. "Is that your *grandpa*???" kids would ask.

It didn't help that my eccentric dad grew out his wild gray hair to make him look like "Pedro Almodóvar meets Ursula from *The Little Mermaid*" as Wyatt once accurately coined.

I was also briefly embarrassed by my dad's thick Italian accent. My mom's accent was softer—she had assimilated more to the flat Chicagoland vowels. Plus, Dad has such an animated way of speaking, which often takes people out of their comfort zone.

I was an average American kid but at first, my oh-so-very midwestern teachers, peers and their parents didn't quite know what to make of my dad, the exotic Italian creature. Once everyone was able to get past that, they realized Dad is a warm hug of a man.

The next morning at my parents' house, I decide to put a pin in everything with me and Wyatt. Today I just want us to have a blast with my family.

After a homemade breakfast feast, we pile into various cars, and the Petterelli caravan heads to each niece and nephew activity.

First, there's Izzy's figure skating practice, where everyone dutifully sits in the freezing-cold ice rink bubble, blowing on their hot coffees.

Next, Mia's karate class makes us all afraid that the impressively rough-and-tumble seven-year-old could kick all our asses.

After that, the tiny-for-his-age Leo shows off his wobbly rock-climbing skills while we all can barely look.

While sitting next to my dad at little Ruby's soccer game, I notice he's wearing his perfectly knotted cashmere scarf and wool sport coat on this oddly cool and windy day. I'm proud that he's not only joining us on this epic family outing at his age (seventy-eight!) but that he looks so damn good while doing it.

When my sisters and I stop gossiping and I actually pay attention to the soccer game, I'm shocked to hear the unfiltered outcries of the parents; aggressive yelling at the ref, shouting impossible commands at their innocent kids ("Hustle, Jaxtyn!" "Step into it, Maverick!") and occasionally swearing at each other face-to-face. It's like a viral video of parents behaving badly come to life.

When I look down the row and see Wyatt at the other end, he doesn't look back; a sign he's still upset with me for not telling him about my job, among other things.

Thankfully, it looks like Wyatt is enjoying the game, laughing with Daniella and Antonia, who are all making fun of one especially overly dramatic set of parents about to have an aneurysm over their mini–soccer players.

"This game is giving me anxiety," I say to my dad.

"Did you eat enough?" he asks. Food. It's the solution to all of our family's problems.

"No, I mean, what if we have a kid who becomes super serious about group sports?"

"Oh, that. Yeah, you were never a team sports kid, kiddo. Let the ex–hockey player lead the way," he says, referring to Wyatt.

"He *begrudgingly* played hockey as a kid because his mom forced him. I don't think he's a team sports kinda guy at heart."

"Then you're both screwed!" Dad says, with his infectious laugh.

"Gee, thanks," I say, watching the kids dominate the field. "Seriously, though, I've avoided sports my whole life and now I'll have to participate."

"Remember Mr. Katrakis?" Dad asks, conjuring the ghost of my hard-ass high school gym teacher.

"He bullied me because he knew I wasn't athletic," I say, feeling sick at the thought.

"What a miserable sonofabitch," Dad says. "I remember you'd come home crying because he'd make you run extra laps or drop and give him twenty for no good reason."

"Dizzy Bizzy. That's what he called me," I say. A wave of childhood trauma shudders through me. My dad ropes his arm around me.

"We should've sued the school," he jokes.

We watch the kids huddle and high-five one another on the field and I'm sick to my stomach. "I need some dad advice, Dad," I say in all sincerity.

"You'll be fine." He clasps his arm in mine. "I had five daughters. You think I knew anything about little girl stuff? It wasn't like I could teach them about cigars and good red wine."

I take this in. "Why not?" I wonder. "Now they all love cigars and good red wine."

"Good point," he says with a snort laugh.

My dad was so good at everything he did. From the designer rug warehouse he owned in Chicago where he poured his heart and soul, to wooing my mom with nights at the theater, to making all of us kids feel extra loved. It didn't occur to me he was lacking in any way.

"Maybe there's a night class where I can study soccer," I joke.

"Watch a YouTube tutorial on how to yell at your kid's little league game," my dad riffs back.

"Siri, how do you tackle a free throw on third base?" I say as we both howl with laughter.

But as the refs whistle and the parents yell, it all still nags at me. I never understood the rules of most sports and faked my way through playing them in school. I'm a former happy-go-lucky theater kid.

"Maybe our future kid will want to take up musicals about sports rather than actual sports," I say.

"*Damn Yankees*, anyone?" Dad jokes. We both laugh as it hits me how my dad always makes me feel safe and secure.

After the kids' activities portion of the morning, it's time for some grown-up fun.

"We could have lunch downtown then hop into a museum?" I suggest. This is completely unplanned but, just like me, my family loves a poorly thought-out, sporadic idea that would most likely revolve around food.

Wyatt and I sit in the back of Zia's SUV. After about twenty-five minutes of singing show tunes with the kids, Wyatt turns to me.

"Wait—downtown means the city?" he quietly asks as Chicago's cityscape comes into focus with the Willis Tower and John Hancock rearing their heads in the distance.

I realize he forgot what *downtown* means.

"Yes, 'downtown' is what people in the suburbs call Chicago," I remind him.

"I was thinking it meant downtown Arlington Heights," he admits. It usually confuses anyone who's not from here.

We park in a garage in the Loop and walk to the museum.

Passing the beautiful Millennium Park, I find myself trailing my family, pairing up with Dad again. He clasps his arm in mine, always in a loving gesture, *molto Italiano*. This time though, I feel there's more than just a display of pure love.

He needs me physically. His reactions are slower than the last time I saw him, and he's having slight trouble keeping up with the fast-moving group. I look at our shoes as we walk. My dad always in those stylish loafers.

"All good, Dad?" I ask, open to him interpreting this any way he'd like.

"I'm fine. How are you feeling, Bizzy boy?" he asks me.

"I'm good!" I say too brightly. It's even windier downtown so I knot the scarf my mom told me to bring like his. Now we're identically dapper.

"Don't bullshit a bullshitter." He grins dryly; the lines surrounding his festive eyes make themselves known.

"*Whaaaat?*" I raise my eyebrows in mock surprise. "Why would you say that?"

"Your mom and I stopped sleeping eight years ago. Now we just stay up all night, playing stupid word puzzles on our computers. We heard everything," Dad says.

I tilt my head toward him. "Everything meaning . . . ?" I ask, continuing to feign ignorance.

"Last night. The job, the baby, your guy. We heard it all."

I pause.

I glance up ahead to make sure Wyatt isn't within earshot. He's three sisters deep, intently listening and laughing as Zia tells another one of her hilarious stories. She has Wyatt laughing so hard, he has to wipe away tears.

I turn back to our shoes. "We're both stressed about the baby coming. It's been a lot to plan for the last couple years."

"You know how much planning your mom and I did with you guys? Zilch. We did it and out you all came. One of you was an oopsie baby. I won't say who."

"Dad, we all know it's Zia. Anyway, you're lucky. We had to test our sperm. Then we had to search for an egg donor. Then have our egg donor medically cleared. Then we had to find a surrogate and have *her* cleared. Medically and legally. And this was all before we even could *think* about transferring our embryo . . ." I could go on.

"I don't understand any of it but I feel for ya, kiddo." He inhales deeply. He seems unsure if he should ask this next part. "But you're serious, right?"

I turn to him. "What do you mean? Am I serious about what?"

Dad sighs and stops walking.

He looks me in the eyes.

We stand there, in front of the Art Institute, between the two giant cement lions adorning the entrance, those larger-than-life icons of my childhood. We stare at each other until the entire family detaches from us, heading inside the museum. My sisters look back at us.

"We'll meet you in there," Dad shoos them off. Wyatt glances at us but continues listening to Zia's story.

With our family inside, Dad looks at me and holds my shoulders, like I'm a life preserver in open water. "What I mean, Massimo, is are you serious about having this baby?"

"Of course I am," I say to him unblinking.

"That wasn't a question for you to answer, Massi. Let me finish," he says, looking into my soul. "I know you. I was the same as you back when I was your age. Wild. Carefree. Always looking for a party. Only caring about yourself."

"That's not entirely—"

"You need fun to feel alive, to feel joy and stay happy all the time. I understand. But you know what's going to bring you the most joy, the most fun, the most happy? It's not an out-till-four-a.m. party-of-the-century artificial high. It's a stroll around the park with your baby. It's seeing him smile for the first time. Watching him laugh. Hearing the baby say your name, watching him grow."

"Or her," I add. "Or they."

"Or five hers," he adds. We both laugh.

"Whatever emptiness you're feeling right now won't be there. I promise. And before you know it, she'll be a teenager off to college and you'll be a crying mess."

Dad lets all this hang in the air. He tightens my scarf and wipes off imaginary lint. Tears in his eyes. "I know you're scared. But stop doubting yourself," he tells me.

I swallow. He hit the nail on the head. I can't bring myself to tell him just how much doubt I've been having. My dad. A tough act to follow.

"I know I'm biased but you're one of the most beautiful, fun-loving, nurturing souls I've ever met in my life," my dad says. "You have what it takes to be the greatest dad. You've got the stuff. You've got more than I ever did when I was your age, that's for sure. I believe in you. We all believe in you. Now's the time you have to believe in yourself."

My dad's faith in me has given me a much-needed jolt of confidence as we turn and walk up the steps into the museum, arm in arm.

# 23

## GIO

### WYATT

**I**T'S ENDLESSLY FASCINATING TO me just how much Biz's family loves spending time together. Biz and his dad splitting off from the group to have their own little one-on-one makes me a little envious. It doesn't even matter what they're talking about. I had zero quality "Dad Time" growing up, let alone any words of wisdom Gio is probably generously giving his son.

Even seeing Gio and Sylvia together all the time—glued at the hip, never afraid to show public affection toward one another—it's both adorable and a foreign concept to me. Biz's mom has a partner to hang around with twenty-four seven. My mom never had that.

I hope Biz appreciates his luck of the family draw.

Biz and Gio finally join us, and the family sustains quiet reverence as we tour the Art Institute together, lingering in front of Hopper's moody and existential *Nighthawks*, Monet's calming *Water Lilies* and everyone's favorite, *A Sunday on La Grande Jatte*.

I direct and take a picture of Biz, Zia and Daniella perfectly imitating Ferris Bueller and friends, standing in the modern wing with their arms crossed, examining works of art.

Devouring deep-dish pizzas later at Gino's East, it's another Petterelli feast. Gio enthusiastically serves slices to everyone as if he made the pies himself. We eat spicy pepperoni and sausage, green peppers and mushrooms. A couple husbands scarf down Italian beefs. Glasses of cabernet flow.

Biz and I barely speak or have eye contact. There's almost zero interaction except for once passing the red pepper flakes.

There's too much chatter and commotion with everyone trying to talk over one another anyway. Conversations start, get interrupted, detoured by tangents and obstructed by random thoughts. Almost no one finishes a complete sentence. It's overwhelming but fun. Even if issues between Biz and me aren't resolved, I can still enjoy his family and not take anything out on them.

Back in the suburbs, it's getting dark as the nieces and nephews hug and say goodbye to us in the driveway before their little bodies struggle to climb into their parents' SUVs.

Like a wedding or funeral procession, in true Petterelli tradition, the sisters and husbands line up to say goodbye, double kissing each cheek. This affection is something I'm definitely not used to. I wonder if Biz will teach our child how to kiss hello and goodbye like a European.

The sisters let the waterworks flow, crying over their baby brother and me, missing us already, demanding photos of our baby immediately out of the womb.

"Thirty-five more days! Thirty-five more days!" they chant as they disappear one by one.

Dinner later is leftover pizza that Biz and I share with his parents at the kitchen table. The house feels too quiet now. No more talking over each other, no uncontrollable laughter. Just the four of us chewing and swallowing. The next couple weeks are on everyone's mind.

"Next time we see you, you'll be fathers," Sylvia says with a mouthful, picking up a stray pepperoni from her plate and tossing it into her mouth. An echo of what my mom said.

*Maybe our families aren't so different after all*, I think.

"I still can't believe it. The kid's gonna have a kid," Gio says with a big smile, tears forming in his eyes. "Which sperm is he gonna come from?"

"Dad!" Biz says, sitting back in his chair, wanting to shut down the question.

"Gio!" Sylvia says practically at the same time. "You shouldn't ask that!"

"Why not? It's a legitimate question," Gio doubles down.

Sylvia shakes her head and chomps down on her perfectly burnt crust.

Biz's eyes roll their eyes. He doesn't want to go there and neither do I. We can agree on that.

"I told you, we won't know," Biz explains, probably for the hundredth time.

"If he has your Roman schnoz we'll know," Gio says.

I can see Gio doesn't want to let this go, so I try a more direct approach. "We decided to have a dual sperm source, so potentially, the child could come from either of us. But we don't want to dwell on it. We're a family no matter what happens. When the kid is old enough, and if they're curious, they can meet their egg donor."

"The mom?" Gio asks, puzzled.

Sylvia's jaw drops. She's not on board with her husband's line of questioning.

"I've told them all this," Biz says to me, exasperated.

"We opted for an open egg donor versus an anonymous one in case the kids want to meet her," I explain, hoping this will satisfy Gio.

"But it's *like* she's their mom, right?" Gio asks, still grasping to wrap his head around the concept.

There it is. I love Gio but I can tell he's never going to one hundred percent understand this modern feat of technology; certainly not two dudes having a kid together without a mom. He's a product of an older generation. He's okay with it all—ecstatic is more like it—for his son and his son's life partner to have their own kid with the help of science. But neither of us have ever expected Gio, or even my mom for that matter, to fully grasp every detail.

"It's not their mom. Our child will have two dads. End of story," Biz explains in the plainest of terms, officially done with this conversation.

"I get that. Yeah, I understand." Gio tells himself this more than us, clearly still trying to understand. "But I'm just realizing that my grandkid won't have a mom. Not saying that's good or bad. Just hadn't thought about it."

"Well, now you have," Biz says, getting annoyed and defensive with his parents in a way I haven't seen.

"Either way, I know you two will be the best dads on the planet. I can feel it," Gio adds. He wants us to know we have his full support. He picks up the last slice of pizza, and in the most casual of ways, says, "Okay if I have the last piece? Could be my last one for a while."

A confused look forms on Biz's face. I try to play it cool even though I fill with dread.

"Gio, my god, don't say things like that," Sylvia says with a sigh, picking up our plates and carrying them to the sink. "They still don't know."

"Know . . . what?" Biz asks, tensing up, bracing for the unknown.

"Should we tell 'em?" Gio asks Sylvia, clearly wanting to tell us.

"Cat's outta the bag," she says.

Gio munches on his slice.

"Tell us what, Dad?" Biz almost grows upset.

"Don't worry. It's treatable," Gio says, skipping over the headline as if we know what he's talking about. But I can guess.

"Dad, what are you talking about? What's treatable?" Biz leans in, full of fear.

"It got me. The goddamned C word. Can you believe it?"

Biz has no words. I can see his dad's entire life flash before his eyes. "Like *cancer*?!"

"Oh, don't say that *word*! Basta!" Sylvia says, stacking the dishwasher in defiant anger.

"What kind? How bad is it?" Biz asks.

"The good kind," Gio says, wiping grease off his mouth.

"The good kind? It's not like an avocado and the good kind of fat, Dad. There is no good kind," Biz says.

"He means it's stage one. It's in his stomach. It could be worse," Sylvia explains.

"They're gonna laser beam it out. How cool is that?" Gio says, trying to downplay it.

"Do the girls know? Why didn't you tell me before?" Biz asks.

"We just found out the other day. We told all your sisters right before you got here."

"How the hell did they all keep that secret?" Biz is in shock. Like me with my mom, Biz assumes his dad will magically live forever. Parents are immortal until they're not.

With that, Biz erupts into tears. Gio stands behind him and puts his hands on his shoulders to console him. Sylvia sits next to him with both of her hands grasping his face.

"Don't worry. The doctor is great and said he'll be okay," Sylvia says.

"You gotta face the facts that your old papa is getting even older, kiddo," Gio says.

They hold their son as he sniffs and wipes his tears, like Biz is a kid again, only this time he's an adult, looking directly at his parents' mortality for the first time.

I want to grab Biz and hold him and tell him everything will be okay.

Biz grabs his dad by the waist and buries his head, sniffling into his cashmere sweater.

I look down at the vintage salt and pepper shakers on their kitchen table, feeling heartbroken, knowing we'll always remember this exact time and place.

"You're gettin' snot on my shirt," Gio says to Biz as we all laugh through our tears.

# 24

## YOU NEVER FORGET
## HOW TO DODGE A BIKE

**BIZ**

IN THE BLINK OF one night, my entire world view of Mom and Dad changed.

We saw it with Wyatt's mom too.

I can't stop myself from crying in the driveway the next morning as we say our farewells to my parents.

I know my dad's surgery won't be easy; my mom will have an equally hard time taking care of him while worrying that nothing bad is going to happen to her.

"I hope I live to meet my grandkid," my dad jokes.

I shoot him a deadpan stare, not ready for any gallows humor but secretly thinking his delivery is kind of funny. Wyatt stays focused on loading up our car.

"Enough, Gio!" my mom says. She's annoyed but also can't help but laugh as she loops her arm through my dad's.

"Four more weeks!" I playfully remind them.

We hug and kiss and squeeze and hug more, profusely thanking each other for all the fun.

Nothing but love between us.

Our furry daughter reluctantly jumps into the car with us and we pull out of the driveway.

My parents stand in front of their garage, waving, uncertain of their own future but feeling fortunate they'll be around to meet their new grandkid.

I wave and watch them become smaller in the rearview mirror until we can't see each other anymore.

Virginia Woolf needs gas so I drive us to my local childhood gas station . . . *which is now a Dunkin' Donuts?* "When did that happen?" I ask.

"I was hoping you wanted to fill us up with a dozen glazed donuts," Wyatt says.

"I think we've eaten enough for the next six months," I remind him.

We drive to the next nearest gas station, where I remember fueling up my mom's car as the sun came up after a night out with friends hitting the gay bars in Chicago while I was home from college.

I pump the car full of unleaded and exhale, my dad's health now weighing on top of everything else.

Back in the car, I take the wheel again. "Colorado, here we come."

"We should get to our hotel in Nebraska in just under seven hours," Wyatt says. Thankfully we'd agreed to split the drive in half and stay overnight somewhere.

"Music?" Wyatt asks as GPS lady tells us to zig through back roads I don't recognize.

I eye Wyatt. "Don't you want to talk about what's going on? With your dad? With my dad? With us? With anything?"

Before he can answer, we hear our fur baby in the back seat chewing on something and I glance behind us. I squint.

Matilda gnaws on a brand-new rawhide bone that's as thick as her head.

"Did you give her that?" I ask.

"No, did you?" Wyatt asks.

"Oh, crap. My mom must've tossed that in right before we left."

"Always spoiled by Grandma." Wyatt grins, watching how much Matilda loves it. "I guess we should take it away before it makes her throw up?"

Neither of us move.

We both have no intention of taking something away she loves this much.

"You know what. Just let her have it." Wyatt relaxes on our rule of never feeding Matilda during a drive.

"Should we check on Flora?" I suggest.

"Good idea. I think she had her doctor's appointment yesterday."

Wyatt props up his phone and dials Flora.

"How are the two pre-daddies?" she answers through speakerphone, sounding in a bright mood.

Personally, I'm exhausted, anxious, feeling out of shape, dreading the long drive, worried I'm going to be the world's worst dad and now the news about my own dad is making me feel like life is about to extinguish my last nerve.

"We're great!" I blurt out.

"Where are you now?" Flora wonders.

"We're just heading out of my parents' house and trying to

find the highway," I say, suddenly not sure of my bearings. We pass a new subdivision I've never seen before, but I'm too side-tracked with our conversation to course correct.

"I thought you were going to Michigan?" Flora is still on our original itinerary, not yet aware of our impromptu detours.

"Actually, no. Biz wanted to stop and see his family even though we were scheduled to go to Saugatuck. We're heading west now, a little behind schedule," Wyatt chimes in, irritated that I don't know where I'm going.

"That's because Wyatt wanted to stop at his mom's before this, even though we were supposed to go to P-town, but we didn't and we'll probably never go there again," I counter, tinted with a little bitterness.

*Where are we?*

"It's not that I *wanted* to stay at my mom's. Are you forgetting my brother got into an accident so we went there to support my mom?" Wyatt asks.

"I'm just telling Flora we went to your family's house and then we went to my family's house," I manage.

"Maybe tell Flora you're being passive-aggressive and making it seem like it's my fault our plans changed. Like I did it all on purpose to hurt you or something," Wyatt lets out.

"That's not at all what I'm saying to Flora—"

"Um . . . guys?" Flora thankfully slaps us both through the phone.

"Sorry. We just have road trip fatigue," I try and paper over our real issues.

Wyatt breaks the silence. "How was the doctor?"

"Actually . . ." Flora says softly.

We quickly eye each other, detecting concern in her voice. We shove our bickering aside and listen.

"What's wrong?" I ask, admittedly a bit too dramatic.

I do a double take as we pass a small cemetery that doesn't look at all familiar. I am officially lost in my hometown.

*Are we even still in my hometown?* I wonder. There are so many new stores, houses and repaving of the streets that nothing looks familiar. I'm so used to only going home during the holidays when it's covered in a blanket of snow with holiday lights on every house. Seeing it in the summer, now with everything green and in bloom, is making me disoriented.

Flora sighs, never a good sign. "I met with her again yesterday."

Wyatt and I share another look with each other.

"Okay," Wyatt says delicately.

My pulse quickens. I try to swallow my anxiety.

She continues. "She said my stomach is still measuring small at this stage. The baby's abdomen is tinier than it should be. So she's sending me to a high-risk doctor to get a level-two ultrasound. The baby hasn't gotten any bigger in the last few weeks. So there's talk of inducing me early."

"How early?" we both say in unison.

Wyatt mutes us. "Watch out for that dude on a bike," he says to me, always the backseat driver, then unmutes us.

"Just a couple days before the due date," Flora reassures us.

I screech to a halt at a red light, narrowly avoiding the cyclist's back tire. The cyclist is decked out in spandex everything, speeding through the crosswalk as he flips us off.

"Jesus," Wyatt says, alarmed by the near collision. He glares at me and puts on a cheery voice for Flora. "I mean—that's perfect because we'll be there a couple weeks before the due date."

"Wonderful. My appointment's tomorrow and we should know more then."

"I don't understand. If the baby is smaller, why wouldn't they leave them in longer to like . . . bake more?" I ask, still stuck on the issue.

"We're having a baby. Not a batch of chocolate chip cookies," Wyatt says.

Even after all our research, we never stop learning about pregnancy.

The light changes to green and the cyclist stands across the street, bike by his side, staring us down as we drive past him.

"It's because the baby will get more nutrients outside of the womb. The doctor keeps reassuring me the baby's fine, so don't panic, guys."

"We're not panicking," I say, panicked. The menacing cyclist isn't helping.

Wyatt looks behind us. The cyclist starts riding toward us at full speed, eventually catching up to us. "Biz, I think you should speed up. This guy's a lunatic and he wants revenge."

"What?" Flora asks, confused and thinking Wyatt is talking to her.

How is Wyatt always three steps ahead of me when *I'm the one* driving?

I check my rearview mirror. Sure enough, the cyclist is gaining speed.

He's becoming larger and larger in my mirror, like an angry Hulk in biker shorts.

"What's he gonna do, rear-end us with his ten-speed?" I ask.

In one quick second, the cyclist vanishes. We breathe.

I think we've lost the guy until he pops up on Wyatt's side, pedaling as fast as I'm driving.

The cyclist has a look of murder in his eyes, gritted teeth, practically foaming at the mouth as he grasps Wyatt's door.

"Guys?" Flora asks, sensing we're, uh, multitasking.

"Can we call you right back, Flora? We're kind of in a pickle right now," Wyatt says as calmly as possible, careful not to distress anyone.

*Pickle?* I mouth to Wyatt.

"You guys focus on driving," Flora says. "I'll keep you posted after the doctor," she adds.

"Sounds perfect, Flora. Thanks for the update," Wyatt squeaks out.

We must not have hung up yet because she hears Wyatt tell me to take a sharp left and try to lose this creep. "Wait—is everything okay?!" Flora, with her perfect maternal instincts, knows we're definitely not acting normal.

"Everything's fine. We're just being chased by a psycho killer on a bicycle," I offer.

"Biz!" Wyatt tries to hush me.

"*What?!*" Flora is genuinely concerned. "Do you need me to call 9-1-1 or something?"

"You have bigger issues to deal with than us being murdered," I say.

Wyatt throws up his hands in defeat at my bluntness. "Just keep us posted on what the doctor says," he says calmly.

"I will, of course. Drive safely, guys."

Wyatt ends the call. He stabs it over and over to make sure we've hung up so he can properly freak out. "Do you know how to get us on the interstate?!"

"I'm eighty-three percent sure I can cut through here to get to the highway. Fine, forty-three percent sure." I have no clue where we are.

Wyatt frantically tries opening his map app. "My reception's not great."

I hook a left, heading into an unfamiliar subdivision and the cyclist stays on us. We drive through a quiet residential area with 1970s ranch houses and handwritten signs warning "Drive Like Your Children Live Here!"

It's a maze we can't escape.

"We're Shelley Duvall and this asshole's Jack Nicholson with an axe," Wyatt says, whipping his head in every direction. The cyclist barrels after us.

I take a right, then a left.

We're forced to slow down for a stop sign, not wanting to piss off any residents, or worse, scare a kid. We turn to see the cyclist right next to my window.

Again, his eyes are terrifying.

We both gasp and I hit the gas.

"I'll kill you!" the cyclist spits at us.

I turn right. Then left. He's out of sight. For now. But we still can't find our way out of the subdivision maze.

"We don't have eyes on him," Wyatt pants. "Aren't you *from* here? I thought you knew where you were going!"

"I know exactly where we are." I absolutely do not know where we are.

I pull up to a stop sign. Three kids of various sizes on scooters cross.

Before we know it, our windshield is sprayed with some kind of red liquid.

In an epic anticlimactic twist, we turn to see the not-at-all-intimidating cyclist next to us, emptying the contents of his red sports drink all over our car.

"Is that . . . *strawberry Gatorade*?" Wyatt asks.

The cyclist has a little bit of a pot belly with one of his bare-skinned rolls protruding through his spandex top.

"Cool, cool. Are you happy now?" I say with renewed confidence, realizing we outnumber this guy.

Our orange Virginia Woolf is covered in red liquid as the light turns green.

"Thanks for the fruit punch!" Wyatt says.

"Bike safely!" I call out.

We can't help but laugh as we finally escape the subdivision and gun it onto the highway.

Both of us look back one last time to see if the cyclist is behind us.

Just to make sure.

# 25

## A VERY SPECIAL EPISODE

**WYATT**

DRIVING FROM ILLINOIS THROUGH Iowa into Nebraska with its miles of flat, uninterrupted terrain will give us some much-needed peace after the Bicycle Incident. The *Simpsons*-blue skies spotted with misshaped marshmallow clouds give us a calming energy that we happily invite. But like the smooshed bugs on the car's grill and windshield, our relationship angst still needs a good wash.

As Biz drives, I close my eyes for a second, feeling a little spent.

"Should we call Flora back?" Biz asks.

I check our phones to see if there are any messages. "Let's give her some space. She'll update us after the doctor."

"I just hope everything's okay."

"It will be," I say, unsure. "Let's stay positive. Flora's doctor is the best."

Biz nods in agreement as we try to push forward.

"Do you want to talk about anything?" Biz asks.

"Like what?"

"Baseball statistics," he jokes. "What do you think?"

"I'm happy just staying quiet for a while." I shut my eyes
meditatively. I know this isn't the answer Biz wants to hear but
a car nap is calling my name right now, which happens so rarely,
I feel like I should give in to it.

"Fine with me," Biz says a few seconds later, waking me up
this time. "I can totally do quiet . . ." He shifts in his seat. "Yep,
I love it . . . Just pure unadulterated silence . . . No talking
whatsoever . . . Zero sound . . . You can hear a pin drop over
here . . . All quiet on the Western Front. Or should I say *Mid-*
western Front? . . . Quiet as a snowflake landing on a mouse,
sitting on a lamb in a soundproof—"

I open one eye and point it at him. "Biz?"

"Sorry," Biz whispers. A minute later: "Not even some music? Maybe some yacht rock? Christopher Cross? *Saaaailiiing . . .*
*Takes me awaaaay . . .*"

"Seriously? I just need quiet right now." I shut my eyes again
and it seems like Biz finally gets the memo. I desperately want
to fall asleep, but I'm not like Biz, who could sleep anywhere,
slumped over, mouth open and probably snoring with just the
perfect amount of drool. He's like a "funny" stock photo of
someone sleeping.

My body shifts into a dozen positions. It's impossible to get
comfortable inside this cramped car.

I'm also slightly concerned that Biz might even fall asleep at
the wheel. I pop my eyes open every once in a while, making
sure he's still awake. I'm impressed he's not multitasking with
his phone anymore, keeping both hands on the wheel when I'm
not looking.

And now I can't get that Christopher Cross song out of my head.

We drive. And drive. Then we keep driving after that. I doze in and out of sleep. When I'm awake, I anguish over how I'm going to address my father's letters with my mom. And what does my brother know?

In between my tiny naps, we decide to stop at a gas station car wash to clean up the Gatorade bomb that's still bright red and probably sticky all over the hood of Virginia Woolf.

Slowly exiting the car wash dryer, we joke that we're about to see the cyclist standing there, lying in wait to make good on his promise of murdering us. Luckily, he's gone forever.

Conveniently, Matilda throws up the second after we leave the car wash.

Halfway through Nebraska, I spot a billboard for Burger King advertising something called chicken fries. They look incredible. Maybe it's the way they're breaded and deep-fried, mozzarella sticks–esque. Or maybe it's the appealing packaging of the french fry container with a cute face of a cartoon chicken on it. Either way, my whole world is suddenly about them.

"Can we pull over?" I ask Biz, who's still driving. "I have to go to the bathroom." I actually do have to go to the bathroom, but I also want those chicken fries, and I don't want Biz judging me for wanting fast food again.

He looks at me suspiciously. He knows if I had my way while driving long distance, we would never stop. I'd prefer it if we drive straight across the country without ever eating, drinking, sleeping or peeing. It's like a commercial production. I just want to power through.

"You need to wear a diaper," Biz jokes, imitating my joke to him whenever he wants to pull over.

This particular Burger King is a straight shot off the exit ramp. We don't want to disturb a napping, snoring Matilda in her cozy bed in the back seat, so we leave our angel undisturbed and head inside.

Walking toward the cashiers, I notice the only people inside the restaurant are elderly folks.

"Retirement community?" I ask Biz, trying to guess where the group is from.

Biz narrows his eyes and tries to guess. "Book club," he says.

"I'm changing my guess. They're an Alcoholics Anonymous group," I say.

"Maybe a sober book club from a retirement community," Biz says as we both laugh.

Biz looks up at the menu. "Ugh. *Cheetos* chicken fries? All this food looks like it would make you constipated."

"Today's the day I'm going to make you understand the pleasures of fast food," I confidently declare.

We order our food—chicken fries and Whoppers—and take our trays outside, sidling up to a picnic table in the back. We check on Matilda, who's still fast asleep in the car.

"Aren't they good?" I say to Biz, as we chomp into our chicken fries. After several bites, I see Biz's mind churning, trying to figure out his take on what he's eating.

"Don't analyze it. Just enjoy it," I tell him.

"My job is literally to analyze food," Biz says. "Was." Biz goes quiet for a moment, sinking his teeth into his Whopper. I can't tell if he thinks it tastes good or not but he's going back in for more.

I turn up an I-toldja grin.

It doesn't seem like Biz is focused on the food. He looks up from his burger. "Remember that one very special episode of *Back in the Saddle* I did . . . ?" Biz starts, fondly remembering his teenage television years. "Where Kaylynn reveals to the gang that she's dyslexic?"

"I can't say I'm super familiar with that one," I admit, wondering where this is going.

"Well, that storyline got press at the time. They called it groundbreaking. But it was the same episode where Cole, the older owner of the ranch, passes away. The actor had a three-episode arc," Biz continues.

"I didn't realize Disney shows had episode arcs," I say, finishing my chicken fries.

"Anyway, I found out later the head writer on the show was dealing with the death of his own dad so he worked through it by writing it into the show. I just remember getting that script and we all sat around reading it out loud for the first time at the table read. When we reached the end where we're all talking about Cole's death, I burst into tears," Biz says, reliving the emotion from that day.

I hear the pain in his voice. "Were you thinking of your dad?" I ask.

"It brought up the fear of my dad passing away. Since he was older, losing him was something I thought about a lot growing up. He wasn't going to live as long as my friends' dads. Plus, that actor looked like the cowboy version of my dad; it was eerie. And when they brought him in just to kill him off, it was slightly traumatic for me," Biz says, contemplating another bite of his Whopper.

"That's so hard," I say, feeling bad for the kid in Biz. "You were so young."

"There was even a funeral scene," Biz goes on.

"Wasn't this a sitcom for tweens?" I ask. I know the answer but I'm just making sure.

"It was. We shot the funeral and scattered his ashes on the ranch," Biz says.

"Kinda heavy," I say.

"I know. When we wrapped though, I cried again. The whole cast did. I had to call my dad just to make sure he was okay, and that my mom was fine, and I made them promise me that nothing bad would happen to them while I was away."

"Oh, Biz," I say, heartbroken.

"This news of my dad's health I've sort of been waiting for my whole life. It's just a thing I'd always prepared myself for and now that it's here . . . You just can't be prepared for something like this, ya know?" Biz looks up from his food at me, wanting answers.

"I know it's not what you want to hear but you just have to treasure every moment with your dad while he's still here. You're lucky. I was never able to do that with my father. You still have time," I say. The absence of my dad has given me a lifetime of perspective.

"You're right," Biz says, thinking it through.

"Say everything you want to say to him now. Talk to him on the phone every day. Reply to his dumb funny emails and jokey puns that he texts you. I know you do that anyway but appreciate him every day. Be present for him. Have your parents stay with us when the baby's born. We'll go to Chicago too so they can see their baby's baby," I suggest.

This makes Biz smile.

"Your dad gave you the best blueprint for parenthood you can ever have. I didn't get one. I have to figure out how to write my own version of being a father."

"Thank you for that," Biz says appreciatively. "It's amazing you grew up without a father and yet you have all this wisdom about being a parent."

"You can't know what you're missing until it's gone," I say, letting Biz interpret this about his father, about us, about all of it.

Biz eats his chicken fries, savoring them, really enjoying the taste now.

"And don't give me a hard time about fast-food places anymore," I add. "I can tell you love those fries."

Biz throws an entire chicken fry into his mouth and chews. "They're okay," he feigns indifference.

I slow clap, feeling proud that he can do what he puts his mind to. Both with his dad and the chicken fries.

We finish our food, immediately feeling sick to our stomachs from all the grease, and mosey our way back to the car only to discover something extremely shocking and terrible.

Matilda is missing.

# 26

## MATILDA: THE BOOK: THE MOVIE: THE MUSICAL: THE MOVIE AGAIN: THE DOG

### BIZ

**T**HIS IS NOT GOOD. This is bone-crushingly bad.

We ping-pong back and forth about who left which window open and why.

"We need to put our heads together and find our dog," Wyatt says calmly.

"You're right," I say, taking a deep breath. "You check White Castle. I'll check Arby's." We take off in opposite directions.

I run inside Arby's, which is practically empty except for a teenage couple with piercings wildly making out in a corner booth. I ask the too-cool assistant manager behind the counter if he's spotted a dog anywhere, but he blankly shakes his head no.

I dart to the gas station, a sprawling mecca made up of dozens of gas pumps with a parade of cars and trucks coming and going. It's anchored by a strip mall–like building that houses a convenience store the size of a supermarket.

I run in circles, sweating, in and out of the pumps, looking in every direction, realizing Matilda could be anywhere at this point.

"MATILDA!" I yell, panicked.

A woman trucker overhears me and jumps out of her rig with a look of concern, an upstanding citizen who wants to help.

"Y'all lose your wife or kid?" she asks.

"Our dog is missing," I blurt out, starting to hyperventilate over the words I just said.

"You try whistling?" The trucker sticks a bunch of fingers in her mouth and unleashes the loudest, most impressive whistle imaginable, screaming, "Ma-TIL-da!"

The two of us look around. Nothing.

"Not sure if she's ever responded to whistling before."

"Worth a shot." The trucker whistles again, somehow louder this time. Instead of Matilda, Wyatt sprints toward us. "You find her?" he asks, out of breath.

"No. Nothing at White Castle?" I ask, desperate.

Wyatt shakes his head and we lock eyes. We both want to cry. I grab Wyatt by the shoulders and pull him into a comforting embrace.

"I'm sorry," I say, our cheeks smushed into each other.

"Why are you sorry? I'm sorry," Wyatt says. "This whole trip has been one huge thing after another."

"I know. I'm just so distracted by everything," I say. "This is my fault."

"It's no one's fault. Let's just try to find our girl," Wyatt says as we take off running together.

When Matilda first came into our lives, we were in P-town

for the annual Spooky Bear Halloween weekend, between the summer crush of people and the dead of winter.

I remember the streets were covered in red, orange and brown leaves and the autumn air was almost supernatural. The weekend's events usually included dancing, haunted houses, impromptu after-parties, all culminating in a costume ball.

The town was swarming with people in costume.

Sexy superheroes. Sexy cartoon characters. Sexy blue-collar workers. Sexy biblical characters. Or just a sexy person.

We shared a house in the West End with four friends, which was owned by two queer women who were both retired bankers turned sculptors.

There was the main house where me, Wyatt and our friends stayed and the smaller carriage house, where Shannon and Katya would sit on their porch and drink IPAs, laughing at six grown men running around the house, getting dressed up for Halloween.

After a night of carousing at various venues, all of us dressed as sexy Teenage Mutant Ninja Turtles, we headed to Spiritus Pizza, where the P-town ritual of buying a slice of pizza after a night of boozing was still in autumnal full force.

We sat on the curb, our green face paint fading.

"Ninja Turtles eating pizza is a little on the nose," Wyatt shrewdly said. We all laughed.

After chatting up four sexy UPS men, a Lucille Ball, a ZZ Top with a ZZ Bottom and a zombie Barbra Streisand, we eventually called it a night. It was a beautiful, starry sky and the moon was in the shape of a perfectly eerie crescent.

Halfway down Commercial Street, it was breathtakingly quiet. We lost our friends and Wyatt stopped me so we could appreciate the silence. Then he slapped me on the ass and yelled

"Cowabunga!" the famous Ninja Turtles catchphrase, as we ran full speed down the empty street, free and exuberant.

We stopped, out of breath, in front of Captain Jack's, a small pier made up of a dozen colorful cabins, all shapes and sizes, cobbled together to form a unique lodge.

The moon hung over the small beach to the right of the wharf. Wyatt's face brilliantly lit.

"How are you so handsome?" Wyatt asked me.

"Even dressed like a turtle?" I wondered.

We laughed and Wyatt grabbed my hand as we tiptoed down the side of Captain Jack's, under the dock and all its sleeping guests. We leaned on a pole as our bodies pressed up against each other, our mouths fusing together. We fell onto the sand, tearing off each other's costumes, kissing, moving rhythmically, hoping no one would see us.

Or who cares if anyone did see us. That's P-town!

"I have green paint in my mouth," Wyatt said in between love bites.

"Never knew I could be so horny for a turtle."

Our shirtless bodies tangled up in each other. Our hearts pounded in unison. Our combined warmth cut through the pre-November chill. We made each other feel more spectacularly alive than ever before.

When we arrived back at our house, we were surprised to see Shannon and Katya still up, sitting on the porch of their cottage. They'd moved on to sipping whisky.

Their dog, Pancake, a beautiful Airedale terrier, had just given birth to a litter of eight puppies of various brown and black markings a month before. The puppies were all by their mother's side, sleeping and acting adorable.

"The pups started wobbling around tonight," Shannon said.

"They look like Bambi on the *Titanic*," Katya joked.

"You want one?" Shannon asked us. We laughed at how casual she sounded but she was dead serious.

As if to say, "pick me," one of the tinier ones broke off from the pack, waddled up to me and Wyatt, nipping at our green Birkenstocks. She yawned and scurried back to her cuddle puddle.

Everyone let out an "awww" at the same time.

When Wyatt and I went to bed that night, we held each other tight, thinking about our hot encounter under the pier, while staring at the moon through our window.

"What if we brought a puppy back to Brooklyn?" I asked.

"We're so not prepared for a dog, let alone a rambunctious puppy," Wyatt said, of course. "If you really want a souvenir, I'll buy you a Race Point Beach hoodie."

"Come on, it'll be fun. We can be fur daddies. Pawrents! It'll be cute." I immediately became obsessed with bringing a puppy home.

"Are you still thinking about being a real parent? To a human?" Wyatt asked, hopeful.

"I've always wanted to have kids. You know that," I said. Wyatt knew I wanted to recreate my large family. Our mutual goal to have kids was another thing that attracted us. "Maybe a dog is a first step? A trial run for having kids," I suggested.

"Dogs and babies aren't the same," Wyatt said. "It's a lot of responsibility and having a dog in New York is extra hard. No backyard for peeing and pooing. You really want to wake up every morning and take the dog out? Then go out three or four more times a day?"

"We can figure it out." I threw Wyatt a smile that always made him smile back. "I mean, how many times are we going to be presented with a free adorable puppy? Come on. Let's get a dog, then we'll get married and have kids." I smiled again.

"You're irresistible." Wyatt gave me a huge, wet kiss. "Let's sleep on it."

With that, Wyatt turned on his side and pulled me in close behind him as his big spoon.

"How about the name Matilda? Like the musical," I said, holding on to Wyatt, eyes closed, grinning, hopeful.

"It was a book first. Roald Dahl," Wyatt said.

"I know. Then it became a movie in the nineties."

"Then it was a musical."

"And then it became *another* movie. Based on the musical. Based on the book."

"Sleep on it," Wyatt murmured again, spent, fading.

"*Matilda* was the first Broadway show we saw together," I reminded Wyatt.

"Duh. I remember. Now please sleep," Wyatt said and then whispered, "I love you."

"I love you too." We held on to each other, falling asleep, thinking about our future.

The next afternoon, we would never forget the look on Pancake's face when we scooped up the tiny puppy that waddled up to us the night before. The protective mom signaled a worrisome look that was tempered by all the humans around her.

"The boys are gonna take good care of your baby, Pancake," Shannon said as she knelt down and scratched behind Pancake's ears.

Matilda, the book, the movie, the musical, the movie again, was now a puppy.

We had no idea how much attention we were about to receive.

Taking the lovable three-month-old Matilda on walks in the city reminded me of when I was younger, at the height of my television career, when kids and tweens made their parents stop me on the street to snap a pic and bashfully say how much they loved me on the show.

Now people stopped me on the street but they didn't recognize that kid from the Disney show. All they wanted to do was say hi to our cute, clumsy, overly friendly, little dog. I was lucky if they gave the human attached brief eye contact.

Even though Matilda chewed up our gym shoes, gnawed on the legs of our kitchen table and destroyed all our socks, we were and are forever in love.

Back at the convenience store, we're worried out of our minds.

"What do we do? Start putting up flyers? Call the police?!" I ask naively, more desperate.

"Let's check the convenience store again?" Wyatt says, unsure.

An older woman with a spray tan and a side ponytail jogs from the convenience store toward us. She looks like a sixty-year-old, washed-up cheerleader. "You two lose your dogs?"

"Yes!" I almost jump her.

"There are a couple dogs behind the store," she says, out of breath. "I just saw them by the bathroom there." The woman points to the side of the convenience store and takes a hit of her vape pen.

We run as fast as we can.

Behind the store, sure enough, there's Matilda chasing another fluffy, medium-sized dog in circles. The two are fast friends and not going anywhere anytime soon.

Tails wagging. Open-mouthed smiles. It's love at first sniff.

I scoop up Matilda as she licks my face, squirming with excitement over our reunion. She lets out a sharp, gleeful yelp, as if introducing her new friend. Wyatt steps in and we both hold her tight, never wanting to let go.

Wyatt and I look at each other and smile affectionately, trauma bonding and feeling grateful. My relief doesn't last long. My chest tightens, feeling like I'm the one to blame.

We look down at the other dog, peering up at us with forlorn eyes, tail wagging, craving affection. The fluffy ball of fur circles us three, wanting in on our love fest. He has an adorable face and he's mostly beige with some patches of white.

"He looks like a miniature version of the lion in *The Wizard of Oz*," Wyatt says.

"What a cutie. He's like a cross between a Chow Chow and a Husky," I say.

"A Chowsky? Chusky?"

I kneel down and pull the stray dog in close. No collar, no tags, no way of finding his owner. We carry him around the gas station, asking people if they know the dog.

"Didn't you just lose a dog? Now you have an *extra* dog?" the gas station attendant asks.

"He's a stray we found in the back with our dog. Know anyone who's missing a pup?"

"Looks like yours just got a friend," the attendant says. We laugh and head back to our car. It dawns on us that we can't just leave this dog here alone.

"What should we do?" Wyatt asks as I set the dog down and we watch Matilda and him get along famously.

We stare at the dogs playing, then we look at each other. That time in P-town when we first met Matilda flashes in my mind again. We look back down at the dogs.

"They love each other," Wyatt says.

"I guess . . . we have room in the car?" I say.

"Maybe we'll find a shelter to take him to," Wyatt says. "Is this a bad idea?"

Without further discussion, we pack the two dogs in the back and take off.

As we drive, the dogs harmoniously lie together in Matilda's bed, staring out the windows in silence, watching the landscape fly by like two tired little kids.

The dogs let out the same heavy sigh and fall asleep within seconds of each other. It's extra baggage and we'll have to find a home for this little guy once we have our baby.

"What should we call him?" Wyatt asks.

"How about Pancake? In honor of Matilda's mom."

"I love it."

We drive in silence as Matilda and Pancake sleep, tucked into their bed together, each appreciating their new companion.

Wyatt and I squeeze each other's hand with a renewed bond for each other, realizing the fragility of our little family and understanding that it could fall apart at any second.

# 27

## CALRISSIAN COTTAGE

**WYATT**

**O**N THE ROAD AGAIN. No, literally; we're listening to "On the Road Again" by Willie Nelson. It only seems fitting that while we cross Nebraska toward Colorado, one of the first states to legalize marijuana, we should listen to the Prince of Weed sing his heart out.

Temporarily losing our dog in the middle of the country made us emotional wrecks, but finding her unharmed, with a delightful new companion, has emboldened us. Like Biz and I could endure anything together.

We feel in sync for the first time in a while as we happily sing together, *"The life I love is making music with my friends! And I can't wait to get on the road again!"*

"I can't wait to hit the dance floor," Biz says, thinking ahead to our friends' wedding.

"I need a bed," I admit, too exhausted from driving all day to even think about physical activity.

"We're going to party our asses off. I'm gonna get DRUNK."

Biz awkwardly pumps his fist in the air. "I wonder if there's a dance remix to this song."

There it is again. I silently worry that Biz is reverting back to his teenage party years.

I know we're both hoping that we can find a happy medium between fatherhood and not abandoning fun forever but sometimes I feel like Biz is running in the opposite direction of where we're going.

Biz checks Spotify and lists all the "On the Road Again" covers. "Alanis Morrissette did one?" Then I hear an unwanted tune.

"Do you hear . . . a gurgle and a rattle?" I ask.

"Gurgle and rattle. Isn't that a U2 album?" Biz asks, buried in music.

"No, the car. It's making noises. Like a gurgle and a rattle." I grow concerned. I know nothing about cars and Biz knows even less. Matilda knows more about cars than us. One time, a friend of ours was talking about his Lexus and I thought he meant an antidepressant.

Biz looks up from his phone, his eyes scanning back and forth, searching for the sound I hear. Every few seconds it becomes more pronounced.

"There. Hear that?" I ask.

"That time I did, yes," Biz says.

It's probably a good idea to drive in the slow lane, I decide. If there's something wrong with Virginia Woolf, we need easy access to the shoulder of the highway. We drive and listen to the rattling that sounds off every four seconds.

*GrrrrrrrrrTKTKTKTKgrrrrrr.*

After a few minutes, the rattling stops. But maybe the gurgle's still happening?

"There. We fixed it," Biz says, hoping we won't have to eventually fix it for real.

"Teamwork," I say. "Seriously, if it happens again, we should probably pull over and get it checked out."

"We're aligned," Biz says.

After four peanut butter granola bars, a giant bag of Flamin' Hot Cheetos, one stop at a pet store to buy dog food, a new collar and leash for Pancake, and the entire album of *Hamilton* played twice, it's pitch dark.

As much as I want to drive all the way through to Colorado, we follow the plan to check into a motel and start fresh, first thing in the morning.

We spot a Super 8 sign along the highway and I pull off the exit.

Our modest and perfectly fine motel room fits the four of us nicely, and as we get ready for bed, I start to worry about Flora and the baby.

"We should call her to check in," I say.

"Her doctor's appointment is tomorrow," Biz says. "There's not much we can do."

"Yeah, but just to see how she's doing? I know it's late there but she might appreciate us thinking about—"

I turn to see Biz is asleep. The dogs are passed out, comically sprawled over the bed in a pile with Biz. It's time for all of us to sleep as I snuggle in next to them and shut my tired eyes.

- - - - - - - →

EARLY THE NEXT MORNING, WE HIT THE ROAD AND ARRIVE IN EVERGREEN right on schedule. The breathtaking mountain vista is the perfect antidote to yesterday's flat scenery. The looping road on the way to Patrick's house nestles us in high altitude that makes our ears pop.

Biz has taken the bulk of the drive so I text Patrick to let him know we're close. He texts back immediately:

PATRICK

**Welcome to Colorado! The gate code is 9601**

"He just sent us his *gate code*," I say, barely comprehending our friend having a gate.

"His house has a gate?" Biz asks.

"I knew it was a big house but I didn't think it was this big."

We turn into a driveway with an enormously grand double gate.

"Looks like his gate has a gate," Biz jokes.

On one side of the gate is a bronze plaque that reads, "Calrissian Cottage."

"Is that some *Star Wars* reference?" Biz asks.

We playfully roll our eyes at our friend's well-known *Star Wars* fandom. Biz enters the code and the iron doors slowly swing open into a grand driveway.

There's another vibration on my phone and this time it's my mom calling. My stomach nosedives. I haven't spoken to her since we left, and I have a mental white board cluttered with unresolved theories, questions and mysteries surrounding my father.

I swipe to answer and hope I can control my emotions. "Hi, Mom," I say, flatly, making sure she knows I'm not entirely happy with her at the moment.

"Where are you now?" my mom sounds like her usual

energetic self. Then again, she would probably sound like this no matter what news she's calling to share. She always has her game face on.

"We're just arriving at Patrick's house in Colorado." We look ahead and all we see are rows of thick pine trees on either side with no end in sight. "I think."

I stubbornly don't want to say anything more to my mom. My resentment right now is as high as the Rockies. Plus, *she called me*. This is her show. "I'm putting you on speaker, Mom."

"Hi, Bev," Biz chirps. We both wonder if there's an end to this long-ass driveway, which seems more like an airport runway inside a forest.

"Hi, Biz," my mom says with a heavy sigh. "I just . . . I guess I wanted to talk to you about your boxes. And what you found. I see you took some of your father's letters."

I look at Biz solemnly. His mouth drops open, ready for the drama. This is the exact opposite kind of energy we need right before the beginning of a wedding weekend.

There's so much I need to say to her and it's going to have to wait because now Flora's name pops up on my phone.

"Can I call you back, Mom?"

"Honey, there's never a good time to talk about this and we just need to address this once and for all," she says, almost in a scripted way. She's never been this forthcoming about my father.

"I'd love to, Mom, but Flora's calling," I say, hoping she'll remember our priority right now.

"Is everything alright?"

"I don't know. That's why I probably should answer her call. Can I call you back?"

I hang up with my mom and answer Flora as Biz stops the

car at the end of this road/driveway. We can see a giant house peeking through the trees in the distance.

"Hi, Flora," I say into the speakerphone.

"I'm just about to go into the doctor's office," Flora says, sounding nervous.

"Do you want to video conference us in?" I ask, trying anything to make her comfortable.

"I'll be fine. I just wanted to hear your voices, I guess."

"You're gonna be great," I say.

"Why, should we worry?!" Biz almost yells into the phone, way too anxious. I mime turning the drama dial down a notch.

"You got this, Flora. We're with you in spirit," I encourage her again.

"Call us the second you're out," Biz says, in a little more supportive tone.

"I will. Thanks, guys," Flora says.

We hang up. Biz and I look at each other, feeling helpless. There's only so much we can do long-distance.

Our quiet reflection is interrupted by Patrick exiting his house. Strike that: his mansion.

Climbing out of the car, tight hugs all around, we look up and feel dwarfed by the palatial structure. The dogs jump out of the car and chase each other around the ornate fountain in the middle of the driveway, happy to be free. As difficult as it is, I try to focus on the present.

"Now I get it," I say. "Calrissian Cottage is ironic. Because it's *not* a cottage."

"This is unbelievable!" Biz says, taking it all in.

Our jaws fall to the circular heated driveway. What we see before us is outside of anyone's imagination. The three-story house disappears into the forest on either end.

"Funny, you guys don't *look* like freaked-out dads-to-be," Patrick greets us. Now with a full beard since the last time we saw him, he looks very Bradley-Cooper-moved-to-Colorado-and-became-a-gay-bear. The small gap in between his two front teeth has always given him a little extra relatable quirk. "How do you two always look so fresh?"

"We have two dogs now. They keep us young," Biz says, not joking.

"You said this place was big but I wasn't thinking MGM Grand big," I say.

"Four years in the making," Nathan adds, exiting the house and coming at us with big hugs. Nathan is Patrick's husband-to-be, with an equally bushy beard, bear vibes and hairier than an average werewolf.

"You guys must miss New York," Biz says, looking around.

"We have ten acres of land here, but yeah, we totally miss our Hell's Kitchen one bedroom," Nathan jokes.

"Please tell me you have a casino in there," Biz says.

"Apologies if the bowling alley, basketball court and petting zoo aren't enough for your tastes," Patrick says.

"You do not have a petting zoo," I say, unsure.

"You'll have to come in and find out," Patrick says.

"I never pegged you as indoor basketball court guys," Biz says.

"We have a gift-wrapping room to even it out," Nathan says.

"If there's a Beanie Babies room, I'm checking into a Red Roof Inn," Biz says.

"Why do I direct commercials? I need to get into cryptocurrency," I say.

"First you need to *google* cryptocurrency," Biz says, more accurately. Everyone laughs.

As we pull our luggage from the trunk, I see Patrick not-so-subtly slip Biz a plastic baggie of what I presume are drugs. I try to ignore this exchange and call for Matilda and Pancake, who zoom around the driveway.

"You know we sold the business, right?" Patrick asks us.

Patrick and Nathan spent their formative years together in New York before building their dream home closer to Nathan's family in Denver. They'd created a string of successful tech start-ups together that were all moneymakers but totally unclear to us. *Some kind of software company? A film data marketing exchange maybe? A geolocation infrastructure app thing?* Whatever they touch turns to gold. They briefly explain their current business, which makes me feel like I should've studied harder in school.

Inside we're greeted by a statuesque man in a tight black T-shirt serving us a specialty cocktail. "Spicy cucumber margarita?" he says with a heavenly deep voice.

"Sure!" Biz is the first one to take a glass. He raises an eyebrow at Patrick after the butler (*maybe?*) disappears around a corner.

"We hired some staff for a couple days so we didn't have to do everything ourselves this weekend." Nathan shrugs, trying to stay humble despite everything around him being anything but humble.

After the grand tour of the compound, which takes forty-five minutes, the four of us sit in the living room and surround the largest charcuterie board known to man. Patrick is originally from Houston and does everything oversized.

"How's your gaycation so far?" Patrick asks, chomping down on spicy soppressata to go with his spicy marg.

"Hasn't been super gay," Biz says. "Except for two days in

P-town. But it's been pretty great." Biz seems happy with our detours and no longer missing our original plan.

"We made some last-minute stops in Boston and Chicago to see our families so we didn't even get to the places we were supposed to visit. Totally unplanned but they were great. Mostly," I add, remembering my father's letters.

"Wow. The man who used to make Excel spreadsheets to map out his ten-year career plan took detours?" Patrick roasts me.

Our bedroom is cozied away in our own separate cottage, one of four such buildings, just opposite the main house. The couple's family members are staying in the other cottages. It's surreal that a peer of ours—not even just a peer, a close friend—could afford this type of luxury while we're scraping by to make our Brooklyn rent and have a baby. Now with Biz out of a job, our struggle feels more real.

"I can't believe we have our own little house," I say, inspecting every inch. Our house is not so little. It's two stories and looks like it was kissed by a production designer on a Nancy Meyers movie.

I admire a tiny golden ceramic Laughing Buddha on the dresser. I rub the Buddha's belly and make a wish that Flora's doctor's appointment goes well. That's exactly when Biz and I get a text from her. We both read our phones.

FLORA

The doctor said everything is great!

She decided not to induce me early.

She's continuing to monitor me but we're back on track with the same due date! ☺

"Such a relief!" I say out loud to Biz as I type the same thing to Flora. We can rest easy tonight and enjoy the casual rehearsal dinner Patrick and Nathan have planned.

"That makes me feel so much better. We should check in with her again after the wedding," Biz says, exhausted, falling into the luxurious bed. "Isn't it wild those two are getting married tomorrow?" Biz asks as he sighs with a pang of heartbreak. I know Biz wishes this could be our wedding. I fall onto the bed next to him.

We stare at the beamed ceiling and listen to Matilda and Pancake find a spot together in a corner of the room. It's cute we have this huge room and they choose to nap together.

I'm feeling uncontrollably sleepy and I can tell Biz has heavy thoughts on his mind. "Do you wish that . . . maybe we were the ones getting married?" he asks.

It's the last thing I hear before everything fades and sleep takes hold of me.

# 28

# THE BEHEADING
# OF A GRIZZLY BEAR

**BIZ**

**T**HE NEXT NIGHT, THE wedding ceremony is just Patrick's and
Nathan's families and a limited number of close friends, so
we feel lucky to be included.

Under a big white tent in the beautiful backyard, there are
shimmering paper lanterns with candles and several million
colorful flowers everywhere.

A storybook dream of a wedding.

Throughout the ceremony, my thoughts turn to our own
non-marriage. Of course Wyatt started napping as I was trying
to talk about getting married. I'm hoping the wedding itself
will inspire Wyatt to reconsider getting officially hitched one
day soon.

After hearing the news about my dad's health, having a giant party with our friends and family to celebrate our love is
something I want more than ever.

But Patrick and Nathan's themed wedding is nerdier and

quirkier than I'd expected. We're all dutifully seated as the quartet plays the main theme song from *Star Wars*.

"Oh my god. Look at his groomsmen," I say. Patrick's two brothers stand by his side wearing stormtrooper helmets with tuxedoes.

Their groomsmaids wear dusty rose dresses but with Princess Leia buns in their hair.

Their four-year-old niece and nephew ring bearers don fuzzy little Ewok costumes.

The wedding officiant is a woman in a Chewbacca suit.

The groom and groom appear at the altar dressed as Luke Skywalker and Han Solo.

"Love is love is intergalactic love," I whisper to Wyatt and we both quietly laugh.

By dinner, Wyatt the movie expert informs me that we've heard the entire musical oeuvre of the famed *Star Wars* composer, John Williams, everything from *Close Encounters* to *Indiana Jones* to *E.T.*

Sometime after the speeches, the nerd fantasy melts away and the romance of the evening finally kicks in. Patrick and Nathan ditch their lightsabers and turn into earthly beings who just want to smoosh wedding cake into each other's mouths.

Even though the cake is in the shape of the Millennium Falcon, I'm envious of this act of commitment I want so badly to share with Wyatt.

A dance remix of the "Imperial March (Darth Vader's Theme)" comes on and I head to the bar to soak my envy in more champagne. I stand there, taking in the joy on the dance floor as wedding guests show off their best moves, when Wyatt joins me.

He's returning from the bathroom after a stormtrooper

groomsman had accidentally spilled red wine on him on the dance floor.

"Looks like you got it off," I say, noticing the wet spot on his jacket lapel.

"I'll send my dry-cleaning bill to Yoda," Wyatt says before asking the bartender for a glass of champagne.

We notice Patrick's mother strutting her stuff on the dance floor, surrounded by her son and new son-in-law. She's a vision in all white, wearing an elaborate hat worthy of a royal wedding. She tosses a pinkie wave at us and we hold up our champagne glasses to her.

"I like his mom's hat," Wyatt says.

"Is that supposed to be a *Star Wars* costume?" I ask, dead serious.

We look around and I realize the entire party except us are grinding and twerking and vogueing on the dance floor.

Wyatt turns to me. "You look so handsome in that suit," he says. He's not getting me on the dance floor right now. The idea that we're about to have a baby but still not married has been eating me up inside all night. This event is highlighting it. "Do you want to dance?" he asks.

"I'm okay just watching for now," I say, trying to navigate my feelings. Wyatt turns away from me, disappointed. Then an idea pops into my head. "Wanna get lost inside the house?" I ask. "No one would find us."

Not one to pass up a self-guided tour of someone's mansion, Wyatt smiles conspiratorially.

We push our way through the gourmet kitchen, past the chefs and cater waiters, and take the elevator downstairs to the four-lane bowling alley.

Lights flicker on to reveal a vintage jukebox full of dance

party anthems, an overhead disco ball, a legit hot dog stand and a rack of fluorescent-colored bowling balls.

We find Robin S.'s "Show Me Love" on the jukebox and flip the switch on the disco ball.

It's a competitive game of bowling between the two of us, lit up by black lights, emitting a purple glow around the entire space. We smile and laugh, teeth ultra white and eyes green from the psychedelic lighting.

I take my rage out on the game and bowl a strike. When Wyatt steps up to bowl, I grab him, our mouths inches apart until I shower him with kisses. He gives in.

We fall to our knees, in the middle of the lane, making out like we're horned-up teenagers at the local disco bowling alley.

In between our heavy breathing and Robin S. belting it out, I ask, "You know what would be fun?"

"What?"

"The basketball court."

Back in the elevator.

This time going up.

I slam Wyatt against the wall, causing the moving box to jiggle back and forth.

Loosening ties, unbuttoning dress shirts, hoping the thing isn't going to get stuck. We laugh as it dings us into a darkened hallway with plush white carpeting, our mouths still connected.

We slowly zigzag forward.

Reaching the end of the hall in the south wing, millions of lights pop on to reveal the professional-sized basketball court, complete with wooden bleachers. We each dribble perfectly new balls down the court, doing messy layups and free throws. We're only slightly terrible.

I knock the ball out of Wyatt's hand, slap his ass and get in his face, like a teammate about to give an impassioned pep talk. But, ya know, in a sexy way.

"Coach isn't sure you can play with the big boys," I say, role-playing a basketball player.

"Ew. Don't do that."

"Yeah, sorry. That was weird." We laugh and fling ourselves onto each other, falling to our knees, this time onto the hardwood floor in the center of the basketball court.

"That hurt my knees."

"Mine too."

We hold each other tightly, fall backward, make out more, like we didn't get enough the first time around and may never feel satisfied.

"I hope no one comes in," Wyatt says, letting his rational side creep in.

Something burns inside me and it's exhilarating.

"I don't care if anyone comes in," I say.

"We're like two stowaways unleashed into an empty yacht," Wyatt says.

In between lip smacking, I say, "It's too bright in here. Are you thinking what I'm thinking?"

"The ballroom," we say at the same time.

Three chandeliers in the shape of starbursts. They slowly lower from the vaulted ceiling. The illuminated crystals rival the ones inside the Metropolitan Opera at Lincoln Center. Wyatt dims them to perfection.

"It seems the only reason these guys have a ballroom is so their wedding guests could sneak away and have sex inside of it," I say.

"Imagine being so rich you hold your wedding somewhere *other* than your own ballroom," Wyatt says.

We woo each other the old-fashioned way, pretending we're in a costume period drama; quietly noticing each other from across the length of the room with demure smiles.

We move closer toward each other like animals stalking our prey.

Until finally we're a foot apart.

"May I have this waltz?" I fling my arm out, both of us laughing hysterically. We do a clumsy old-timey dance to the music thumping outside under the tent, taking turns on who's leading. We speak in faux posh accents and transport ourselves into a Jane Austen story.

"You're a natural, Mr. Petterelli," Wyatt says.

"Why thank you, Mr. Wallace," I say.

"I'm impressed by your lightness of foot."

"Don't make me blush, your lordship."

We pretend to spot an acquaintance among the polite society across the room.

"Is that Mr. Farnsworth of East Sussex in Derbyshire?"

"I believe it is him, looking rather inebriated and foolish."

We spin around dramatically and draw each other closer, our mouths almost touching, resisting any urges.

"If I may be so bold, Mr. Wallace, I would like nothing more than to ravish you."

"Oh, Mr. Petterelli!"

We slam against the red velvet curtains, smearing each other's faces, necks and chests through our unbuttoned dress shirts with our mouths. We've broken a light sweat from our dance and our bodies against each other become even more heated.

"I've never been quite this invigorated!"

"And I as well!"

"I dare say we move our tryst to somewhere more . . . private?"

"I'm perfectly delighted to oblige!"

We swing open the door to . . . where else?

"Gift wrapping room!" we both say at the same time again.

Every colored ribbon under the sun, bows, boxes, wrapping paper, all organized by someone with severe OCD.

"It looks like a pop-up Christmas store inside a shopping mall," Wyatt says.

I kiss Wyatt on the forehead and lift him up on a marble counter, climbing on top of him, unfastening my belt buckle.

"It's the *un*wrapping room," I badly joke, as I unbutton, unbuckle and unzip Wyatt's clothes in an expert three-pronged move.

*Something has come over me*, I think. It's unlike me to dominate him this much.

Wyatt lets me take control.

I grab his wrists and pin them behind his head. He lets loose an uncontrollable snort-laugh but I'm serious. I'm working out some kind of long-gestating fantasy in this mansion.

"You know where we should go?" I say, now sitting on top of Wyatt, in charge.

"Where?"

Patrick's office is the size of a New York City one-bedroom apartment. The decor is plush CEO working space meets Comic Con just threw up. The room is brimming with paraphernalia from every sci-fi movie, TV show and comic book ever. Costumes of various Jedi masters worn by mannequins inside glass cases. The bust of some purple bug-eyed monster's head on top of a podium. A life-sized, stuffed grizzly bear in killer attack mode.

There's even a framed autographed poster of Patrick's God himself, George Lucas.

A rich nerd's paradise.

I'd swiped a bottle of champagne from the champagne vault on our way through the house and pop the cork. The fizzy Dom Pérignon spills as we gulp straight from the bottle.

"Gummies, anyone?" I dangle the plastic bag full of edibles that Patrick had given me.

Wyatt hesitates. He grabs the bag from me and slips them in his pocket.

"Is that a no?" I ask.

In a power move, like a disgruntled coworker, I wipe Patrick's desk clean with one swoop of my arm.

I push Wyatt on top of the empty desk and straddle him, lying on him to feel the heat between our chests.

I kiss him gently at first and then go to town.

It feels like I'm channeling the grizzly bear that's surveying the entire scene behind us.

The whole thing feels illicit.

"We're like cat burglars but instead of money and jewelry, we're stealing kisses in every room of the house," I say.

"Only two hundred and sixteen rooms to go," Wyatt jokes.

"Stand up," I demand. He complies and I pin his chest against a wall, kissing the back of his neck, brushing my hand through his chest hair.

I step in between his legs to sturdy myself, rubbing our thighs together until he stumbles slightly, our feet knocking into each other.

Wyatt loses his balance, grabs on to the tail of my shirt, tearing it, and falls sideways on top of the grizzly bear statue, creating a loud *thump*.

The bear's head chops right off as it hits the side of the desk.

I try to grab both Wyatt and the bear but it's too late. Wyatt tumbles on top of the bear's body. We're both horrified.

The head of the now decapitated bear rolls toward the door in agonizing suspense.

Panic engulfs us as we hear footsteps outside the door. Only wearing an unbuttoned, torn dress shirt and naked from the waist down, I grab the bear's head and cover my junk.

I turn three shades of red as the door slowly opens.

A woman is silhouetted by the hallway light, and we can't tell who's standing there, witnessing this crime scene.

We're in silent shock.

The woman is wearing some complicated hat thing. Like a flamingo standing on top of her head. Then I realize it's Patrick's *friggin' mom*.

"What is happening in here?" she says in a fizzy way with a laugh, entering the room to reveal herself, barefoot and holding her high heels with one hand.

"Hi, Judith," Wyatt says as he stands, dusts himself off and buttons his pants.

I'm frozen, holding the bear head steady and upside down. Judith arches an eyebrow, trying to figure out what has just unfolded in this room.

"I was just going to the powder room—the one in the east wing because I like that hand soap in there—it's jasmine, so pretty. Anyway, I heard a pop like a gun went off then a crash like someone hit the floor!" she says.

"Oh, that was probably the champagne we opened," I explain, trying desperately to ignore the bear head eclipsing my crotch. Judith eyes the poor bear lying on its side between us.

"And, uh . . . what about this guy? Did he have too much to drink?" she asks, pointing to the injured bear with a half smirk and a tiny laugh.

"No, but we probably did."

Recognition washes over Judith's face.

"Oh my god. Wyatt and Biz! It's you guys! I thought you were Nathan's creepy cousins," she says.

"Nope. Just us. Sorry about the commotion. The wedding is amazing, by the way. So lovely. Congrats to you and Ronald." Wyatt pours on the charm when he wants to.

"Oh, kill me if I ever have to do another one of these. Pat's sister can elope." We all laugh.

She looks at us with a certain nostalgia and says, "Oh, you guys, it's so great to see you and Patrick still connected after all these years." She adjusts her bra straps. "Don't get too wasted, boys." She pinkie waves at us and closes the door behind her.

Once we hear her padding away down the hallway, we dissolve into a giggle fit.

"Oh my god. How are we going to fix this stupid-ass bear? We need superglue. Screw it. Patrick can just buy another one," I say, holding the bear head in the air like baby Simba.

Wyatt turns to me. "Wait." He blinks. Something occurs to him. "Was this a revenge fuck?"

I tilt my head like a puppy trying to understand a human. "What? No."

"We just had foreplay in every room of Patrick's house while he was dancing to Mariah Carey at his own wedding. I've never seen you this . . . aggressive. I mean, I love it but . . . this feels like revenge sex."

"Maybe I wanted to have sex with my boyfriend because we haven't been intimate in months," I say.

"Or maybe you're mad that we're not the ones getting married and you took it out on Patrick's mansion," Wyatt adds.

"This? No. I would never want to get married like this. It's *waaaaaay* too over the top," I say, not convincing either of us. I think again. "Actually . . . I mean, why not? It's still something I would like to do. Maybe I am a little upset this isn't us getting married." I look up at Wyatt, hopeful. "There's still time."

"We can't rehash this. I just want us to have the baby first. Then we can figure that out when the time comes." Wyatt simply isn't ready.

The pain of his parents splitting up is still too much for him.

He doesn't want that to happen to us.

But I'm ready.

For now, I just have to wait and hope that one day Wyatt catches up. We button our shirts in silence, both keeping our eyes fixed on the fallen, headless animal.

# 29

## APRÈS SKI

**WYATT**

*September 21, 2017*

*Dear Wyatt,*

*It's been a few months since I last wrote to you and your brother. All is well here but it's been awfully hot lately.*

*I've decided to retire from the casino as my back has been stiffening up more than usual and my legs have been getting weaker. I'm trying to exercise but it's been a challenge lately. I don't recommend getting old like me. I'm going to try and relax and have a swim in the pool this afternoon.*

*I don't suppose you're getting my letters. Or maybe you are and just don't care to write back. As always, my invitation to come visit me in Las Vegas still stands if you ever find yourself out here.*

*Xoxo*
*Dad*

*P.S. I know calling myself Dad to you boys is presumptuous but "Richard" was starting to feel too formal.*

"Let's not go to Palm Springs just yet," I say to Biz the next morning in bed, holding a freshly brewed cup of espresso I made in our little kitchen in one hand and my father's letter in the other.

This is the first time in a while that I've decided I want to go off script and do something that I haven't planned out.

I am, for once, winging it on my own terms.

Biz sits up and rubs the sleep out of his eyes. He takes a second for himself, massaging his temples. We're both hungover but not in a terrible way; a mix of champagne, red wine and regret that we were caught doing it in Patrick's office. "I'm listening," he says, interested to hear more but cautious. He eyes my letter and climbs out of bed to make his own coffee.

While I'm sure Biz really wants to spend a week with our fellow gays in the desert like we had planned, he seems intrigued and a little excited that I want to do something spur of the moment for once. "What would you want to do instead?" he asks.

I stand and open the curtains, the sun revealing our well-appointed guest cottage. I squint and see the worker bees outside already deconstructing the white tent and round tables.

"I think I want to go to Las Vegas," I say, still marinating the idea in my head.

"You're so not a Vegas person but that could be a blast." Biz fumbles with the unfamiliar and complicated espresso maker. "How does this even work?"

"I know, I've only been to Las Vegas once to direct a Skittles commercial," I say. Staying at a hotel in Vegas is not a fun place to wake up at five in the morning to direct a shoot. There's nothing like seeing drunk people, still out from the night before, stumble around a casino like gambling zombies while you're freshly showered on your way to work. "You have to lift the le-ver thing," I instruct Biz on the espresso maker.

On the other end of the spectrum, Biz went to Vegas a lot when he lived in LA; mostly weekend benders with his fellow cool Disney pals with their fake IDs where they stayed up partying for forty-eight hours, the details of which are still fuzzy.

The espresso machine spits out that sweet brown nectar for Biz.

"The baby is due in twenty-eight days," I say. "Maybe we do Vegas and Palm Springs. Do like three or four days in each city. Plus it would be nice to split up the drive."

"I'm down for that." Biz sips his espresso. "We could see an illusionist! Or maybe an all-male strip show? Those are so gross but fun. Or the Ferris wheel? Or we could like play blackjack while we skydive into a Michelin-star restaurant."

I tellingly don't acknowledge any of Biz's ideas. "We can play it by ear." I expertly make myself another espresso.

Biz sits on the sectional sofa. "Are you feeling okay?"

"I'm fine. Why?"

"You just said you want to play something by ear. That's not your thing. That's my thing," Biz says, detecting something is off. "Did you have something else in mind in Vegas?"

My nervous hand grabs the worn letter off the bed. "His return address has changed a few times on the letters but on the most recent ones it's stayed the same. He lives outside the Vegas Strip." I hand the letter to Biz, who reads it. "He's said in a few letters that I can find him whenever I'm ready."

"Wow," Biz says, studying one of my father's handwritten letters for the first time. "Good penmanship."

"Definitely someone who appreciates order and straight lines."

"Like you," Biz says. He looks up at me. "Are you ready?"

I half nod. "If I'm ever going to do it, I might as well do it now. Before the baby comes and we're too preoccupied," I say. "Plus, seeing him again will be a good lesson in what *not* to do with our own child."

A smile contorts on Biz's lips. "Vegas, here we come," he says. I sit up next to him on the couch as we both quietly reread the letter between us.

- - - - - - - >

ON OUR WAY OUT OF EVERGREEN, AFTER AN ELABORATE *STAR WARS*-themed brunch with the newlyweds, Biz fixates on the wedding. "I just can't believe Patrick and Nathan's whole weekend was based on a movie franchise."

Biz and I know there's a tinge of wedding envy still lingering.

"I've never understood your burning desire to get married," I say, trying not to sweep this topic under the rug for once. "We're life partners, committed to staying together and raising a baby. Do you really need the legal piece of paper and validation from the world?"

"You don't get it," Biz says dismissively.

"Get what?" I ask. Biz just shakes his head. "Seriously, enlighten me," I say.

"It's okay. You don't want to get married and I do. It breaks my heart but it's something I'll have to be okay with," Biz says.

"But why is it so important to you?" I ask again.

Biz sighs. "It's symbolic. It's telling the world you're committed to each other. It bonds us in a deeper way. It gave my parents a more meaningful connection and it's always something I've wanted to emulate."

"I totally get that," I say, turning to Biz. "I have been thinking about it, just so you know," I offer.

"You have?" Biz looks up from his phone with a crooked smile.

"Of course. After we decided on our egg donor, I was looking into wedding venues. I mean, I don't personally need to get married but I know how important it is to you," I say.

Biz deflates. "Such a romantic," he jokes.

"No, seriously. I've been thinking maybe I shouldn't let my parents' separation define me. Maybe I don't know what I'm missing by us not getting married," I say.

Biz turns to me with a smile. We both leave it there and let some music take us away.

A few hours later we've listened to every album of every female singer-songwriter pop star who's ever walked the earth and highlights from a dozen short-lived original Broadway cast albums. After hearing the camp-errific *Diana: The Musical* with Princess Diana singing, *"Harry, my ginger-haired son, you'll always be second to none . . ."* even Biz knows it's time to move on to something else.

"How about a murder podcast?" Biz suggests.

"Whaddaya got?" I ask.

Biz scrolls through his phone, rattling off a few true crime options.

*"A Laci Peterson Murder Update?"* Biz suggests.

"Too overexposed," I say.

*"The Notorious Brides in the Bath Murders?"*

"What year?"

"Early nineteen hundreds."

"Too old."

"*The Shaker Heights Shoplifters?*"

"Too low stakes."

"*The Burger Chef Murders?*"

"We've heard that one!" we both realize together.

"*The Murder of Girly Chew Hossencofft?*"

"Sounds weird and promising."

"Oh, wait—it has UFO conspiracies and light cannibalism."

"Hard pass."

"*The Honolulu Strangler?*"

"I don't want to think of Hawaii in a bad light."

"Do we only want murder?"

"Preferably, yes."

"What kind? Give me a ballpark."

"It should be an unpredictable murder within the last ten years, but nothing too graphic, and it has to have several red herrings and ultimately solved with the serial killer getting a life sentence with no parole or worse, but then the epilogue has a twist that we never saw coming." I turn to Biz and say in a dramatic whisper, "*Or did we?*"

"Okay, that's not specific at all. Let's see . . ." Biz scrolls more on his phone. It's not long before we settle into the cozy, soothing sounds of two determined Gen Z podcasters trying to solve a recent murder that took place in a small town in Vermont where the owner of a year-round Christmas-themed gift shop goes missing.

The extremely detailed episodes are a chance for me to dip in and out of paying attention, letting my mind wander. But I perk up when I hear the podcast host say, "*Maggie had a ton of support from her friends, family . . . even her dog."* I can't help but tear up a little, thinking of my own life with Biz. Things aren't perfect between us right now but I still feel lucky.

My tiny burst of emotion surprises me. I never would've thought a twenty-something woman talking about a Christmas store stalker could make me appreciate my own relationship.

Spending time in the state where Biz and I met, the memories of our first night come flooding back. It was Gay Ski Week in Aspen, the winter after I graduated college. Patrick and I were each other's wingman.

It was our first day of skiing and the mountain air was fresh as we sliced up all the double black diamonds we could find.

Afterward, we met at the bottom of the mountain for a hearty lunch of burgers, truffle fries and beers. I wanted to keep hitting the same trails we'd found but Patrick wanted to nap before the big dance party that night.

It was something called the Gear Party. "Wear your leather gear, snow gear or sports gear for this sexy blowout dance party!!!" the poster screamed. Patrick was all about his newly purchased leather harness, and I showed up in ski pants, suspenders, snow goggles around my neck and an obligatory tight T-shirt.

Once we arrived, Patrick, who kept saying he desperately needed me as his wingman, immediately found someone. This was way before he met the love of his life. "That guy's so handsome," Patrick nodded toward a group of random guys.

I looked at the group and spotted one guy that made me think, *My life is about to change.* He had a one-in-a-million friendly face, a few days' scruff with a fresh haircut and perfect everything. His friends were laughing at something this guy just said, all of them doubling over with giggle fits, in their own world on the dance floor. I was entranced.

"The one on the right?" I asked.

"No. The one on the left," Patrick said to my relief. Before I knew it, Patrick had abandoned me and leapt onto the dance floor with the guy he thought was cute. I didn't even get to clock in for my job as a wingman.

The guy I had my eye on disappeared, so I wandered the periphery of the dance floor, feeling ridiculous in my ski gear getup.

When a dance remix came on, the room was electrified. Depeche Mode's Dave Gahan belted out that he was taking a ride with his best friend and he hopes he never lets him down again.

That's when I spotted the guy again. Right next to me.

This guy turned to me with his forest green eyes. For a second, it was like the music and crowd noise went silent. It felt like the song was speaking directly to the two of us. We grinned at the irony of the song lyrics. Maybe the line wasn't ironic as much it was a prediction. *I could fall in love with this guy*, I immediately thought.

We introduced ourselves. "What kind of name is Biz?" I asked.

"I'll tell you when we get to know each other more," he promised.

A warm glow took over me. "Did you have fun skiing today?" I asked.

"Oh, I don't ski. I'm afraid of heights. And speed. And people skiing into me from behind. I'm all about the après ski. I'm just here for the cozy sweaters and hot cocoa by the fireplace," Biz said.

I laughed, charmed by this romantic, sweet guy. We immediately found that luck was on our side after he asked where I was from.

"You live in New York? *I live in New York!*" he shouted over the music.

When we were back in the city, we quickly started dating and never stopped. It was magical and miraculous to both of us that we met and hit it off clear across the country.

Back in the car, I spot a sign ahead that reads, "ASPEN CITY LIMIT." Here we are now, passing through that little corner of the state where it all began.

"Just like Depeche Mode said, *I'm taking a ride with my best friend,*" I say out loud, knowing how corny it sounds but I mean it. The lyrics ring true then and now.

I look over at Biz, and while I'm trying to connect over our song, our town, our *first moment*, I see that he's completely asleep.

So much for hoping he never lets me down again.

A moment before we pass the Aspen City Limits sign, Biz wakes up, leans over and gives me a sleepy kiss on the lips. "Happy Town We Met In," he says, gripping my thigh before snuggling himself back to sleep. I drive with a smile on my face.

# 30

## MIND READER

**BIZ**

AFTER TEXTING MY DAD to check in and make sure he's doing okay, I think how I've been waiting for the day my tight-knit family would rub off on Wyatt. I'm happy he's decided to finally reconnect with his dad.

"Welcome to Fabulous Las Vegas!" I say to Wyatt, reading the sign as we enter.

The violet dusk sky turns dark, which seems fitting for Sin City.

I feel the desert air rip through the car with the top down as we pass a row of palm trees. Out here, palm trees are like weeds but to us Brooklynites they're exotic.

Ridiculously long stretch Hummers. Dancing fountains. Tourists sipping thirty-eight-dollar, footlong daiquiris through straws while meandering down the street.

I feel hungover before we even start drinking, marveling at the pulsating lights and neon signs of hotels, casinos and restaurants, all screaming for attention.

From Colorado through Utah, Virginia Woolf made the same gurgle and rattling sound from a few days earlier. Every time it happens, Wyatt and I just look at each other, puzzled, not knowing what to do or where it's coming from. Car guys we are not.

The noise disappeared when we entered Nevada so the problem is fixed! (We think.)

We amble down the Vegas Strip as we read a group text from Flora assuring us everything is still okay.

"That's great." I turn to Wyatt.

"Sounds like everything's on the right track."

Wyatt's phone buzzes.

"Flora?" I ask.

"It's my mom," Wyatt says. He lets it go to voicemail.

"Don't you want to see why she's calling?" I ask.

"I really have to pee so I'd rather check into the hotel first. I want to get my bearings and not have to focus on a long-winded conversation about what we're doing in Vegas right now."

My phone buzzes next. "Now your mom's calling me." I look at Wyatt with slight concern. "Could be important."

"Don't answer!" Wyatt's jumpy. "Can we just find the hotel? Seeing all these fountains is really making me have to go to the bathroom."

We arrive at the Venetian Hotel where the large lobby is pure gold and marble. This is not the Italian decor I grew up with.

We found a last-minute deal and booked it on Wyatt's phone while driving and our room lives up to the hotel's promise of "an homage to the Italian opulence."

We settle in. I crack open tiny tequilas I find in the mini fridge, pouring them over ice.

"Are you going to tell your mom you're here to see your dad?" I ask Wyatt as he exits the gold bathroom.

"Maybe later," he says, clearly avoiding any confrontation.

"Should we hit the casino? Maybe go dancing at a club?" I ask. "Oh—I've always wanted to try that José Andrés restaurant where you can grill Kobe beef at your table after devouring cotton candy foie gras."

"Let's not go nuts," Wyatt says.

"We're in Vegas. You have to have a little fun before the heavy stuff tomorrow."

Clink. Sip.

"I was thinking maybe we have dinner at the hotel and have an early night in."

I guzzle my tequila and stare at Wyatt. My gaze turns a little watery as the tequila hits. "Early night in? How about an early night out?"

Wyatt finishes his drink. "You're right. Let's go out," Wyatt says, changing his tune.

Thanks, Jose Cuervo.

More drinks flow during dinner and I think this is exactly what we need before the baby comes. No family or friend obligations. Just the two of us out on the town together, enjoying each other's company, letting go of our inhibitions.

An epic date night.

Wyatt seems preoccupied, probably thinking about his dad, throughout the entire dinner.

All I hear are the conversations around us. "We come here every year on our anniversary."

"Vegas is the only time we gamble."

"We've seen Barry Manilow thirty-seven times!"

During our chocolate mousse dessert, I mention we could

see a show tonight to get his mind off things. Wyatt agrees but seems like he's just going through the motions.

Declan Del Monaco is a resident mentalist/illusionist/hypnotist and the hotel is able to snag two last-minute tickets in the cheap seats for us. We watch as he makes his assistant levitate and hypnotizes an audience member into thinking he's touching him from across the stage.

Before I know what hits me, I'm called up on stage. Mostly because I raise my hand when Declan Del Monaco asks who's game to become another one of his personal puppets.

I stand on stage for the entertainment of hundreds of people and Mr. Del Monaco correctly guesses the name of my true love: "Is it . . . *Wyatt*?" the mentalist asks in his signature dramatic way. A smile takes over my face and the crowd bursts into applause.

I glimpse Wyatt in the audience looking surprised.

After the show, I suggest we hit a club annoyingly called hydr8te (all lower case with the number 8 just inserting itself in there like it belongs).

Snaking our way through the long dark corridor where we hear the thumping house music grow louder, Wyatt and I exchange amused looks.

It's a huge space full of sweaty, writhing bodies with music so loud, I can feel it in the pit of my stomach. I spot someone's drink on a ledge slowly slide off from all the bass.

We weave through the crowd upstairs, where we find a sizable booth overlooking the dance floor.

While everyone around us dances and drinks, Wyatt and I just watch.

I look into the sweaty mass of people and my first thought is, *I'm going to be a dad*. An image of me pushing our baby stroller through our Brooklyn neighborhood enters my mind. It nags at me, the pressure of living up to my own amazing dad.

I turn to Wyatt and see his mind is somewhere else too. His eyes adrift on the crowd. We decide the music is too loud and we can't get a server's attention for drinks so we leave.

Mentalist or not, at this point I could fall asleep at the snap of anyone's two fingers.

We walk through the casino of our hotel just to glimpse the action before bed.

The elevator plops us onto our floor and I follow Wyatt down the gold carpeted hallway.

"So," I say. "Are you ready to meet your dad tomorrow?"

Wyatt slides his key card into our door's handle as the green light pops on.

# 31

## WHAT HAPPENS IN VEGAS?

**WYATT**

OVER OUR BREAKFAST BUFFET the next morning, as Biz scoops up a pile of lukewarm, rubbery scrambled eggs and slides them onto his plate with a wince, we both realize after last night that the tone of our trip and Vegas itself are two very different animals.

Biz is grateful, at least, for a night of fun, with tequila headaches as our cheap souvenirs. I'm feeling guilty that I've made a lot of our trip all about me.

"You don't have to join me today," I say, biting into a toasted everything bagel with scallion cream cheese, savoring the first bite of the morning.

This isn't a test. I really want Biz to have fun doing his own thing. Even though deep down inside I want him to join me. I just don't know what to expect.

"It's totally up to you?" Biz says. "On one hand, it seems like a very big deal to meet your estranged dad after all these years, and I can understand you wanting alone time with him . . ."

"And on the other hand, it would be nice to have you there for support," I finish his sentence.

"I'm here for you either way. You know that," Biz says. "Are you sure he's here?"

I pull the envelope out of my shorts pocket and smooth it out on the table in between our plates of food.

As my father's address sits between us, we both grow anxious, unable to eat the rest of our food. We just stare at the only evidence that my father is somewhere nearby.

We spend the morning inside the hotel gym—I jog on a treadmill and Biz works up a sweat on an elliptical machine. Both of us want to work out any nervous jitters. But really I'm just delaying the inevitable.

Watching some of the older, seen-it-all employees on the casino floor that we pass by on the way back to our room—the blackjack dealers, the cocktail servers, the pit bosses—I wonder if my father knows any of them.

Freshly showered, holding two bottles of green juice and with a clear head, I sit next to a tranquil koi pond in the grand lobby while waiting for Biz. A clutch of bachelorettes wearing swimsuits with pastel-colored "Bride-To-Be" and "Bridesmaid" sashes noisily stomps by in their bejeweled flip-flops and French pedicures, laughing and talking in outdoor voices, disrupting my calm vibe.

After they pass, I take in the serenity of the nearby mini waterfall and let my eyes wander until I spot a turtle swimming upstream in the pond on its own. The little guy struggles along among a sea of homogenous koi fish. Just him against the elements. *Am I this turtle?*

Biz dings out of an elevator and approaches with a sympathetic smile.

"I think maybe I should go alone," I decide, standing and handing Biz his green juice.

"Are you sure?" Biz asks, sipping his juice, thinking this through.

"Yeah, I'm like a lone turtle," I say, referencing my new koi pond friend.

"Turtle?" Biz asks.

"Long story. Anyway, our meeting could go a million different ways. If it goes well, I could introduce you later, if we decide to keep in touch. I don't know. This whole thing is strange. I'm just showing up at his house unannounced. If two strangers show up, it might be too much," I explain.

"Totally agree," Biz says. "You can bring me into the relationship if and when you're ready. Assess the situation first."

"I'll only be a couple hours," I tell Biz, anxiety setting in that I'm actually doing this.

"Perfect. Maybe I'll just sit by the pool, and we can have a late lunch when you're back."

I fill with nerves. I'd rather sit by a pool.

"Do you want one of Patrick's gummies? It'll relax you." Biz dangles the plastic baggie full of edibles that Patrick gave him.

Outside, waiting for the valet to bring Virginia Woolf around, I notice my mom called again. She left four voicemails and at least as many texts asking to call her back. But I know if I call her, she'll probe and I'd have to reveal what we're doing in Vegas. Mom can wait.

It only takes thirty minutes to drive to Henderson, a residential area just outside of downtown Vegas. Every few minutes I hear a new sound: *woob woob woob*. I make a mental note to get the car checked out once and for all.

Now without Biz, Matilda and Pancake, I feel alone. They are my ever-increasing pack, with a new member about to join. I think of the gummy I took at the hotel and realize it's not doing anything to relax me. Then again, those things never work for me.

GPS lady tells me I'll arrive in four minutes, so I decide to touch base with my anchors.

I steer the wheel with my knee and text. I'm a hypocrite for telling Biz not to do this. I send a quick message to Flora in our group text.

WYATT

**Everything good?**

She texts back immediately.

FLORA

**All good. Seeing the doctor again in a couple days.**

Biz and I text back heart and prayer emojis.

It's another ninety-degree day so I hope Biz is enjoying the pool. I text him separately.

WYATT

**Almost here. I'm nervous. 😬😬😬**

BIZ

**ur fine just breathe is the gummy helping????**

WYATT

**Not at all. Don't feel a thing.**

BIZ

weird CBD never works for u

WYATT

Ugh. What if he's a hateful
monster like my mom
always said?

BIZ

lower your expectations

WYATT

Good idea. You're the best.
I love you. I don't know what
I'd do without you.

BIZ

ur literally without me now

WYATT

Oh. True.
I love you.

BIZ

love u too

I turn right onto Sahara Plains Boulevard—my father's street—and slow down; I feel my heart racing through my T-shirt with my production company's logo printed on the front pocket. Sweat forms around my hairline, either from nerves or the heat or both. My jaw clenches.

There's no turning back.

It's time for some closure. Or at least the next step in the evolution of my relationship with the man who left us.

I park on the curb, three houses away. Looks like my father lives in a nice two-story home built in the seventies. I need another two to forty-five minutes to steel myself before pulling into the driveway of my long-lost father, unannounced, after not seeing him for almost thirty years.

And then it hits me. The gummy, that is.

I feel fuzzy, euphoric, suddenly happy—almost giddy. I hold in an uncontrollable giggle and let it out in a huge guffaw. Holy shit. *Was this the CBD*, I wonder? It's making me feel good. Too good. I'm completely high.

Something nags inside my mouth. I make a face like the grimace emoji and check my teeth in the rearview mirror. There's a stubborn poppy seed, leftover from breakfast, stuck between my two bottom right incisors.

"Hi, I'm your son!" I say out loud with a goofy accent, the prominent seed staring back at me like I'm missing my front tooth. I laugh way too hard at my own joke. Then I explode into a giggle fit over the idea of meeting my father totally high with my mouth full of poppy seeds.

It's too hilarious to comprehend.

I try plucking out the poppy seed with my tongue, then my finger, and then finally, the corner of the envelope that contains my father's letter. That does the trick.

I text Biz.

WYATT

**What did you**

**give me?**

BIZ

huh?????? the gummy why

> WYATT
>
> Feels like more than
> just CBD. Are you
> sure it was CBD?

BIZ

that's what patrick told me

> WYATT
>
> Okay. Going. In.

BIZ

wait are u ok????????

> WYATT
>
> I'm fine. I think. Just
> kind of hilarious that
> I'm doing this.

BIZ

maybe wait in the car
til it wears off

> WYATT
>
> Nah. I'm good.

BIZ

u sure???

> WYATT
>
> Yes. What's the best
>
> that could happen?
>
> *whore
>
> *whores
>
> *worse
>
> *worst!!!

*Even my autocorrect is high*, I think.

> BIZ
>
> oyyyyyyy ok im there
> with u in spirit

> WYATT
>
> Love you!!!!!!!!!!!!!!!!!!!!!!!!!!!!!!

I stab out three heart emojis, as if declaring my love to my spouse back home, before going into battle. Biz sends me back a kissy face emoji and a photo of the gorgeous pool.

> WYATT
>
> Looks gross.

> BIZ
>
> disgusting

> WYATT
>
> Pure filth.

BIZ

**garbage trash of a pool—how do**
**people live like this???????**

A guttural, hysterical laugh emerges from the depths of my core. I can't stop laughing.

BIZ

**keep me posted!!!!!**

WYATT

**I will!** 😂 😂 😂 😂

I'll be fine. I think.

# 32

## SWIMMING POOLS
## AND FRENCH FRIES

**BIZ**

**A** LITTLE WEED GUMMY MIGHT be just the thing Wyatt needs at this point.

The dude is always too sober.

I just hope he doesn't need me to help navigate his gummy weed experience like a spiritual guide walking someone through an ayahuasca retreat. He's such a lightweight.

I down the rest of my piña colada and order a club sandwich and fries from the pool guy.

*What am I doing?*

This whole day makes me miss Wyatt. We both love a piña colada and pool fries. This isn't supposed to be our alone time. It's supposed to be our alone time together.

None of this is landing the same without him.

With Wyatt seeing his dad today, I'm missing my own dad, so I give him a call. Of course both of my parents answer on FaceTime.

"Are you coming back to see us again?" my dad answers in lieu of a "hello."

"Massi. Where are you now, sweetie?" my mom asks, stretching her neck so her head is in the frame.

My whole body relaxes and I smile. Seeing my parents always fills me with joy. "You're not going to believe this," I say.

"Don't tell us you already had the baby," my mom says with a slightly panicked look on her face.

"Noooo. Not yet. There was a minute when Flora thought they were going to induce her early but they decided not to," I say, squeezing more sunblock onto my legs and rubbing it in.

"So what aren't we going to believe?" Dad asks.

"We're in Las Vegas. Wyatt found some letters from his dad that his mom had been hoarding in the basement, so he's going to meet him for the first time since he was a kid."

"Wow. That's a lot to take in," my dad says.

"His dad lives in Vegas?" my mom asks.

"Yep. We're doing a stopover before we head to Palm Springs."

"When was the last time they saw each other?" Mom wonders.

"Wyatt hasn't seen him since he was like seven years old."

"I hope he's as loving of a person as Wyatt," my dad says, sounding and looking a little tired. "It's never too late to try and connect with family."

My thoughts shift to my dad's health. "What's happening with you, Dad? Any talk with the doctors?"

My dad sighs and my mom chimes in before he can speak. "We're seeing the specialist downtown next week. Most likely the surgery will be the week after that."

I slide my sunglasses off as the gravity of this sets in. My dad sees I'm silent for a beat too long.

"Don't worry, Massi. I'll be okay and the best thing is I'll be fully recovered in time to meet your baby," Dad says.

"I know," I say, hopeful.

"You can be a little afraid but don't worry so much, kiddo. Your job, your relationship with Wyatt, the baby. Even me. It's all going to be okay, okay?" he says. "Remember what I said to you in front of the museum? Believe in yourself because everyone else does."

"The old man is right," my mom says as we all let out a laugh.

"What are you doing while Wyatt meets his dad?" Dad asks.

"Are you outside?" my mom asks.

"I'm at the pool actually." I flip the camera view on Face-Time and scan the pool area for them to see.

"Looks like heaven," my mom says.

"What are you doing talking to us old geezers? Go get a tan for us," my dad says.

"We love you, Massi," Mom says.

"Love you both back. Keep me posted about the doctor," I say as we all blow air kisses and hang up.

I put my phone back under my towel and across the pool I spot a woman who looks about seven months pregnant. A pool attendant leads her and her two young kids into a reserved cabana. The size of her floppy hat rivals her oversized glasses, and she looks like she sprang from the pages of a fashion magazine.

Diamond earrings sparkling from afar. Gold Cartier bracelets. A white cotton linen maternity beach shirt over a white bikini. She takes her shirt off to reveal a belly so big, it looks like she's pregnant with an entire rugby team.

I'm entranced by her.

I watch as she gets her kids ready for the pool, applying sunscreen on them, slipping on their inflatable arm floaties and ordering lunch. It's an expert move only a seasoned parent could properly execute.

*Will I ever be that kind of parent?*

Just as her kids are about to step into the shallow end, their mom calls them back over. The woman lies back on her lounge chair and draws them both in close. She puts their tiny hands on her large belly as they feel the movements of the baby, their future sibling, all of them giggling together with glee.

I remember the conversation Wyatt and I had: the baby bump is that elusive experience in our *journey* that we never really had.

I'm momentarily heartbroken, a feeling that directly contrasts with the golden sun and glistening swimming pool.

*There will be no feeling our baby kick before they're born*, I think.

Soon, the pool guy brings my club sandwich and fries, along with a postcard for discounts on various Vegas activities. I bite into my sandwich and scan the postcard.

I spot something that makes my heart race and palms go sweaty. Fear sets in and I realize my lazy pool day is about to take an unexpected turn.

# 33

## OH, HIGH

**WYATT**

**WAKE UP FROM A** nap, still in the car, and check my watch. I'd closed my eyes for a second and now it's forty-five minutes later?!

The sun seems even hotter now.

I must've been sleeping sitting upright, like a mannequin with its mouth open.

The weed has coursed through my body: hysterical laughter, unable to move, and then finally, sleep. My head feels fuzzy but at least I no longer feel totally under the influence. I can concentrate on having a conversation. I clear my throat and wish I'd brought some water. The car is even out of snacks.

I step out of Virginia Woolf and walk down the sidewalk when it suddenly occurs to me that I'm betraying my mom's trust. Maybe we should've discussed this before I meet him. It's painful to think about hurting my mom but I have so many questions about my own father before becoming one myself.

The pristine walkway to the house suggests a similar neat

and orderly personality that could easily have the same handwriting as my father's letters.

My finger pushes the doorbell and I mutter to myself, "I can't believe I'm doing this."

I look behind me and almost take off running until I hear footsteps and the front door unlocking.

That's when my father opens the door.

# 34

## REALLY HIGH

**BIZ**

**Z**IP-LINING. TEN STORIES IN the air. Flying like a superhero.

This is the photo I'm staring at on the postcard.

I could never do that. I'm terrified of heights.

When I had to shoot a scene in a hot air balloon for *Back in the Saddle*, I had a panic attack and cried. I wanted to quit. My parents had to fly from Chicago to the set and convince me to stay. We made a pact with the producers that I would only shoot scenes where my feet were firmly planted on the ground.

I stir and slurp the last of my second piña colada.

*Should I zip-line?* I inexplicably wonder to myself.

My palms sweat again just thinking about it. Even the bottoms of my feet get clammy.

To distract myself, I dig for my phone and check in on @quaddaddiez. Today, their photo is the six of them wearing sunglasses surrounding a sandcastle on the beach.

The caption reads We did a thing. Under that are a bunch of

hashtags that read #beachvibes #sundayfunday #playtime #BizIsGoingToSuckAtParenting.

I immediately drop my phone. I want to toss it in the pool. I blink, trying not to let my imagination get the best of me again.

I've had enough sun and too many frothy drinks.

I miss Wyatt and have to keep myself occupied. I pick up the postcard again.

I'm going zip-lining.

# 35

## THE GEOLOGY OF NEVADA

**WYATT**

**M**Y BOYFRIEND AND I are driving cross-country to California for the birth of our child and . . . along the way I found your letters, so I looked up your address and, well, here I am," I manage to say to my father.

There's a pause. He blinks with a slight flash of recognition.

"Come in," he says, looking conflicted. "I'll get us some drinks."

His house is beautifully decorated with tasteful, modern touches and an outpouring of sunshine. Hockney-esque paintings of men lazily lounging around swimming pools colorfully line one wall. I sit on a long minimalist sofa. The house's air-conditioning dries the sweat that's caked on my forehead and now showing through the underarms of my shirt.

Stacked in front of me on the coffee table are expensive-looking books about art and a beautifully large book called *The Geology of Nevada*, which showcases the natural wonders of the state. I flip through its thick pages, my nerves rattling me so

much that I'm unable to process what I'm even looking at.
Mountains? Rocks? The moon?

I feel like a character in a play waiting for the curtain to go
up and the lights to come on so I can finally deliver my opening
line. My palms sweat.

A few torturous minutes pass as I flip back and forth through
the same three pages, when my father enters the living room
carrying two glasses of iced tea.

He's the kind of person I'd cast in a commercial if the casting specs called for "Retired man in his sixties with a friendly
demeanor, full head of silver hair, brown eyes and fit physique.
Fully understands the protagonist's need to become a dad and
meet his estranged father. Minor role but a key character to the
story. Note: no facial hair. Must be a local hire."

I'm a thousand percent sure I could cast him in a pharma-
ceutical commercial and his career as an actor/model/possible-
guest-role-on-a-*CSI*-spinoff would take off overnight.

But something about him isn't right. This man looks nothing
like me.

I'm parched from the heat, the weed, everything, but I'm
too nervous to sip my drink.

My father takes a seat across from me on an artsy chair. The
kind only an architect or someone with an eye for design might
have.

"So I'm guessing it's safe to assume you're one of Richard's
sons?" he asks.

I blank for a second. *Richard's* sons? "Are you . . . not
Richard?"

The man who I thought was my father, who I now realize is
not at all my father, shakes his head. "I'm not your dad, no. My
name's Gordon. Your dad told me about you through the years.

And I'm sorry you two never had a chance to reconnect. He feels awful about everything that happened."

"Everything that happened?" I repeat without rancor. I genuinely want to know my father's side of the story. The objective truth. I try to tune out the abandoned kid in me and hear this guy out as a mature adult.

Before he can answer, something catches my eye; it's centered on the mantelpiece. A stocky, emerald green box outlined with a gold overlay. Its prominence in the room suggests it could be an urn. My heart sinks.

"If you're not my father . . ." I look at the urny-looking thing. "Is *that* him?"

# 36

## SLOTZILLA

### BIZ

**I**T'S BEEN A WHILE since I've been to Vegas. Of course this city's idea of zip-lining isn't cascading over majestic mountains. It's basically inside a mall.

An Uber lets me out at something called "SlotZilla," which boasts itself as the world's largest slot machine. I'm a tad drunker than I'd anticipated, and I feel very out of my element just seeing this monstrosity.

To people on the ground, it looks like a giant slot machine pouring out people instead of coins when you hit jackpot. There's even a goofy *cha-ching* noise that sounds every time a new pair of people swoosh through.

Wyatt would love the thrill of it. Me, not so much.

I already feel a single but persistent butterfly in my stomach.

Making my way to the entrance, I look up and see people strap themselves into neon green harnesses, flying head-first.

A guy who works there—covered in tattoos and wearing a

cowboy hat, probably once dreamed of a life as a recording country artist—sees me approach, wide-eyed.

"It's the largest single slot machine in the world," he tells me. "Ready for some fun?"

I look around, making sure he's talking to me. "Fun?" I ask.

"This is something you want to do, right?" he says directly to me.

"I guess?" I say, unsure. "I don't know why I even came here." I stand there, looking up, paralyzed by fear.

"People like you come up here all the time. Some want to have fun. Some want to overcome their fears," he says wisely. "What brought you here that you're afraid of?"

*I'm afraid of not living up to my potential as a dad*, I think. But I'm not about to tell this to the guy who runs SlotZilla.

"I'm not a big fan of heights. Or speed. Or all of . . ." I motion to the adrenaline screams from zip-liners above us. ". . . that."

"If you can overcome your fear of heights, you can overcome anything," he says.

I blink. Something clicks inside me. Maybe this is why I pulled myself here.

I stare at the guy, who's smirking at me like he knows my type.

Sometimes we find a gentle push off the ledge in the most unexpected places.

I walk upstairs, where an instructor gives me quick, simple directions like a bored flight attendant reciting safety procedures. I want her to have a little more enthusiasm or something to quell my anxiety, but before I know it, I'm in an elevator going up eleven flights to the top of the structure.

It feels higher than I had imagined. I step up and watch

people in front of me fly through the air with total joy, screaming and laughing. I swallow, feeling unprepared.

I'm next in the zip-line queue. I want to run back to the elevator.

Suddenly, I think of Wyatt and how silly it is for him to
meet his dad alone. He probably needs backup. Why am I about
to go zip-lining while my boyfriend is having the most emotionally challenging day of his entire life?

It's too late to second-guess this. It's my turn to fly headfirst,
seventeen hundred feet in the air through a friggin' shopping mall.

The zip-line attendant shuttles off each person as fast as he
can like he's installing widgets on an assembly line with a
watchful boss.

*Hook. Connect. Fly. Hook. Connect. Fly.*

I can't remember the last time I felt so out of my element.

I want to scream before it's time to scream.

Before I can overthink it, I'm dangling in midair, connected
only to a wire. The harness hugs and pulls my junk in an uncomfortable way.

*Hook. Connect.*

Two green lights flick on and a large metal gate opens. It
looks like I'm about to be sent through a human car wash.

*Fly.*

The "slot machine" makes the frightening *cha-ching* knell.
And I'm off!

For about thirty seconds, I fly outside, crossing the street
from a bird's-eye view, wind hitting my face as I zoom into the
open mouth of the mall shaped like an airplane hangar.

It's a dense assortment of casinos, neon lights, hotels, flashing signs, stores, kiosks and . . . some hair band playing live on
a stage? It's a total Vegas blur.

People below look like ants looking up at me.

A delayed shot of adrenaline finally hits me and I realize this is supposed to be fun, so I fling my arms out, feeling like a cheap Superman.

It's only a one-minute ride. The extreme height plus the speed mixed with the alcohol doesn't feel like the right combination. There's an abrupt slowdown as I approach the opposite landing platform.

I see people on the ground cheering me on with thumbs up, and I feel momentarily proud of conquering this lifelong fear.

*Unhook. Unconnect. Stop.*

Another attendant helps me out of the harness and I feel dizzy, my legs weak. One step down the stairs and my knees buckle, forcing me to stumble and fall to the ground.

Something snaps. The unmistakable sound of a tendon. Or a bone. Or something else. A woman yells, "You alright?!"

I give her a cursory nod as my eyes close.

Then everything goes dark.

# 37

## MEN HAVING BABIES

**WYATT**

"THAT'S MY MOM," GORDON says, gesturing to the urn that I thought was my father. "You know that your father and I are partners."

This doesn't compute. "Business partners?" I ask, even though I'm starting to guess what he means.

"Life partners," Gordon says. "Husbands. We've been married for seventeen years."

I'm silenced. Breathless.

"I thought you said you read his letters," he says, perplexed.

"Apparently not all of them," I manage. It feels like I've turned to a pile of dust. Put my remains in that urn and scatter my ashes at sea.

*What did he just say?*

It takes me a full minute to interrupt my internal processing and speak.

"My father's gay?" I ask. A nervous laugh slips out of me.

"Your mom . . . didn't tell you?" he asks with a glimmer of shock on his face.

Memories flood my mind. "I do remember hearing about you. She once said he had a best friend. That you two shared a house. I guess I never . . ." I take a confused breath. Sparks of anger bubble in my chest, thinking how my mom left out the most important part.

How she denied me the truth.

"It's okay," he says, flashing a supportive smile.

"Is he here?" is all I can think to ask.

Gordon tenses up, looks at the floor, then back up at me with concern. "We recently had some setbacks and decided it was best for him to live in a community where he could be monitored and looked after. He's not far from here. It's a twenty-four-hour care facility."

I don't know how to digest all of this news. I flip through a million questions in my mind.

"You know, this whole time—my whole life—for whatever reason, my mom told me he left when I was a kid and wanted nothing to do with us, and we believed it and never questioned it. Then his letters . . ."

I trail off, reaching into my pocket to pull out a letter. "He wrote to me and my brother and I had no idea. There were a bunch of them. We never knew." I'm about to become emotional. Saying this all out loud makes me feel less like myself and more like a sad orphan in a Dickens novel. The foundation of my identity starts to crumble.

Gordon examines the letter. With someone else holding it, I can really see the passage of time in the dusty envelope, the way it's torn, stored for years and recently transported across state lines.

"Do you—would you like to see him?" Gordon asks, knowing I need answers to fill the hole in my heart.

All I can do is think of how much I wish Biz were sitting in the empty seat next to me.

- - - - - - - - >

SILVER DESERT RETIREMENT COMMUNITY HAS A PERFECT RING TO IT. A NICE place to retire in Nevada; even though the engraved wooden sign out front that reads "We're Family" seems ironic for obvious reasons.

I decide it's best that Gordon doesn't join me at first. If Biz isn't by my side, I want to stay committed to my solo endeavor.

Entering the inviting lobby of the retirement community, there's a fragrant lavender smell I wasn't expecting. It's refreshing. A good omen, maybe.

It's not often I have the chance to see something so authentic as this place. As a director, I'm always collecting images in my mind. Real life props, the design of a room, people's faces. It's cute to see two seniors sitting closely on a loveseat, laughing at a video on one of their phones. The joy in their eyes makes them look thirty years younger.

But then I bristle, imagining a time when millennials become geriatrics, all staring at their phones, still liking each other's pictures forty years later. Or maybe by then, instead of "liking a pic" we have to "hug a hologram" or "whisper to an AI" or some other not yet invented term.

A silver-haired woman at the front desk gives me my father's room number, and before I know it, I'm standing in front of a residential door: 402. It stares at me as if my entire life has been leading up to these three little numbers.

I feel my phone vibrate in my shorts. It's Biz. There's nowhere to take a private call in the hallway so I text him back.

> WYATT
> No biggie. About to see my
> father. What's up?

BIZ
NM ur situation is a little more
important than mine

> WYATT
> Why? What's happening?

I see text bubbles appear and disappear a few times, like Biz can't decide what to say. Then his text appears.

BIZ
don't worry about it. call
me after

Now I'm worried about whatever is happening with Biz.

> WYATT
> Are you sure? Do you want
> to meet me here and we can
> talk? I wish you were here
> with me actually.

BIZ
of course

I text Biz the address of the place and tell him to meet me in the courtyard. If things go horribly sideways, Biz can swoop in and save the day.

How long could a meeting with your long-lost father last? We'd have to make small talk before even thinking about dipping our toes into any kind of father-son relationship. I'm not expecting a redo of our entire missed lives together in a single hour.

The best I could hope for is an answer to why he left.

I knock on the door. Before it opens, I adjust the way I'm standing at least ten times: arms crossed, uncrossed, knees slightly bent, standing with perfect posture, two steps back away from the door, one-half step back in. It's hard to know how to act and where to put your hands and how to stand and look and—

The door opens.

I wasn't expecting someone this short. Well, he isn't exactly short but his eyeline is lower than I'd expected.

I tilt my head down to see my father sitting in a motorized wheelchair. This man that seemed larger-than-life in my memory is now so small.

This time, I need confirmation right away. "Richard Wallace?"

Beneath his pair of giant, black-rimmed glasses, like an old-timey Hollywood power mogul might wear, his eyes are sharp and he has a playful smile. "Wyatt Wallace?"

We stare silently at each other for a few seconds, trying to connect all of the lost years between us and everything that brought us back together.

We take our conversation to the beautifully designed courtyard. It's a lush area with flower beds and brand-new paved walkways. Patio tables with yellow umbrellas surrounded by stately palm trees offer protection for its citizens.

Richard—I'm not ready to say Dad—speaks first. "I was wondering what you'd look like," he says, taking in my face, reconfiguring his brain to understand that I'm not a kid anymore. "I've tried googling you over the years but could never find much."

"Yeah, I don't have much of an online footprint. My social media is just pictures of our dog. Oh, and I take a pic of my director's chair once in a while."

"Before you tell me about your dog and your job, you say there's a *we*? Are you married? Your mom never replied to me through the years. I don't know anything about you boys."

"Not married." I guess now's the time to come out to him. "Partnered. Boyfriend."

"I'm so happy you found someone," he says without missing a beat.

"Yeah," I say, staring at the thorny base of a nearby palm tree. "You too. Gordon seems so great."

At the same time, we smile, realizing it's kind of a gift that father and son are both gay. A fact that's still blowing my mind. But at least we're one step closer toward bonding that might not have otherwise existed.

"He's the best. Been by my side for almost twenty years," Richard says.

"Wow. Amazing," I say, astonished at how little I know about him.

"What's your guy's name?"

"His name is Biz. His real name is Massimo? He's Italian? And was nicknamed Biz as a kid?" I have no idea why I'm suddenly saying everything like a question. Nervous energy can take strange directions. "And we have a baby on the way."

"No kidding!" Richard grins with tears in his eyes. "When?"

"Due in a few weeks. That's why we're here. We drove from New York and the baby will be born in California."

"And then back to New York?"

"That's the plan."

Richard bites his quivering lower lip to keep from crying tears of pride for his son having a baby. He takes a deep breath and looks up at the deep blue sky for strength.

"I suppose you want to know . . . everything," he says, diving into the past.

"That would be helpful," I say sharply. Of course I want to know everything, to question him, to poke and prod and fight and debate and argue until I know every last detail of how, why, what, where, when.

Richard sighs with a weight he's been carrying. "Right around the time your brother was born, I was diagnosed with MS. Been living with it for decades now but . . . it was mild at first. I was able to keep it under control with the right meds. After I left Boston, I met Gordon. We've had a great life. Lately, it hasn't been much fun though. My needs started taking up our days. It took a toll on both of us. This place was the closest to home where I felt comfortable, and he visits me every day." He flashes a smile. "Getting old isn't for cowards."

I blink. Part of me feels bad. He's had it rough. But I wonder if I somehow missed the part where he abandoned us and why Mom never spoke of him.

But I think I know why.

Realizing my hands are clasped too tightly to the seat of the bench, I release them. I need to just free-fall and not plan exactly what I'm about to say.

"So . . . when you left, was I—"

"It wasn't you or your brother's fault, just so we have that clear," Richard says, putting a gentle hand on my knee, making sure I know this emphatically.

"No. Yeah, I know. I maybe thought that when I was younger but . . ."

"It wasn't just one thing. It was a perfect storm." Richard lets the floodgates open. He explains to me what happened as much as he reminds himself. "Me being gay and marrying your mom was obviously the main thing."

"Which me and Alex had no idea about."

"It was a different time, that era. Back then, if you wanted to fall in love, get married and have kids, you'd marry a woman. We didn't have surrogates. Adopting wasn't in the picture. Neither was saying you had a boyfriend. None of it was the norm the way it is now. And so . . ."

"You blew it." For a second, I was going to just nod and take it all in. But I decide not to forgive him that easily.

"I don't know if that's fair to say," Richard says. His posture stiffens.

"Why not? To leave us kids and Mom with nothing? She had to completely start over." I swallow, nervous adrenaline kicking in. "Sorry, but it's time to let out my bitterness and frustration and astonishment and hurt. I'm no longer a kid, sad and missing my dad. I'm an adult now, speaking to another adult. Why didn't you just come out to Mom and hang around for the sake of your two kids?"

"Like I said, different era. Coming out and being openly gay wasn't an option. I left because that wouldn't have been fair to your mom. And I needed to be honest with myself and live an honest life."

"But clearly that hurt Mom. And it definitely hurt me and Alex. You broke an entire family. Growing up, we took three separate paths. There was barely any communication of any-thing real. No cohesiveness. None of us recovered from you leaving. Not really," I explain.

I can see he's hurt, but he's willing to accept the truth.

"I'm not saying Mom is innocent either," I continue. "It's wrong that she could never really tell me why you left. Or that you'd been trying to reach out."

"I eventually told her I was gay," he says. "When I finally admitted it to myself. It's why I started writing you guys letters. But by then she had already cut me off completely. She didn't stop talking to me because I was gay. She stopped talking to me because I hurt her."

"I just can't understand how you both kept up all the lies," I say, my cheeks starting to burn. "You waited so long to tell her who you really are, and she could barely bring herself to tell me about your letters. I had to discover them."

"We both screwed up. It didn't start perfect and it ended worse," he admits.

My head throbs thinking how I came out here in search of answers, only to learn more than I could've ever imagined.

I remember all the Father's Days, the hockey games, the snow days when all the kids and their parents met at the park and went sledding, wishing I had my dad with me.

In an instant, I decide I don't want this to hurt me anymore.

I think of the long road ahead that Biz and I are about to have with our baby. I can't replace the memories I don't have, but I can create new ones.

As much as I want to dwell on the fantasy of what could've been with my father, what should've been, there isn't enough time. I have to accept that colossal mistakes were made and that all those years between us are gone. This is our new reality.

I realize this jigsaw puzzle in my mind is always going to have a few missing pieces.

Richard chooses his words carefully. "Look at you. You turned out so great."

"That's because I chose this path. I didn't choose anger because I didn't want your absence defining me. I could've held in only so much more resentment until it cracked me and turned me bitter or rebellious. Getting to this point in my life hasn't been easy. I don't know where I got the tools but something helped me along the way," I say, realizing all of this for the first time.

"I'm sure your mom had something to do with it," he adds softly.

I nod, knowing her force of nature helped my brother and I push through a lot.

We let a quiet breeze linger for a moment as the only sound between us.

"I gotta say, no matter what you think of me, it's so damn good to see you, son," he says. Hearing him say that word sends a shock through my central nervous system. It sounds so foreign coming from someone who's not my mom.

I turn to look at this man. Really look at him. Underneath his black statement glasses, I'm struck by how much we look alike, like Dave meeting his future self at the end of *2001: A Space Odyssey*.

I realize that I'm a perfect mix of my parents. I have my mom's blue eyes and fair Irish skin with my dad's full lips and the same prominent jawline. Strong genes run deep. I'm happy to see that he still has a full head of hair, a wild whip of gunmetal gray, like a news anchor on vacation. There are cracks around his eyes and deep lines around his mouth where he smiles often.

Most noticeably, the heart on his sleeve yields to a lifetime of regret.

"So where do we go from here?" I ask.

"If you follow this path, it takes you to the north parking lot," Richard says.

"I mean bigger picture."

"That was a joke. Sorry. My dry sense of humor," he explains.

"I was joking too. 'Cuz I knew you were joking. Guess we're both dry."

"Wow. You really played that real. Good one," Richard says.

We smile at each other with an identical playfulness in our eyes. Both trying to move past the nostalgia of each other.

"I think it's up to you," Richard says. "I realize we could never make up for lost time, but I'd love to stay updated on your life. Check in, just to chat." Richard doesn't want to overstep. "If you want."

I'd have to give our future relationship more thought. "That's a good first step," I say.

We look up at someone approaching. "My god, they're getting younger and younger in this place." We spot a figure struggling to walk toward us, backlit by the sun, almost in silhouette. The man is using a walker? Or a cane, maybe? Like he's trying to learn to walk again.

When the man clears the hedges, I can't believe who I'm looking at. I stand and see the man is on crutches with a big black medical boot on his foot. My heart sinks.

"Biz?"

# 38

## GERSHWIN

### BIZ

**T**HE THREE OF US sit at a round table under a yellow umbrella in a corner of the garden as I explain my dumb zip-lining accident.

"So, yeah, it's nothing. Just sprained," I say, trying to downplay it.

Wyatt has a shocked, sympathetic look on his face. He rubs my back, making me feel a little better.

"But aren't you supposed to land safely when you zip-line? It's not like you were parachuting." Wyatt senses there's more to the story, but I'm not about to tell him I'd been drinking in front of his long-lost dad.

"I just landed weirdly. It's a minor fracture."

"I thought you said it was a sprain," Wyatt says with mild confusion.

"I did. But then I upgraded it to a fracture, which is more accurate. It's fine."

"From now on, I'm not letting you out of my sight," Wyatt jokes.

"Maybe we're better as a team," I say to Wyatt as he pulls me in for a hug.

This man, who I presume is Wyatt's dad, feels slightly embarrassed, out of place, watching us. It's my window to redirect the conversation.

"Anyway, it's nice to meet you," I say to Richard. "I'm glad you're not a complete monster." For a moment, the three of us aren't sure if what I just said is wildly inappropriate or funny. We all lightly chuckle.

"I'm just happy you're making my son happy," Richard says, beaming to finally share this moment.

It's striking for me to hear Richard refer to Wyatt as his son. I'm sure it's going to take a minute for Wyatt to call him "Dad," but it's a nice step to reconciliation.

As impending dads ourselves, we're all too aware of the meaning of that word. I fish for Wyatt's hand under the table and give him a good, supportive squeeze.

Another man appears in our little corner. He arrives with a smile and a large brown bag.

"Gordon! Grab a seat," Richard greets him as they give each other a smooch on the lips. It's a beautiful thing to see two older gay men have affection for each other and—

*OH MY GOD.*

I'm just putting two and two together. The wind is knocked out of me.

*Is Wyatt's dad gay? And this is his husband? What is happening right now?*

Wyatt glances at me with a slight smirk, communicating to me that he'll explain it all later. I can't help but think of how Wyatt's mom is going to react to this whole meeting.

After Richard introduces his *husband, Gordon,* confirming

my suspicion, Gordon takes out some sandwiches and the four of us split a late picnic lunch.

I want to stare at these two. I need to gawk. I suppress my urge to yell, "You're gay?!"

The main topic of the day has been set aside for a moment while we enjoy our food, the beautiful afternoon sun and each other's company.

"I guess we both needed a little backup," Richard says to his son about their partners, now sitting comfortably by their sides.

"Did you bring the box?" Richard asks Gordon.

Gordon takes out a small keepsake wooden box and hands it to Wyatt.

"What's this?" Wyatt asks.

"Just some things I've been wanting to give you. Since I wasn't even sure if your mom was getting my letters, I didn't want these to get lost in the mail. You can open them later."

Wyatt seems touched. He smiles appreciatively, but at the same time, he's clearly conflicted and overwhelmed.

The faint strands of music start to play. Richard motions for all of us to check out what's happening.

The four of us walk, crutch and wheel around a line of bushes to find a small group of the community's residents have set up chairs to enjoy live music.

Violins, cellos, flutes, even a conductor.

I put my arm around Wyatt to let him know I'm here for him during this wild ride. Richard and Gordon stand next to us, an imperfect, strange new family that will take some time for healing. But for now, we all listen to the beautiful little symphony play George Gershwin's "The Man I Love."

# 39

## RICHARD

**WYATT**

THE MOST VIVID MEMORY of Richard/my father/Dad took place in a car. I was six or seven years old, I think. I vaguely remember going to this local elementary school, which was—at the time—a three-story brick building with giant pillars out front.

It was before he left us and we were forced to move to a less expensive part of town.

Every Sunday morning, the four of us would pack into the car and go for a drive. Mom and Dad in the front seats, and me and Alex in the back of our tan Volvo station wagon with matching tan cloth seats.

It was my dad's day off from the bank. I never really knew what he did there. Mom always said he was "down at the bank," or "going off to the bank" and "thank god the bank's closed today."

We usually took a leisurely spin around suburban Boston—literally Sunday drivers—looking at houses bigger and fancier than ours, trying to imagine other people's lives. In retrospect, this was when my mom's real estate expertise was born because she always knew where to find the biggest, most interesting houses.

One particular Sunday, after seeing all the houses, my dad announced we were going on a secret impromptu road trip. Even Mom didn't know about it.

One hour and two naps later, we arrived in the bustling city of Boston. The skyline was aglow with the magic of city life. We had a late lunch at a popular waterfront place. I remember my dad pretended it was my birthday (which was probably months away), so we had free chocolate cake with a candle while the entire restaurant sang to me. I was full of joy; I couldn't stop laughing.

Afterward, my parents took us to a magnificently restored art deco movie theater with its signage jutting up into the purple night sky. They were showing a Hitchcock classic, one of my father's favorite movies: *Vertigo*. The red curtain opened to reveal the magical moving images as I sank into the plush red seats.

My brother and I didn't understand any of the movie, but in between popcorn, peanut M&M's, Twizzlers and Coke, I became moved by the experience. I'd occasionally look up at the projector, wondering where those magical images came from. That movie and that theater became the birthplace of my desire to be a director.

I guess in a weird way, I have my father to thank for that.

– – – – – – – ▸

WHILE SITTING IN THE PASSENGER SEAT AS BIZ DRIVES US TOWARD OUR final destination of Palm Springs, I decide to do something as spontaneous as my father did that day. A chance to create an unexpected memory with Biz.

"Let's go to the desert," I suggest.

Biz tries to keep his eyes on the road. "What do you mean? We *are* going to the desert. Palm Springs."

"Forget Palm Springs. I want to do something off the beaten path."

Biz glances at me and thinks. I can tell he's immediately game for something spontaneous. "Okay, where? We can't just find a place in the desert."

"Why not? Let's just go hang somewhere in the middle of nowhere. Clear our minds," I suggest.

"Like Joshua Tree?"

"Or somewhere deeper in the desert. Quieter. More remote. Not obvious," I say.

"Quieter than Joshua Tree? Okay, you wanna look up something?"

"Nope. No planning. Let's just fucking go." I want to chase the free feeling my father brought that day on our trip to Boston. I realize now that this is the spirit Biz brings to, well, everything.

Biz's mouth curls into a smile as he steps on the gas.

– – – – – – – →

TWENTY-FIVE MILES LATER, THE RATTLING FROM VIRGINIA WOOLF IS NOW too consistent to ignore as we head toward an undetermined spot in the desert. We decide to find the closest mechanic to figure out the problem if we want to make it there safely without worry.

There was no room in the car for Biz's crutches, so he'd returned them to the hospital. With the dogs and eventually a baby, something had to go. The doctor gave Biz the option to use crutches or not, and it wasn't a problem for him to hobble around in his medical boot.

We wait at a car repair shop in the middle of nowhere. A dusty, family-owned operation that looks like it was established in 1802, but we don't have too many options.

According to the name tag stitched into the mechanic's greasy, navy blue coveralls, his name is Dale. He looks like he eats cigarettes whole—with his severely purple smoker lips and sallow complexion. Dale is friendly and likes to overshare, spending more time talking about himself than actually working on our car. *It's not like being a mechanic was my dream—I played ball in college till I busted my ACL. I tried living in Reno once but those big cities ain't for me.*

He says something about fixing the engine belt, or taking a look at the suspension system—maybe it was the rear axle? While we wait for the expert to do his thing, we reflect again on the meeting with my father, feeling conflicted but mostly good about the whole experience.

"I seriously cannot believe he's gay. I mean, I can believe it. But I can't," Biz says, leafing through a ten-year-old *Car and Driver* magazine in the wood-paneled waiting room. There's even a small convenience store that houses guilty pleasure snacks and, of course, a wall of slot machines. Only in Nevada.

"You and me both," I say, still wrapping my head around the entire idea.

"Your mom never said anything?" he asks.

"Never. I don't think it even crossed my mind either," I say.

"It's bizarre how much he looks like you too," Biz says about my father. "I just can't believe your mom kept all of this hidden for so many years."

"I know but I'm not going to blame her. We all have our traumas to work through. She saw him more as a man who betrayed her and not the father of her kids," I say.

"Ironic that you've wanted kids your whole life," Biz says.

"That's probably *why* I want kids. To be the dad I never had."

I decide to go outside to call my mom while Biz stays inside the mechanic shop, buying snacks and bottles of water from the vending machine.

I have to tell my mom that I just reunited with my father; it's time she knows.

But first, I remember the wooden box my father gave me. I walk to the side of the shop and open it. Inside are a few treasures: several photographs of Richard holding me as a baby, a necklace with my name in gold, a pair of bronze cuff links and a beautiful silver ring.

I hold the ring up to the sun, matching the perfect circles.

I pace the unpaved road just outside the repair shop, waiting for my mom to pick up the phone. I hang up—deciding maybe it's better if we could see each other—and FaceTime her. After one second, she picks up. She isn't her usual coiffed self: no makeup, hair twisted into a knotty, messy bun on top of her head and . . . a *sweatshirt*?

"Are you okay?" is the first thing I can think of, seeing her this out of character, dressed so casually. At least it's a sweatshirt with her real estate company logo embroidered on it and not a bargain-basement number with pizza stains, otherwise I'd have to fly home.

"Hi, baby," Mom says, looking tired.

"Everything okay?" I ask. She spots the dry, dusty background.

"Where are you?" she asks, ignoring my question.

"Nevada?" I say, testing her.

"*Nevada?* I thought you were going to Palm Springs." For the first time, I see the web my mom has spun all these years. She never knew how to tell me that my father is living in Las Vegas, trying to connect with me.

"Actually, Mom, you probably know the reason why we're in Nevada," I say, waiting for a response. Absolute silence. Her face says it all. She does know. Moms always know. "We came here because . . . I wanted to meet him." I pause. She's letting me have the floor, staring at me with sympathetic eyes. "All those letters in my boxes . . . I had to track him down and see him again."

"Oh, honey." She sits on the sofa and hugs her legs. "I think that's wonderful."

"You do?"

"Of course I do." She softens. "I think it should've happened a long time ago."

I'm not sure if I heard that right. I think this through, shifting the phone from my left hand to my right hand. "What do you mean? Then why didn't it ever happen?"

She sighs. "I've thought about this for a long time. All those years I went back and forth, do I or don't I want him in the boys' lives. For me, I couldn't separate the husband from the father. He wasn't a good husband to me back then. And, honestly, he wasn't the best father to you both. I did all the work when you were babies."

I sigh, feeling terrible for my mom.

"He didn't want to be married to me and he wanted children even less. It was the fair-weather father that I didn't want in my life and your lives. You were too young to remember but he wasn't committed to any of us. I didn't think it was fair to you and Alex. I wanted stability for you both. So I cut off our relationship completely."

I take this all in. "But when did you know? I mean, when did he tell you that he was gay?"

"I was naive. I always knew things didn't feel exactly right with him. But I didn't know if that was how relationships were supposed to be. Or maybe I blamed myself."

I feel bad for all of us.

"Sorry. But it's true. When you were in high school and Alex was in middle school, he contacted me to tell me he was living with another man. It was before you came out. In hindsight, I should've done things a lot differently."

I spot an abandoned rickety old rocking chair on the sidewalk and take a seat. I nod, trying to understand. "Honey, I was so hurt when he left me. I was a single mom. I just had to keep moving forward and start my business. For you guys." She collects her thoughts. "I've only always wanted the best for you two. And remember, your father didn't reach out until you were in college. It would've been a distraction."

In the distance, I look up and see Biz slapping the broken vending machine inside the repair shop with his palm while the dogs run in circles around him. Our little family, holed up together at the end of the earth.

That's when I decide not to let any of us stay trapped by the past. "Mom," I interrupt her. "It's okay." I fill with a sudden lightness. "You did your best, which was more than we could've asked for. And he . . . it sounds like he needed to figure some things out, especially with his health."

Mom wipes her teary eyes with her sleeve. "How does he look?"

"Honestly? Like an old gay," I say, as we both laugh a little. "He's in an electric wheelchair. But he can move around better than me."

"Is he doing okay?"

"The MS has caught up with him for sure. But he's living through it." I'm not sure if I should say this next part but our wounds need to heal completely. "And we met his husband."

"Oh . . ." she says, trailing off into silence. She stares off. "You know, in the past, those words would've been hard for me to hear, but with you, Wyatt . . ." She feels relief, connecting with me through our screens. "I never imagined talking about this with you could be so easy."

"It's not easy, Mom," I say. "I want so badly to be angry with you for omitting so much and hiding those letters, but you gave us so much more in return. Maybe it's the desert air talking but I don't want to be mad at you. Because we're in this together," I say.

Mom shakes her head, shuts her eyes tight, trying to will away her tears. She can't help but let them flow. Through her sniffles, she manages a warm, appreciative smile.

"Thank you for saying that, Wyatt," she says, wiping her nose with a tissue, trying to compose herself. "What's his husband like?"

"Nice. Artsy. Actually, he's literally an artist. Talented. Great guy," I say. "I don't know if we're all going to have Christmas together anytime soon but . . ." I trail off with a small laugh, thinking of the absurdity of it all.

"I'm happy you're in touch," Mom says. "It's long overdue that I support you no matter what kind of relationship you want to have with your father. I hope you know that."

My heart fills with love. There's one more thing I have to know. "Did you . . ." I hesitate. "I mean, the boxes you told me to sort through . . ." I wait for her to interject but she's wondering where I'm going with this. "I found Dad's letters in those boxes. Is that why you kept telling me to go through them?" It feels weird for me to call him *Dad* but it's okay for me to try. I've never had the chance to call anyone Dad. Why can't I now?

"His letters were in those boxes? I must've forgotten. There's just a ton of crap in that basement I gotta go through." She waves this off.

Mom claims she didn't tell me to go through my boxes so I could find Dad's letters. But maybe she did too. I know the truth is probably somewhere in the middle.

We say our goodbyes and I hang up after promising to call her once the baby arrives.

Biz saunters out of the repair shop with a smile on his face, snacks in hand, followed by the dogs running after him. I feel okay with my mom and the situation with my dad, not sure where the next phase will lead us.

Now it's time to focus on building the family I'm about to have.

# 40

## NEON TO NATURE

**BIZ**

**V**IRGINIA WOOLF IS AS quiet as a library. We're back on the highway.

Our next destination: unknown.

The TMI mechanic did the trick. He fixed whatever needed fixing. But not before he told us an elaborate story about an alien ship that descended upon his garage with their UFO in need of repairs, which—shocker—turned out was all just a dream he'd had the night before.

With Wyatt behind the wheel, I suggest staying at a roadside motel or even one of those luxury tent glamping situations. "We can rough it under the stars surrounded by majestic mountain panoramas, left to fend for ourselves—but you also get like free Kiehl's products or some shit. Super roughing it," I say.

"Sounds tempting," Wyatt says. "Let's just find a place when we get there, dog policies be damned."

"You're really taking this spontaneous thing seriously. I like it," I say.

I've always loved Wyatt's me-against-the-world attitude. But making that initial step toward peace with his dad feels like a weight has been lifted.

I text my own dad, now more appreciative of him than ever.

BIZ

i love you dad. that's
all i wanted to say.

GIO

Dear Massi,

He always texts me like he's writing a formal letter.

GIO

I love you too. Love, Dad

He concludes with three heart emojis.

We pass a metal sign that reads "The Heart of the Mojave." Feels like crossing into a new dimension. The bright lights of Vegas are a distant memory. Now it's red rocks and a Joshua tree forest; the shaggy branches of the trees look like people raising their arms to the sky.

With the top down, the heat intensifies, like swimming in hot sauce. The desolate highway feels like we're the only two people on Earth plus two dogs.

Wyatt spots something in the distance and slows down.

"What are you doing?" I ask.

"Just trust me," he says. We pull to the side of the road as a cloud of dust kicks up.

"Didn't you just pee?" I ask, looking ahead at the infinite nothing.

"I don't have to pee," Wyatt says.

"Then why are we stopping again?"

"Have you noticed Matilda hasn't thrown up since we picked up Pancake?" Wyatt asks.

We look back at the two content dogs, napping. Matilda opens one eye to see what all the fuss is about, then decides it's not worth it and shuts her eye to continue napping.

"Oh my god. You're right. Pancake has a calming effect on her," I say.

"Or maybe because *we're* more relaxed than ever," Wyatt realizes.

I smile, thinking he's right. "Let's share this moment of silence in honor of Matilda not barfing anymore," I say. We stay still for a second.

Then Wyatt points to a sign that reads "Mojave National Preserve."

The old Wyatt would've been predictably keeping us on a tight schedule. But the more relaxed West Coast Wyatt, this new version that's starting to emerge, doesn't have anything planned.

Motoring down a dirt road, we weave around a grove of tamarisk trees, past the juniper trees filled with berries, getting farther and farther away from civilization.

I smile, knowing neither of us know where we're going.

I turn to look at Wyatt driving. He has his concentration face on—slightly biting his lower lip. A mild crinkle on his forehead, just above his eyebrows. Excitement in his eyes too. Like he's discovering a new part of himself.

We hit a small puddle that splashes mud on the car.

"I don't think Virginia Woolf is equipped for off-roading," I say. We're traveling on a road that's not a road, and at this moment, it doesn't matter. "But I trust you!" I blurt out.

Wyatt glances at me and lets out a chuckle. "Good!"

We're both committed to winging it.

We pass an abandoned mine, maneuvering gently around a jackrabbit that's just squatting in the middle of our path. We're careful not to disturb her.

The sun sets behind the glorious mountains.

Wyatt pulls next to an oversized Joshua tree with its wild outstretched arms creating a playful shadow on our faces.

He cuts the engine. I check my phone. "No service out here."

"Are you nervous?" Wyatt asks.

"No, are you?"

Wyatt smirks and shakes his head before stepping out of the car to let the dogs loose—happy again to escape the moving box. Both dogs pee and chase each other in circles around the car, smiling from ear to ear in their canine way.

"Good doggies!" Wyatt calls out to them.

"Don't go too far!" I add.

I stretch my legs next to Virginia Woolf, my cumbersome medical boot anchoring me. The sunlight hits me from behind, projecting my shadow on the ground.

"You look like a logo for a yoga apparel company," Wyatt says.

Wyatt grabs me from behind, mid–hamstring stretch, spins me around and starts kissing me. I'm quickly worked up, my excitement showing through my sky-blue corduroy shorts.

He stops as quickly as he'd started.

"What was that for?" I ask.

"Because I love you. I want to share everything with you. And we're about to have a fucking baby together. I just wanted to mark this moment out here in the middle of nowhere." Wyatt is intoxicated by the nature therapy.

"You know how much I love you," I say.

We sit cross-legged on the ground and look up. The early evening sky puts on its nightly free light show and we have front-row seats. Fiery reds and oranges and pinks and yellows seem to shoot out from space.

This time the silence between us is comfortable, safe.

I take out two bottles of water I picked up at the repair shop.

I sip and make a face. "What is the worst bottled water and why is it Dasani?"

Wyatt laughs, which makes me laugh. We break into hysterics, causing the dogs to run over and joyfully lick our faces, getting in on the fun.

I look up at the sky again. "It's amazing."

"Incredible."

"I might cry."

"It's giving me a boner."

Without taking his eyes off the sky, Wyatt grabs me closer, our thighs entwined.

I take out my phone and play "Sound & Color" by Alabama Shakes.

"Oh my god. This song with this sky and you. The sky is so . . . *vibrant*. Isn't it vibrant?"

"Stop saying vibrant," Wyatt jokes.

"Oh! I have an idea." I play another song.

"*Take your time, think a lot. Think of everything you've got. For you will still be here tomorrow but your dreams may not,*" Cat Stevens sings.

"'Father and Son.' Nice," Wyatt says. He plays another song on his phone. "Cat's in the Cradle," the equally laid-back song with a similar father-son theme.

"Another Cat Stevens!" I say.

"Harry Chapin. You're confusing 'Cat's in the Cradle' with Cat Stevens."

"Oh. Right." The chorus comes and we stand, belting it out as loud as we can. We harmonize together, our own desert karaoke.

"*And the cat's in the cradle and the silver spoon. Little boy blue and the man in the moon . . .*" We point at the moon and laugh, our shining beacon spotlighting our performance with an audience of two bewildered, sleepy dogs.

"*And all I remember is your back.*" I change the song to Kelly Clarkson's "Piece by Piece." "*Walkin' towards the airport, leavin' us all in your past . . .*"

"Are there any songs about fathers that *aren't* depressingly sad?" Wyatt asks.

"At least this one is a bangin' dance remix."

Both of us have equally sick dance moves to the song, trying to one-up each other. Wyatt, sexy, slow-moving, hips shaking. Me, higher energy, playful. We laugh at how good the other dances until tears stream down our faces.

Before the song ends, I slowly turn down the volume until it's completely silent.

"Nice fake fade-out!" Wyatt shouts.

"When it's a seven-and-a-half-minute remix, you're simply left with no choice but the fake fade-out."

Next, I play "Papa Don't Preach" by Madonna. *"Papa, I know you're going to be upset. 'Cause I was always your little girl."*

"Um, that's a song about teen pregnancy?" Wyatt reminds me.

"Well, it's father-daughter so . . ." I play Fleetwood Mac's "Landslide" instead.

"That's a father and son song?" Wyatt wonders.

"It is now." We sing every word together in unison, waving our phones in the air like we're at a stadium concert. *"But time makes you bolder. Even children get older. And I'm getting older too . . ."*

"Oh!" A song pops into my head that I can't find fast enough. Sondheim's "Children Will Listen" from *Into the Woods.*

Wyatt lets me, the former musical theater performer, take this one. *"Careful the things you say. Children will listen. Careful the things you do. Children will see . . . and leeeeeeearn."* I break character to remind Wyatt, "I was—"

"The Baker, your junior year of college," Wyatt recites back to me like he's heard this a thousand times before. "I know."

I have an idea. "Maybe after the baby comes we could go to LA for a few days. I can try to reconnect with some of my old cast members, maybe try to set up a few meetings with agents or managers while we're there. I need to think about what I'm going to do next."

"Definitely." Wyatt thinks this through. "I could stop by the LA office and see my reps there. They're trying to produce more film and TV stuff. Not just commercials."

"Look at us. Making career moves like a couple of bosses," I say.

Wyatt grabs my phone with another song in mind.

Steel drums play, conjuring a lazy Caribbean scene. Then comes John Lennon's dulcet voice singing "Beautiful Boy."

*"Close your eyes. Have no fear. The monster's gone, he's on the run. And your daddy's here."* Wyatt quietly sings along, telling me his mom used to sing this to him.

I go silent.

The lyrics strike a chord with me and I'm finally ready to let it out. "I've been afraid of some things," I say.

Wyatt tilts his head. Waiting for me to finish my vague thought.

"I'm scared I'm not going to make a good dad," I admit.

Wyatt's entire face changes to empathy. Like this is the key to unlock our future relationship potential.

"What?" he asks. "Why didn't you tell me this before?"

"I don't know. I didn't want *you* to question if I would make a good dad, I guess. But I'm still afraid," I add.

"Afraid of what?"

"Of living up to my own dad," I say. "And honestly? Living up to you. I've been afraid to say that out loud but somehow it feels good now, but . . . I feel like you're going to out-dad me. I know it's not a competition but . . ."

Wyatt's lips curl into a smile, clearly thinking this is absurd. "Biz, you don't even realize how great of a dad you're going to be," he says. "You're going to be the best. I know for a fact. You're going to make the kid laugh and do funny voices and you'll be more loving and nurturing than me because it's what you know from your dad. I'm going to have to learn from you how to do all of that." He lets out a short laugh. "I can't even believe you would have that worry."

"I didn't know this but that's exactly what I needed to hear you say."

"So is this what the babymoon was all about?" Wyatt asks, lifting his brow.

"What do you mean?"

"You didn't just want this babymoon for the fun of it all, did you," Wyatt says.

I look into the horizon for a moment, gathering my thoughts. "I did want to have fun but at the same time . . ." I turn to Wyatt. "Maybe I was running away from my fears," I say, figuring this out as I speak. "Maybe I thought the more fun we could have, the more I could escape feeling afraid that I wouldn't be a good parent."

Realization washes over both of us.

"I'm afraid too," Wyatt admits. "Of being a father."

"You are?" I ask, in complete shock.

"Of course. You had the blueprint for a good father. Not me," Wyatt says. "But who wouldn't be afraid? It's the biggest thing that could ever happen to anyone."

My heart races with excitement. Suddenly, I don't feel so alone. "I guess we both just have to dive headfirst," I say.

"And hope we don't break an ankle," Wyatt jokes as we share another laugh.

A funny thought pops into my head. "There's this insufferable Instagram account I look at sometimes. They're called quaddaddiez."

"quaddaddiez are the worst!" Wyatt squeals.

"What! You know quaddaddiez?! You're never on Instagram," I say.

"I dabble from time to time. What about them?"

"They're this completely unattainable idea of parenthood," I explain.

"Trust me, I've thought the same thing," Wyatt says. I'm stunned. "But none of that is real life. They just have really good lighting."

We laugh. "I know. They're everything I don't want to be," I go on. "But at the same time, they're everything I *do* want to be. I want the ridiculously posed family photographs with our kid and the matching Christmas onesies and the elaborate Halloween costumes. I want story time and to go on baby playdates at the park and stay up all night with them while they're crying to make them feel better. I want to do it all with you."

"That's all I want too. And that's all I needed to hear," Wyatt says.

My heart grows three sizes, rockets to the moon and back.

"Are you still going to say the opposite of what I say all the time?" Wyatt asks with a glint in his eye.

"What do you mean? I don't say the opposite thing all the time," I joke.

Out of nowhere, I goofily howl at the moon. Wyatt follows suit as the two dogs join in, a veritable symphony of humans and animals.

We laugh and Wyatt's body melts into mine as we fall onto the ground, kissing each other's faces, necks, chests. All of our limbs stretched out underneath each other as we toss one another around. My whole body tingles.

Matilda and Pancake practically roll their eyes as their elbows fall to the ground, planting themselves firmly into their new sleeping positions.

The dogs sigh and look away as their owners do unspeakable things with each other under a sky that morphs into lavender in the middle of nowhere.

# 41

## GETTING THE BOOT

**WYATT**

"THE MILKY WAY IS EPIC!" Biz shouts, lying next to me on the hood of Virginia Woolf, staring up at the night's stars. We're naked, covered in sweat and grime from rolling around on the earth, luxuriating in our afterglow.

I've never seen so many stars. "Like, what even *is* the Milky Way, ya know?" I ask.

"Technically, a candy bar," Biz jokes.

"There are a gazillion bajillion stars," I contemplate, "and we're just so inconsequential compared to all of . . . them." I wave my arms toward the open sky like a QVC model. "I am truly humbled."

Biz cracks up at my sincerity. "Mmm, now I wish we had candy bars."

"I wish we could make s'mores."

"Oh my god, yes!"

"C'mon. You know how to build a fire. Be the daddy and get it going."

"I think there are designated areas for that."

"I want a burnt marshmallow real bad."

Biz crosses and uncrosses his legs. "How do people in movies lay on their cars and watch the stars, this is so not comfortable."

"I know. My back is trashed right now."

We both tumble off at the same time, groaning like elderly men.

"I wish we had a tent," Biz says, sliding on his boxer briefs.

"We could sleep in the car." I pull on my boxers.

"What if we get mauled by a bear?"

"Are there bears out here?"

"I have no clue. Are there snakes? Or spiders? I think I read once there are baby tarantulas in the desert."

"Scorpions are a thing out here too. I think."

We've both lived in the city too long to know what current neighbors we're dealing with. I wouldn't be surprised to see a pigeon. Our Brooklyn is showing.

"Whatever's out here, Matilda and Pancake will protect us." We turn to see both dogs curled up in balls of innocence, incapable of hurting a fly, fast asleep.

There's a faint cool breeze. Thankfully, the temperature has dropped so it's not too steamy. In one big swoosh, Biz spreads out a blanket on the soft ground where we hold each other and cuddle under the dust of constellations.

The silence is abundant. It feels like we should whisper.

"I feel like we're in an episode of *Naked and Afraid*," I say.

"Except we're in an episode of *Boxer Briefs and Semi–Freaked Out*."

Biz grabs me, flips me on my side, flings his leg around my

hips and turns me into the little spoon. Matilda and Pancake lazily waddle and plop down next to each other at our feet.

I grin from ear to ear, listening to Wyatt, Matilda and Pancake all breathe heavily, dreaming together; our little family. Our bodies blur together and we all find sleep.

- - - - - - - >

SOMETIME AROUND EIGHT THIRTY THE NEXT MORNING, I WAKE UP SURprised to find Biz already awake. The night owl is up before the early bird.

"How are you awake?" I ask, rubbing sleep out of my eyes, sitting up. My mouth is dry and my brain feels swampy. I crave black coffee. "This might be the first time I've ever seen you up before me."

"I guess I sleep better in the middle of the desert," Biz says. "And snuggled next to you."

I smile as the dogs stretch and shake the dirt off their fur.

The blinding sun is high and bright, moving over the surreal, ragged mountains towering in the distance. It feels hotter and dryer than yesterday and it's time we find indoor relief.

"Is there any more water?" I ask, putting on shorts and a T-shirt.

"I just poured some for the dogs. There's a little left."

"Shit. Okay. We should get going." I start to panic slightly.

"Relax. We'll be fine." Biz starts doing yoga poses to wake up.

"I'm serious, Biz. I don't wanna die of dehydration out here. I saw a roadside motel on the way here that looked decent. We can check in, shower, get breakfast and stay the night."

"Or we can just buy a tent and come back to this spot."

"I'd rather have a little more civilization tonight," I decide.

"Okaaaay," Biz says, making sure his disappointment comes across.

"What?"

"Nothing. You're completely diminishing last night but that's fine," Biz says.

"How am I diminishing it?"

"By saying you want more civilization," Biz says, standing up. "I thought it was magical for both of us."

"It was. That's not what I'm saying at all. Last night was a total blast but today's a new day and it's time to focus."

"I should've known your spontaneity was temporary."

I watch him abruptly fold the blanket and put away the dog bowls. I wonder how this went south so quickly.

"C'mon. Stop. It was my idea to detour out here," I remind him.

Biz unfastens the thick Velcro straps—four of them—on his medical boot and slips it off with a sigh of cathartic relief, like undressing after a day of skiing.

"Thanks for agreeing to keep that on while we did it last night. That was kinda hot," I say, trying to win him back.

"You have a medical boot fetish, I guess?" he says.

"Apparently." I watch Biz massage his foot and ankle, which is sweaty and still swollen. "I still can't believe you did that. I feel so bad."

"It's okay. I'm mobile. And the whole experience was a breakthrough for me," Biz says. "But don't drink and zip-line at home, kids."

I turn to him with a quizzical look. "What do you mean? You drank before you went zip-lining?"

"I told you. I was at the pool. I just had a couple piña coladas," Biz says.

"You did not tell me that." I shake my head. "That's just . . . that's unbelievable."

"Okay, you don't have to judge me," Biz says, offended.

"I'm not judging you. I just don't understand when that's going to end?"

"Aaaaaand the magic desert party is officially over."

"I'm serious, Biz. I mean, you seem to make the same mistake over and over again."

"What mistake?" Biz demands.

"Being irresponsible! Enough, already. You're about to be a *dad*," I say.

"I'm pretty sure dads drink. The entire concept of a beer was made for dads."

"That's not what I'm saying at all."

"What, you meet your actual dad for one day and suddenly you're the expert? Why do you have to be so uptight when it comes to literally everything?" Biz asks.

This stings.

"I'm not claiming to be a dad expert. And I'm not uptight. It's called responsibility. We're about to have one of the most profoundly life-changing events, and we're in the middle of the desert fucking off like we're in *college* without a care in the world. I'm just saying maybe it's time we grow up a little. Not everything has to be fun fun fun. That's not really how I want to live my life, and I don't want to be shamed into thinking I'm some uptight monster."

"That's not what I'm saying," Biz says.

"You just did."

"*I* wasn't the one who wanted to pick a random spot in the

desert to sleep. Please don't put that on me." Biz has a point. This was my idea.

"You're right. But I'm constantly feeling all this pressure from you to do something outrageous like that so . . ."

"When have I ever said I want you to be outrageous?"

"You haven't. It's just always implied. You make me feel like *I'm* the parent sometimes."

"And you make me feel like I'm a kid."

"Maybe because you're acting like one." I'm seething. "With you losing your job and not even telling me about it—"

"I tried to tell you and there was never a right time," Biz says.

"Again, all I ask for is transparency in this relationship."

"Says the guy who isn't exactly the best communicator," Biz comes back at me.

"You really don't understand how all the pressure is on me now. I'm going to have to take so many shitty directing jobs and I'll never see our baby," I say. "I honestly think sometimes you just don't want to be a dad."

We stare at each other for a moment. Neither one of us backs down.

Biz stands. He limps barefoot, crossing through the dogs, and sits on the car's back fender. I watch as he struggles to slip his medical boot back on, tightening the Velcro straps.

He throws on a single sneaker, a pair of shorts and pops on a T-shirt.

"What are you doing?" I ask.

"Leaving. You can have the rest of my Dasani."

A laugh slips out before I realize he's serious. "Wait—*what?* You're taking the car and leaving us out here? I don't think that's—"

"No. You take the car. I'll walk." Biz kneels down to pet the dogs. They wag their tails and lick his face in unconditional loyalty. I can't hear what he whispers into their ears but I know it's something like love. I imagine Biz is waiting for me to call his bluff.

Wiping the fresh dog slobber off his face, Biz stands and slowly, comically, limps away toward the horizon. He's awkwardly getting nowhere fast. And he's not looking back.

I raise an eyebrow, watching him, incredulous, half amused. The farther Biz walks away, the more my stomach pools with a mix of dread, anxiety and that familiar fear of abandonment.

There's no way he could actually leave. *Can he?*

"Biz?!" I call after him. "C'mon. You just can't limp all the way to civilization from here. Can you stop so we can talk?!"

One minute in and I can see Biz is already out of breath from the rising heat. Now he has to commit to walking away to maintain his pride.

"You're just going to walk out on your unborn baby?!?" I shout at him, going for the jugular.

"You said you don't think I want to be a dad, so . . ." Biz shouts back.

I immediately regret my words.

He's going to prove a point to me, even if it means dying of heat exhaustion.

I think of running after him as the dogs sit on their hind legs and whimper, wondering where their other daddy is going. But he surely can't get far on one good foot.

When Biz disappears behind a clump of ancient Joshua trees, my uncertainty grows.

I let out a long-winded, frustrated sigh.

It would be the biggest mistake of my life to let the love of my life walk out. Especially now. I can't let Biz wander through the desert only to get torn limb from limb by wild jaguars or leopards or coyotes or lions. Okay, I have no idea what kind of animals are out there in the desert, but I'm pretty sure they might be lions.

I throw on some clothes and hop into Virginia Woolf with the dogs. The car seats are boiling hot, even for cloth. Just as I'm about to start the car, somehow my phone has reception and I get a call. It's Flora.

I keep my eyes focused on the horizon in search of Biz as I swipe to answer it.

"Flora! How are ya?!" I arrange the tone of my voice to sound casual and upbeat, because my boyfriend *definitely* didn't just leave me stranded in the middle of the desert. We've been waiting to hear from her so it's good she's finally calling.

"Hi, Wyatt. It's me," Gabrielle says. Flora's wife. I tense up. It's not normal for Gabrielle to call us. In fact, she's never called or texted us alone before.

"Oh hi, Gabrielle." I start to freak out but want to project a level of calmness.

"You guys are harder than shit to get a hold of. We left you five thousand messages."

I look at my phone and don't see one message. I'm hanging by one teeny-tiny bar of service. "We've been on the road and service is spotty out here. Sorry about that."

"Okay, don't freak the fuck out . . ." Gabrielle does not have a way with words or with people. Her tactless, devil-may-care approach brings with it a certain charm though. "Shit's going down." Maybe not *charming* exactly.

"What do you mean? What's happening? Is Flora okay? How's the baby?" I'm done with being calm.

"You need to relax, dude, but here's the scoop. We're with the doctor now, and she's saying the baby's not getting any bigger so they need to induce her early."

"Induce labor early?" I ask. "Flora said the doctor decided against that."

"The doctor changed her tune. The baby's not getting enough nutrients inside the womb so we can't wait," Gabrielle says.

"The baby's due in three and a half weeks. How early are they thinking?"

"Today."

I stop breathing. My jaw clenches. I scream inside.

The dogs look at me and whimper. They sense stress and it makes them uncomfortable.

"I know you guys are driving cross-country or some shit, so Flora wanted me to call you. The baby could be here this morning."

I swallow and try to regain composure.

"We'll be there," I say, not knowing if this is true or not.

"Where are you?" Gabrielle asks.

"Currently? Mojave Desert."

"Oh, killer. Wait—what? Don't answer that. Just meet us at the hospital asap."

"We're in the car as we speak. Thanks for letting us know."

"See you soon I hope," she says.

She hangs up.

I exhale sharply three times like I'm the one having a baby, and now I have to find Biz. I pack everything up, slam the car door shut and quickly turn the keys in the ignition.

The engine sounds like a chainsaw. I shake it off and try

again. Same thing—chainsaw. The dogs cower under the strange noise.

"Oh, come on," I say out loud.

I try again to turn on the engine. Chainsaw. Virginia Woolf has met yet another tragic end for herself.

We're not going to the hospital anytime soon.

My phone has no signal. I start running to find Biz. I'm panicked. There's no way in hell we drove all the way out here only to miss the birth of our baby. We've spent a lifetime building up to this moment. And I need to tell Biz how I feel about him.

Sprinting through unknown terrain, I pass one Joshua tree so quirky and beautiful that I briefly think about stopping to take a picture. I make a quick mental note to shoot an athletic shoe commercial on location here.

A flicker of some kind of prayer crosses my mind, hoping Matilda and Pancake will stay tied to the tree I knotted their leashes around.

The only sounds I hear are my heavy breathing and the pitter-patter of my shoes hitting the cracked earth. I run fast but my thighs feel heavy, my core blobby and bloated and my calf muscles could cramp at any moment. Stuffed in a car, driving cross-country while eating fast food is not the training I need to run a half-marathon through the desert.

*Did Biz hitchhike a ride from a stranger? Fall into a well? Is that brown thing on the ground a stick or a snake?*

After several minutes of running, my momentum slows when I spot an old two-story house that I don't remember on our way in. I head toward it instinctively, needing shade. I also need to hydrate. The house could have a water fountain or hose, or at the very worst, a bottle of Dasani. It's a weathered home-stead cabin that looks like it's been baking under the sun for three hundred years. No sign of life anywhere.

I sit on the ground, out of breath, cradling my knees to my chest. I fill with despair.

Maybe it's the heat but I stare into the sky and vividly imagine a conversation with our future sixteen-year-old. After graduating from Harvard early, where our little genius majored in climate change and minored in saving the planet, they would hop in a self-flying car:

*Dad: Congrats, kid. I'm so proud of you. Your other dad would've been proud too.*

*Kid: Yeah . . . about that . . . were you guys there for my birth?*

*Dad: No. Sorry, kiddo.*

*Kid: Why not?*

*Dad: Well, we got into a fight and I never saw him again.*

*Kid: I hate you.*

Snapping out of my daydream slash hallucination, I stand and focus, staring at the house. My phone repeatedly chirps and I'm now getting full service. Twenty-six text messages appear on my screen along with four voicemails, all from Flora.

One second later, my phone powers down, out of battery.

"Hey!" It's the sound of someone shouting.

I wipe sweat off my forehead with my bare arm, spin around and spot Biz sitting behind a cement wall inside a patio around the back of the house. He pierces me with a deeply disappointed look in his green eyes.

I hurry onto the patio to find a glistening swimming pool and a bubbling hot tub. A heavenly oasis. Next to Biz appears a smiling twenty-something couple wearing matching denim rompers. They have identical long stringy hair down to their butts and both look like Jared Leto.

"There you are! We have to go!" I say, trying to convey urgency in my voice.

Biz gives me a condescending look. "Okay, rude. Wyatt, I'd like to introduce you to our hosts first," Biz calmly says, not aware of any urgency.

"Biz—seriously . . ." I can't get the words out quick enough without Biz interrupting me.

"This is Plum and Cosmo. Plum and Cosmo, I'd like you to meet Wyatt." Biz speaks way too slow and I'm losing patience. "Plum and Cosmo are on a silent retreat for two months so they can't speak out loud right now."

I look at both of them, unsure of who's who. "Nice to meet you both," I say, rushed.

As advertised, the couple doesn't speak and just solemnly bows their heads, making a prayer gesture with their hands. After way too long, they finally raise their heads with enlightened grins like they've been tickled by their god of choice.

"Okay, great. Biz—"

"They just asked if I wanted a sound bath and a prickly pear margarita," Biz says.

I glower at Biz. "I thought you said they couldn't talk."

"They wrote it down." Biz looks around. "Wait—where are the dogs?"

"They're fine. They're leashed to a tree," I say. Off Biz's confused look, I can't hold it in anymore. "Flora called and they're inducing her. She's having the baby early!"

"*What?!*" Biz is full of shock and excitement.

"The car's broken. It doesn't work. That idiot mechanic must've been talking too much because he didn't fix it properly.

It's too far to walk back to the dogs, then walk out of here. My phone died so we need to call a cab or something," I say.

"A cab to drive us all the way to Baker? That's like three hours from here. And my phone died too," Biz says.

We both turn to the couple.

# 42

## SEA SALT WHITE

**BIZ**

THREE AND A HALF HOURS LATER, WE arrive at the hospital in Baker. Plum and Cosmo drove us, staying committed to their vow of silence the entire way. Thankfully they're not on a luxury SUV sabbatical.

Wyatt and I weren't exactly speaking to each other either.

"You guys, thank you so much," I say to our new best friends as we climb out of the car with the dogs.

"You're lifesavers. Truly," Wyatt says, focused on unloading our luggage and the baby seat.

Plum and Cosmo step out of the car to give us warm hugs. Plum, or maybe Cosmo, writes something in a small, tattered journal. She rips the paper off and hands it to me.

*You are a beautiful family unit.*

Her penmanship is flowery and loopy, like a little girl's.

Cosmo adds to it, his handwriting almost illegible, like chicken scratch: *don't forget . . . communication is key.*

Wyatt and I wish them luck, and as we go, we look at each

other, stifling smiles at the irony of this couple who took a literal vow of silence telling us we need to communicate more.

– – – – – – →

## THE HOSPITAL IS BRAND-NEW AND STATE OF THE ART. SPRAWLING.

It looks like its ambitious architectural plans come to life.

We pass under a giant cantilevered roof and enter a beautiful, triple height, all-glass lobby that's filled with natural sunlight.

The dogs' fingernails click along the polished linoleum floor, trying to keep up with their anxious daddies.

"Hi. Maternity?" Wyatt spits at the woman behind the front desk.

"Allow me to translate into polite English: we're looking for the maternity ward?" I say to the friendly, seasoned-looking receptionist, who throws us a knowing, warm smile, all too familiar with dozens of similar freaked-out, would-be parents.

"Of course," she says. "I'm assuming your cuties are service animals?" The receptionist raises her eyebrows, hoping we catch onto her harmless little scheme.

"Yes?" I say, which is very much a lie that everyone is in on.

"Good. Just in case anyone asks. I'm a dog lover too. Got two Siberian Huskies and a Jack Russell Terrier who's deaf and blind," she says conspiratorially. "Fourth floor."

The way Wyatt breathes inside the elevator—three quick exhales, three quick inhales—you'd think he was the one about to have a baby.

Our newly charged phones are fully operating. We both text our moms to tell them what's happening and they reply immediately.

Exciting!!!

Here we go!!!!

Keep us updated!!!!!

Send us pics immediately!!!!!!

After checking in, we find several comfortable-looking love seats in the empty waiting room. We each take our own love seat, like two dads-to-be who happen to arrive at the same time.

Silence between us. Later, crunching.

Wyatt blankly eats a bag of classic Lay's potato chips, slowly chewing them one by one, like a sloth. My breakfast of choice is quickly stuffing my face with Pepperidge Farm Goldfish.

*Munch, crunch, crunch, crunch, swallow.*

Next, pacing.

I meander in circles in front of a wall of windows, staring into the tranquility pond outside, my hand massaging my own neck, occasionally stretching out a leg or two.

Wyatt, arms crossed, stares into his own thoughts, marching back and forth along the wall of couches like a determined general going to war.

And then napping.

I'm curled up in a fetal position on my love seat falling in and out of sleep, mouth open, snoring exiting my face.

Sitting in the opposite love seat, Wyatt tries to maintain an upright position, fighting sleep as the weight of his head falls forward, then backward, then forward. Each time he catches himself, midsnort.

Finally, coffee.

I create coffee theater, making a huge production starring a packet of raw sugar, costarring a generous pour of almond milk, with special guest stars including a drip—no, three drips—of vanilla syrup and a cameo of cinnamon.

Wyatt pours himself a recycled paper cup of hot black coffee, blows on it and gulps.

We sit and sip. Both of us come alive. We savor the liquid energy.

The waiting area steadily fills up with families waiting for news from their loved ones.

With time running out, Wyatt finally breaks the silence between us. "Biz," he whispers. "I'm sorry."

I'm too emotional to respond. We both stand, meet halfway and give each other a warm embrace. People start watching us but we don't care.

"I regret saying what I did in the desert," Wyatt says into the crook of my neck. "I take it all back and I didn't mean it. I know you want this just as much as I do."

"It's okay. I'm sorry I called you uptight."

Creeping into my mind is how Wyatt's highly organized schedule has been blown to pieces. I pull us out of our hug and we sit.

"We can't check into our house rental for another week or so," I remind Wyatt.

"I know," Wyatt says.

"We're gonna have to rent a new place," I realize.

"Yep."

"We don't even have a crib or diapers or literally anything yet," I say.

"I know."

I look over to find Wyatt completely casual and calm. It throws me off.

"You seem like you're okay with all of this?" I ask.

"I guess I am," Wyatt says, looking at me, even surprising himself.

"Actually, you seem totally calm. How is that possible?"

"Maybe it doesn't matter anymore," he says. "The planning. The organizing. Having everything exactly perfect and in the right order." Then out of nowhere Wyatt asks if I remember that weekend we painted the baby's room.

"Of course," I say. "That was a blast."

Remodeling our spare bedroom into the baby's room was pure joy. One rainy Labor Day weekend, we spent three days painting, making it perfect for our little one. Sitting on the paint-splattered drop cloth on the floor and eating Chinese food out of white cartons "like a commercial cliché," Wyatt said, I brought up the idea of getting married.

"I just think it would be nice for the kid. To say their dads are legally married," I said, trying to defend my idea. "And it's a celebration of our relationship."

"It feels like you just want an excuse to have a party," Wyatt said.

"That too." We laughed. True! "But it's also something I've wanted since I was a kid. I used to read my sisters' bridal magazines and dream of the big day. The ceremony. A huge, fun party with a cheesy DJ. Lionel Richie's 'Dancin' on the Ceiling.' With all of our friends and family. I mean—I realize my Italian cousins would make up two-thirds of the guest list but . . ."

"More than two-thirds." Wyatt bit into a piece of sweet-and-sour chicken and arranged his thoughts while he chewed. "I understand wanting to get married before having a kid. It's the traditional thing to do. But we're having a kid in the most nontraditional way. Maybe we'll get married when the kid is six or seven or thirteen, and they can be there and remember it too. Not to mention, we'll hopefully be able to afford a wedding by then."

*Every excuse in the book.* That's what I thought at the time.

Matilda sauntered into the room and plunked down in Wyatt's lap. "That's my little monster," I said. "Also, hey, Matilda."

Wyatt laughed.

"I still love you even if you don't really want to get married," I said.

"I'll only love you if you let me have that last egg roll," Wyatt said.

"Deal," I said, feeding him half the egg roll.

As we crunched and smiled at each other, something felt off. We both knew we weren't going to see eye to eye on the whole getting married thing. But I was willing to focus on the baby before the wedding, if there ever was going to be one. Ultimately, I knew our life together was fulfilling in so many other ways.

Then something felt really off.

"What is it?" I asked Wyatt.

"Look at the wall," he said.

I looked at the one wall we'd finished painting. The afternoon light was shining in and the color seemed to have morphed before our eyes.

"Is that the off-white we wanted?" Wyatt asked.

"It's starting to look yellowy."

"I think they gave us sand dollar yellow instead of sea salt white," Wyatt said, turning to me. After our initial disappointment, we turned back to stare at our newly yellow room as laughter erupted from our guts.

- - - - - - →

**BACK IN THE MATERNITY WAITING ROOM, WAVES OF EMOTION FLOW** through us both remembering that weekend.

I feel the warmth of the sunlight through the windows projecting onto my face. Wyatt turns to look at me, leans in and lands a sweet kiss on my mouth. I wasn't expecting it.

"I know you're not irresponsible. And that you're going to be a great papa. And I know I need to learn to let go of my control issues."

"You think?" I joke. Wyatt laughs at his own expense. "I know you've sometimes doubted my commitment to this but . . ." I want to say the right thing. "I'm one thousand percent committed, but you just have to give me a little more credit and trust me more. I'm ready for this. I'm ready for the little one to get here and ready for our family to grow," I say.

Even though it's the biggest day of our lives, we both arrive at a place of calmness.

We can't stop staring at each other, our smiles bigger than ever.

"Guys?" Gabrielle is standing there, half smiling at how ridiculous the two of us look, gazing into each other's eyes like this on such a stressful day. We don't break away at first.

"Hey! Earth to love birds. Wake the eff up. It's happening."

# 43

## PUSH

**WYATT**

FLORA IS PROPPED UP in bed wearing a sky blue hospital gown with patterned white daisies. Her face is flushed with a happy glow, and, if I'm being honest, I can sense a small part of her is ready to move on with her life.

Next to her are various machines and monitors, one to check the baby's heartbeat and another to check Flora's contractions. The room is larger than I thought, but not a sterile operating room like *Grey's Anatomy* or something I'd expected. I immediately take note of every detail in case one day I need to direct something that takes place in a delivery room. There's even a couch along one wall in case one of us needs to faint.

After excited hellos and tired hugs, Flora and Gabrielle want to know all about our trip.

"Well, we were *going* to spend a week in P-town, but then Wyatt's brother got into a mountain bike accident. So we got *all the way* to P-town, that's when Wyatt's mom called—"

I have to interrupt. "Can we maybe give them the abbreviated highlights? They don't have time for the five-hour story." Everyone laughs and Biz concedes. "We want to know how *you* are."

Flora exhales. "Besides horrible back pain, mild heartburn, these heinous veins popping up all over my arms and neck and having to pee like *all the time*, I'm great. Oh, but if one more person calls me a *trooper*, I'm gonna slice their thumbs off," Flora says, exhaling. "Thank god your little one is doing fine. Totally active. The last ultrasound they said it looks like the baby's giving us the peace sign. So that's cool."

We smile at her with sympathy and gratitude, unable to express how much all of this means to us. Any of the issues we've had with each other seem inconsequential compared to what this woman sent from heaven is about to go through. For us.

Flora puts her hand on her large belly. She waves us over. The three of us each stack our hands on Flora's stomach. It's like a shot of serotonin. We feel a sizzling sensation electrifying our hands and arms, straight to our hearts.

We're finally able to feel Flora's extended belly in person. We sit there in awed silence until Flora points out specifically where we can feel the baby's head, feet, legs and arms. We look up and lock eyes, quietly laughing, tearing up. Then we look at Flora and the three of us have nothing but love for each other.

"Oh, shit," I say, remembering something. "We forgot to tell the photographer the baby's coming early. Shit, shit, shit." I had arranged for a professional photographer to meet us at the hospital to document every moment. Normally, I would've obsessed over this misstep but now? I wave it off and press on. "I'm not worried. One of us will just snap some pics along the way."

Flora turns her head for us to see that Gabrielle has been

filming us with her phone the whole time. "Already on it, champ," Gabrielle assures us.

"That's my girl," Flora says.

"Just let me know if you want to direct me." Gabrielle looks at me. "I know how you are, Scorsese."

"It's all you," I reassure her. "You're the director now."

Flora makes a face like she's impressed that I'm not trying to take control of the situation per usual. "What did you do to him on your road trip?" Flora jokingly asks Biz.

"Fatherhood is not something perfect men do, but something that perfects the man," Biz says. Everyone is impressed with Biz's wisdom until: "I just read that on a brochure by the coffee station."

A cute, scruffy male nurse named Kirk enters the room to check on Flora and her various machines. He says with a gentle Southern accent, since she's dilated at ten centimeters, "It's time for y'all to push."

"Push what?" I ask.

Kirk laughs and points at Flora's belly.

"It's the . . . final leg . . . of your *journey*!" Flora says in between breaths, fully in on our private joke. Leave it to Flora to lighten the mood even in the middle of the most intense and life-changing activity another human being can go through. "Okay, boys. Let's get this beyotch outta me!" Flora looks up to see everyone is slightly stunned. "Sorry. That was aggressive."

Kirk and another labor nurse prepare Flora.

"Oh my god. Seriously? This is really happening?" Biz keeps saying even though everyone, including Flora, is ready. "Like *now* now?"

I rope my arm around Biz to calm him.

- - - - - - - ➤

NOTHING COULD HAVE PREPARED US FOR THIS MOMENT. NOT THE YEARS of planning or the doctor meetings or the sperm analysis or the genetic testing or the number crunching or the trips to buybuy Baby or scouring the Internet for baby names or hate-scrolling through @quaddaddiez or babymoon road-tripping that went a little sideways. Not even the advice from our own sisters and brothers and moms and dads.

And yet, we are fully prepared. We're ready for the diaper changing and the middle-of-the-night crying and the teething and high fevers and the not knowing what the baby needs and their first word and choosing which one will be Daddy (me) and which one will be Papa (Biz) and all the snuggles and the giggles and the kisses and affection. Because we're ready to love this baby and we're truly in love with each other.

Almost immediately, Flora starts pushing. Heavy breaths, big squeezes, some slight groaning. Biz and I stand on one side of the bed cheering Flora on while Gabrielle stands on the other side, squeezing Flora's hand, filming the big moment.

Feeling helpless, Biz grabs my hand. We turn to each other with tears of worry and joy and excitement in our eyes.

For the next hour and a half, the nurses move Flora in several different positions in order to get the baby moving down the birth canal: on her knees, on her left side, right side, on her back, until finally she's sitting fully straight up. Flora's breathing is more labored now and her eyes are shut tight. The room smells like literal blood, sweat and tears.

Without giving it so much as a minute's thought, I seize the emotions in the room and decide Biz-style that I'm going to do something spur of the moment again.

That's when my hand slips out of Biz's hand and I fall to the floor.

Biz panics. He doesn't know what's going on, like Sandra Bullock accidentally letting go of George Clooney's hand in *Gravity*, hanging from the side of a space satellite as I drift off into the black nothingness forever.

Flora, Gabrielle and the nurses check to see if I've fainted. Flora breathes through it, wondering what's happening.

"Are you okay?" Biz asks, bending down to try and help me off the floor. I squat down on one knee, take something out of my shorts pocket and stare up at Biz with dreamy, teary eyes.

In my hand is the silver ring my dad gave me. I could let it become a painful memory of his absence all those years or the consolation prize for not having a father.

Instead, I'm putting it to better use.

"Massimo Biz Petterelli?"

Biz's eyes go wide. "Oh my *god*."

A second later, everyone else's eyes go wide.

"You're doing this *NOW*?" Flora shouts, alternating from exhausted to giddy and back again. The doctor, nurses, Gabrielle, even Flora, all stop to watch.

"Do you want to have a ceremony and a big celebration with all of our friends and family and our newborn baby but not have it be *Star Wars*–themed?"

Biz covers his open mouth in shock.

"Ask the *fucking* question!" Flora shouts.

"Will you marry me?" I fling out.

"Great! Now answer!" Flora says, laughing, in pain, happy, distressed and sweating out a hundred more emotions.

"Yes! Please! Yes! Holy crap! Yes!" Biz shouts.

I slip the ring on Biz's finger, and it's too big but we don't care. He extends a hand and lifts me off the floor in a big bear hug. We kiss each other's faces all over as everyone showers us with cheers and applause.

"Can we focus on me now, please?" Flora asks. The tears of joy and laughter are flowing. The nurses instruct Flora to pull her knees up to her chest and she gives one final big push.

# 44

## BIZ
### SIX YEARS LATER

**F**OUR SUITCASES SIT NEXT to each other on our bedroom floor.

It's difficult to finish packing while Matilda is flopped inside Wyatt's bag with her chin resting on his folded shirts like it's the most comfortable spot in the world.

This is our dog's new thing. The mere sight of our bags used to make Matilda dart around in anxiety circles. Now she fully embraces going on a road trip.

"Matilda! That's Papa's bag," Finch playfully yells as his four-year-old sister, Rose (named after both our grandmothers), runs in with Pancake. Matilda jumps from Wyatt's bag and chases Pancake out of the room.

Our son Finch Beckett Petterelli-Wallace's first name comes from my favorite literary character, Atticus Finch, from *To Kill a Mockingbird*, and one of Wyatt's favorite movie directors, David Fincher. Also, when Finch was born, he looked tiny, like a little bird: a finch.

His middle name is Beckett for no real reason. We agreed it just sounded cool.

Thankfully, Wyatt and I agree on a lot more these days. Like leaving Brooklyn and moving upstate to the Hudson Valley in our sweet little house where we're living now so we could have more space.

Tomorrow morning, we leave for a family road trip to Door County, the same coastal area in Wisconsin I went to with my family every year as a kid. The kind of trip Wyatt wished his family would've taken when he was growing up.

This time we only have one stopover before our final destination: Millie and Dennis's bed-and-breakfast in Ohio.

Hopefully.

After packing and eating a delicious dinner that I made, Finch asks to rewatch the video of the magical day he was born. He laughs every time, watching his dads sweat as their eyes pop out of their heads during the graphic parts.

Mostly, it's Wyatt's eyes bulging. He looks like a deer in headlights when Kirk hands him our baby.

"Why are you both crying?" Finch asks us, eyes glued on his video.

"We were so happy to meet you," Wyatt says.

"I'm so tiny," Finch always says, watching himself in awe.

"You're perfect," Wyatt and I always remind him.

"Where's the stork?" Rose asks.

"The stork was just off camera," Wyatt says, pulling Rose and Finch close under each of his arms.

"Can you see him in my video?" Rose asks.

"He might have a cameo," I say.

"What's a cameo?" Rose wonders.

The four of us continue to watch the video. A close-up of

Wyatt. His cheeks are flushed and you can literally see sweat dripping off him.

"Look at me. I'm a mess. I can't believe you thought I'd be the calm and collected one," Wyatt says.

Wyatt hands me little Finch for our first skin-on-skin contact. I'm in a state of bliss.

"I can't believe I was freaking out so much before this," I say.

"You look like an old pro. Like you've been a dad your entire life."

"I don't know what came over me. I was so relaxed and it felt so natural."

There was no shadowy figure tapping me on the shoulder and telling me I was out of my league. The doctors and nurses didn't start laughing at me, saying I was doing fatherhood wrong. Wyatt didn't take Finch away from me forever, telling me I wasn't good enough.

"We still have Finch's little lavender blanket," Wyatt says, seeing them swaddle him in the video. "In a very organized box in our basement, thank you very much."

I grin as we snuggle next to each other on our big bed. We're beaming as we watch the video of us beaming at Finch.

We look up at Flora and start to cry more like a baby than Finch.

There's just nothing we could possibly say to Flora for our gift, and I think she knows how much she means to us. She helped us do it all over again two years later with Rose. We went with Mackenzie again too, our same egg donor. Never underestimate someone whose special skill is making dolphin noises.

Wyatt and I are still in negotiations on baby number three.

After we settled upstate, I went back to my roots and started acting again. I booked a lot of TV and movie roles in the city, and I'm making my Broadway debut later this year with rehearsals starting after we get back from our trip. In a weird twist of fate, the show is a musical based on *Mrs. Dalloway*, the famous Virginia Woolf novel.

Wyatt directed a commercial for the Super Bowl that made a big splash. His thirty-second stories became sixty-minute stories, and lately he's been directing episodic television.

My phone buzzes.

GIO

Dear Massi,

What's your ETA tomorrow?

Love, Dad

Dad is cancer-free now and as long as he continues to text like he's writing a formal letter, I'll know he's fine.

Speaking of dads and writing letters, Wyatt checks in with his dad sometimes. We invited Richard to our wedding, but he can no longer travel so he wasn't able to join. We haven't been back to see him in Vegas yet, but we will one day soon while the kids are still young.

I text my dad back.

BIZ

we get there thursday
midmorning, remember?
tomorrow we spend the
night in ohio

My dad sends back a string of kissy emojis.

This trip is the first time my entire family and Wyatt's family are all spending time together since our wedding.

We've even graduated from Virginia Woolf to an embarrassingly large SUV, which comes in handy when you have luggage for four humans and two dogs.

The video ends and Wyatt and I glance at the four suitcases in front of us, going over our mental checklists, excited and eager for the early morning drive.

"Think we have everything?" Wyatt asks, turning to me.

I look around to see two kids sleeping in between us with a couple of snoozing dogs at our feet, and I turn to Wyatt with a grateful smile. "I think we do."

# ACKNOWLEDGMENTS

Now that my second child has made its way into the world, there are so many people I'd like to thank who helped make this baby a reality.

I feel incredibly lucky to work with the imprint of Berkley and everyone at Penguin Random House. Thank you to Craig Burke, Loren Jaggers, Kristin Cipolla, Hannah Engler, Kim-Salina I, Elizabeth Vinson and Dache' Rogers for your talent and kindness. My editors, Cindy Hwang and Angela Kim, thank you for shining your bright minds on this and helping me push this story in surprising directions. Thank you to Tal Goretsky for your brilliant cover designs that I can't stop showing off. It's a pure joy to work with all of you.

To everyone at Writers House, including Torie Doherty-Munro, who always makes my day with your emails, thank you. To my book agent extraordinaire, Dan Lazar, a million thank-yous for sharing your intelligence, honesty and thoughtful guidance hashing out every story idea, big and small.

Thank you to my UK team at HarperCollins, including

Lucy Stewart, Lynne Drew and especially to Katie Seaman for your incredible attention to detail as I was refining this book.

An endless thank-you to everyone at Lit Entertainment, my film and TV management team, including Shelby Eggers for your enthusiastic insight on an early draft. A special thank-you to Adam Kolbrenner, one of the greats, for cheering me on at every turn in the marathon of this business. This is the second book that would not have existed without you. I'm forever grateful for your clear-eyed perspective, your creative thinking and, above all, your friendship.

To lifelong friends who show their support in person and virtually, including but not limited to Nina Goodman, Emily Heller, Mike Hoffman, Daniel Kaemon, Sari Knight, Mark Landsman, Scott Landsman, Jennifer Livingston, Lisa Krit Randall, Sara Weiner Rubel and Peter Alexander. To Jessica Zoller Kaplan and Asher, a wow, thank you for making the trek to New York for my book event and narrowly escaping fire in the sky. You are all my fellow theater geeks, road trippers, Ravinia crew and "my chunk."

Absolutely no one is sick of hearing me thank John Hughes for making movies in my hometown and inspiring me to write.

Thank you to my writing group, Anything But Poetry.

A massive thank-you to all the booksellers, libraries, podcasters, bloggers, morning talk show hosts, late-night talk show hosts, public radio talk show hosts, Bookstagrammers, fellow authors and readers who have championed *Best Men*.

To my friends: Melissa Roth, thank you for reading and always saying exactly what I'm thinking. Lara Shapiro, thank you for your pep talks and trusty advice.

At the heart of this book is a story about the different versions of families and I'm eternally grateful for my own brothers and sisters, Anita and Jimmy, Jo (for reading several drafts), Julie, Nicky and Miriam and Butch and Nancy. The extended Karger and Placent families have been the greatest support system and I'd like to thank you all for your unconditional love.

Writing about two characters who are trying to become parents would not have been possible without my own amazing mom and dad, Cookie and Frank Karger, the best in the biz. My dad instilled in me a love for reading the entire end credits in movies, which is why I appreciate a good acknowledgments page. Several of my mom friends cite Cookie as their guiding light, which makes me happy-cry. Mom and Dad, if you could stick this book on your refrigerator under a magnet, I know you would. I hope I'm making you both proud. Long live our blue station wagon.

To Zelda for taking me on walks, hiring me to manage your Instagram account and making us smile.

My deepest gratitude goes to my co-pilot, Jean-Michel, who helps navigate all of our twists and turns. I'll ride anywhere with you and I can't wait to see where our little family goes next. Your heart is a gift.

Author photo by Josh Touvim

**SIDNEY KARGER** is an award-winning screenwriter for film and television. His debut novel, *Best Men*, was published in 2023 and featured on *Good Morning America*, the *Today* show and *Watch What Happens Live with Andy Cohen*. He currently lives in New York City with his partner and their Australian Labradoodle, Zelda.

### VISIT SIDNEY KARGER ONLINE

SidKarger.com
🐦 SidKarger
📷 SidKNY

Ready to find
your next great read?

Let us help.

**Visit prh.com/nextread**

Penguin
Random
House